# IF NOT 4 U
## and Some Shoes

# IF NOT 4 U
## and Some Shoes

Laurie Henson

# IF NOT 4 U AND SOME SHOES

iUniverse books may be ordered through booksellers or by contacting:

iUniverse
1663 Liberty Drive
Bloomington, IN 47403
www.iuniverse.com
1-800-Authors (1-800-288-4677)

ISBN: 978-1-4917-7019-1 (sc)
ISBN: 978-1-4917-7020-7 (e)

Library of Congress Control Number: 2015911084

Print information available on the last page.

iUniverse rev. date: 07/22/2015

When a picture paints
*more* than a thousand words . . .

# foot note one

New shoes, new shoes,
Red and pink and blue shoes.
Tell me, what would you choose,
If they'd let you buy?

Buckle shoes, bow shoes,
Pretty pointy-toe shoes,
Strappy, cappy low shoes;
Let's have some to try.

Bright shoes, white shoes,
Dandy-dance-by-night shoes,
Perhaps-a-little-tight shoes,
Like some? So would I.

—Frida Wolfe

WHEN I WAS FOUR YEARS OLD, CURLED UP IN MY FLUFFY WHITE
bed, waiting for lights-out, I first heard Frida Wolfe's poem "Choosing
Shoes," as recited by a redheaded, curvaceous, wacky babysitter
named Ella. The happening not only marked the moment when girlie

1

footwear began registering on my radar but also awakened me to the fact that the opposite of ordinary was what flipped my pancakes—a revelation further affirmed by other stuff Ella exposed me to, such as well-strung words in pop songs, the quirkiest wardrobe known to humankind, the intricate body ink decorating her limbs, cool Amazonian wildflowers depicted on the Internet, and evening snacks displayed fancifully on a plate. God, that girl was too cool for cool. God, I was bluer than blue when her family moved away only two years into our companionship.

When I was eight years old, shopping at a mall in the company of my look-alike mother (the petite, brunette, girl-next-door-type Claire Lanoo), I encountered a flamboyant, outrageously attired department-store shoe salesman bearing the name tag Mark, who slipped onto my feet a pair of three-strapped metallic-gold Mary Janes that he claimed had "fairy-tale princess" written all over them. That happening not only impressed upon me the fact that shoes could speak volumes about the wearer but also instilled in my brain the notion of exceptional footwear becoming my *it*, my expression, my chase. Though I expected many people (including my three-years-older, not-interested-in-fashion sister, Brigitte, and my three-years-younger, save-the-earth sister, Talula) might view the fixation as silly, I didn't care, because walking around in those shoes that day made my internal happy meter register an all-new high.

When I was fourteen years old, I met someone who gave my footwear affinity a clear purpose. The encounter took place just before the start of ninth grade, on a sunny Sunday afternoon in downtown's City Center Park. I was in the company of my best gal pal, the red-haired, fine-featured, long-legged Phoebe Crane; two other gal pals, skinny, cute blonde Beatrice Nelson and willowy, borderline-Goth Silvia Reece; and my best guy pal, Patrick Needle, a baby-faced, lanky, awkward-like-me blond sweetheart I've known since I was a toddler. The five of us were wandering along a dusty pathway, doing a whole lot of nothing—because that's what teenagers do in the small, middle-of-nowhere midwestern city of Riverly Heights—and became so unbearably overheated we headed to the park's scenic riverbank to join a few others wading in some knee-deep water. It was an activity that everyone decided to do barefoot, except for me, because I was determined to put a layer of protection between my feet and the slimy crawlies of the world (bug hater that I am). Long story abbreviated, while I was wading, I slipped, went bottom-up, got saturated from head to toe, and turned my tank top and short shorts into a second skin. For sure, that was reason enough to go home to change my clothes, but after my friends sold me on the quick effects of sun drying, I decided to tough it out at the park's popular open green space, where the intense sun was sure to rid me of my clothing woes in a matter of minutes. That strategy turned out to be the best decision ever, because on that green space, a pickup football game was in progress, involving the most gawk-worthy guys I'd ever seen. One of them, in particular, was so through-the-roof mesmerizing he caused an electric charge to ripple through every fiber of my being.

He was standing in a huddle about twenty feet away from where we sat on the grass, and the instant I laid my cocoa-bean-brown eyes on him, I knew my life would never be the same. Maybe it was because his angular facial features looked as if an artistic master had sculpted them or because his flouncy light brown hair was begging to be played with or because his gleaming, rock-hard muscles were reflecting sunlight into my eyes. Even the shoes he wore—cool retro sneakers in gray suede with white stripes—stood out as spectacular. Regardless, the sum of his parts equaled nothing short of amazing, telling me with certainty that (a) Cupid was not a myth and (b) I'd need to tweak my happy meter to include the level infinity.

Feeling bubbly inside and out, I, for the first time, discarded my uneasy-around-boys ways and murmured to Phoebe, "Boom-chica-wow-wow, would you look at that guy?"

Giving me a light shoulder bump, she replied, "Yeah, he's about as first-worthy as they come."

With eyes locked on his every move, I whispered the boldest statement I've ever made: "I call dibs."

Minutes later, near where we were sitting, the object of my affection made an impressive catch, completed a wicked body roll, and came to an abrupt halt with his head mere inches from my flip-flopped feet. Any other day, that type of kerfuffle would have caused me to scurry away like a frightened puppy, but not that day—not with him so close. Rather, as cool as a cucumber, I watched as he lifted his upper body away from the turf, looked at my feet and then at my face, and— simultaneous to the sun peeking from behind a cloud—exposed what has become my yet-to-be-surpassed bliss inducer: his eyes.

Holy crap, they were stunning: large, perfectly round, emerald green, and so bright they made the gems on my dangling earrings look like dusty rocks.

Mesmerized, I barely heard when he softly said, "You know, there's an ant crawling on your cute flip-flop."

But I could not have cared less, because the only thing that mattered in that moment was that I be allowed to stare.

And he stared back until one of the other football players yelled, "The game's still on, lover boy!"

"Yeah, I'm aware, Ben," said the guy with the green eyes as he stood up and brushed the grass from his clothing.

"Berkeley, make sure you grab the ball," the guy named Ben said.

As he yelled, "Got it," I whispered, "Berkeley," and watched him toe-flip the ball into the air, jump up, and catch it—the coolest maneuver of the day.

Patting Berkeley on the back, Ben said, "Nice snag despite the hot distraction."

Glancing at me over his shoulder (at least I think he was looking at me, but I guess he could have been looking at Phoebe), Berkeley gripped the ball firmly with both hands and replied, "Making sure the hot distraction didn't get a ball to the face is what gave me the wherewithal to make the snag."

With my eyes gleaming because I'd just heard a teenage guy use the word *wherewithal* in a sentence, I mumbled, "Oh, to be that ball right now."

And as if my words had hit Berkeley on the head, he looked back at me and flashed the most-fantastic grin I'd ever seen.

From then on, I was utterly spellbound.

An hour later, when the football game finally wrapped up, I felt frantic that I might never see Berkeley again, so I told myself to get up, walk over to him, and say something—anything. But as I sat there running opening lines through my brain, Phoebe, of all people, blindsided me by springing to her feet, darting toward Berkeley, and initiating the conversation I should have started. Evidently, she had not heard me call dibs.

Devastated as well as uninterested in witnessing what might develop between someone as awesome as Berkeley and someone as boy-magnetic as Phoebe, I shifted my focus to my other friends and started babbling. When, soon after, I overheard Phoebe's dialogue morph into full-out flirtation, I sighed and stated, "Time for this banana to split."

"I'll walk you home," Patrick said.

"That'd be nice," I replied.

"Let's grab ice cream for the stroll home."

"Brilliant idea," I said with a pat to his back.

From about fifty steps away, I checked over my shoulder to see if Phoebe was making any inroads with Berkeley and thought I saw him peering past her, watching me leave. Maybe yes? Maybe no? Maybe it was just wishful thinking?

Maybe it didn't matter, because I knew a guy like Berkeley was way out of my league.

I was pleased to learn from Phoebe later in the evening that no sparks had ignited between Berkeley and her. How weird would it have been for me to watch them date? It would have been unbearable, torturous, the worst.

Surprise, surprise—two weeks later, I ended up seeing Berkeley again, on the first day of ninth grade, in my designated homeroom. Just as I took a seat at a desk bearing my name tag, I glanced toward the door, and lo and behold, he sailed smoothly into the room.

Murmuring, "Holy crap, we go to the same school now?" I followed his every move as he casually wandered to the back of the room and took a seat.

Discovering via a stolen glance that his eyes were equally as awesome even under the screaming-white classroom lighting, I told myself to head in that vicinity to grab a tissue or sharpen a pencil—*anything*. But as I readied myself to make my move, cute and bubbly Colette Manner cut me off at the pass as she rose from her seat, slinked toward Berkeley, and settled her forearms on his desk.

After taking a deep breath, I returned my gaze to my desktop and started doodling on my binder, whispering, "Maybe tomorrow?"

Unfortunately, I didn't make a move that day either, because in what could only be described as "well played," Colette strategically switched desks to the one directly in front of Berkeley, thereby commanding his attention for the entire semester.

If only I'd thought of that.

Over the next couple of months, as it became clear that half of the girls in my school were as hung up on Berkeley as I was, I accepted that I didn't have it in me to compete—I had no relationship experience, I was too uncomfortable in my own skin, and I didn't know the meaning of the word *provocative*—so I threw in the towel.

From then on, I did everything in my power not to dwell on the guy: I darted in the opposite direction if I saw him heading my way; I pretended not to get caught up by everything he did (playing guitar with his band in the school's talent show, reciting poetry at the front of the classroom, or running past my house during one of his early morning runs); and I even forced myself to look deeply into the eyes of a few other guys in search of something equally impactful, but when the practice had no measurable effect, I abandoned the effort.

Eight weeks of Berkeley avoidance later, aware that my ability to function normally was still every bit as hampered by the slightest sighting of him, I hatched a plan to speak to the guy, thinking the icebreaker might make me less anxious in his midst. So one morning, I woke up, dressed up, put on my shoes and lipstick, and headed to school with the plan of walking up to him and nonchalantly quipping, "Nice sneakers—too bad we don't share the same shoe size." But in what could only be described as an extreme case of bad timing, I came around a corridor corner at the exact instant Berkeley did from the opposite direction, collided head-on with him, and sent our bodies— butts first—onto the hard tile floor.

He cursed, I cursed, and books went everywhere. Pens rolled away and tripped a few other people. Lunches exploded into food fragments no longer edible.

In the aftermath of the side-by-side crawling around to gather our stuff, I took a deep breath, smelled Berkeley's freshly showered scent, and became so flustered that I mumbled as we were face-to-face, "Nothing like a big bang to start the day."

Though he laughed, I was so embarrassed that I stood up, ran away, and repeatedly exclaimed, "Oh my God, why did I say that?"

Plunking into a seat at the back of my first-period classroom, smack dab between Phoebe and Patrick, I confessed, "I have a secret longing that's affecting my ability to think straight."

"You're crushing on someone?" Patrick asked.

"Maybe. Yes. Okay, so I am."

Grabbing my shoulder, Phoebe said, "Let me guess: Berkeley Mills."

"How did you know?"

"Because every time that guy is in your midst, you nearly hyperventilate."

Following a shared pity-filled laugh over the telling of my big-bang story, they insisted on getting involved, Phoebe with a plan to make me more noticeable and to keep me well informed on all Berkeley-related gossip, and Patrick with intention of dragging me anywhere Berkeley might be.

When New Year's Eve rolled around, I went one step further by announcing three solid resolutions: "I'm going to hit the party circuit more often. I'm going to quit loitering in the back wings. And I'm going to speak to guys not only when spoken to."

The next thing I knew, I was out there, first on a date with a cute guy named Riley and, a week later, on one with a guy named Fielding. Though both outings ended with a one-and-done good-night kiss, they instilled enough confidence in me to stop running in the other direction whenever Berkeley was in the vicinity. That newfound courage proved beneficial because it enabled me to watch with interest as he ditched Colette, moved on to a cute ginger named Corinne, and eventually settled on his current fling, blonde and beautiful Catharine Armour, leaving me to wonder, *Do I need to change my name to Crancie to put myself in the running?*

At the start of second semester, when I learned I had a class schedule identical to Berkeley's, I realized I had an open door for all of six hours a day, five days a week. In theory, that should have set the stage for an easy verbal opener. Right? Wrong. By the end of the second week, I still hadn't uttered a single word to him, not even a returned "hi" when the two of us entered the room at the same time, although I did regularly muster a smile.

When Phoebe learned of my plight, she took hold of my shoulders and said, "Okay, shrinking violet, I'll give you exactly twenty-four hours to say something to that guy, or I'm going to do it for you."

With pursed lips, I exclaimed, "Don't you dare!"

Sporting a devilish smirk, she said, "Surely you know by now that I do my best work when I'm dared."

Because I did know, I exhaled and mumbled, "Okay, fine. I'll talk to him."

The next morning, when I arrived at school, Phoebe held me to my word, arming me with a sixteen-ounce energy drink, instructing me to consume it in one long gulp, and ushering me to the door of my classroom.

"You look like you're going to faint," she said.

"I hope I do so I won't have to go through with this."

Giggling, she said, "Just relax. You'll be fine."

All abuzz, I sat down at a desk beside Berkeley, looked his way, and boldly said, "What I would give right now for a pair of those fake eyes, the ones that fit over your own to make you look awake when you're not."

Looking my way, he smiled and replied, "But then, Ms. Lanoo, how would you know which guys in the room are checking you out?"

Rattled and feeling a little woozy—probably because my latest beverage had taken full effect—I lost all ability to speak or think. Zooming my eyes to the front of the room, I blocked out the rest of the world for one full hour and swore never to consume caffeine again.

The good news was that after that, Berkeley and I regularly said hello when we walked into the classroom together, always smiled at each other from across crowded spaces, and even exchanged contact information. Best of all, we became science partners—at his suggestion—enabling me to spend the last period of every school day working within two feet of him, an hour I grew to love because it left me with enough of a Berkeley fix to carry me over until the next morning.

On the upside, during that time, I learned that Berkeley's inner awesomeness perfectly matched his outer. On the downside, during that time, I learned that the chances of me making any kind of impression on him were slim to none, because the other girls vying for his attention were exceptionally skilled at maneuvering next to Berkeley and pushing me to the periphery.

In mid-May of ninth grade following an art class, Berkeley strolled over to me at the sink, grabbed some of my brushes to help clean them, and initiated the most-unexpected—and cutest—conversation.

While glancing at my aqua tie-up platforms (eye-catchers because they had lavender-ribbon laces that looked like wings), he said, "Those shoes have 'bird lover' written all over them."

Broadly smiling, I replied, "Uh-oh, my secret passion has been outed."

Smirking and shifting his sweet-smelling body toward me, he responded, "So out of curiosity, what kind of shoe has 'Francie Lanoo' written all over it?"

Accidently brushing my forearm against his, and thereby losing all sense of time and place, I had a flashback to the Frida Wolfe poem, and replied, "'Dandy-dance-by-night shoes,' I expect they'll be."

It was a stupid, ridiculous thing to say—I know. But it did prompt Berkeley to say, "Well, if you need a partner to do that dandy dancing, feel free to give me a call." Then he hung around the sink with me well into the lunch hour.

Ever since that day, two things in my world have noticeably changed. First, I can't put on shoes without thinking of Berkeley, and second, I regularly catch Berkeley glancing at my feet, leading me to wonder what might happen if I find my *me* shoes and strut around the school wearing them.

That's the reason, effective today—my first day of tenth grade—I am a girlie girl on a mission: I'm going to find the shoe style that has me written all over it, and I'm going to show it to Berkeley to see what he has to say. I've even come up with a plan to make it happen: basically, every time I step into noteworthy footwear, I'm going to analyze the style for features that reflect me, and when I'm lucky enough to find one, I'm going to record it in a database (one point at a time) until I've compiled a comprehensive and well-rounded list. Following that, I will imaginarily mold the adjectives into something tangible and scour the retail world for its earthly equivalent.

Of course, I have no idea how long this shoe-volution will take—perhaps until I'm super old, like twenty. Maybe it will never even reach an end, because there are millions of shoe styles out there, and a girl's only got so much time. But I plan to have some fun with it, and for a shoe lover like me, that's got to be worth my time.

# foot note two

THE FIRST FOOTWEAR I'M ABOUT TO ANALYZE ON MY SHOE QUEST is a pair of black high-heeled wedge lace-ups that started out as my sister Brigitte's. She handed them down to me after she overwore them and got sick of them. To inject a bit of me into them, I changed the laces from black to bronze and glued dozens of tiny metallic studs onto the sides. Voilà—rebirthed as the Debut-Taunters.

I'm wearing them tonight to the first dance of the school year, in combination with a stylish, form-fitting, bell-sleeved black minidress, which is a bit extroverted for someone like me but was pretty much forced upon me by Phoebe, who claimed it was a requirement for attracting the attention I was seeking.

I went all in and heightened the visual drama by turning my typically unpampered long dark brown hair into a mass of loose, flowing curls; enhancing my pouty lips with some hot-pink metallic gloss; and making my big eyes bigger with a heap of smoky makeup and thick mascara.

Taking one last look at my skinny body in the mirror and wishing I were a few inches taller and a few inches curvier, I sweep my always-dangling bangs away from my face, admire the fact that I hardly recognize myself, and exclaim, "You do *not* look fifteen!"

As I insert a pair of large hoop earrings, I sigh with relief that my father is away at a legal convention this weekend, because if he were to see me looking this enhanced, he'd nail every door and window of our house shut.

I hear the doorbell ring. It's probably my date for this evening's festivities.

No, it's not Berkeley (*God, if only!*). Rather, it's blond, hunky, hazel-eyed pretty boy Daniel East, whose arrival is causing my heart rate to go off the charts because he's about to escort me to where Berkeley will be.

The minute I walk through the arched doorway of the school's auditorium, I dart toward my three favorite gal pals, initiate a warm hug, and admire their enhancements.

Touching Beatrice's arm, I say, "Please let me borrow that retro romper sometime soon."

"Sure," she replies, and after adjusting my sleeve, she adds, "You should wear your hair like that all the time. It looks amazing."

"Thanks," I respond, smiling and then turning to the always-clad-in-black Silvia to say, "You look twenty-one tonight."

With devious eyes, she responds, "So do you, which is why we should try to get into a nightclub later."

I lean into her. "What a rush that would be."

Turning to the seductively dressed Phoebe, who is proudly showing off the legs every teenage girl dreams of, I quietly say, "You know, a pic of you right now would garner a cazillion likes."

Raising an eyebrow—because, of course, she knows that—she points out, "Based on the fact that half the guys in the room are gawking at what you've got going on, so would a picture of you."

Rolling my eyes, I say, "Whatever," and when I realize that many guys are staring at me, I dart my eyes to the floor.

Nudging me with her elbow, Phoebe asks, "Hey, where's Daniel?"

My eyes shift to the entryway. "Oh, I completely forgot about him."

Leaning into my ear, she notes, "I still don't understand why you're on a date with one guy when you're totally hung up on another."

Biting my lower lip, I respond, "Because one guy knows I exist, and the other doesn't."

Rolling her eyes, she says, "Well, if this new look you're sporting doesn't blow the mind of the guy you think doesn't notice you, then it's time to accept he's senseless."

Shrugging but also feeling adrenaline rush at the reference to the guy I'm crazy about, I perk up and become a heat-seeking drone, panning the room for what I most crave. However, when the effort yields nothing, I turn my attention to the hundreds of silver streamers dangling from the rafters above and observe.

Transfixed by one caught up in an air swirl on the far side of the room, I follow its erratic maneuvers here and there, watching intently as it eventually descends and settles in the vicinity of—*Oh my God, Berkeley is here!*

Feeling as if I've just swallowed a net full of butterflies, I pause for a moment to catch my breath and then use one of my well-practiced side glances to observe guys and girls alike swarming him, all no doubt hoping his sweet, cool, outgoing aura spreads to them.

Though I'm only able to see his athletic silhouette from behind, I know he's looking awesome tonight. He always is.

As large hands grip my shoulders from behind, I wince and cower, but when I realize they belong to Daniel, I exclaim, "Hey! There you are."

Flashing his recently whitened grin, he says, "What happened to you? I turned around, and you were gone."

"Sorry. I guess I got swept up in the crowd."

Circling around to stand torso to torso with me—*Whoa, that's so close*—he says, "You left me high and dry in the lobby, where I got held by some cheerleaders who insisted on showing me a new routine."

I grin. "Well, at least you didn't end up lonely."

"No, that's never been a problem for me," he responds, sliding a muscular arm around my waist and then adding, "I'm gonna grab us some drinks. What can I get for you?"

After taking a deep breath, I answer, "I'm up for anything."

Leaning into in my ear, he murmurs, "I'll keep that in mind for later."

"Charming," I mutter to myself.

Rejoining my gal pals so that we can watch Daniel walk away, because it's definitely worth our time, I ponder what it would be like to be the girlfriend of a guy who easily scores 9.5 on the visual scale (the 0.5 deducted because he wears sneakers so obnoxiously bold they require sunglasses to view). Would I grow to enjoy his cocky behavior? Would the boldness of his shoes always distract me? Would it be fair to spend time with someone when, all the while, I'd be daydreaming about someone else, as I am again now?

Grasping my arm, Phoebe says, "Earth to Francie."

I stand at attention. "Yeah, Francie to Earth."

"Berkeley's here, you know, standing under the school bell."

"I know."

"You should go over and say hi."

"No, I can't."

"Why?"

"Because I become too awkward around him."

She smiles. "If he saw you right now, I don't think he'd label you awkward."

Shrugging, I say, "No, I don't want to get lumped in with all of his other aficionados hanging around over there, like Catharine, who just glued herself so tightly to Berkeley a piece of paper couldn't squeeze between them."

Taking hold of one of my shoulders, Phoebe says, "As much as Catharine looks awesome with her Marilyn hair, dress, and shoes, just watch closely: whenever she moves toward Berkeley, he edges away."

I squint. "That is true."

Before Phoebe has a chance to comment further, Daniel reappears with a drink in each hand. They're orange, of course, the loudest color. After handing me one, he starts manhandling me again.

Rolling my eyes, I wriggle away, reach to the floor, grab a couple of streamers, stand up again, and peek in the direction of the guy I would never wriggle away from.

At the same time, as if by an act of my will, Berkeley turns around and looks at me.

He smiles. I smile. He waves. I wave. Then, for some reason, he keeps staring at me despite the fact that his guy friends are engaged in a conversation with him.

I can't stop staring either, and I watch like a hawk as he grabs his phone and sends a text, which comes to me, inquiring, "Hey, Ms. Lanoo, what's up over there?"

Taking further steps away from Daniel, I reply, "Typical teenagery."

He smiles and replies, "Same here. Got any suggestions for something atypical?"

I think and reply, "Grading geeky dance moves on a scale of one to ten?"

He shakes his head and texts, "No, too many to keep track of."

I pause and reply, "Spotting the hidden flasks?"

He shakes his head again. "No, the teachers are already on that."

I look to the floor and say, "Stringing streamers?"

His face scrunches up. "Elaborate, please."

Feeling as if a spotlight has been aimed my way, I set my drink on the floor, retrieve a handful of the coiled strands from the floor, and start decorating myself with them. I put several around my torso, a few around my wrists, and one around each ankle, making sure my actions are in perfect time to the beat of the music. I even loop several around my neck and sway from side to side to make them dance.

When well wrapped, I strike my best attempt at a chorus-line pose and text, "Ta-da."

Grinning, Berkeley texts back, "Clap, clap, clap."

So I take a bow, grab more streamers, and gesture that they are all his, watching intently as he says something to his friends and starts walking.

Alarmed by the fact that he's heading toward me (*Is he heading toward me?*), I retrieve my drink, sashay toward Phoebe, and say, "Will you keep Daniel occupied for a few minutes?"

"Sure," she answers, smiling when she notices the direction of my gaze and then nudging me in the back to make sure I don't chicken out.

Deep in the middle of the crowd, Berkeley scoops the streamers out of my hand, places them on the top of my head, and says, "Belle of the ball."

Tweaking my new headgear, I say, "Thanks! My outfit needed that."

Looking me in the eyes, he says, "Ms. Lanoo, your outfit needs nothing tonight. You look amazing."

"Thanks," I reply, getting lost, as usual, in his dreamy gaze.

Calmly, he looks at his feet and says, "Umm, you know, you're dripping."

Noticing I've tipped my beverage and am pouring it onto Berkeley's loafers, I step back and say, "Oh no, I'm so sorry!"

As I crouch down and use some of the floor's streamers to clean his shoes and bare ankles, he says, "Don't worry about it, Ms. Lanoo. It's all okay."

"Are you sure?"

"I'm sure," he replies, taking my beverage, setting it on a nearby ledge, and discreetly shifting us away from the mess.

Turning to face me, he says, "So, Francie, would you like to, umm, dance?"

Flustered because Berkeley has never before called me Francie, I stupidly blurt out, "Right here? By myself?"

His face contorts. "No, not by yourself, bozo. With me!"

I sputter, "Well. Okay. Sure."

Shaking his head and grabbing my hand, he says, "Come on, Miss Oblivious. Let's find a better spot."

"Sure," I say, feeling a little woozy because the feel of his hand clutching mine is beyond amazing.

As we weave through people, I nervously mumble, "I'm just now realizing that I agreed to go to a dance with a date I have absolutely no interest in dancing with."

Smirking, Berkeley notes, "Maybe next time, you should be pickier with your dance dates."

"A rookie mistake," I say, blushing because I probably should have kept the comment to myself.

Stopping us at a quiet niche near the steps to the stage, he asks, "How's this?"

I look from side to side. "I can shake a leg pretty much anywhere, so this is definitely fine."

With a nod, Berkeley responds, "Well then, start shaking."

So I do, and I say, "Feel free to upstage me."

Eyeing my every move (some of them are good ones, thanks to my many years of dance classes), he notes, "That's impossible on every level imaginable."

I grin. *Nice!*

When the upbeat song ends, a mushy, slow one begins. As the words "Baby, I want you" are sung, Berkeley takes a step toward me and says, "The DJ must have read my mind, because I was hoping the tempo would switch about now."

I glance up. "Yeah, but now you're at great risk of having your feet stomped on by mine."

"No." He smiles. "I've seen you shake your legs many times, so I know my feet are safe."

*Nice, again!*

Confidently taking hold of my hands, he eases me toward him and commences a smooth sway, our bodies moving in perfect unison, as if we have the same beatbox installed in our heads.

Feeling Berkeley's torso touching mine, I nearly lose my mind, and I think, *Hold it together, sister, because this moment is unlikely to get repeated.*

Midsong, I feel the urge to memorize every detail of Berkeley's extraordinary face. Nonchalantly, I sweep my eyes upward, and to my surprise, I discover that he is looking down at me.

Overwhelmed and immediately overheating, I unleash a case of verbal pointlessness. "Whoa, who cranked up the thermostat? Hey, Mr. Marshall obviously time-traveled to borrow that suit from the seventies. And surprise, surprise—Edell is here with Boone."

Berkeley says, "And you're here with Daniel."

"Yeah," I reply, locating Daniel alongside Phoebe. "But only because the guy kept following me around the school, asking me over and over and over to be his date for tonight, so I finally said, 'Okay, I'll go to the dance with you if it'll make you stop asking me!'"

Loudly exhaling, Berkeley asks, "So are you with him now?"

"No! I'm not with him. I'm just his escort—in the not-for-hire kind of way."

His head tilts. "Funny thing—until I saw you with Daniel, I thought Patrick Needle was your go-to guy."

I snap my head back. "No! Why would you think that?"

"Because he's always with you."

"Only because we've known each other forever."

"And he's never tried to date you?"

I shake my head. "No, the closest he and I ever came to that was at last year's Christmas dance, when someone held mistletoe above our heads."

"What happened with that?"

"Patrick kissed me, and I got the giggles."

"Interesting reaction."

"That's what he said."

Tensing his shoulders, Berkeley says, "Listen—I suspect I'm stepping out of bounds by saying this, but your date tonight has the reputation of being a serious Casanova."

"Oh, a Casanova. Should I be worried?"

"You should definitely be on your guard if you let him take you home."

Tipping my head, trying to ignore my recent hands-on experience, I hesitantly say, "Don't worry. I'll manage."

Berkeley stops moving. "FYI, Francie, Daniel is six feet tall, weighs a hundred and eighty pounds, and could hoist your featherweight body over his head with one hand."

I clear my throat. "Well, you probably could too, so maybe I should hire you as my bodyguard."

Pulling me close, he responds, "I accept."

As my heart begins to race, I say, "Don't you first need to clear it with your girlfriend?"

Sweeping the hair off my shoulders, he answers, "No, because I don't have a girlfriend."

"You don't?"

"No."

As my stomach flutters, I say, "Well, just so you know, if you assumed the role of bodyguard, you'd have to ride on the roof of Daniel's car when he takes me home, because you know, he drives a two-seater."

Berkeley restarts our swaying and replies, "No problem. The windblown look suits me just fine."

I grin. "Out of curiosity, what are your bodyguard services going to cost me? Because in this pocketless dress, I couldn't stash any cash."

He smiles. "For you, Ms. Lanoo, my bodyguard services are free of charge."

As I get lost in his gaze, Berkeley takes a deep breath and says, "Here's a thought."

"What?"

"Why don't you just take Daniel out of the picture tonight?"

"Meaning what?"

"Meaning let your new bodyguard take you home."

Thinking, *Holy crap, I'm in way over my head,* I say, "Well, let me first ask you something."

"Sure."

"How good are you at piggybacking?"

He smiles. "I'm extraordinary."

"Good to know," I say, pinching myself to see if it hurts, because I can't tell if this is reality or another one of my Berkeley daydreams.

As a fast-paced tune starts blaring over the airwaves, the crowd starts bouncing as one—except for Berkeley and me, because we can't stop staring at each other's faces. Only when someone abruptly elbows Berkeley in the back do we snap out of it.

"So," I ask, "how exactly does it work—swapping out a date for a bodyguard?"

He places his hands on my hips. "You give me your hand."

When I offer it for a handshake, he instead meshes his fingers with mine, sports a grin that sets my insides on fire, and leads us away.

The moment seems euphoric until Daniel shouts from across the room, "Hey, Mills, what are you doing?" and starts moving toward us, the crazy expression on his face causing the hairs on my forearms to stand on end.

Berkeley doesn't respond and continues bobbing and weaving us through a sea of active bodies.

"Where are we going?" I ask.

"Outside to get some air."

I swallow. "Air is good."

Glancing over his shoulder, Berkeley says, "How close is our tail?"

Looking back and noticing a fist-clenched Daniel about ten paces behind but caught up in an erratic crowd bounce, I answer, "You don't want to know."

Peering at my feet as we exit out the door, he adds, "This escape would have been so much easier if you'd worn sneakers."

I look down. "But these *are* my sneakers."

Chuckling, he says, "Suddenly, I'm foreseeing a lot of piggybacking in my future."

"The reason I asked if you were any good at it."

Smiling, he leads us across the open grass and says, "Who knew I'd have to actually scheme to spend five minutes in Francie Lanoo's company?"

My forehead crinkles. "Berkeley, you spend five minutes in my company every day of the school week."

He smiles. "I meant alone."

I giggle. "Why? So you can retaliate for the orange-pop incident?"

He sighs. "Sure, if it means I get to fondle your ankles the way you just fondled mine."

As I sheepishly grin, we arrive at the base of a humongous oak tree in the middle of the school's front yard, where Berkeley, in one fell swoop, lifts me up and into it.

Following suit, he parks himself face-to-face with me, takes a deep breath, and sweetly chants, "Francie and Berkeley, sittin' in a tree."

As I blush, the school's exit door swings open, causing a startling bang.

Looking toward it, peering through thick leaves, we watch Daniel scramble around the moonlit school grounds, shouting expletives clearly aimed at us.

When the racket finally fades, Berkeley leans into me, ties my necklace streamer into a bow, plants his palms on the tree trunk behind me, and commences a spine-tingling, over-the-moon, intense, mint-flavored lip-lock that makes me feel as if I've never been kissed before.

As all of me starts to vibrate (even my fingernails, eyelashes, and earlobes), I realize Berkeley is even hotter to kiss than I've imagined—and believe me, I've imagined. Unable to help myself, I whisper, "Please do that again."

He does, pulling my body so close to his that I can feel his heart thumping as fast as mine.

Hovering his face an inch away from mine, he quietly says, "I kid you not, Ms. Lanoo—my legs just went weak."

Taking hold of his ripped upper arms, I respond, "It was probably all that running."

He slowly shakes his head. "My condition has nothing to do with running."

Flustered by his closeness, I start swinging my feet and say, "You run really fast."

He smiles. "You move surprisingly fast too, especially considering you're wearing shoes with heels."

I give him a cute glance. "Running well in heels is a skill all girlie girls are proficient at."

He lightly laughs. "Adding to the long list of your notable traits."

"Adding to my long list of *weird* traits."

He locks eyes with me. "Ms. Lanoo, *weird* would be the last adjective I would use to describe you."

I tilt my head upward. "So give me one you think fits better."

"I'll give you several," he says. "You're irresistible. Gripping. Addictive. Sirenic."

Dipping my chin, I lightheartedly say, "Anything else?"

"Yeah, you're cute as hell," he replies, descending to the ground and helping me to do the same.

Following a quirky-conversation-filled saunter all the way to my house (much of it involving piggybacking because my feet were done like dinner), Berkeley gives me a good-night kiss with such sizzle it enables me to travel up the stairs and into bed as if my feet aren't touching the ground.

Under the covers, with clothes still on, I lie there, wide-eyed and stunned. As an uncontrollable grin erupts on my face, I reach my hand toward the floor and transfer this evening's shoes onto the pillow beside me.

While briefly recapping the last hour of my life, I ask a question that's certain to become a shoe-wearing ritual: "Does anything about the Debut-Taunters reflect me?" Let's see. They did garner the only attention that matters to me, so that's a plus. However, they also caused at least four blisters that I'm going to have to nurse for at least the next week. Shaking my head, I enter into my phone the first of my me-shoe criteria: *hurtless.*

Then I drift off to a new dreamland, imagining what's up next for my feet and for me.

# foot note three

AM I AWAKE OR DREAMING? I DON'T KNOW. I'M LYING IN BED faceup, staring at the ceiling, but my eyes aren't able to focus. After rubbing them with my fingertips, I turn my head to the side and, in the dimness of the early morning light, see a pair of shoes sitting on the adjacent pillow. As my consciousness hints at returning, I deduct that I'm half choking because a streamer is tied around my neck, and I'm half mummified because a dress is wound tightly around my waist. Attempting to free myself, I hear my phone ping on the nightstand. Fumbling to grab it, I ramble, "Five a.m.? On a Sunday? Who texts at this hour?"

Propping myself up on my elbows, I discover that apparently, many people do—roughly ten over the course of the last few hours. Fully raising my eyelids, I read the current sender's name: Berkeley Mills.

"Berkeley Mills!"

As an intense recollection of recent events hits like a tsunami, I bolt upright and exclaim, "Holy crap! I was with him last night."

Squinting to see my phone clearly, I read his message slowly and distinctly: "I'm awake and thinking about your freckles."

Murmuring, "Could that guy get any more adorable?" I text back: "I'm awake and thinking about your minty-fresh breath."

After a few seconds, I hear a ping and read, "Available to breathe on you 24–7."

Smiling so widely my face hurts, I turn my phone off, plant my head face first onto my pillow, and force myself to go back to sleep.

I must because I cannot comprehend the mind-blowing possibility that I might be Berkeley Mills's latest girlfriend.

What? How? Why?

Monday morning arrives, and again, I open my eyes to the sight of shoes perched on the pillow beside me. As my nervous system fires up, I feel tinges of pain from several now-enormous blisters caused by those shoes, prompting me to finally accept, to my disbelief, that the events of Saturday night were not a dream.

Yesterday I wasn't the least bit convinced, which is why I spent the entirety of the day off the grid. And I would love to implement that same avoidance mechanism today, but I can't, because I have to take a first-period precalculus exam, and I have be in a classroom to do it.

I peer at my phone. It's seven o'clock—time to get vertical and face my new reality, regardless of how unreal it feels.

I grab my Debut-Taunter shoes, hobble across the room, stare at the many shoes on the shelves inside my closet, and say aloud, "It's amazing that babysitting earnings could amass such a collection." Then I set my prized footwear in a place of honor, top and center. Adjusting the shoes so that they're perfectly straight, I note, "To remind me that I got kissed by that guy more than once."

As visions of kissing Berkeley dance around in my head, I check out my marred bare feet and contemplate today's footwear case study. *Hmm. What options do I have that are both blister-friendly and eye-catching?*

Hit with an urge to call Berkeley to say, "Holy Hannah banana, you have hot lips," I grab my phone from the nightstand, turn it on, and start reading the messages I ignored during yesterday's hiatus.

First up is Silvia: "Spill the details! I've barely slept, waiting to hear from you."

Next is Beatrice: "See?! That hairstyle opens all the right doors."

A message from Phoebe reads, "I take it back; the guy isn't senseless after all."

One from Catharine Armour says simply, "Bitch."

"Whoa, that's harsh," I say aloud.

Next, I read several sent by some of Berkeley's fanatical devotees, all of whom, in a nutshell, imply that I'm undeserving.

Lastly, I listen to a voice message from Daniel that says, "I can't believe *you* ditched *me*."

Never having had a peer conflict in my life, I set the phone down, run my fingers through my hair, dart into the bathroom, and slink into the hottest shower I can handle. Midshampoo, I mumble, "I didn't know being with Berkeley had a downside," and I consider how I'm going to get through the day.

As my head fills with an image of me wearing a prosthetic nose borrowed from the drama department, I hear my mother hollering, "Girls, I've got a building to design today, so ready or not, your chariot is leaving in five minutes!"

Rushing from the bathroom to my bedroom, I exclaim, "What to wear? What to wear?"

Realizing it's not in my best interest to do anything to draw attention to myself today, I clad myself head to toe in stealth: black skinny jeans, a black turtleneck, and low-heeled black boots, soft soled and silent. After a final glance in the mirror, I say, "Dull as dirt," and then I tear down the stairs and out the door to where my mom awaits. The only thought running through my head is that my inability to cope with real-world issues might turn Berkeley Mills into my third one-and-done date, which would be heartbreaking on many levels, including the fact that I don't yet have photographic proof I was ever with him.

In the front seat of my mom's SUV, my brown-haired, hazel-eyed sister Brigitte, who is wearing masculine eyeglasses that hide her pretty face, says, "Francie, you look like a badass bandit today."

"I'm good with that," I say, glancing to the left and finding my fair-haired, cute, shy, and mousy sister Talula looking at puppy pictures on her phone.

Glancing toward me, she quietly says, "You look nice whatever you wear."

"Thank you, sweetie pie. So do you."

As my mom starts rambling about the latest movie releases, I hear my phone ping.

It's a text from Berkeley, saying, "If I don't see you before school starts today, I'm gonna lose my mind."

Opening my eyes wide and sitting up straight, I do a quick lip-gloss application and reply, "I'm fond of your mind, so please don't lose it."

He responds, "Hanging on to it by a thread."

Smiling for the first time today, I reply, "I'll be at the front gates in five."

Swiftly, he responds, "It'll be the longest five minutes of my life."

Stepping out of the vehicle, I pan the glistening landscape, and the sight of Berkeley leaning against my now-favorite oak tree makes me as awestruck as I was the first time I saw him—and the last time I saw him and every time in between. Pushing all of my morning angst to the back burner, I take a deep breath and beeline toward him.

"Hey," I say softly.

Taking hold of my hands and pulling me toward him, he sweetly asks, "How are you?"

"Better all of a sudden."

"Me too."

I manage a tiny smile. "How was your yesterday?"

"Frantic!"

My eyes spring open. "Why?"

He broadly smiles. "Because I was running around town, buying up breath mints."

I look to the ground. "I have no idea why I mentioned that. I mean, I really like having you breathe on me, but you probably didn't need to know that."

He dips his face so that it's directly in front of mine. "I'm glad I left an impression."

"More than one," I admit as the two of us start walking toward the school's main entry.

Tightly by my side, Berkeley says, "I tried to call you a couple of times yesterday, but you must have had your phone turned off."

"Yeah."

"I hope you weren't avoiding me."

"No, not at all. In fact, the lack of you actually made my insides hurt."

"Same," he murmurs with a sweet grin.

Glancing to the side, I say, "I turned my phone off because I was suffering from some kind of post-Saturday-night stress disorder."

"Why?"

I clear my throat. "Well, partly because I've never actually dated anyone before."

He says, "No worries—it's not hard."

I look at his face. "But mostly because you're you."

His brow furrows. "I have no idea what that means."

I squint. "You would if you walked into any of the girls' washrooms and read what's been written about you on every stall wall."

His face flushes. "Have you written anything?"

"No, of course not."

He shrugs. "Then there'd be no point in me reading."

I smirk. "Well, you should, because it's wildly informative."

Wiping his brow, he quietly says, "Okay, now you've got me curious. Give me one example."

Withholding a grin, I respond, "Well, there's a general consensus that your scent is intoxicating."

Grabbing my hand, he says, "Is it?"

I blush. "Yes."

He grins. "Well then, I'm gonna keep up the good hygiene."

After giggling, I take a deep breath and say, "Also adding to my list of stresses, your last girlfriend messaged me and implied that she's not happy you moved on."

His eyes perk up. "Catharine contacted you?"

"Yes, as did several other girls, whom I'm guessing are the writers of the messages on the bathroom stall walls."

He sighs. "I hope they didn't rattle you."

I frown. "Yes, they did, which is why I intend to get lost in the crowd today."

Eyeing my outfit, he responds, "You do know that that's physically impossible for you, right?"

"Why?"

He smiles. "Well, for starters, you currently look hotter than Catwoman."

As my cheeks heat up, I catch sight of my Saturday-night date entering the school through another set of doors. "Crap," I mumble.

"What?"

"Daniel's here, and I have no idea what I'm going to say to him when I inevitably cross his path."

Opening one of the school's doors, Berkeley replies, "Out of worry that your inaugural relationship is getting off to an alarmingly troubled start, why don't you let me handle all of this stuff? Okay?"

Giving him a sweet look, I say, "I don't expect you to fight my battles for me."

Wrapping an arm around me as we enter the building, Berkeley sweetly responds, "It's what any good bodyguard would do."

Amid a shared smile, Berkeley and I come face-to-face with a crazy-eyed Catharine Armour.

Poking her long-nailed index finger into Berkeley's chest, she shouts, "That's it? You break up with me on Friday, and a day later, you move on to a new tart?"

Calm as can be, Berkeley says, "You do realize what you just implied, right?"

Rolling her eyes, she says, "Whatever."

As I'm wondering, *Did she just label me a tart?* Berkeley says, "Sorry, Catharine, but I don't have time to get into this right now."

But apparently, she does, because she gets in my face, blocks me from walking, and says, "Who knew you had it in you?"

Too startled to respond, I freeze in place and let her stare me down.

Gripping my upper arms from behind, Berkeley eases me around Catharine, sets us on a speedy course down the corridor, and says, "See you around, Catharine."

From a distance, she shouts, "A word of warning, Francie: your boyfriend swaps out his arm candy on a bimonthly basis."

Shifting so he's walking alongside me, Berkeley murmurs, "Please ignore that."

Wanting to but unable to, I say, "Well, when you do decide to swap me out, rest assured I'll go more quietly than that."

Gripping my hand, he responds, "FYI, Ms. Lanoo, I'm feeling pretty optimistic that my days of swapping are officially over."

Warming from head to toe, I ask, "Why? Because I dazzled you on Saturday night with my ability to run in three-inch heels?"

Looking me square in the eyes, he replies, "Because you dazzle me always."

The happy vibe instantly dissipates when Berkeley and I arrive at my locker and find Daniel shouldered into it with his arms crossed.

Into my ear, Berkeley whispers, "Someday you need to explain to me why you went out with that guy in the first place."

Before I can respond, Daniel abruptly shouts, "Well, look at you two!"

"Sorry, Daniel," I mumble. "I just didn't—"

"Hey, man," Berkeley interjects, "I really want to apologize for my behavior on Saturday night. It crossed a line."

Standing erect, Daniel exclaims, "Don't for a minute think I'm gonna let you off the hook for what you did!"

Shuffling me out of harm's way, Berkeley responds, "Seriously?"

Then, right before my eyes, Daniel lunges and initiates the only fistfight I've ever witnessed—or caused.

As I'm opening my locker to see if there's room for me to climb inside, Berkeley steadies Daniel against a wall and says, "Don't make a bigger deal of this than necessary, Daniel."

With gritted teeth, Daniel replies, "What's necessary is that I make your pretty face so ugly that no one will ever want to date you."

"Jesus," Berkeley says. He then looks at me and says, "Francie, if Daniel turns my face ugly, will you still date me?"

"Yes."

Suppressing a smile, Berkeley says, "Sorry, Daniel. She'll still have me, ugly or not."

As I gawk and try to contain a grin, Daniel eases up, walks away, points toward his torso, and says, "Fine, Francie. But this is your loss."

"I understand," I say quietly.

"Have a happy life," he shouts, heading toward a pack of girls that are eagerly awaiting his attention.

Looking to Berkeley, I say, "Thank you for that."

He tentatively smiles. "No problem."

I shake my head. "I can't believe you got in a fight for me."

Leaning toward me and pressing his forehead onto mine, he responds, "For the record, Ms. Lanoo, after Saturday night, I'm fairly certain I'd eat bees for you."

I look into his close-up eyes. "Bees?"

He steps back. "Yep."

I smile. "For the record, I would never expect you to."

He moves toward his nearby locker. "Good, because I once swallowed one while cycling, and I did not enjoy it."

As I chuckle, the second school bell rings to signal the start of class. With books in tow, Berkeley and I scurry hand in hand down the bustling corridor, and along the way, we receive a few gawks—some with surprised grins, some with approving nods, and some aiming their puppy-dog eyes only at Berkeley. One guy from the football team slaps Berkeley on the back and says, "It's about time you found the nerve."

Feeling as if a hundred pounds of worry have just floated away from me, I think maybe Berkeley won't be my third one-and-done date.

Stopping at my classroom door, Berkeley puts a hand on my back and quietly says, "So tonight I have to go to dinner with my parents, tomorrow night I have to go to a football fund-raiser, and Wednesday night I have this photography-club event."

"You're so busy."

Walking backward away from me, he says, "At the risk of exposing how smitten I am, I was hoping you'd be busy with me tonight, tomorrow, and Wednesday."

Withholding a jump for joy, I ask, "Are you sure several nights in a row won't make you sick of me?"

He shakes his head. "Not seeing you for several nights in a row is about the only thing that would make me sick."

I smile. "Okay then, I'll be busy with you."

His eyes gleam. "All righty then. So we're doing this?"

I peer from around the classroom door. "I guess we are. See you at lunch?"

Nodding, he responds, "Already thinking about it."

Taking a seat in the back of the classroom and feeling as if I'm about to float to the ceiling, I slip my feet out of my footwear to check out my blister situation, smile because these shoes have inflicted no further damage (in fact, my wounds are starting to heal), and whisper, "Okay, did you or did you not enlighten me about me?"

Pondering the fact that while wearing them, I discovered I'd rather be stricken with the plague than deal with conflict, I decide on the next of my me-shoe criteria: *harmonious.*

Sneakily entering the descriptor into my phone, I tune into the teacher's explanation about gravitational forces and say under my breath, "How apropos." I think ahead to this evening and accept that a little bit of angst won't hamper my happy world too much if a lip-lock with Berkeley awaits me at the end of the day.

# foot note four

TODAY IS THE TWO-MONTH-PLUS-ONE-DAY MARK OF ME DATING Berkeley, which means I'm able to finally put aside Catharine Armour's warning that a Berkeley girlfriend has a two-month shelf life. Not all of them do.

To celebrate, I'm wearing my latest footwear acquisition: a pair of black suede booties inspired by the groovy 1960s. I'm calling the style the Amaranthine, partly because it means timeless and everlasting but mostly because it sounds cool. I like this bootie's look because it's a retro throwback but still feels contemporary. I love this look because when I strutted into school today wearing it, Berkeley looked at my feet and my face and said, "If I had my way, I'd do nothing but stare at you all day every day."

It's words like those that explain why my face now bears a permanent grin; why I'm drawn to mushy love songs, romantic poems, and rom-com movies; and why my mind prefers steamy thoughts of Berkeley to a good night's sleep.

It might also be why I'm doing stuff that I would never have had the nerve to do pre-Berkeley, the most notable being my first entry into an art competition, a prestigious annual event at the Metro Gallery downtown.

Berkeley is the one who first read about it in one of our school's general e-mails, and while watching me complete an abstract sculpture for my art class (he loves to hang around when I'm creating art), he said, "You have to get involved in this; if not, you'll be depriving the world of your awesomeness."

After witnessing how lit up his remarkable eyes were, I could not disappoint.

The submission was a ton of work, though. I had to be prequalified based on grades and prerequisite classes by our school principal, Mrs. Bouchard. I had to write an essay about what art means to me. I had to put together a list of my future goals. I had to acquire three reference letters from people familiar with my artwork and bundle that with a transcript of my grades. Lastly, I had to slave for many hours on a series of eight original artwork pieces—my concept being eighteen-by-twenty-four-inch portraits, each featuring a compelling male figure in an action pose, each an attempt to bring to light the awesomeness of the subject it depicted (yes, they were all inspired by Berkeley).

Officially, I entitled the collection *Figures in Motion*. Unofficially, I refer to it as *Holy Crap, I Get to Kiss This Guy!*—a thought that blows my mind every time I do.

The technique I used for the artwork was new to me: thick hand-drawn lines in charcoal, cubist-like shapes filled in with bold watercolor washes, and overlaying shadows done in complementary pastels. The net result was whimsical, surreal, and a little bit odd, prompting my school art teacher, Ms. Kapp, whom I summoned to do a critique for me, to state I'd simultaneously channeled Matisse, Modigliani, and Picasso. Her comment made me smile despite the fact that I was unsure if it meant the images were good or bad.

Of course, I highly doubt my work will make the competition's top three (awards that will be announced next March—a full four months away) or put me in the running for some art-school program that the competition is linked to; however, the experience was good because it made me want to create more.

All of this is thanks to Berkeley, who, by the way, has had a stellar two months plus one day too. Aside from demonstrating daily that he's the ultimate bodyguard, ensuring that no badness ever comes my way, in October, he was named to the city's all-star football team; two weeks ago, he won an award from the photography club; and yesterday he was appointed editor of the school newspaper for next year.

There is a lot of mutually good stuff going on too. Berkeley and I talk about anything and everything in conversations that sometimes carry on for hours. My friends and his friends have blended together into one big heap. Both of our families light up when they see us together. My already-art-filled bedroom is overflowing with sketches of Berkeley. His bedroom is plastered with photographs he's taken of me (all goofy ones, much to my chagrin). We even do homework together, so clearly we will do anything to be in the same room. Yesterday, while lying in my backyard's fabulous string hammock, my all-time favorite place to hang out with Berkeley, we discussed the future—how I'd like to someday study fashion design and how Berkeley will one day take over his family's local newspaper business.

His admission surprised me, I have to admit, because I know he'd be way better suited to a career in photography or music or both—he's so bloody talented.

I chose not to mention that though, because I'm pretty sure that one day, he'll draw the conclusion on his own.

As we walk home from school, Berkeley—laughing at me because I'm taking exaggerated strides to try to keep up with his energetic pace—looks at my footwear and asks, "So how goes the shoe hunt?"

Smiling, I respond, "I'm plugging away at it, and in fact, I think I'm going to add a new descriptor, inspired by these booties."

"What would that be?"

"*Timeless.*"

"Why's your rationale for that one?"

"I like the idea of something being lovable for all eternity."

Putting an arm around me, Berkeley says, "I think it'd be awesome if you one day designed the Francie Lanoo shoe all by yourself."

Scoffing, I say, "But I don't have the slightest clue how to design a shoe."

Pulling me close, he says, "Then when you go to college, that's what you should study."

Feeling my face warm, I stop in my tracks and reply, "You know what, Mr. Mills? I think you just found my calling!"

"I can't think of any profession more well suited to you," he responds with a proud smile.

"Thanks for that."

"Happy to help."

After arriving at home, I pull out some drawing tools, muttering, "Francie Lanoo, is your ideal shoe buried somewhere within you?"

I retrieve my laptop and source an online tutorial on the basics of shoe design, and then I start sketching. Though every one of my ten attempts ends up in the recycling bin, I grin and say to myself, "This could be fun."

# foot note five

IN A MATTER OF HOURS, I'M DESTINED TO SLIP INTO A TERRIBLE slump. Berkeley is leaving early in the morning to travel to London, England, with his parents for two full weeks—the entire Christmas break—which will mark the first time in three months that he and I will have gone more than an overnight without seeing each other.

As an experiment to see if uplifting footwear will minimize the free fall, I've purchased the most-dazzling shoes this city had to offer: a pair of low-cut, square-heeled metallic-silver slip-ons, each with a faux-diamond gemstone on top. I'm calling them the Anti-Dismals and am hopeful that when I slip into them, they'll inject my disposition with a quick-fix dose of merriment.

The tactic proved to be costly, I will admit, depleting every last penny of Grandma Lanoo's Christmas money. But if not shoes to fill the enormous void of Berkeley Mills, then what?

He should be here at nine o'clock this evening, right after basketball practice.

*What to wear with my fantastic footwear? Hmm.*

It's a Tuesday evening in the confines of my own home, so I don't want to be too fancy; however, 'tis the season, so I don't dare underdress.

The doorbell rings. I look at the time. "He's fifteen minutes early."

In a state of frenzy, I throw on a fitted sweater, funky chandelier earrings, and slim black pants. After stepping into my silver sensations and smiling when they boost my mood as planned, I slink out of my bedroom and down the stairs.

Berkeley is in the living room, a silver-streamer-drenched, compact Christmas gift in hand, sitting in the big red Womb chair opposite my parents, who are sitting side by side on the sofa. The three are immersed in a smile-inducing conversation, which is a good sign, but when Berkeley catches sight of me, he ceases speaking, bolts to his feet, and says, "Hey, hi."

"How are you?" I respond, making my way across the room.

"Great. How are you?"

I coyly smile and jest, "A little worried my parents are boring you half to death."

"Not at all." He grins. "They were just giving me some background info on you."

"Oh?"

His eyes light up. "I had no idea you were named after your mom's favorite doll."

Tilting my head toward my mom and my lean and prematurely gray but seriously handsome-for-forty-something dad, I moan, "Really, Claire and Bennett? That's what you felt the need to share?"

My dad lifts his chin into the air. "We shared a lot more than that." I smirk. "Oh really?"

My mom clears her throat. "Next time, don't take so long to get ready." I shoot her a look. "Next time, I'll have Berkeley wait on the front step."

Chuckling, my dad says, "I doubt that'll change anything now that Berkeley has shared his contact information."

I grab Berkeley's hand to drag him away, suppress a smile, and say, "Dad, don't you dare become text buddies with Berkeley."

"I can if I want to," he says, flashing a devilish grin.

Shaking my head, I murmur to Berkeley, "I hope you know it's a date crime to befriend your girlfriend's parents."

Laughing adorably, Berkeley reads an incoming text (no doubt from my father) and distractedly replies, "I promise I'll only use the link for the greater good."

"Yeah, I bet."

En route to the family room, Berkeley veers to the left, grabs his outerwear, and catches up with me.

I eye his coat. "Did my father just instruct you to go home?"

Berkeley smiles. "No, I'm going out into the backyard—with you."

"What? Why?"

He throws an arm around my shoulders. "To show you something."

I slump. "But it's cold outside."

He pulls me closer. "Don't be a sissy. Go grab your stuff."

"Can't I just observe from the window?"

"You could, but I'm not going to let you."

"Argh."

He squints. "How can you not love hanging out in your backyard? It's a snow-blanketed, magical wonderland out there."

I coyly say, "If it's not hammock weather, it's not Francie weather." Noticing he's donned the cutest expression ever, I murmur, "Fine," and leave to grab my stuff.

When I return, Berkeley waves his arm toward the patio doors and says, "Hurry, hurry. This is a time-sensitive matter."

I scurry and say, "How can you be so enthusiastic about the prospect of freezing your ass? *My* ass?"

He shakes his head. "Stop fretting. Your ass will remain perfectly fine."

"Promise?"

"Promise."

After flinging the patio doors open, Berkeley charges to the middle of the yard, flops backward into a fresh layer of snow, lifts his head to observe me standing in the doorway, and grins ear to ear. "Get your perfectly fine ass out here."

Whispering some quiet curses, I suit up, step outdoors, and moan, "Don't for a minute think I'm going to lie in the snow."

He smiles. "Just plunk down on top of me, and the suffering will be kept to a minimum."

As I settle in, he says, "Be sure to look straight up, because the sight overhead is not to be missed."

Swinging my eyes to the sky, I exclaim, "Oh my! Those are some serious stars."

As the dazzling display of sparklers shines upon us, Berkeley explains, "It's a moonless, clear night, which is optimum for stargazing."

"Huh! I did not know that."

"It's crazy cool, don't you think? Like being watched by thousands of eyes."

I smile. "Just like when you walk around the school."

Squeezing me tightly, he replies, "That comment should have come from me to you."

I smirk. "No way. You're far prettier than me."

He huffs. "If you believe that, you're delusional."

I giggle. "Care to take a poll?"

"No, I don't care to."

For many minutes, we linger, until Berkeley says, "I could make a habit of this, hanging out with you under the stars."

I turn my head to look at him and quip, "If my face wasn't frozen, I'd smile at that comment."

"I'll unfreeze your face," he says, rolling me onto my back and breathing fresh, minty, warm air onto my frosty cheeks.

"Thank you. I needed that."

He smiles and then warms me even more with a long, drawn-out kiss, after which he says, "FYI, you just made my insides so hot that I think I'm about to melt the entire backyard."

"I can help you with that," I reply, throwing snow onto his face and scrambling away.

Wiping his eyes clean, he hollers, "You know, you're the only person on this planet I'd let get away with that."

I smile. "Thanks for the tip."

Standing up, he replies, "Like you didn't already know."

Back in the family room, Berkeley settles on the sprawling sectional sofa, grabs his gift off of the end table, and says, "This is for you."

My eyes feel as if they're going to burst out of my head. "Thank you!"

"I made it."

"Yay," I say, taking the box and nestling beside him. "And you tied about a hundred streamers around it."

"Yeah, that's because everything looks good draped in streamers."

"Ha-ha. Cute."

He chuckles. "For the record, I'd happily let you give me another face wash if you showed me those streamer-stringing dance moves again."

I wrinkle my nose. "Highly doubtful."

"Hang on to the streamers just in case."

"Sure."

He leans a shoulder into mine. "I hope you like it."

I smile. "Is it an announcement that your vacation has been canceled?"

"Sorry, no."

"Then evidently, Santa didn't get my wish list."

Pulling me into his lap, Berkeley says, "I'll make it up to you next year."

"I'm gonna hold you to that."

Into my ear, he murmurs, "Feel free to hold me anytime."

Offering up a sugary-sweet eye roll, I respond, "Thank you. I will."
He winks.

Opening the box, I find a paper scroll displaying a list of songs and a series of black-and-white photos of Berkeley wearing a ridiculous expression on his face.

I read aloud the scroll's title: "Songs to Take Your Mind off This Dude."

He says, "My favorite is the one called 'Shoe-Stomping Revenge.'"

"This is the best," I warmly say, grinning when I notice that every photo suits the accompanying song name.

"I scoured every music library out there to compile the best worst songs."

I place my forehead against his. "You have outdone yourself."

Smiling, he replies, "I hope it'll accomplish what it's supposed to."

I pull my head away from his. "Unlikely, but I will listen regardless."

Setting my gift on the table, I say, "I have something for you too, which I also made."

He smiles. "I like that we're on the same wavelength."

I giggle. "You'll be saying that again as soon as you see what I made."

I wander toward the nearby Christmas tree, grab a large, tubular Christmas cracker, sit back down close to Berkeley, and say, "But unlike your present to me, this one is meant to keep your mind *on* me—literally."

Reaching inside the tube, he says, "Sounds like Santa got my wish list." He smiles when he finds a customized pillowcase bearing a life-size selfie of my face that I took about a week ago. It's kind of cute, if I do say so myself. I have bed head and sleepy eyes. I'm wearing a red-and-white nightshirt. I have tinsel in my hair, bobbles dangling from my ears, glitter adorning my cheeks, and garland coiling down my arms.

"This is fantastic!" he exclaims, holding it up in the air.

I smile. "Maybe you could take it to London so that you think of me every time you hit the hotel pillow."

He says, "So I can *obsess* about you every time I hit the hotel pillow."

I lean into him. "You don't think it'll be a little creepy having a face staring at you while you sleep?"

He smiles. "On the contrary. I may never get out of bed."

I giggle. "Nice!"

Setting the pillow to the side, he adds, "It's great, Francie. Thanks for making it."

"You're welcome," I reply, lifting my shoed feet onto the sofa.

Watching, he says, "You know, those shoes have 'Christmas ornament' written all over them."

I chuckle. "Yes, but if they got put on a tree, my feet would become very sad."

"I've never seen sad feet before. What do they look like?"

"Like any other fifteen-year-old feet," I reply, slipping off one of my shoes, thanking the stars that I got a glittery pedicure yesterday.

Taking a closer look, he exclaims, "Whoa! Your feet are really nice, like they were swiped from a porcelain sculpture."

My face twists. "Okay?"

He grins. "Seriously, you should hire them out for barefoot modeling gigs."

I giggle. "As a shoe devotee, that would feel like an act of treason."

Playing with my toes (*Wow, that feels nice!*), he asks, "Where did your passion for shoes come from anyway?"

I sigh. "I don't know. I think it's just one of those unexplainable things. You know, where something just clicks."

He nods. "I can relate."

I perk up. "To *your* shoes?"

He looks me in the eyes. "No, to you."

My cheeks flushing, I solemnly say, "You know, you've got some pretty good lines for a fifteen-year-old guy."

He sighs. "Thank you, and just so you know, there's more corniness where that came from."

I smile. "The cornier the better."

He eases me toward him. "I'll remember that."

As the two of us get lost in each other's eyes, Berkeley exhales and says, "I know this is the worst case of bad timing, but I have to leave in about five."

"Seriously?"

"Yeah, I'm being dragged to the airport at the crack of dawn and haven't packed yet."

I slump. "But if you go home right now, you'll thwart my plan of making you miss your flight."

He gets up and helps me do the same. "Even better would be if you came with me."

Slipping my shoe back on, I respond, "Why not? It wouldn't be hard to stash petite me into your suitcase."

Pulling me into his arms, he responds, "I'm game if you're game."

I giggle. "Although, there is the issue of all the shoes I'd need to bring with me, not to mention the subsequent extra-baggage fees."

"You and your shoes would be well worth it."

I flutter my eyelashes. "I think so too."

Walking toward the front door, Berkeley whispers into my ear, "Of course, the bigger reason not to stow you in my luggage would be your father."

I nod. "Yeah, the old guy would probably go berserk with me in your hotel room."

Berkeley smiles. "Which is really too bad, because over the next fourteen days, I am going to miss you a lot."

"How much?"

"Hmmm. Like a pencil misses lead?"

I think for a second and add, "Because there would be no *point*?"

He smirks, steals a kiss, and says, "You make my day, Ms. Lanoo."

46

I flash a cute look. "Well, if you'd like me to make it again tomorrow, you should call me as soon as you land in London."

"How about I'll call you when I get home in ten minutes?"

"Please do!"

He does, and we talk the entire time he packs.

Readying myself for bed, I remove my footwear, think about my ongoing quest, and make a quick observation: as lovely as these shoes are, they don't possess a single quality worth noting on my list. I can't say why specifically. Perhaps because they will forever be associated with the crater-sized hole that just formed in the center of me.

To slow the downward slide I can sense lurking, I reminisce about one of this evening's highlights—the romp in the snow—and draw upon a different source of inspiration, adding another adjective to my me-shoe criteria: *sparkly*.

"Because isn't it every girl's dream to walk into and light up a room?" I say to myself, carrying my shoes to the closet.

Climbing into my bed, I hear my phone ring.

It's Phoebe, asking, "How was your evening?"

"Fantastic. I just wish Berkeley's holiday was over already."

"He hasn't even left yet."

"I know."

"Want me to do something with you tomorrow to cheer you up?"

"Sure, as long as you don't mind that I'm going to make you wear a Berkeley mask."

She laughs. "Francie, you sound like you're smitten."

I rub my eyes with my fingers. "I think I might be."

She clears her throat. "Be careful going down that road until you know whether or not Berkeley is on the same page."

"Too late. I'm already in a free fall."

She sighs. "Well then, I hope it works out for you."

I take a deep breath. "Me too."

# foot note six

FOR THE PAST TWO WEEKS, I'VE DONE NOTHING BUT OBSESS ABOUT my first Valentine's Day spent with a boyfriend. I wondered, *Do I buy a gift or a card?* I went with the card. *Do I call him on the morning of to say something mushy?* I didn't have to, because he beat me to it. *For this evening's dinner, do I dress like any other day, or do I wear something that has "valentine" written all over it?* Sappy as I am, I went with the latter.

For my feet, I chose a pair of low-heeled hot-pink cloth slip-ons that I recently treated as an art canvas, meticulously hand-painting heart murals all over them. I'm calling this style the Amore, and though it's far from masterpiece material, it's a creation I will forever treasure.

For my attire, after earlier indulging in a chocolate-covered, marshmallow-filled treat my mom left for me, I chose white jeans, a white T-shirt, a long chocolate-brown faux-fur coat and pink patent-leather gloves. Yes, I'm paying homage to a tacky and cheap treat. No, I don't expect Berkeley to pick up on it. However, I will be thrilled to the gills if he notices I'm wearing delicious strawberry-flavored lip gloss and my first-ever spritz of perfume (as suggested and provided by Phoebe).

In celebration of the occasion (which falls on a Wednesday, so I have a curfew of eleven o'clock), Berkeley and I are celebrating with some friends at Jule's Pizza. Phoebe will be there on a first date with a guy named Will. Beatrice will be there with her current steady, Jack. Berkeley's friend Pierce, who is almost as good looking as Berkeley but has dark hair and dark eyes like me, will be with his girlfriend, Jenn. As per the restaurant's longstanding tradition, all of what's being served for the occasion will have an underlying heart theme. Though I know it could prove corny or sappy, I'm excited about it because heart-shaped food will be a first for me, and firsts of anything tend to form my best memories.

All evening long, despite being surrounded by hokeyness, Berkeley and I get swept up in romantic gestures: staring into each other's eyes, playing footsy under the table, and webbing our fingers together (which makes my heart race).

After consuming our heart-shaped pepperoni pizza, heart-shaped strawberry shortcake, and fizzy drinks with heart-shaped ice cubes, Berkeley slides a Valentine's Day card across the table to me. "This is for you."

"Thank you!"

Inside the pink envelope, I find a close-up picture of a half-eaten apple with the caption "From the very core of me, I'm sweet on you."

"Nice!"

"And true."

With an ear-to-ear grin, I hand Berkeley a card and smile in anticipation of his reaction.

Removing the envelope, he discovers the picture of two cartoon lizards looking at one another with tiny pink hearts positioned above their heads. Opening it, he reads, "Hey, Valentine! Iguana be with you night and day." He smiles. "Right back at you."

Pointing to the female iguana, I say, "FYI, my back is not that scaly."

"Thanks for letting me know," he says, staring into my eyes, seemingly thinking about something. I don't know what. Maybe about my back?

A wind gust from an opening door sends the iguana card to the floor. Bending over to pick it up, Berkeley looks at my feet and says, "I like your shoes."

"Thanks. I painted them."

He sits upright. "I can tell you did. They have your unique style written all over them."

My eyes widen. "I wasn't aware I had a unique style."

"Yes, you do, and speaking of, have you heard anything about that art contest you entered last fall?"

I shake my head. "No, and I won't until the ides of March."

He smiles. "I have a good feeling about that."

"Why?"

"Because you, Ms. Lanoo, are destined to go places in life."

I smile. "And what about you? What are you destined to do?"

He looks to the tabletop. "Well, if I had my druthers, I'd pursue music in some capacity, but because such skills are not applicable to the newspaper business, I'll probably just do so as a hobby and, you know, follow the career path that's expected of me."

I dip my head to bring his gaze back to my face. "Have you ever discussed with your parents the fact that you have your own aspirations?"

He shakes his head. "No, because I might disappoint them, and they don't deserve that."

As I consider where to take the conversation from here, the well-fed, well-liked restaurant manager, Julian, cheerfully announces, "Attention, lovebirds, it is now closing time."

"Say it isn't so!" several people around us say in unison—an almost-nightly response at this beloved, near-the-school establishment.

I smile at Berkeley. "Thanks for bringing me here this evening."

"Thanks for the conversation."

"Too bad it got cut short."

"Yeah, too bad."

I raise an eyebrow. "Well, if you ever want to resume it, please know I'm all ears when it comes to you."

"Thanks," he says, smiling and grabbing my hand as we stand up to leave.

During our casual-paced stroll home, I check my phone and realize it's fifteen minutes past my curfew.

Sauntering up the front steps of my house, I whisper, "The minute I open this door, my parents are gonna pounce all over me."

He inhales. "No, you'll be okay."

I squint. "Don't be so sure."

He smiles. "I *am* sure, because I texted your dad earlier and got you an extension."

"Really?"

"Really."

"Well, thanks for doing that!"

He dips his chin. "To be honest, I had selfish motives for my actions."

"You did?"

He moves closer to me. "Yeah, I was gunning for some alone time with you."

I ease into his arms. "Well, your gunning just got you some."

"Finally!" he exclaims, pulling me toward him, offering up another one of his knock-my-socks-off gazes. *Jesus, how does he do that?*

As if energized by his aura, I lift onto my tiptoes and do something I've never done with a boy before: I kiss him.

Sweeping my bangs away from my face, Berkeley stares into my eyes for several seconds and quietly says, "I love you, Francie."

As my heart nearly bursts out of my chest, I reply, "Well, that's really good to know, because I love you too."

He smiles and steps back. "I'm really happy to hear that."

I lean against the iron railing. "I'm really happy to say that."

He looks toward the landscape. "You know, for months, I've laid awake at night, thinking about where and when to tell you how crazy-mad I am about you."

"For months?"

"Yes, approximately five of them."

As my eyes pop open (because five months is how long we've been dating), I smile and whisper, "Wow."

He smiles. "Yeah, you've made me altogether smitten, Ms. Lanoo."

Dipping my chin, I softly reply, "Well, at least we're in the same boat."

Moving toward me and pressing his forehead onto mine, he quietly says, "You'd better go inside. It's getting late."

"Yeah, I'd better."

"I'll see you tomorrow, okay?"

"Sure."

Walking away, he spins around and says, "By the way, I think those shoes deserve placement in a hoity-toity museum somewhere."

I giggle. "You do?"

"Yeah, they're something special."

I grin. "I just wish they weren't so flat."

His forehead crinkles. "Why is that?"

My eyes dance. "Because it's important that I keep the distance between my lips and yours at a minimum."

He chuckles. "I like the way you think, Ms. Lanoo."

"I like it too."

He waves. "See ya."

I wave back. "Good night."

As his silhouette fades into the darkness, I slip inside my house, lean against the inside of the door, and marvel that every inch of me is tingling.

"Did you have a nice evening?" my dad asks out of the blue from the nearby den.

"I did," I say, popping my head around the corner.

Smiling, he adds, "I was impressed when Berkeley sent me a text earlier this evening, to let me know you'd be home late."

"He's pretty upstanding."

"Yes, it appears that way."

I coyly smile. "It sure does."

Exhaling, he notes, "Just be sure to pace yourself, Francie, because you know, you're only fifteen."

I take a deep breath. "Thanks for the advice, Dad. I'll take it under advisement."

He stands up. "I'm just saying, sweetheart, your sister Brigitte is a full three years older than you and is still weighing her relationship options."

I shrug. "Maybe that's because she doesn't know what she's looking for."

"Are you implying you do?"

I shrug. "What's the worst that could happen if that's the case?"

He raises an eyebrow. "You could get hurt."

I purse my lips. "Berkeley's not going to hurt me."

"He'd better not."

I roll my eyes. "Good night, Dad."

"Sleep tight, Francie."

Removing what I'm about to relabel the I Love You shoes, I make my way up the stairs, into my bedroom, and onto the bed.

Ignoring what my dad said, rehearing what Berkeley and I professed to each other, and giggling about the silly comment I made regarding the distance between Berkeley's lips and mine, I search for something to add to my criteria and settle on *uplifting*—to the tune of at least three inches.

Ready to call it a night, I decide to show these shoes some

appreciation by keeping them on my feet while I sleep. That way, when I wake tomorrow morning and feel them in place, I will instantly be reminded that Berkeley Mills loves me.

I sigh, smile, and hug my pillow.

# foot note seven

IN CELEBRATION OF BERKELEY'S SIXTEENTH BIRTHDAY, I'VE assembled a lineup of footwear to wear in his company. Boldly, I'm labeling the series the Subliminal Seductresses, which seems befitting because they're all a little bit flirty but not in-your-face slutty.

For daytime at school, I'll be wearing a pair of low-heeled, calf-hugging black suede boots that have an elongating effect on my not-elongated legs. It's early March, and there's still snow on the ground, so I went for something in the practical realm to keep my feet warm for most of the day.

For early evening, I'll be wearing a pair of black patent square-toed, square-heeled, superstyling ankle boots that Phoebe and I fell in love with at first sight a week ago and desperately wanted to own, but because there was only one pair remaining in stock at the store—in my size, not hers—I went home with them. This evening will mark their inaugural strut.

Lastly, for later in the evening, I'll be wearing a pair of perky, flashy coral-colored flip-flops that I bought to accompany the outfit I'll be wearing them with. More on that impractical choice later.

If, in combination, the three footwear styles net me a single characteristic worth noting in my quest, I'll be thrilled. If, in combination, the three help to make Berkeley's birthday spectacular, I'll be ecstatic. A happy Berkeley equals a happy me.

Lying in bed with insomnia, noticing it's six o'clock in the morning, I decide to call Berkeley so that my voice is the first one he hears today. Hitting number one on my speed dial, I hear four rings followed by some fumbling on the other end of the line.

"Yeah, hullo?" he murmurs.

I clear my throat and start singing a personalized rendition of a birthday song, and though my raspy morning voice sounds sleepy and lacks rhythm, it does what it's supposed to: it makes Berkeley laugh.

As I hold on the last note, he says, "You need to start a band."

"I'm sensing sarcasm."

"What? Never."

I giggle. "So how does the age of sixteen feel?"

"A little blurry."

"Are you ready for a day of surprises?"

"That depends. Will there be more singing?"

"Maybe later, if I'm feeling saucy."

"Saucy?"

"Well, it *is* your birthday."

"I've never seen you saucy."

"Feel free to let your imagination run wild."

"Believe me, I am."

My cheeks heat up. "Hey, what time will you be at school this morning?"

"Not until at least nine thirty. My driver's exam is at eight thirty."

"Hmmm. I was hoping to see you beforehand so I could transfer some good-luck vibes your way."

"Sorry to mess up your plan."

I smile. "No worries. I'll instead use mind waves to fire them to you through the airwaves. Can you feel your body vibrating?"

He sighs. "When it comes to you, yes, pretty much every minute of every day."

"Nice."

After a moment of silence, I loudly say, "Hey, birthday boy, are you still there?"

He exhales. "Yeah, I'm here; I'm just preoccupied with thoughts of you being saucy."

I lightly shake my head. "Get out of bed, Mr. Mills."

"I am, and I'm turning the shower on to freezing cold thanks to you."

I laugh. "Break a leg, but don't break the car."

"Thanks. I'll try not to."

Hanging up, I cross my fingers that Berkeley obtains his driver's license today, not just because it'll make him happy but also because it'll make it easy to get him to where he needs to be this evening: his friend Pierce's house for a surprise party. I didn't plan it, and I haven't been told a lot about it (perhaps because Pierce was worried I'd slip the secret), but I do know that swimsuits are suggested, which is interesting because there's still snow on the ground, and that a fire pit is involved, for which Phoebe was given the task of bringing stuff for s'mores.

Whatever the details, I know Berkeley will have a good time because he loves hanging out in the company of friends, and friends love hanging out with him. In fact, Berkeley's easygoing, charismatic, and quick-witted personality usually is the life of the party.

The suggestion to bring a swimsuit explains my choice of flip-flops in the wintertime—this evening's shoe selection will perfectly complement the skimpy, pretty bikini I bought exclusively for this celebration. Because this will be the first time Berkeley sees me in a swimsuit, I'm pulling out all stops to make a lasting impression, even though I'm at risk of having him look at me and think, *That girl is shaped like a Popsicle stick.* To be clear, I don't resent that I'm thin.

In fact, it's the body shape I'd have chosen, if given the option. But I definitely don't fit the mold of Berkeley's previous girlfriends, all of whom must have hit puberty at age ten.

*Man, I can't wait to see Berkeley today. Man, it seriously sucks that he and I do not have a single class together this semester.*

At noon, when Berkeley and I finally cross paths in a bustling school corridor, I grin from ear to ear at the sight of him carrying an armful of newly discovered balloon animals that I planted in his locker before school started.

He walks up to me, leans in, plants a kiss on my forehead, and says, "I found your friends."

I sport a silly grin. "They're your friends now."

He shakes his head. "I knew there'd be a consequence to sharing my locker combination with you."

I dip my chin. "I give you my word that I will only ever use privilege to make you happy."

He smiles. "Just remember, I know your lock combination too."

"Message received." Petting one of the creatures, I ask, "Hey, did my good-luck vibes do their job this morning?"

"Yes, they did. I passed."

"Yay!" I scream, jumping up and down.

Making the balloon creatures walk all over me, he says, "And guess what else."

"Did you crash your dad's car?"

He gives me a twisted look. "No!"

"Okay, what?"

"My parents gave me a car."

"Oh, wow! You are so lucky!"

"I know. Come on. Let's go for burgers."

"Sure!" I say. "Birthday lunch is on me."

"I'm good with that," Berkeley replies, flashing a cute look that naive me spends the next thirty seconds clueing into.

For the next hour, driving around in Berkeley's new wheels (a compact dark green car with plaid upholstery and a stick shift), we tour nearly every inch of Riverly Heights' downtown core, munching our supersized fast food and playing loud music as Berkeley's balloon friends stare at us from the backseat. Occasionally, we glance back at them; however, when Berkeley almost sideswipes the mirror off of a parked car, we agree it's time to safely return us all back to school.

I don't see Berkeley for the entirety of the afternoon or after school, because he has a photography-club meeting, but he picks me up at seven so that we can join his parents for dinner.

When I come down the stairs to meet him, he's in the dining room with my parents and sisters, who are feeding him a birthday meal before he has a birthday meal. My mother even prepared him a cupcake with a candle. *Too cute.* As he stands up to greet me, I notice he's looking even more irresistible than he did earlier in the day—he's freshly showered, sporting a styling haircut, and wearing fashion-magazine-quality attire.

Relieving him of food overload by escorting him to the front door, I say, "You're gonna get birthday kisses from complete strangers looking like that."

Setting his dreamy eyes onto my face, he responds, "Impossible when I intend to spend the entire night lip-locked with you."

"Ready when you are."

His mouth upturns at the corners. "Saucy so soon?"

"It is your special day," I say, following up with what I hope is the first of many lip-locks this evening.

We join Berkeley's parents for dinner at the Rosemont, a well-known, quaint café situated on the old part of Main Street. It's a cool place because it has many private booths, red-vinyl seating, gold-glitter tabletops, and an old-style jukebox.

Berkeley's elegant and eloquent mom, Sarah, has her midlength brown hair pulled back in a neat knot, is dressed in a sleek green pantsuit that matches her eyes (and Berkeley's eyes), and is so perfectly polished she could easily grace the cover of *Vogue* magazine. Berkeley's handsome and distinguished dad, Archer, could be on a magazine cover too, with his lean physique clad in a dapper linen suit, his graying hair newly cut (I'm guessing he and Berkeley went to the stylist together today), and his face tanned and pretty much wrinkle-free.

During the hour we spend together, we keep the conversation lighthearted and varied in topic, and we laugh often. All the while, Berkeley keeps one of my hands warm by holding it tightly under the table.

When it's time for us to leave, Mr. and Mrs. Mills stand and each give Berkeley a warm hug and offer a heartfelt birthday wish and an "I love you."

As I'm smiling and admiring how perfect a family they are, I'm unexpectedly pulled into the embrace and made to feel as comfortable as I do with my own family.

"Have a memorable evening, you two," Sarah says when we part ways.

"I always do with this girl," Berkeley responds, throwing an arm around my shoulders.

"Be on your best behavior, Son," Archer says.

Rolling his eyes, Berkeley responds, "I will, Dad. No worries."

Back in the car, I extract from my hobo bag a flat, rectangular wrapped package that I set on Berkeley's lap.

"Something for you," I say. For the record, I did not wrap up my bikini, although the thought did cross my mind.

He picks it up. "You didn't have to get me anything."

I exhale. "Well, I kinda did, because I've kinda got the hots for you, and that's kinda what people in my situation do."

He keeps his eyes on mine. "You *kinda* have the hots for me?"

I flutter my eyelashes. "Correction: I *really* have the hots for you."

"Really?"

"Just open your present."

"Then quit distracting me with your provocative folly."

"Provocative folly?"

"Yeah, something you're very good at."

I squint. "I'll reply to that once I've consulted my dictionary app."

"It means you get me going."

"And the problem with that is?"

Shaking his head and eyeing my goofball expression, Berkeley removes the paper to find a stack of thin notebooks. "What might these be?"

"Open one."

He does. "Oh! They're for writing music."

"Yes, for some future songwriting. Sometime. Someday. Whenever. If you please."

"What a great idea."

"I know, right?"

He smiles. "You know me well."

"Which works to my advantage in my quest to make you happy."

"Maybe someday, I'll write a song for you to make you happy."

"Maybe that would be so cool!"

He exhales. "First, I'll need to come up with something that rhymes with 'provocative folly'."

I smile. "Sweet as a lolly? Creepy crawly? Round and jolly?"

He grins. "Definitely the last one."

I giggle.

As we cruise around our neighborhood, I casually say, "We should stop by Pierce's house sometime tonight."

"Why? Is something going on there?"

I bite my lower lip. "Yes. According to Phoebe, the making of many s'mores."

Berkeley shrugs. "We could head over there now."

My eyes grow large. "Sure!"

*Yay. Easy peasy*, I think as I discreetly send Phoebe a heads-up text.

After parking in front of Pierce's house, we walk along the side yard toward the gate that leads to the backyard. All the while, I stick tightly by Berkeley's side, anxious to see the reaction on his face when he realizes many of our classmates are waiting for him in the bushes, behind patio furniture, and alongside the hot tub.

Just as we pass through the gate, all of them jump up and yell, "Surprise!"

As I flinch, Berkeley calmly looks at me with a cute expression that quickly turns puzzled when several hunky guys swarm him, strip him down to his boxer briefs, and throw him into the steamy water.

As everyone in the backyard goes crazy with cheers and someone cranks the music up to full volume, I stand far away from the action with my hands covering my mouth to mask a cringe.

When Berkeley resurfaces, all eyes are on him as he shakes himself free of water, exposes his perfectly sculpted physique, and runs his hands through his dripping-wet hair. I too gawk, never having seen him like this before. When he lifts his eyes and looks at me, I feel vibrations going on in my body in places I didn't know vibrated.

Releasing a smile and pointing at me, Berkeley says, "You're next, young lady."

I shake my head. "Not while wearing my snazzy boots."

Leaning over the edge of the hot tub, he says, "I'll give you thirty seconds to get out of them before I come get you."

"Fine," I reply, exhaling to cool my insides down.

By the time I return from the nearest bathroom—dressed in my swimsuit, flip-flops, and two large, mummifying towels—I find seven other people already in the tub.

Sighing, I announce, "Uh-oh, too crowded. Off to make some s'mores."

But as I turn around to go elsewhere, Berkeley bursts out of the hot tub, dashes toward me, discards my towels, and throws me over his shoulder. Despite my giggles and futile attempts to break free, he plunges both of us into the middle of the water, dunking me and laughing the entire time.

Resurfacing, entangled in Berkeley's limbs, I observe a large crowd of people watching and cheering. Shaking my head, I faux scowl and say, "You will so pay for this, Mr. Mills."

"Take your best shot," he replies, sitting on the hot tub's bench and lightly splashing water onto my torso.

Returning the gesture, I mumble, "I can't believe you tossed me in."

He smiles. "It's way warmer in here than out there, so it was for your own good."

"Smart-ass," I say, pushing hair off my face, rubbing mascara off of my cheeks, and fixing my bikini so that it's where it should be.

Around me, the number of people in the tub swiftly increases to twelve, and we pack in like sardines. As Berkeley eyes me, as if he's in a trance, I make my way from the middle of the hot tub toward him, spin around, and ease onto his lap. As he gently wraps his strong arms around me and kisses me on the side of the neck, I realize this is the closest we've ever been with almost no clothes on. Considering what thoughts are going on in my head right now, I can only imagine the ones going on in Berkeley's.

An hour later, Berkeley clutches my thighs and says, "You look like a lobster."

I glance at my legs. "Whoa, you're right. My skin matches my swimsuit."

He gives my body a squeeze. "We'd better get out of here."

I coil. "But it'll be so cold outside of the water."

Murmuring, "No worries, I've got you covered," he steps out of the tub, wraps himself in a towel, and holds another towel up for me.

After grabbing his clothes and my bag, he leads us toward the house and into the closest bathroom and locks the door behind us.

As I stare at Berkeley's still-wet torso and, for a split second, imagine fondling it, he pulls a snug-fitting T-shirt over his head and says, "This feels so much better."

Noticing that I'm not moving, he walks toward the bathtub, slides open the semisheer shower curtain, and says, "Here—why don't you change behind this?"

"That'll work," I reply, smiling as he helps me shuffle over the bathtub's edge.

Locking eyes with him as he closes the curtain, I quietly add, "Thanks for being respectful of my good-girl-ness."

Sighing, he says, "If you could read my mind right now, you would not find me the least bit respectful of your good-girl-ness."

I coyly grin. "Care to share?"

"No, sorry. That's not going to happen."

Peeling off my swimsuit, I say, "For your information, my only experience of being naked in front of a guy is with Patrick Needle."

"Oh?!"

"Yeah, back when he and I were toddlers, playing in each other's paddling pools."

"I wonder if he remembers that."

"He does, and he mentions it often."

Berkeley smirks. "I should go outside and have a conversation with him about trash-talking my girl."

I giggle. "Please do."

As I'm towel drying—and wondering what Berkeley is able to see through the thin film—I ask, "Out of curiosity, do all your dates change behind a curtain?"

"Uh, I only have one date."

I smile. "Well, what about your previous dates?"

He takes a deep breath. "Where are you going with this?"

Sorting through my clothes, I respond, "I'm reminding you that on the relationship scale, I'm a novice."

"I'm aware."

Biting my bottom lip, I add, "And I guess I'm wondering where you rank."

"Well, what are the categories?"

I think and respond, "Let's see. Ascending from the beginning, there's monastery bound, which is self-explanatory. Then there's novice (i.e., me). Then there's dabbler (i.e., most of my gal pals). Then there's—what's a good word? Maverick. And at the end of the spectrum, let's see—there's crackerjack."

He exhales. "Well, I'm not a novice, and contrary to what you might have read on the washroom walls, I'm not a crackerjack either. So I'll peg myself as a dabbling maverick."

"Okay."

He adds, "One that, despite your irresistibility factor, can be totally trusted while you're standing naked behind a curtain."

I grin. "You're pretty decent for a teenage guy."

"That's because my mother is relentless about manners."

Slipping into my clothes, I say, "Remind me to compliment her on that."

"No, I won't, because it'll only fuel her."

Wryly smiling, I sweep open the curtain, stand there with my shirt open, and say, "My fingers are pruned. Would you mind doing my buttoning?"

Taking slow steps toward me, Berkeley asks, "Is this a test to see if I can keep my dabbling-maverick urges in check?"

I grin. "No, it's a test to see what your dabbling-maverick urges are all about."

Swallowing, he reaches for my shirt and replies, "Okay, but be sure to say *when* if I do anything that crosses a line."

"Ditto," I say, running my hand down his rock-hard chest,

triggering the hottest activity we've ever gotten into, which occasionally results in laughter as we awkwardly squirm around on the cold bathtub floor.

A loud knock on the door startles us, as does a male voice hollering, "Hey, can I get in there?"

Shyly gawking at each other, Berkeley and I say nothing. But when a second knock sounds, I abruptly shout, "We'll be out in two!"

"Fine," the door knocker says.

Standing us up and resuming the buttoning of my shirt, Berkeley quietly says, "Sorry, I got carried away."

My eyebrow arches. "For the record, the word *when* did not once cross my mind."

Taking a chest-heaving breath, he replies, "Regardless of that, next time I'm locked in a room with you, I'm gonna need handcuffs."

"For use on you or me?"

Sweeping the wet hair away from my face, he says, "I'm gonna be up all night thinking about that."

Giggling, I grab my stuff and drag a flushed-faced Berkeley by the hand out the door, neither of us saying a word as we pass a lineup of gawking, curious friends.

Outside, as we join those gathered around the raging fire pit, Berkeley sits on a log stool, pulls me into his lap, wraps his arms around me from behind, and asks, "Do you want my jacket?"

"No, you took the chill right out of me a few minutes ago."

He tightens his hold on me. "Yeah, I'm contemplating pouring ice down my pants right about now."

As I giggle, Phoebe sits on a log beside me, grabs one of my booted ankles, and says, "Why is it that my feet aren't as cute and petite as yours so that I could at least borrow those beauties once in a while?"

I grin. "Maybe it's because you stand four inches taller than me."

She smiles. "Then grow, would you? So we can share all the contents of each other's closets."

I look her way. "Believe me, if I could will my ten-year-old-boy figure to fill out and stretch, I would."

As Phoebe chuckles, Berkeley says, "For the record, I think you're perfect exactly the way you are."

I glance over my shoulder. "You don't mind that I'm stick-shaped?"

He tightens his hold of me. "I wouldn't mind if you had a polygonal or a trapezoidal or a triangular shape. You'd still steam up my sunglasses."

Phoebe stands up. "Berkeley, you're the only guy I know who could make geometry sound sexy."

Berkeley chuckles. "Blame Francie. Her unending allure has given me a one-track mind."

Walking away, she replies, "Yes, Berkeley, we are all aware of that."

Rotating to face and straddle Berkeley, I wrap my arms around his neck and say, "Out of curiosity, what would you say is the highlight of turning sixteen?"

He inhales. "Hmm. I'd have to say the sight of the flip-flops you were wearing earlier."

I grin. "So a simple pair of flip-flops has made your day."

He blushes. "Yup. I didn't even notice the bikini you were wearing with them."

Feeling warm all over, I rest my chin on Berkeley's shoulder and linger there for many minutes, relishing the fact that no one could ever make me feel as special as he does.

Swinging my booted feet to the beat of a romantic song, I get hung up on my silly me-shoe search, wondering whether there's a deeper purpose to it besides extracting characteristics that are supposed to magically come together to form a shoe that reflects me. As I'm recapping some of the descriptors I've amassed thus far—*hurtless, harmonious, sparkly*—and replaying in my mind the steamy encounter Berkeley and I just had in the bathtub, I come to realize that my quest is only minimally about unearthing footwear. It's mostly about unearthing me.

# foot note eight

I LOVE SPRING, ESPECIALLY THE FIRST DAY OF IT, AND I HAVE A theory that the season is the reason toenails evolved, because after all, there is nothing more uplifting than showing off a pretty pedicure following many months of tootsie concealment.

Complementing today's nail polish shade of Metal Lavender is a pair of skin-toned gladiators chosen because I wanted them to blend with my feet so that my toes would stand out. I've labeled this style the Metamorphosis because the word seems to go hand in hand with the day. Walking into school, I get a buzzing feeling that these shoes are about to become part of a memorable day. I have no idea why, but my shoe intuition is telling me I'm going to feel different after a day of wearing them.

During lunch hour, I substantiate my wacky premonition when I receive a message from the school's principal, requesting I meet with her regarding something very important.

As Berkeley and I sit side by side outside on the school cafeteria's outdoor patio, I quietly ask, "What do you think Mrs. Bouchard is going to tell me?"

After swallowing a bite of an apple, he replies, "That you're getting an award for being the cutest student ever."

I grin. "No, because that would go to you."

He smirks and tips his head to the side. "She probably wants to talk to you about that art contest you entered last fall."

"Yeah, that'd be my guess too."

"Maybe you won it."

Shrugging, I say in my most-syrupy voice, "Will you wait for me after school?"

"Of course. I want to be the first to hear what Mrs. B had to say."

"Don't expect too much."

He smiles. "It'll be good news. Wait and see."

At the end of the school day, I arrive at the admin office, and after finding an unattended front desk, I wander toward a private office bearing the nameplate "Mrs. Bouchard."

Her short graying hair is the first thing I see as I stand in the open doorway, but when the sound of my light knocking interrupts her, she stands up (all six feet of her), puts on her glasses, and adjusts her conservative blue suit.

Gesturing for me to take a seat, she says, "Hey, Francie. Thanks for making yourself available on short notice."

"No problem, Mrs. B. I've been eagerly anticipating this meeting all day."

She sits down and smiles. "I've got some exciting news for you."

I squirm in my seat. "Oh?"

She takes a deep breath. "Yes, it's with regard to the Metro Gallery's art competition, the one you entered last fall."

"Yes," I respond, sheepishly smiling at the recollection of my work's unofficial title: *Holy Crap, I Get to Kiss This Guy!*

Mrs. B continues, "Late yesterday, the gallery's executive director, Mr. Reid, called to tell me that you've been awarded first place."

"Really?"

"Really."

"Wow, I can't believe it!"

Mrs. B's face lights up. "The official announcement will be released to the press tomorrow, which is why I needed to talk to you about it today."

As I sit frozen and speechless (*Me, in the news?*), she adds, "Congratulations, Francie! You should feel very proud."

"Yes. Thanks. I do."

She smiles and leans forward on her desk. "There's one more component to all of this that I'm happy to share."

My eyebrows rise. "What's that?"

She inhales. "As you know, there's an educational program associated with this competition that utilizes a patron's grant to place artistically talented high-school students in exclusively art-oriented learning environments."

"I remember."

She looks at a paper. "The specific program Mr. Reid referred to is called Idea Incubatrice."

"Cool name."

"It comes from the word *incubator,* I'm told."

"So is it a summer camp or an after-school thing?"

She smiles. "No, it's a high-school level facility that focuses on skill building in the areas of art and design."

"That sounds impressive," I say, wishing I'd stop fidgeting.

"Mr. Reid also said that students who've gone through the program are typically offered outstanding postsecondary opportunities."

"I can imagine."

Mrs. B takes a deep breath. "The reason Mr. Reid has explained all of this to me is because he thinks you're a worthy candidate, and he'd like to offer you the opportunity to attend the school."

"Really," I reply, abruptly coiling because I don't know if that's a good or a bad thing.

She reads on. "The letterhead describes the facility as a 'creativity laboratory for high-school students, aimed at developing new directions in design, art, and communication.'"

"Okay."

"The placement would commence next term, late August."

"Uh-huh."

"And your tuition, room and board, and school supplies would all be paid for."

I swallow. "I see."

She looks up. "You'd be away for nine months, for the entirety of eleventh grade."

I chew my bottom lip. "All righty."

She flips a page. "And let me see … It looks like the facility is in—oh, wow—Florence, Italy!"

"Whoa!" I gasp.

She dips her head to the side. "Oh, Francie, how fantastic for you!"

"It sure is," I reply, heating up inside and taking short breaths so that I don't panic and run out of the room.

Straightening the papers into a neat pile, she adds, "Obviously, you'll need time to discuss this with your parents before making a decision, but know one thing for certain, Francie: opportunities like this are rare, so unless you've got a reason not to, you should thank your lucky stars and dive headfirst into this."

"Yes, I should."

"One last thing: you have until the Friday before spring break to decide."

"Sure. No problem."

Standing up and shaking my hand, she says, "Congratulations, Francie, on being given an opportunity that is sure to be life altering."

"Thank you," I reply, scurrying out of the room as fast as I can.

Glancing down the now-deserted school's main corridor, I see Berkeley sitting on a chair, his eyes fixed on his phone.

At the sound of my footsteps, he looks up, abruptly stands up, and asks, "Hey, how'd it go in there?"

"Fine."

Walking alongside me, he says, "So what did Mrs. B have to say?"

After taking a deep breath, I reply, "She told me I took first place in that art contest."

"Fantastic!" Berkeley exclaims, lifting me off the ground in a hug, spinning my body in a circle, and transforming my limbs into wings.

Setting me on the ground, he says, "This is so incredible!"

"Yeah, I guess it is," I murmur with the enthusiasm of oatmeal.

His face lights up. "What a great day this is!"

"Uh-huh."

He squints. "I can't believe you're not freaking out right now."

I exhale. "That's because Mrs. B mentioned something else."

"What?"

I look at a bank of lockers. "That I've been offered a bursary to attend some fancy art-and-design school."

"Really? Where?"

Pressing my lips together, I mumble, "Florence."

"Florence, as in South Carolina?"

"No. Florence, as in Italy."

Berkeley steps back. "Oh, wow."

"Yeah."

"When?"

"Next fall, for an entire school year."

He runs his fingers through his hair. "That's really soon and really lengthy."

"Yeah, which is why I'm in favor of declining the offer."

"What? No! You can't decline an offer like this."

I squint. "Why?"

"Because the experience will be great for you."

I resume walking. "Sixteen is pretty young to be on your own."

Grabbing my hand, he notes, "Bear in mind, the place will have dorms, cafeterias, chaperones, and lots of other students in the same boat."

"Yeah, and it'll be very far away."

He twists to face me. "It's not, Francie. I've been there. It's an overnight flight to Rome and then a quick train ride a few hours north."

I shrug. "But it would mean separation from my family and you."

Berkeley puts a hand on my shoulder. "Not a lot of it, because you'd make trips home, and we'd make trips there."

"So you're saying you'd be okay not seeing me for months at a time."

"No, I'm saying that I think this is a big deal and that I'm willing to do whatever it takes to make it happen."

Looking to the ground because I'm on the verge of tears that he's not begging me to stay or claiming he can't live without me, I say, "I guess I just need time to let it sink in."

He sighs. "Yeah, I'm sure that's all it is."

The only chatter on the ride home comes from the car's radio.

As Berkeley parks in front of my house, I stare at the building's boxy shape and say, "Did I ever mention that my mom designed this house?"

Dipping his head to view the structure through my window, Berkeley replies, "No, but I just assumed that because she's an architect, she must have."

Smiling, I add, "I love living in it. And in Riverly Heights."

Berkeley grabs my hand. "Yeah, but it's okay to leave here, knowing you can always come back."

"I guess."

"How long do you have to decide on the Italy thing?"

"Two weeks, on the day I go skiing with my family."

"Well, that gives you lots of time to figure out what'll make you happiest."

"I already know what'll make me happiest."

Shifting toward me, Berkeley asks, "Are you going to make me pack you up in a suitcase and take you to Italy myself?"

"Only if you want to get rid of me."

He shakes his head. "Nothing could be further from the truth."

As I shrug, he says, "Just think it through, okay? That's all I'm saying."

My brow furrows. "Why are you pushing me so hard on this?"

He leans back. "Because I think fate just served up your destiny on a silver platter."

As I slump in my seat, he adds, "And because I think you'll learn more about art in Italy than you ever would here. And because I think you'll love touring the museums, eating the pizza, and shopping for shoes."

When I do not respond, he says, "Come on, Francie—how many reasons do you need to see how fantastic an opportunity this is?"

Climbing out of the car, I reply, "None. I get it."

As I walk away, Berkeley opens up the passenger window and yells, "You know I'm right about this."

Looking over my shoulder, I shout, "And if I prove you wrong?"

He smiles. "Then I'll eat those fantastic shoes you're wearing."

I suppress a smile. "But I like these shoes."

"Then don't give me a reason to eat them."

I smirk. "Whatever."

After Berkeley drives away, I walk inside the house, peel off my sandals, and head toward the family-room sofa. Flopping onto it facedown, I bury my head under several cushions and mutter, "Why did I enter that competition in the first place?"

Lying there, trying to will myself to fall asleep so that I don't think about how my family is going to react to my news, I hear little voices in my head—pretty female voices—that I've never known to exist before. *Am I developing multiple personalities?*

One whispers, "Maybe flipping a coin is in order."

Another says, "You do love Italian food."

A third says, "It would mean a winter without snow."

No longer interested in sleep, I flip over, stare at the ceiling, and do some considering of my own: I'd be in a part of the world I'm dying to explore. I'd make a bunch of new friends. I'd have access to shoes for my ongoing quest that I would never find in Riverly Heights.

However, when I do not see Berkeley in any of my visions, I switch to the cons and develop a headache, because that list is endless.

During dinner with my family—I'm barefoot because shoes remind me too much of Italy—I do little but play with my food and knot my fingers under the table. Several times, I attempt to enter the conversation to mention my news, but no words will form. All the while, I listen patiently to my mom talking about her latest nightmare client and to my father rambling about the court arguments he used this morning in a nasty divorce case. I even tune into Brigitte barking at Talula about the disheveled state of our shared bathroom.

When dessert is served and the room goes silent, I take a deep breath and say, "I have an announcement."

Everyone stops eating, looks my way, and waits for me to speak. However, for several seconds, I don't. I can't.

Touching my arm, my mom asks, "What is it, Francie?"

After taking a deep breath, I say, "I won an art competition."

"What? Wow! Great! Super!" the four reply, their words blending so that I don't know who's saying what.

As the racket subsides, I add, "And I've been offered a bursary to complete eleventh grade at an art school in Italy."

"That's incredible!" my mom exclaims, pulling on my dad so that they can jointly smother me with well-wishes and mushy hugs. Despite the fact that I haven't even mentioned if I'm accepting the placement, my mom and dad start making plans for a celebration party and discussing who'll accompany me on the flight overseas. They mention buying me some nice luggage.

Seeing such extreme happiness on their faces, I slump in my chair and say nothing further. When we finish dessert, I get up, complete the table cleanup, wander into the family room, and stare out the window. Smiling at the realization my father has strung my beloved hammock between its customary two trees, I imagine a variety of potential strategies that might work to get me out of my predicament, such as causing Riverly Heights' airport to shut down for the next year so that I'd be unable to depart, falling into a mineshaft and being stuck there for at least six months (yet I'd still be afforded the comforts of home), or painlessly spraining both wrists so that I'd be unable to do art until I'm in well into twelfth grade.

Finished with my stroll down Crazy Street, I wander into my bedroom, sit at my desk, and scribe on paper what school in Italy versus school at home is really about: pursuing me or pursuing Berkeley—but not both.

Whispering, "Eeny, meeny, miny, moe, I've got two weeks to tell the world what I already know," I lean back in my chair and rub my face with my hands.

# foot note nine

*DO I GO TO ITALY OR NOT? ON THIS, THE DAY BEFORE DECISION DAY,* that is the question, and though I'm pretty sure I've got the answer, I'm keeping it locked deep inside of me because I don't dare release such critical information ahead of the deadline, out of fear someone will convince me otherwise.

I tell myself, *Hold your ground today. Don't let anyone tell you what to do today. Do what's right for you today. Stay stern.*

With that in mind, my footwear choice, as I stand here ready to head to school, is a pair of Brigitte's low-heeled bright red loafers—my intention in wearing them is for some of her don't-tell-me-what-to-do attitude to rub off on me. I'm calling this style the Frank, which I hope to be today.

It's now day thirteen of listening to people's advice on what I should do next fall.

Beatrice told me, "I hear the guy gawking in Italy is worth the trip alone."

My mom said, "Florence is the birthplace of the best art on the planet, and you'll be able to view it anytime you like."

My sister Talula said, "If it's shoes that turn your crank, then why wouldn't you go where they're plentiful?"

Phoebe told me, tongue-in-cheek, "I'd be happy to keep Berkeley occupied while you're away, to make sure no one else does." I know she meant it in a platonic way (I trust her wholeheartedly), but regardless, it was unsettling to hear.

Even teachers I've never had a class with have congratulated me.

Even a janitor I've never spoken to in my life gave me a high five.

Most regularly, it's Berkeley who has tried to sell me on what to do: downloading onto my phone an Italian-language tutorial app; photoshopping pictures of me superimposed on an Italian backdrop (some of them hilarious); playing Italian opera music while we're driving around in his car; and showing me photographs taken from his trip to Italy a few years back.

Don't get me wrong—I know everyone's gestures are well intended, which is why, at the end of each sales pitch, I usually nod and smile. Or in the case of Berkeley, I kiss him and whisper dabbler-level stuff into his ear, which makes him lose track of any topic being discussed.

I'm aware that if Berkeley didn't exist, I'd be packed for Italy already. However, Berkeley is real and is unlikely to maintain a relationship with me if I live on the opposite side of the planet. It'll be too hard for him, with wannabe girlfriends certain to make themselves visible the minute I step on the plane—something I have no doubt about, because the washroom-stall commentary involving Berkeley has heated up over the last couple of weeks, and I know that's not coincidental.

Spring break begins at the end of the day tomorrow, which means the countdown to the big reveal is at the twenty-four-hour mark. As I head out the door to school, I look to my feet and say to Brigitte's bright red shoes, "Do whatever you have to to give me the backbone I currently lack."

The day at school ends up being quiet and uneventful in terms of the Italy rhetoric. Working in my favor is the school's defective fire-alarm system, which keeps going off, disrupting classes, aggravating students and teachers alike, and separating me from most of my friends when I exit a door they don't.

During the car ride home from school, Berkeley grabs my hand and says, "I'm running some errands for my dad for the next few hours, but I was hoping you and I could do something together later tonight."

"Sure, want to go for dessert?"

"Sounds great. How about I pick you up around eight?"

"Works for me." To avoid going down Italy Road, I add, "I can't believe tomorrow is the start of spring break."

Berkeley smiles. "I can't believe I'm going to be deprived of you for more than a week."

I blush. "I wish you were coming skiing with me."

"I do too."

I sigh. "You're such a great skier."

His brow furrows. "When have you seen me ski?"

"On the ninth-grade ski trip. I escaped the cold by hanging out in the chalet, where I spent most of my time watching you race around."

He grins. "Well, that explains a lot, because I spent most of my time racing around to find you and couldn't."

"You were tracking me?"

He glances my way. "Francie, I've been tracking you since the first time I saw you."

"Oh?"

His face flushes. "Yeah, it started in a park one afternoon a long time ago. You probably don't even remember."

"I remember."

"You were sopping wet for some reason, and the sunlight was reflecting off of your skin, and oh my God, the sight of you blew my mind."

"I was covered in slimy lake water."

Running his hand down my arm, he adds, "I remember I was

playing football, and after catching a long toss, I crash-landed very near you."

"Yes, you did."

"Afterward, I heard you say something cute—directed at me, I hoped—which marked the first of about a thousand times I wanted to kiss you before I knew you."

"Seriously?"

"God, yes! For the longest time, the sight of you drove me mad."

"Why didn't you say something to me?"

"Because I was a wreck around you."

"But you're the calmest guy I know."

He smiles. "Now I am, because I'm no longer chasing you."

As I giggle, he says, "One day, I think it was last December, I was wandering around the school, looking for you, and noticed in a glass-wall reflection that you were headed toward me from around a corner. So I rushed to casually meet up with you, but in my haste, I misjudged your location and ended up knocking you to the floor."

I press my lips together. "Yeah, the big bang."

He coyly smiles. "After that, I waited for you to say something to me, which, by the way, took the longest time!"

I squint. "I can't believe I didn't notice you noticing me."

He gives me a look. "That's because you fail to see most of the gawks you get."

"Only yours matter."

"I like hearing that."

"I like saying that."

He takes hold of my hand. "God, I wish you were coming to the Bahamas with me."

"I wish I was too, because I much prefer swimsuits to ski suits."

He squeezes my fingers. "On you, I do too."

Getting the warm fuzzies inside, I take a deep breath and think about the prospect of attending school somewhere other than the home of Berkeley Mills. I would have to be insane to do that, which means I know what I need to do.

Looking to Brigitte's shoes, I sigh and smile because they *are* transferring into me a gutsy, confident vibe. I can feel it.

However, I know they won't factor into my ongoing shoe quest, because they're fire-engine red, a color too angry and aggressive for me to ever warm up to.

If I could, I would rebirth these shoes in the color magenta, cherry, or, best of all, fuchsia—the happiest version of the red family and also the color I wear best. I decide to add *fuchsia* to my me-shoe list of criteria.

*Good. Settled. The Francie Lanoo has a hue.*

Berkeley just sent me a text to say that for this evening's dessert outing, he's taking me to a new Italian bistro downtown called Cielo Turchese. I checked out the translation of its name: "turquoise sky." *Nice.* I also checked out its website, discovering that the place has a bold turquoise ceiling (apropos), many multicolored blown-glass lights, cool furniture, and amazing replicas of famous Italian art. Though I think it might be the most-beautiful restaurant I've ever seen, because it's Italian, I will not share that sentiment with anyone.

For the occasion, I've decided to use the tactic of seductive distraction, dressing as sexily as my wardrobe will allow: a short, tight black skirt and a fitted, long-sleeved white blouse, minimally buttoned. I'm still wearing Brigitte's red shoes, because so far so good in them today. I've not had to face the topic of my decision on Italy even once while wearing them.

When Berkeley arrives to pick me up around eight, looking as irresistible as ever in fitted jeans, a black button-up, and a plaid windbreaker, I open the door, flash him a provocative smile, and ask, "Ready for something sweet?"

He smiles and kisses me on the cheek. "I'm already looking at her."

I take his hand and head down the steps. "Are you sure you want to go to a restaurant? Because we could always go somewhere less public."

Exhaling, he says, "As tempting as that sounds, I've got something to talk to you about, and I think it's best I'm in a locale where you're least likely to affect my concentration."

*Crap.* My plan has already encountered its first hiccup.

On the car ride to the restaurant, I talk nonstop to Berkeley about a variety of non-Italian topics: the amazing sunset; my intention to avoid skiing when I'm in the mountains; and tomorrow's math exam, which I haven't yet studied for.

Walking into the restaurant, I look around and dreamily say, "Wow, I love it in here."

When Berkeley, sharp as ever, retorts, "I bet you love it here because all things Italian agree with you," I start sensing defeat.

Sighing, I say, "The art of persuasion is in play already, I see."

As we take our seats, he says, "And I've got plenty more where that came from, but I'll hold off until your mouth is too full to argue."

"I can eat and battle you at the same time."

Taking hold of my knees under the table, he quietly responds, "I loathe the thought of ever battling with you."

"Good. Then we're going to get along just fine tonight," I say as we both smile.

After a pretty red-haired waitress takes our orders in the most-drawn-out manner imaginable, chatting with Berkeley as if I don't exist, Berkeley's green eyes light up, and he announces, "I have something for you."

"You do?"

"Yep, right here in my jacket pocket."

"Is there a particular reason for such a lovely gesture?"

Pulling a small, rectangular box out of his jacket, he says, "Just to remind you that I'm madly in love with you. That's all."

I reach across the table to touch his hand. "That is so sweet."

Handing me a narrow box tied with a fuchsia ribbon, he says, "I hope you like it."

Grasping the tag, I read, "Property of Francie Lanoo's Atelier." Looking at Berkeley, I say, "That sounds so formal. What does *atelier* mean?"

"It's a fancy word for an artist's studio."

"Lovely."

"My dad suggested it."

"Your family is so good with words."

"Words are what we do."

Nodding and glancing at the box, I ask, "Did you tie this bow all by yourself?"

"Yes, I did, because bows are a thing for me."

"I do know that about you."

He grins. "It might have something to do with the fact that I was able to tie my own sneakers at age three."

I look him in the eyes. "I bet you were the cutest child ever."

He shrugs. "I'm told I was the most active."

"Some things never change."

"It's my nature to move around. What can I say?"

Removing the gift's ribbon and lid, I lay my eyes on the most-beautiful antique fountain pen imaginable—quill shaped, alabaster finished, and bevel tipped, with a series of gemstones that form a circle on the face. As my eyes gleam, I exclaim, "Oh my!"

"Do you like it?"

"How could I not like it? It's beautiful!"

"I'm glad you think so."

"May I touch it?"

He smiles. "Of course you can touch it. It's yours."

Lifting it out of the box, I ask, "Where did you get this?"

"My great-grandmother gave it to me several years ago, after my great-grandfather passed away."

Running my finger along the tip, I add, "I've never seen anything like it."

"It was one of several unique pens the old guy used when he started the *Tribunal*."

"Did he write newspaper articles with it?"

"Yeah, and he wrote letters, and he doodled, and he did calligraphy."

"So the pen is multifunctional."

He smiles. "Yes, which is why it's perfect for you."

Sitting back in my seat and shaking my head, I say, "Berkeley, I can't keep this pen. It's a family treasure."

He reaches over and squeezes my hands. "But I want you to have it so that you can transfer all of your crazy shoe ideas onto paper."

I dip my head to the side. "That's really thoughtful, but seriously, there is no way you should trust me with this."

"Why not?"

I place the pen in his hand. "Because I could lose it."

"I could lose it too."

"Which is why the pen should be kept in a safe place somewhere."

"To do what? Collect dust?"

I sigh, pause, and then reply, "I bet you could find a purpose for it."

He furrows his brow. "Francie, I have to get a journalism degree so I can work with my parents, the tool of which will be a computer, so I have no practical use for a fountain pen."

As our waitress returns and serves me tea and tiramisu, all the while stealing glances at Berkeley, I smile and remark, "You could write cute notes with it to give it a practical use."

As our server finishes setting down Berkeley's water and lemon gelato—he always orders the healthiest option on the menu—he bats his eyes at me, takes hold of the pen, and says, "Give me your hand."

"Okay."

After dipping the pen into an accompanying tiny inkwell,

Berkeley webs his fingers with mine, flips my left palm upward, and begins scribing.

"That tickles," I say.

"Hold still," he replies.

"I'll try," I say, suppressing a laugh.

Finishing with an emphatic dot, he releases my hand and asks, "How's this?"

Glancing downward to see that he has ornately written, "B ♡ F lots," I feel my insides warming as if they're nestled beside a fireplace. As a single tear forms in one of my eyes, I quietly say, "And you wonder why I'm hesitant to leave here."

Putting the pen in the box and pushing the box toward me, Berkeley says, "Let's settle on this: you take the pen on loan and return it to me when you come back."

I stare into his eyes. "You're very persistent."

"And you're very resistant." Watching me roll my eyes, he notes, "I'm serious, Francie. I want you to have the pen with you in Italy, if for no other reason than it'll remind you of me occasionally."

I tip my head to the side. "Alternatively, if I stay here, I won't need any reminders."

With a mouth full of gelato, Berkeley exclaims, "What is it about going to Italy that's scaring you?"

I inhale a deep breath. "I'm not scared; I'm not even sure that art is what I want to pursue in life. I have lots of things that interest me."

He shakes his head. "You and I both know this is not about art."

I groan. "So?"

He runs his hands through his hair. "So why are you letting one minor detail overcomplicate a critical juncture of your life?"

I huff. "I'd hardly call you a minor detail."

"In the big picture of things, I am," he says, turning his focus to his dessert and finishing it.

I do the same, and for many minutes, we sit quietly, unable to find more words.

As the waitress slowly clears our dishes, Berkeley shifts his upper body toward me and says, "Please don't make me the reason you don't do this."

"Why?"

"Because if I make you miss out on something this fantastic, I'll be bothered by it for the rest of my life."

I yank on my hair. "Argh! Can we just talk about something else?"

Leaning back and crossing his arms, Berkeley says, "Fine. But before you give Mrs. B an answer, you'd better consider what you'd be giving up by not going."

"All right. I will when I get home." After taking a sip of my drink, I try to switch gears and say, "So how's the training going for the track-and-field meet on Saturday morning?"

Exhaling, he replies, "Really well. I think I'm ready."

"I'm sure you'll do great. You always do."

Staring into the distance, he says, "Why don't you come by our practice tomorrow morning before school starts and cheer me on?"

"Sure."

Shifting his eyes back to me, he replies, "Okay. Good."

As we hit another lull in the conversation, Berkeley pays the check, and we stand up to leave.

Noticing me glancing at the inscription on my hand, Berkeley grabs the boxed pen off of the table and says, "Don't lose this."

I smile. "I promise I never would."

Wrapping an arm around me, he adds, "I'm going to buy you a giant inkwell so that you have enough goop to last the entire time you're away."

Biting my lip, I force a grin and reply, "Thank you."

Back at my house, as we stand face-to-face on the front steps,

Berkeley softly kisses me on the cheek and says, "Please, please, please do some deep thinking tonight about Italy."

"I will."

"Good," he says, darting away as if he just started a race.

I wait for him to wave good-bye from the car, but he doesn't. When he drives off, he squeals the tires, which leaves me wondering, *Is he mad?*

Standing in a bit of a daze, second-guessing every thought running through my head, I remove Brigitte's shoes, dangle them from my fingers, and mumble, "Maybe I should go to Italy because it's what Berkeley wants me to do."

*Crap. Now I'm even more confused.*

# foot note ten

I PROBABLY SHOULDN'T BE DWELLING ON SHOE CHOICES ON THE most-stressful day of my life, but they're a good distraction from what I woke up contemplating: the up-and-coming disgruntled look on Berkeley's face, the soon-to-be terse expression on Mrs. Bouchard's face, and the inevitable disappointment on my parents' faces when today's announcement enters their ears.

*Should I wear flats, sandals, or flip-flops? Or should I wear boots because the temperature dipped overnight?*

As I lie in bed and imagine specific options, my phone rings. Noticing that it's Berkeley, I feel my blood start pumping, and I mumble, "Here we go."

Picking up, I say, "Hey, hi."

Energetically, as if he's just run a 5K—and he probably did— Berkeley says, "Hey, sleepyhead, it's seven thirty. Aren't you coming to my practice?"

After clearing my throat, I reply, "Actually, I ended up studying until two and haven't showered yet, so I might have to catch up with you at lunch."

"What time are you meeting with Mrs. B?"

"Eight thirty."

He exhales. "Did you spend some time last night thinking about your decision on Italy?"

"I did."

"Is it a yes or a no?"

"It's an 'I'll tell you when I see you.'"

After pausing to breathe deeply, he says, "You know what? It's really important that I see you before you talk to Mrs. B, so why don't you meet up with me around eight fifteen outside the guys' locker room?"

"Sure," I say quietly.

"Rise and shine, Francie Lanoo."

"I am right now," I mumble, dragging my butt out of bed.

Crossing paths with my parents in the kitchen, I say, "Morning."

"Morning," they say in unison.

Giving me a hug, my dad says, "Big day today for you."

"Yeah."

"Did you make a decision yet?"

I shrug. "I'm leaning toward staying here."

Pouring a cup of coffee, my mom says, "I guess it's a little late for me to reiterate that you're passing on a fantastic opportunity."

I nod. "Yeah, but if I really do have talent, I'm sure other art-related opportunities will come my way; and if for some reason they don't, I'll pursue something else."

"Whatever makes you happy," she replies.

I smile. "Thanks for saying that."

After showering, I select the outfit I know Berkeley is quite fond of—a teal-print, form-fitting sweater dress. For my feet, I choose something meant for speed, because I'm already running late: adorable wine-colored ballerina flats. Unfortunately, I don't have time to label them, but I'll come up with something appropriate for them when I come home.

By the time I enter the school, it's already 8:12 a.m., so I commence sprinting, rehearsing in my head the words I can't wait to say: *I choose you.*

Heading down the stretch of corridor leading to the guys' locker room, I smile at the thought of seeing Berkeley's freshly showered face, bouncy hair, and mesmerizing eyes. However, as I hit the final stretch, my grin turns upside down, because Berkeley is standing face-to-face, adjacent to the door, with a girl named Shanna Wells—a willowy brunette wearing too-tight clothing and gaudy footwear—who's made it no secret she's been hung up on Berkeley since the beginning of ninth grade.

As my eyes zoom in further, I notice Berkeley has his back pressed against the lockers, and Shanna is edging toward him, her beady eyes looking at him like a cat eyeing its prey. Though I can only see Berkeley in profile, I don't think he's doing anything to encourage her. On the flip side, I also don't think he's doing anything to discourage her.

Just as I whisper, "Why is Berkeley with her?" I witness the unthinkable: Shanna leans in and kisses Berkeley square on the lips.

I gasp and exclaim, "No!"

I count out the lip-lock's duration—*One, two, three, four, five seconds—are you kidding me?* As my heart shrivels to the size of a raisin, I say the only thing that matters: "He's letting her."

As the blood drains from my face, I turn and start running. In my haste, I knock over a garbage can, causing an earth-shattering, echoing boom. Scrambling to stand the tub upright, I glance over my shoulder and notice Berkeley looking my way.

As our eyes lock, he immediately moves Shanna out of the way, bolts in my direction, and yells, "Francie! Wait!"

With tears pouring down my face, I ignore his plea. Rather, I dart as fast as my legs will allow, thanking God I wore flats, or I would never be able to escape Berkeley's speed.

Bursting through the administrative offices' door, I say to the pudgy, elderly receptionist, "I'm Francie Lanoo, and I'm here to see Mrs. Bouchard. She's expecting me."

Eyeing my tear-drenched cheeks, she asks, "Are you okay?"

I nod. "Yes, I'm fine. It's just my allergies."

"You should see a doctor about that," she says with a puzzled expression, and then she adds, "Yes, Mrs. B is expecting you, so why don't you head into her office? I'll let her know you're here, so she can join you as soon as she's done with her coffee."

"Thanks," I say, rushing into the room, closing the door behind me, and ignoring the muffled sound of Berkeley's voice trying to talk his way into seeing me.

Mumbling, "Good. For once, his irresistibility is failing him," I find a tissue in my schoolbag, wipe my face, and cringe as I see my morning makeup application become a depressing smear of gray, black, and pink.

Thankfully, I have a few minutes alone to control the blithering and sort of fix my face. When Mrs. B finally walks in, I force my eyes wide open, fake a smile, and say, "Good morning."

"Good morning to you too, Francie. How are you today?"

"Fine, thanks. And you?"

Closing the door and looking at me, she says, "Whoa. Are you okay?"

I sit up straight. "Oh yeah. I've just got a huge piece of dust in my eye, and it's causing quite the irritation."

"Do you need to use the ladies' room?"

"No, no, no. I'll be fine."

"Okay then. Let's start talking Idea Incubatrice."

"Ready when you are."

Taking a seat and riffling through some papers, she notes, "What a big day this is for you!"

"It sure is."

Leaning forward in her chair, she says, "Let's cut to the chase: Have you made a decision?"

Faking a delighted expression, I exclaim, "Yes! I'm definitely going."

Sighing, she replies, "I'm so happy to hear that."

"Thanks."

Without delay, she briefly reviews some of the program's details, all of which take my mind elsewhere, dull my senses, and kick-start some happy imaginings of my impending new life.

To prolong my stay in this free-from-Berkeley environment, because I'm worried he might be lurking nearby, I ask some pertinent questions, such as, "What are the living arrangements? How soon do the documents need to be signed? What will happen with class credits when I return to Riverly Heights for twelfth grade?"

Mrs. B answers as best she can, but after looking at her watch, she says, "We'll have to arrange another time to finish this, because I have another meeting scheduled in five minutes."

"No problem."

Standing up, she says, "Before you go, Francie, I just want to emphasize what a phenomenal experience the next year is certain to be for you—full of intrigue, growth, and all kinds of adventure."

Keeping up the facade, I widen my eyes and reply, "Yes, I can't wait to see what awaits me around the next corner."

Escorting me to the door, she says, "Mr. Reid, from the gallery, asked me to call him once you made your decision."

Smiling, I say, "I'm really looking forward to meeting him soon."

Dipping her head to the side, she says, "You know what? I know he wants to meet you too, so if you think it would be okay, why don't I invite him here—say, at three fifteen today—for a quick get-together?"

"Sure," I say. "Although I'd have to be out the door by three forty-five because I'm heading on a holiday later today."

"No problem." She nods. "I'll keep the session brief."

"Thank you."

"Enjoy your day, Francie."

"Thanks. You too, Mrs. B."

Before exiting the admin office, I fiddle around in my schoolbag and kill a few more minutes of time. When the corridors appear to be all clear, I wander out the door, head to my classroom, feel a foggy haze invading my head space, and mumble over and over, "I can't believe Berkeley would do this to me."

Entering the biology lab, I explain why I'm a few minutes late, take a seat at an open spot at the back of the room, reach for my cell phone, delete several messages, and turn the device off for what I'm sure will be forevermore.

Taking a deep breath, I lean back in my chair and force myself to absorb Mr. Hanson's ramblings about how the human brain processes information and how it recognizes pain via the nervous system—words I can relate to because I feel like a voodoo doll in a wrestling match with a porcupine.

Closing my eyes, I kick off my ballerina flats and push them toward the back wall, never to look at them again, let along label them. Only then does it occur to me that a choice between pursuing me and pursuing Berkeley Mills was just made for me and not by me.

"So me and my shoes it will be," I whisper, shaking my head at the irony that I'm currently barefoot.

At eleven o'clock, after noticing my feet are disgustingly black on the soles, I head to the dreaded lost-and-found bin and rummage through the left-behinds in search of something wearable. Deep in the dingy pile, I find a pair of cheap white flip-flops in a size close enough to my own. After washing my feet in the washroom sink and pursing my lips at the sight of so much disgusting grime going down the drain, I slip the hand-me-downs in place and murmur, "All I need to make this day complete is to catch a toenail fungus."

I spend the remainder of the day staying clear of everyone I know.

I speak to no one; I eat my lunch alone behind an outdoor storage shed; and I hide inside a washroom stall until the afternoon bell rings and clears the corridors. I even make a point of walking around with my books covering my face, and by doing so, I learn how easy it is for someone as petite as me to get lost in a high school with fifteen hundred students.

At three o'clock, I slink out of my desk, walk to the front of the classroom, and say to my English teacher, "I have to leave a few minutes early because Mrs. Bouchard has scheduled a meeting with me."

"No problem," she replies with a smile. "Enjoy spring break."

"Thanks. You too."

Walking down the quiet hallway, I pass by the school's illuminated trophy showcase. Panning my eyes across the numerous plaques bearing Berkeley Mills's name, I start to get weepy again and murmur, "I hate you." Giving my head a quick shake, I inhale a series of deep breaths, lift my chin into the air, and whisper, "God, I wish it was August."

Inside the admin offices, Mrs. B greets me and escorts me into her private office, where I notice the presumed Mr. Reid is already seated. He's about fifty years old; has graying hair and a compact physique; and is wearing a stylish navy suit, a white shirt, a geometric-print tie, and an interesting pair of brown retro eyeglasses.

Seeing me, he stands up, smiles, and, in a voice as smooth as velvet, says, "Hi! I'm Sean Reid. It's a pleasure to meet you, Francie."

Shaking his extended hand, I reply, "It's a pleasure to meet you too."

Pulling out a chair for me to sit on, he says, "I know we're pressed for time, so let's dive right into the topic at hand so that I have time to answer any questions you might have."

"Sure," I reply.

As if reading from a well-rehearsed script—but he's not—Mr. Reid conveys his faith in the Idea Incubatrice program, the many accomplishments of those who have previously attended, and his confidence in my future success. He even spends several minutes gushing about what he knows of me and how unique my artistic style is, making me forget, for a moment, that this is the worst day of my life.

Lastly, he says, "You have all the potential to go through this program with flying colors, Miss. Lanoo."

Blushing, I respond, "That's very kind of you to say."

Standing up, he says, "I look forward to meeting with you again before you spread your wings and fly away."

I fake a giggle. "Sounds good."

Sauntering down the corridors toward the school's exit doors, I'm surprised to find myself nearly smiling, partly because I'm now excited about what I'm diving into and partly because I'm relieved there isn't a soul around—which shouldn't surprise me, because it's already fifteen minutes into spring break.

Reaching the exit, I glance out the vestibule windows, take note that a gray sky has descended, notice the coast is clear, and open the door. But as I start walking, I unexpectedly jump out of my skin when a person emerges from around the corner to confront me.

"Jesus, Berkeley! You scared me half to death!"

Stepping back and throwing his hands into the air, he meekly replies, "Sorry, Francie, but I really need to talk to you."

I say nothing, walk around him, and scurry down the steps.

Hot on my heels, he asks, "Francie, will you please hear me out?"

Scowling, I retort, "What's the point, Berkeley, when it's pretty obvious you've moved on?"

"Francie, what happened outside the locker room is not what it looked like."

"I know what I saw."

Taking a deep breath, he explains, "What you saw was Shanna congratulating me for breaking a school track record. That's all."

"How nice she was able to be there for you."

"Francie, she means nothing to me."

I inhale a giant breath. "Well, she just monsooned all over my parade, so she means something to me."

Berkeley runs ahead, walks backward so that he can face me, and exclaims, "I'm so sorry, Francie! Please believe me when I say that what happened today was not what was supposed to happen today."

I scrunch up my face. "I have no idea what that even means, but whatever. Message received."

After mumbling several expletives, Berkeley says, "Please stop walking for two minutes so I can explain something."

Avoiding contact with those amazing eyes because I'm well aware they can talk me into anything, I say, "I can't. I have to go."

Taking hold of my upper arms and making me face him, he calmly says, "Francie, you have to believe me. The last thing I would ever do is hurt you."

Looking into his eyes, feeling compelled to fall into his arms but restraining myself, I say quietly, "I'm sorry, Berkeley, but I'm not convinced."

Placing his forehead against mine, he looks to the ground and says, "You have to believe me when I say that you mean more to me than anything and that I just got stupid today, wanting so badly for you to do that Italy thing."

I pull away from his hold. "So what? Are you telling me you staged this?"

After pausing, sighing, and sputtering, he replies, "Yes, I did. I had to. It was the only way I could think of to coax you."

I shake my head. "Well, mission accomplished."

His eyebrows rise. "So does that mean you're going to Italy?"

"Yep. The deal is done and dusted," I say, walking away.

Keeping pace with me, he says, "Please don't leave before I have a chance to clean up this mess."

Increasing my speed, I reply, "My mom's waiting at the corner, and I'll be on an airplane in a few hours, so I'm sorry, but my time with you is now done."

"What does that mean?"

"I don't know."

Spotting my mom's SUV, I dart toward it, open the passenger door, and scurry inside.

As my mom looks at my face, she says, "You look exhausted. Were you just running or something?"

Leaning back and closing my eyes, I say, "No, I've just had a crazy day, and I want to get out of here."

"Are you feeling okay?"

I take a deep breath. "Yeah, I'm just frazzled because I said yes to that Italy thing."

"You did?"

"I did."

Turning bubbly and ecstatic, she starts woo-hooing with ridiculous jazz fingers, exclaiming, "That's fantastic to hear!"

Mindlessly gazing out the side window, I say, "Great, another person thrilled to get rid of me."

As the vehicle turns a corner, I glance back and see Berkeley standing there, watching me leave. Noticing his face seems to have lost all of its life, I rub my eyes and wish for a do-over in which I don't sleep in and subsequently leave Berkeley wide open. Closing my eyes, I hear one of the little voices in my head again, chanting the words "Look forward, not backward."

Grabbing hold of my knees and pulling them tightly to my chest, I glance at my palm, and with pursed lips, I furiously rub away the ink that my morning shower left behind. As my skin becomes inflamed and raw, I lean my head against the side window and mumble, "It's been a life-altering day all right."

Nearing home, I yank the white flip-flops off my feet and throw them into the backseat, categorizing them as the second pair of footwear I never want to see again. Staring at my yet-again bare feet, I start thinking about my me-shoe research and consider whether there's anything from my day that might be of relevance.

Stepping out of the vehicle and accidentally walking through a patch of moist dirt, I conclude only that, clearly, I'm far from knowing what I'm looking for.

# foot note eleven

FOR MY TRAVELS TO THE SNOW-PLASTERED DESTINATION OF Whitefish, Montana—it's a place I'm less than thrilled to be visiting, but I'm happy it's not Riverly Heights—I'm wearing bulky, boot-camp-style, sheepskin-lined brown suede boots made ugly with their inch-thick waterproof soles. I didn't buy them, nor did I choose them. I never would. My mom did, specifically for this vacation, after claiming I owned nothing "ski-trip appropriate."

I have no plans to factor them into my shoe quest, because I hate the way I look in them, and I hate the way they alter my strut, but I am pleased that as I charge down the airport concourse wearing them, they seem to release a fraction of my tension with every decisive stomp.

As a bonus, the added ten pounds of weight is exhausting me, and I expect by the time I settle into my airplane window seat, I will have no trouble falling asleep for two long hours of thinking nothing, dreaming nothing, and feeling nothing.

At a holiday resort buried deep in the mountains, I walk through the double doors of my family's hotel suite, expecting to find a typical wood-paneled ski-lodge atmosphere, but my eyes open wide when

I instead see a tranquil setting of white everything—walls, floors, ceilings, furnishings, accessories, and even the television.

Looking at my mom, I say, "You did well picking this one."

"Thank you," she replies with a smile, already setting up her home-away-from-home office on the living room's white desk.

Wandering toward the massive floor-to-ceiling windows, I look out and realize that the room's decor perfectly complements the serene winter wonderland outside. Smiling, I quietly say, "I like it here. I can de-stress here." Afterward, I kick off my dreaded boots; drop myself into a body-wrapping leather armchair, which is also white; cover myself with a cozy white angora blanket; and contemplate what's in store for me during the week ahead.

"You're awfully quiet," Brigitte says, mussing my hair.

"I'm just thinking about stuff."

Talula says, "Missing Berkeley already?"

"No, just tired," I mumble, pressing my lips tightly together to withhold sharing the mess that has been my day, out of fear my dad will say, "I told you that you could get hurt."

As everyone but me unpacks and gets organized, my dad hollers from the master bedroom, "Why don't we head out to a restaurant to grab a bite?"

Faking a yawn, I reply, "I don't have an outing in me. Would you be able to bring me some takeout?"

"Sure," my mom says.

Smirking, Talula says, "Let me guess—pizza?"

Faintly, I reply, "Yes, please."

"Call us if you need to," my mom says.

Taking a deep breath, I reply, "I can't. I forgot my phone at home."

Squinting, my dad says, "That's odd for you."

I shrug. "It's an experimental thing. To see if I miss it."

Checking my forehead for a temperature, my mom says, "Use the hotel phone if you need to."

"I will."

As the four of them head out the door, I wander into the kids' bedroom, flop onto the bed nearest the window, and climb under the mounds of fluffy white bedding. Coiling into a compact ball, I relish the fact that there's not a sound to be heard, a smell to be inhaled, or a nonwhite element to command my attention.

Nestling my head into a double stack of pillows, I glance outdoors and notice that the ski resort is abuzz with activity; night skiers are enthusiastically shushing their way down the slopes. Captivated by the fastest one of the bunch, because he reminds me of someone, I unwittingly suffer a barrage of memories of the events from earlier today and go down a road I promised I wouldn't.

Withholding tears, I mumble, "Are Berkeley and I done?"

Taking a moment to consider the possibility and realizing a breakup is the most-probable outcome after a boyfriend smashes his girlfriend's heart into a thousand pieces, I pick up the hotel phone and call Phoebe, cringing at the thought of disturbing her at a family gathering.

She picks up on the first ring and, in a hushed voice, says, "Who is this?"

"Francie."

"Oh, hi, I'm at my aunt's house for the wedding-eve party, and there's a toast to the couple going on right now."

"Sorry to disturb. I won't keep you for long. Are you having a nice time?"

"No, I'm miserable because there's not one single guy in sight."

"Sorry to hear that."

Sighing, she says, "Hey, I heard through the grapevine all about your disastrous day. How are you?"

"Managing."

"Did I read correctly—you and Berkeley broke up?"

I squint. "Not that I'm aware, unless you read a post from Berkeley, which would be a cruel way to formally dump me, but I guess it's possible."

"No, he's not the source."

"Then someone must have seen us arguing on the school grounds."

"Probably, because as you know, Berkeley's many stalkers have eyes on him at all times. Which leads me to a word of advice: stay away from your computer until this all cools down. Okay? Because reading all of the social chatter about Berkeley Mills, allegedly single and on the prowl, will only make you feel worse."

"Thanks for the tip."

"You're welcome. You know I've always got your back."

"Yeah, thanks for that."

"So are you okay?"

"I'll survive."

After taking a deep breath, she says, "I can't believe Berkeley would do anything to hurt you, when it's written all over his face that he's flat-out mad about you."

Shaking my head, I say, "Yeah, I'm surprised by what he did too."

"I think it's just proof that big boobs and seductive lips will distract even the most devoted of the male species."

I look at my less-than-stellar bosom. "Thanks. Now I do feel worse."

She sighs. "Sorry. I guess the bottom line is this: Are you willing to forgive and forget?"

Glancing at the still-irritated palm of my hand, I say, "Maybe? Yes? No? Who knows? The guy did claim he set up the incident as a means of making me say yes to school in Italy, so maybe his misstep isn't as malicious as I first thought."

She smirks. "The guy needs to work on his tact, though."

"Yeah, why did he have to kiss someone?"

"Yeah, especially someone like Shanna, who has kissed pretty much every guy in the school—probably even the janitor."

"Eww."

As Phoebe's mom babbles in the background, Phoebe says, "Listen, I've gotta go. It's my turn to say something poignant about the happy couple."

I smile. "Okay. See you when I'm back."

"Call me again if you need to."

With my mind now restless, I turn on the bedside lamp, grab my tote bag from the floor, retrieve my sketchbook and Berkeley's pen (I'm surprised I felt the need to bring it), and ponder something to draw. Realizing I have yet to make an attempt at a Francie Lanoo shoe, I start scribbling one quickly and furiously: a midheight heel made from an industrial spring; a top made of overlapping layers of clear acrylic, to resemble shards of glass; a sole of steely silver; and an instep labeled "frigid-blue satin." To add finishing touches, I render some texture and some shadows and scribe a stylized version of my signature in the bottom right corner.

Analyzing its boisterous and edgy design, I find it interesting that I've pretty much ignored the characteristics on my current me-shoe list—there is nothing timeless, sparkly, harmonious, or fuchsia. However, I did create something that my currently pained mind feels a kinship to, so I set my work stuff aside, lean back, and envision placing the style on my foot.

As my eyelids start to droop, I drowsily announce, "I'll call it the Artsy," and as I drift off to dreamland, I smile when an imaginary adventure starts coming to life.

# foot note twelve

My sleeping mind takes me to a space that's pitch black, quiet, humid, and warm. I assume the location is indoors—the floor is solid, the air is calm, and the ambient sound is hushed.

Using my hands to feel along a wall, I find a doorknob and turn it. Walking through the open door, I discover a well-lit space with white wood floors and high white walls. Panning the empty space, I hear noise coming from around a corner, so I walk toward a mix of conversation, laughter, and acoustic guitar music and find a crowd of well-dressed people milling about. What strikes me as most interesting about them is that they're not reality based, nor is this place. Rather, all that surrounds me is animated in a style I believe has originated from my own hand. Did I climb into one of my drawings?

As I stand and decide where to go and what to do, a group of four females—ageless, ethereal, willowy, psychedelically clothed, and bizarrely coiffed—wander toward me, exhibiting movement as graceful as sailboats on calm water. Though their faces seem vaguely familiar (thoughts of Beatrice, Silvia, Phoebe, and Catharine Armour—*What?*—come to mind), I sense they are strangers and wait for them to speak to me first.

Without saying a word, one of them takes my hand, and they lead me through the crowd, deeper into the room. As I traverse, I catch sight of myself in a large wall mirror, and only then do I realize I'm animated too.

Somewhere in the midst of this strange menagerie of animation, I pause and inquire, "How did I get here?"

In a voice that I'm sensing recently made an appearance in my actual head, one of my close companions says, "You arrived by will."

Squinting, I say, "Why are you here with me?"

Another answers, "Because we're your escorts, your entourage, your sages. Whatever term suits you best."

"What are we doing here?"

Another says, "We're going to find you a suitable dance partner."

"Do I need one?"

The first one responds, "Yes, for your dandy dancing by night."

"Yes, of course." Speaking more loudly to drown out the sounds of the surrounding crowd, I ask, "What's happening here?"

With excited eyes, the second one replies, "A celebration."

"Of what?"

"Of your debut."

"What am I debuting?"

Grasping my hand, one of them energetically says, "Come along, and I'll show you. Everyone is waiting to meet you."

"They are?"

"But of course."

As the foursome lead me around another corner, a round of applause erupts. Initially, I'm startled, but when I see that everyone is smiling, apparently at me, I can't help but smile back.

Looking beyond them, I view expanses of long white walls adorned with ornately framed drawings hung at even intervals. Squinting to see the images, I discover that each drawing is of a person—some are female, some are male, and all are faceless—wearing the most stylish of shoes. Though I don't remember ever creating them, I know they originated from my hand, which reminds me of my most-recent creation, causing me to glance downward to see my feet. "The Artsy," I quietly say.

As my eyes work their way up the rest of me, I notice I'm wearing a sleek dress at the height of fashion, as well as a beaded string necklace that bears an unusual pendant: a miniature alabaster pen. After admiring its intricate detailing, I slip it under my blouse to protect it, softly grinning because I know it's precious, meaningful, and mine.

Looking up again, I feel a hand grasping my shoulder from behind. After spinning around, I see a stranger, a guy about the same age as me, animated, dark haired, dark eyed, handsome, impeccably dressed, and well groomed. In a foreign accent (Italian, I think), he says, "It's delightful to see you here."

I smile and say, "It's nice to see you too," realizing that though I don't know him, I do know he is ooh-la-la.

"This is your debut art show, no?" he asks.

Noticing my companions seem to have dissipated, I reply, "I believe it is, yes."

"You love art."

"I do."

He grins and shows off his lovely white teeth. "Well then, you and I have a great deal in common."

"If you say so," I reply, unable to stop admiring his desirable lips.

Seeming to do the same, he smiles and says, "What do you plan to do with your talent?"

"Design shoes."

"Well then, you must do so in Italy, where all the best shoes find their inspiration."

"So I'm told."

"Have you ever been?"

"No."

He smiles. "Well then, allow me to tell you about the place, because it is, without a doubt, heaven on Earth."

"Okay."

For many minutes, this cool guy escorts me on an imaginary tour, filling my head with images of cool galleries, fine restaurants, live performances, and gourmet delights.

Unexpectedly, I find myself craving more of what he's saying and more of him in general, so I say, "Would you like to view my artwork?"

"Yes, I'd love to," he replies. He takes my hands and leads me along.

Strolling past each piece, he points out several details I've never considered: a line change here, a heel-height tweak there, a decorative element added in an optimum spot.

Viewing the final example, he says, "The night is young. You and I—we should go dancing."

My eyes widen. "Right now? You want me to leave here?"

"Yes, I do. Will you?"

Wanting to because I'm attracted to this boy like a magnet to steel but not knowing how I got here or what's expected of me, I reply, "Before I can answer, I have to ask my escorts. Will you give me a minute to find them?"

He smiles. "Of course, but I'm sure they won't mind, because after all, they brought me here to be with you."

"They did?"

"Yes."

Squinting and glancing around the room but not seeing anyone familiar, I say, "Okay, but I still need to tell them of my plans."

"No problem. I'll wait right here."

Passing through the middle of the room, I see a buffet of food along the wall, so I distractedly head there in search of something sweet. Near an array of gorgeous desserts, I spy another guy my age, with an arrestingly perfect outline, taking hold of a plate. When he turns his head and exposes his profile, I get the feeling I know him from somewhere. However, because I'm in a strange place and surrounded by strangers, I can't possibly. Can I?

Grabbing a plate of my own, I move closer to him and say, "The crème caramel looks delicious."

Without looking my way, he responds, "It is. I've already tasted it. Here—let me pass you some."

"Okay!"

As he extends a food-filled spoon in my direction, we both sneak peeks at each other's faces.

Stricken by the sight of the most-dazzling green eyes imaginable, I become startled and drop the plate.

Simultaneously, he drops the spoon and spills creamy stuff all over my left foot.

Letting out the quirkiest of yelps, I say, "You just slimed me."

He gasps and rambles, "Oh crap! I'm so sorry. I didn't mean to do that. I'm not usually this much of a klutz."

Amused by his sweet demeanor, I reply, "No worries. It feels pretty good, actually."

Grabbing a stack of napkins and crouching down, he says, "I should have been more careful."

Watching my foot and shoe get cleaned, I say, "It's nothing that can't be rectified."

He glances up. "These shoes have so many nooks and crannies. I'm gonna be here awhile."

I smile. "Yeah, they are pretty ornate."

"*Outlandish* is a better descriptor."

I giggle. "Yes, they are outlandish."

Gently taking hold of my ankle and returning the shoe where it belongs, he adds, "You know, if all humans had feet as beautiful as yours, I don't think shoes would ever have been invented."

My eyes dance with delight. "What a nice thing to say!"

"It's true."

I smile. "But if not for shoes, everyone's feet would be covered in calluses."

He shakes his head. "Not yours, because guys would be lining up in droves to piggyback you wherever you needed to go."

Laughing loudly, I say, "Of course, without shoes, my sense of world order would be thrown totally out of sync."

His eyes soften. "You must be a shoe lover."

"Yes, since I was little."

He stands up. "You should meet the artist whose work is being exhibited here. The two of you probably have a lot in common."

"Yes, I bet we do."

As my eyes glance to the floor, he asks, "You wouldn't, by chance, be the artist who created these drawings?"

I look up. "Yes."

His large eyes grow even larger. "Oh, wow! You are so talented!"

"Thank you!"

As I'm about to ask him his name, my concentration is broken with a grip to my shoulder. Turning around, I see the artsy guy from earlier and smile. "Hey, hi."

Grabbing my hand, he says, "The night sky awaits us. Shall we depart?"

I look to the guy with the green eyes and become too fixated on his beautiful face to respond. I proceed to stare silently.

I only stop when the artsy guy nudges my arm and says, "We only have an hour before dawn sets and the stars disappear, so we must run."

Taking my other hand, the guy with green eyes says, "Are you leaving?"

Looking back and forth, I exclaim, "I don't know!"

Holding my gaze on the green-eyed guy, I say, "Do you like to dandy dance?"

Before he's able to answer, I'm hit with an arm slap from my sister Talula, who's sleeping in the hotel bed next to me, and abruptly brought back to reality.

Taking a deep breath, I get out of bed, look out the window, and discover a sky that's beautifully blanketed with stars. "So many eyes."

With a newly formed smile on my face, I return to bed and find pizza and a drink waiting for me on the bedside table. "Nice." As I consume the much-needed nutrients, I retrieve my latest drawing from on the floor and reimagine the crazy dream it inspired. Realizing I'm seriously missing the green-eyed guy, I lose some of the pain I've been feeling since yesterday's incident and hug my pillow. But strangely, at the same time, I think about the artsy guy from my dream and wonder what it would be like to meet a reality-based version of him.

Worried about what this unexpected longing might be telling me, I close the pizza box, bury myself under a heap of blankets, and go back to sleep.

# foot note thirteen

IT'S THE FINAL DAY OF MY SKI VACATION, AND WHAT A WEEK IT HAS been. The only upside worth mentioning is that I'll be leaving this place in altogether different footwear than I arrived in, the explanation of which is not one I would have ever predicted.

First, after having the dream about the artsy guy and green-eyed guy, I woke up with a desire to check out some real guys and, after convincing Brigitte to come along for the adventure, headed to the ski resort's quaint town square to do some shopping and gawking. Lo and behold, while doing so, a serious stunner did materialize, one who fit the term *ski bum* to a T. He was cute and tanned, had sun-bleached blond hair and blue eyes, was dressed in the latest snowboarder fashion, and looked like he pumped iron for a living.

His name was John—I heard his clone-like friend call him that—and after crossing paths with him for the fourth time, I started noticing him and started smiling at him and may have started flirting with him just a smidgeon.

Regardless, while walking away from him, after he said, "Maybe we could ski together tomorrow," I looked back; got my foot caught on a boot scraper; lost my footing; fell onto a sheet of cold, hard ice;

felt unbearable pain; and watched in horror as blood started oozing out the top of my ugly boot.

Hearing my yelps and moans, Brigitte looked my way, had a mini-panic attack, and started screaming for help.

John—and probably everyone else in the town—heard her, rushed to my side, swept me into his arms as if I were made of toothpicks, ran me to a nearby medical clinic without even breaking a sweat, and stayed at my side until my parents arrived.

And that is all there is to say about him. Done. Finished. No more discussion.

My foot, on the other hand, will be a hot topic long after this trip is over. Oh, the irony that I've damaged the one part of my body I care most about, leaving me to wonder, *Is this my punishment for the fantasies that were going on in my head at the time of the mishap?* After all, I'm still the girlfriend of Berkeley Mills. At least I think I am.

Unsurprisingly, I haven't been able to look at my injury. However, I've seen the facial expressions of those who have, so I know it's awful—twelve stitches' or staples' worth of awful, stretching right across the bridge of my ankle, placing in jeopardy my desire to ever wear pretty shoes again.

Lying in my hotel bed, struck with the latest sharp jab delivered by my nervous system, I fumble to grab my meds bottle but knock it to the floor. Watching it roll away, I sigh and holler into the living room. "Mom! Dad! Are either of you awake?"

From the living room, in unison, they respond, "What's wrong?"

I take a deep breath. "I hate to be a bother, but I could use some help, please."

As my dad opens the curtains, my mom grabs the medicine bottle from the floor and says, "I still can't believe that you, of all people, ended up with this injury."

Brigitte stirs in the bed next to mine. "Yeah, trust Francie to get a ski-trip injury while shopping."

I say, "I tripped over that boot scraper *outside* of a store."

She smirks. "You forgot to add 'while admiring a mannequin of the live variety.'"

I furrow my brow. "You were the one who said, 'Check out the ten out of ten.'"

Crawling out of bed, she says, "Only because he kept following us and staring at you and making it known he was interested in you."

I mumble, "Nothing happened with him."

"But would something have, if not for the injury?"

"Go take a shower, Brigitte," my mom says.

"Going," Brigitte says.

Rolling her eyes, my mom says to me, "One thing I know for sure: you won't be able to wear home the boots I bought for you."

Closing my eyes, I exclaim, "Yay, my wish came true!"

Grinning, she jests, "So you're admitting this accident was a grandiose ploy to dump those boots."

My face twists. "Yeah, I mangled my foot to protest the fact that you shoe-shopped for me."

She chuckles. "And guess what? I shoe-shopped for you again."

"Buying what?"

"These," she announces, tossing a gift bag between me and comatose Talula.

With a smirk, I open it to find a pair of pretty beaded moccasins, one in my size and the other in what's probably my father's. Lightly giggling, I say, "You bought singles?"

"Yes, because apparently, foot injuries are pretty common around here."

Examining the intricate hand stitching, the warm fur trim, and the roominess, I murmur, "Actually, these are very doable today. Thank you, Mom."

"You're welcome. Now, let's get you out of this bed and ready to roll, because we leave for the airport in an hour. You too, Talula—time to get up."

"Sure," she mumbles, sleepwalking her way into the living room.

As my mom helps me get up, she asks, "How did you fare going a full seven days without your phone?"

I shrug. "It wasn't horrible, but I'm ready to reconnect."

"To sweet-talk with Berkeley, I bet!" Talula yells from the next room.

"Maybe," I say, releasing a smile, because after being detached for seven days, I'm ready to face my reality.

*Berkeley.* I wonder what he's doing right now on that hot and sunny tropical beach. I wonder if he's thinking about me right now. I wonder if he'll cringe at seeing my marred foot—the one that he inadvertently caused, because if he hadn't kissed Shanna, then I surely wouldn't have had the dream that prompted me to go on a boy hunt.

Okay, I admit that pinning this injury on Berkeley might be a stretch, but I will forevermore associate the accompanying scar with him.

Moving forward, I guess I'll have to embark on a new era of shoe selection, with emphasis on camouflaging, cloaking, and shrouding. Or maybe my injury is a sign telling me to scrap my love of shoes altogether.

As my family and I make our way out of the hotel lobby, my dad pulls out his phone, snaps a picture of me hobbling, and forwards it to someone.

Squinting, I ask, "Who did you send that to?"

"Berkeley."

My body slumps. "Why would you do that?"

"Because he just asked me your shoe size, and I thought that a photo of you and your nonmatching feet worked well with my response: 'Right foot, petite. Left foot, extralarge.'"

I moan. "Thanks for showing me at my worst."

"Francie, that boy is too blinded by love to see a microbial-sized flaw in you."

"A three-inch flaw is hardly microbial."

Smiling, my mom adds, "I bet that boyfriend of yours has gone out of his mind not having seen you in a week."

Pouty-lipped, I say, "He's been on a Caribbean island, basking in sun, so I doubt he's done any suffering."

Her eyebrows rise. "That was terse."

I slump. "Yeah, it was. I take it back."

She sighs. "If you're missing Berkeley, why don't you use my phone and call him?"

Shaking my head, I reply, "No, I can wait until I get home."

Back home, my dad helps me into my bedroom, and I retrieve my phone from a drawer, turn it on, and start scrolling.

A message from Beatrice says, "Shanna feels like a loser for what she did."

One from Phoebe says, "All teenage guys are morons."

Silvia says, "Quit being a moron, and turn on your phone."

Catharine Armour says, "Welcome to the swapped-out club."

At the bottom of the list, I see Berkeley has contacted me just once, with a text that reads, "I'm an idiot."

As my eyes light up at his inherent cuteness, I tell myself that by the end of this day, I will wipe my memory clean of last Friday morning between eight fifteen and eight thirty.

Why?

First, my takeaway from this week away is that I'd rather have Berkeley in my life than not. Second, I'm intuitively sensing that Berkeley's heart was in the right place when he turned into an idiot. Third, I'm now aware I can be an idiot too.

# foot note fourteen

AWAKENING IN THE MIDDLE OF THE NIGHT TO THE FEELING OF MY own pillows and fluffy blankets, I first sigh but soon cringe as my injured foot starts severely throbbing. Aware that my meds have worn off, I pop another batch into my mouth and, now wide awake, contemplate my impending attempt at walking later today. This leads me to thoughts of footwear, and I realize none of my inventory will make the cut, not even yesterday's moccasins, because the extralarge one slipped off somewhere between deplaning and baggage pickup, and I never saw it again.

Wondering if my beloved sheepskin boots will fit over my enormous extremity, I sit up, stumble to my feet, hobble across the room by using furniture as my support, and try to squeeze my left foot into one. *Nope. No go.*

Suddenly feeling lightheaded—either because of the strong meds or the lack of sleep—I return to bed, crawl under the covers, and instruct my mind to do some happy meandering. Because what else does one do when wide awake at five o'clock in the morning? Unsurprisingly, my thought process shifts to Berkeley.

As I snuggle under my covers and wish he were here, I become even more awake, which is horrible because I'm exhausted, my foot hurts, and I know I need sleep to heal.

Waiting for the meds to thoroughly kick in, I start thinking about my shoe quest and whether or not I should I stick with it, when it's obvious that a beautiful shoe will look less than beautiful on a far-from-beautiful foot. Sighing, I whisper, "Hold off on a decision until after you've built up the nerve to look at the disaster zone."

Moving on, I wonder, *Why have I never considered my sheepskin boots as my ideal footwear?* I love them dearly; I can't live without them; and best of all, they hide everything. If only they weren't so chunky, the decision would be a no-brainer. *Hmmm. Maybe ten years from now, if I still haven't uncovered the real thing, I'll award them the championship trophy by default. Good. I have a contingency plan. Moving on again.*

This cozy room is my safe zone, the only bedroom I've ever known—a space I hate the thought of not retreating to at the end of the day. Thinking about my surroundings leads me to thoughts of my dorm room in Italy and what it will be like. No doubt it'll be ancient and small, stuffed away at the end of a dark hallway. It will have peeling plaster walls and a noisy heater, if there even is one. The floors will creak, especially when walked on by many ghosts. The bed will be lumpy. The chest of drawers will be hard to open. And the wooden chair won't be comfortable, even after I've added a cushion to it. Chances are the room won't contain any shoe shelves or a closet. Will it have a window? Maybe, but it'll be too small to enable an escape.

*Moving on, before I change my mind about going there.*

I think of my future classmates. I wonder what they will be like. Some will speak English, some will be quirky, and some will teach me a thing or two about style. One might even resemble the artsy guy from my dream, but when I imagine him, I exclaim, "Enough!" which brings me full circle to Berkeley.

I want to speak with him right now, to figure out where he and I stand. Should I call him? *No, not yet. Wait five more minutes. God, I hate the wait.*

Making fists out of my hands, I agitatedly stare at the time on my phone, watching each minute click away. Unable to wait a minute more, I hit the call button. Hearing a click on the other end of the line, followed by fumbling, rustling, and clinking, I feel my heart doing a loop-de-loop and my face breaking out in smile.

His faint voice says, "Hullo?"

"Hey. It's me."

"Francie!" He gasps. "Hi. How are you?"

Imagining what he looks like—his hair is crazy, his eyes are trying to open, and his mouth is upturning into a grin—I say, "I'm okay."

"Are you home?"

"Yeah, we got in late last night."

"How was your vacation?"

"Very, very, very cold. How was yours?"

"Horrible."

"Why?"

"Because you weren't there. Because I felt sick about what happened last week. Because I was so freaked that you'd never speak to me again."

"Trust me—that will never happen."

He exhales. "I'm so glad to hear you say that."

"Me too."

After a pause, he whispers, "I need to see you."

I grin. "It's five a.m."

"I don't care."

I say, "You might care that I haven't slept in two days, have knots in my hair and bed wrinkles on my face, and ..." I hesitate. "In case you didn't hear, I'm also now marred."

He sighs. "I did hear, and I'm really sorry that happened to you."

"Don't be. It was my fault. I got clumsy."

"How does your foot feel?"

"Sore."

"How does it look?"

"I don't know. My mom's been changing the bandages to spare me the visual."

"It'll heal."

"It'll leave a scar."

"Francie, even a scar will find a way to look amazing on you."

As tears fill my eyes, I murmur, "I've missed hearing stuff like that."

"I've missed saying it."

Exhaling, I quietly say, "I can't wait to see you."

To the sound of the shower spraying, he says, "Let's go eat some pancakes drenched in syrup."

I wipe away a rolling tear. "I don't know if I can leave the house. I don't have any footwear that'll fit my monstrosity."

"No worries. I've got you covered."

"With what? A pair of your clodhopper sneakers?"

"No, with something new, because I went shoe-shopping for you."

"You did?"

"Yeah, I did."

Giggling, I reply, "That's really sweet of you."

"Thanks. So how soon can you be ready?"

"I can be on the doorstep by five thirty."

"Then I'll be there at five twenty-five."

Unable to stop grinning, I say, "Okay. See you shortly."

Sighing, he adds, "Thanks for calling, Francie."

I take a deep breath. "Thanks for answering, Berkeley."

Faster than I ever have, I shower, hobble back to my bedroom, slap on some makeup, and speedily dry my hair. Aware that jeans won't fit over the blob on the end of my leg, I slip into a loose-fitting dress and cover it with a sweater coat. Catching a quick glimpse of my barefoot self in the mirror, I note, "You've seen better days," and then I shrug because I do not care.

Stepping outside and feeling the crisp spring air slap me in the face, I see Berkeley's car waiting alongside the curb and then watch him fling open the driver's door and dash toward me.

Bubbling over inside, one-legged bouncing on the spot, I smile as he approaches, hold on tightly to the handrail, and say, "Hey, you."

"Hey, you, back," he says, taking the three steps in one motion and standing before me, smiling. "You look great."

"Thanks."

Gently pulling me into his arms for a soft bear hug, lifting me off the ground, and giving my foot some much-needed relief, he adds, "I've never been happier to see anyone."

As my body easily meshes with his, I respond, "Me neither."

Tightening his embrace, Berkeley buries his face in my hair and says, "I'm so sorry, Francie, about everything that happened last week, and I promise I will never do anything so stupid for as long as I live."

I look him in the eyes. "I believe you."

"Thank you. I needed to hear that."

Pressing our foreheads together, we kiss sweetly and softly for a long time.

Afterward, Berkeley asks, "How's that foot holding up?"

Looking down at my dangling limb, I reply, "See for yourself."

Glancing at the swell bursting beyond the bandages, he exclaims, "Whoa! That's gotta be hurting."

"Yeah."

"And it's gotta be freezing cold too."

"Uh-huh."

Transferring me into a piggyback position, he heads down the sidewalk and remarks, "I can't believe you didn't even put socks on, when the temperature out here is below freezing."

I sigh. "Not even socks would fit over such a big blob."

As I watch his streetlight-illuminated face break out in a smile, I run my finger along his temple and say, "Nice tan line. Do you have any others?"

He laughs but doesn't respond with one of his playful quips. Rather, he bashfully smiles, brushes off the comment, and helps me get seated in the car.

Inside, he hands me a shoe box and says, "For your collection."

I grin. "I can't believe you bought me footwear."

"I'm a guy after your heart. What else would I apologize with?"

"A valid point."

Opening the box, I burst out laughing at the sight of the most-bizarre shoes I've ever seen: puffy, shiny red-vinyl slippers in the shape of boxing gloves. Noticing that one is large and the other is enormous, I say, "Nice!"

"Comfy too."

Grabbing his hand, I say, "You should wear these; you're such a clown."

Squeezing my hand, he replies, "I bet you wish you'd had them a week ago so you could've kicked my ass with them."

I look him in the eyes. "I could never maim you."

"Even if I deserve it?"

"Even if."

Carefully slipping the footwear on, I note, "Berkeley, these feel really good. Thank you."

He smiles. "For the record, I still intend to carry you around until you're all healed."

I grin. "Trust me—no girl in her right mind would ever decline that offer."

Seated in a diner booth, I ask, "So was it my dad who told you about my accident?"

"No, actually. Brigitte posted a photo."

"She did? Argh! I'm gonna strangle her."

He smiles. "In her defense, the pic was less about you and more about some hunky blond guy."

"Oh?"

"The caption read something like 'If I'd known a ten out of ten was going to come to the rescue, I'd have gotten injured too.'"

I blush. "I'm not sure what she meant by that, because I didn't check the guy out."

"By the look on his face, he definitely checked you out."

My eyes dart to the tablecloth. "No worries. He lives thousands of miles away from me."

Berkeley webs his fingers with mine. "Yeah, but in a few months, so will I."

I look up. "This coming from the guy who saw no downside to me moving away."

His forehead wrinkles. "Okay, I admit I may not have thought this Italy thing through."

I twist his hand. "So the eating of my shoes may very well become a reality."

Squinting, he responds, "I wonder if they'd taste better salted."

"I think syrup is the ticket."

Flashing me a coy grin and shifting his eyes to the plates of food being served by another Berkeley-gawking waitress, he responds, "God, it feels good to be back in your company."

"Ditto."

Munching on superstacks, Berkeley and I begin to fall into a familiar groove, with one small change for me: two weeks ago, I was convinced I'd never survive a day away from him. Today I'm less worried about it. Maybe after seeing him do the unexpected, I removed my rose-colored glasses to see that everyone has flaws. Or maybe I've come out on the other side of this episode more focused on what works for me. Or maybe I've clued into the fact that to be happy, I don't need to be with Berkeley every minute of every day.

Berkeley seems a bit different too: he's quieter and less playful and has a couple of wrinkles around his eyes, which might have something to do with getting too much sun.

Staring at his face and swimming around in those incredible eyes of his, I say, "I had an interesting dream last Friday, and you were in it."

He smiles. "I dream about you all the time."

"You do?"

"Yeah, when I'm asleep and awake, which is probably why your face has become my brain's permanent wallpaper."

"Is that good or bad?"

"Trust me—there is no downside to having your face burned into my brain."

Chuckling, I respond, "I wonder if my face will be there while I'm out of sight and out of mind in Italy."

He looks me in the eyes. "Etched, sealed, and locked."

"I like hearing that."

Pouring more syrup, he asks, "So what was your dream about?"

Not wanting to ruin the moment by discussing some artsy Italian guy, I simply say, "You were admiring my feet."

"As I do whenever I'm with you."

My forehead tenses. "Will you still?"

Saying nothing, he slips his hands under the table, takes hold of my left knee, works his hands down to my ankle, and gently removes my clown shoe. He drops it to the floor and gives my bandaged foot a wonderful, heartwarming caress, locking his eyes on mine the entire time. Sweetly smiling, he says, "Grade eleven had better go by quickly, because I'm gonna lose an ounce of sanity for every day not spent with you."

Sighing, I respond, "The very reason you'd better visit me while I'm there."

He nods. "I will. Often."

"Really?"

"Yes, because I cannot bear the thought of another beefcake rescuing you when I'm not around."

Smiling, I say, "Did I mention that the beefcake told me I had the prettiest crying face he'd ever seen?"

"No, but in response to that, did I mention I'm seriously considering locking you in my closet for the next twelve months?"

I giggle. "FYI, if you had offered that up two weeks ago, I would have jumped all over it."

Shaking his head, he says, "Like I said, I'm an idiot."

On the drive home, Berkeley asks, "Is there any chance those clown shoes will impact your shoe quest?"

Giggling and then shrugging, I respond, "Speaking of, I'm not sure I'm going to pursue my me shoe anymore."

"Why not?"

"Because paying attention to pretty shoes will be a reminder that a part of me is now gruesome."

"You're kidding, right?"

"No."

Grabbing my hand, he says, "I think I'm going to make it my project to toughen you up and help you find your tenacity."

"I don't have tenacity."

"Yes, you do. You've just never used it."

"Nor do I want to."

Exhaling, he responds, "Well, if that's the case, just so you know, I never drop the ball on anything. And since I'm feeling somehow attached to that shoe search of yours, please be advised that if you dump it, I'm going to pick it up and run with it."

"So what are you saying? You're gonna shoe-search for me?"

"I will if I have to."

"Will there be more clown shoes?"

"Probably."

I look at my feet and smirk. "All right. Fine. I'll keep going with it."

"Good decision."

Suppressing a smile, I say, "We'll see."

# foot note fifteen

A gentle knock on my bedroom door awakens me, as does my parents' flopping onto my bed to exclaim, "Happy Birthday, Sweet Sixteen!"

Rolling over and hugging my pillow, I grin and groggily respond, "Thank you!"

Smiling, my mom adds, "It's a beautiful June Saturday morning, exactly what you like on your special day."

"Yay!" I say.

"Sandal weather," she adds.

Shrugging, I say, "We'll see," because although my injured foot has healed enough for mobility purposes, it has yet to heal enough for visual purposes.

"Brunch is at ten," my dad says.

"I'll be ready."

Walking out the door, my mom asks, "Want me to bring you a glass of juice?"

"No, I can wait until ten."

"Don't fall back to sleep."

"I won't."

With the door reclosed, my senses start to fire. Crawling out of bed, I feel different from the way I felt when I went to bed at midnight.

Curious as to whether or not some age transformation took place while I was unconscious, I turn on the light, wander toward the mirror on the wall, and stare.

Shaking my head because I see the same image I remember from twelve hours earlier, albeit more disheveled, I hear my phone buzzing on the nightstand.

Rushing to the bedside, I discover it's Berkeley, smile, and pick up. "Good morning!"

"Happy birthday!"

"Thank you!"

"How are you?"

"Old like you. How are you?"

"Dreading the first half of the day spent at my grandfather's retirement party, because it means time missed with you."

I flop onto the corner of my bed. "When do you head out?"

"In about half an hour."

"When will you be picking me up?"

"About six o'clock. My mom is planning to have your dinner ready by seven."

I smile. "Excellent. That gives me nine full hours to make myself birthday ready."

"You don't need nine minutes."

"I wish."

Yawning, Berkeley asks, "Hey, do you mind if I ask a favor of you?"

"Fire away."

"For a photography assignment due Monday, I need to take a pic of a body part, and I was hoping the subject could be part of you."

"Which part?"

He chuckles. "That's a question with many don't-get-me-started answers, but I was hoping for a foot."

"Not my hideous one."

"Yes, that one."

"Why?"

"Because I want to capture what I think is your most-distinguishing characteristic."

I scoff. "You and I have totally different meanings for the term *distinguished*."

"According to my app, it means 'made conspicuous by excellence.'"

I grab my phone. "According to mine, it means 'different.'"

Sighing, he adds, "As much as I'd love to get into a battle of words with you, I'm running late and need to shower."

"All right, I'll see you and your camera later."

"A word of warning: around you, my camera's eye might wander."

Smiling, I giggle and say, "Good-bye, Berkeley."

"Enjoy the first half of your day, Francie."

Setting down my phone, I start the process of looking sixteen by turning on some upbeat music, scooting back to the mirror, shaking my hair with my hands while bent over, and standing up perfectly straight. Propping onto my tiptoes to try to look taller but quitting when I experience a sharp pang in my ankle, I plaster my lips with a thick coat of pastel-pink lipstick, flash the most-provocative expression my fresh face can muster, and strike a seductive pose. Unfortunately, when my eyes catch sight of my still-visible scar, I sigh and note, "You *will* need nine hours."

After showering, I begin the makeover process by rifling through my closet, assessing my makeup drawer, viewing fashionistas on my laptop, and researching the best ways to make a scar fade. *Note to self: buy some emu oil.*

Wandering into my room to wish me a happy birthday, Talula hugs me and says, "What are you doing?"

"Trying to look sixteen."

Offering her thirteen-year-old wisdom, she says, "Maybe a fancy hairstyle would make you look more mature."

"Sure, I could add some curls."

"Maybe some expensive perfume would make you smell older."

I giggle. "I'll see if Phoebe will let me borrow some."

"Why don't you get one of those push-up bras to help give you shape?"

I laugh and say, "But what would I push up?"

"Good point," she replies, giving me a hug before she heads elsewhere.

With the door again closed, I start pondering my biggest dilemma of the day: my shoe choice—something that has been bugging me all week, because I've pinpointed today as the official deadline to stop wearing camouflaging socks. With winter gone, I'll look ridiculous with them under my flip-flops, sandals, or espadrilles. With spring here, I run the risk of people catching sight of my unsightly wound and staring at it in disgust. *Damn that ski trip.* Taking a deep breath, I slip my bare feet into a pair of dressy flip-flops and my body into a ground-sweeping sundress that fully covers my feet. Glancing downward, I say, "A baby step will do."

For the next couple of hours, outside on a restaurant patio in a tree-filled park, I endure a short-lived spat between my two sisters, followed by teenage humiliation, beginning with my parents embarrassing me with stories of the day I was born. Then a group of way-too-perky waiters sing an action-filled birthday song, and finally, the restaurant manager snaps a photograph of me munching my crepe, claiming he'll post it on the restaurant's website before the end of the day. Throughout it all, I think happy thoughts about seeing Berkeley later in the day and spending some one-on-one time with him, which we haven't had much chance for during the last three months. He went on a school ski trip, but I couldn't because of my injury; he's been busy with basketball and the photography club and working part-time for his parents; and he seems more interested in hanging out in larger groups versus being alone with me.

As I munch on my candle-topped slice of birthday cake, I say to my mom, "For my evening with Berkeley and his parents, I want to wear something summery on my feet, but at the same time, I want to hide my scar. Do you have any suggestions for making it look more discreet?"

Evidently overhearing, Brigitte says, "You and your beauty issues. God forbid a real crisis should strike you someday."

"Enough, Brigitte," my mom responds, and after retrieving a large silver gift bag from under the table, she says, "Maybe this will help. Happy sixteenth birthday, my dear."

"Thank you."

Smiling, my dad adds, "It's a milestone, turning sixteen."

I nod. "And soon I'll be living on my own halfway around the world, getting into all kinds of shenanigans. How many gray hairs is that going to give you?"

"The very reason there's a GPS ankle monitor in that package."

"Rhinestone covered?"

Brigitte shakes her head. "Open your present already."

"Okay!" I reply. I peek inside the bag, realize it contains a shoe box, and say, "Is it chocolates?"

Talula replies, "No, but we'd be happy to do an exchange if that's what you were hoping for."

I grin. "No, I think I'll stick with whatever's waiting for me behind lid number one."

Opening the box, I find the most sophisticated, grown-up shoes I've ever seen: they are made of blue-gray silk and have rounded toes, platforms, and wide, pearl-covered ankle straps that I know will hide exactly what needs hiding.

Smiling, I exclaim, "Oh, wow! Thank you! Thank you! Thank you! I love these!"

Lightly clapping, Talula says, "Yay! We didn't screw up!"

Hugging the shoe box, I ask, "What world did you find these in?"

My father replies, "The world of the Internet."

My mother adds, "Involving an extensive group-search effort."

Grinning, Brigitte says, "I was the one who said New York shoe stores would have the best options."

Pointing her chin in the air, Talula adds, "I was the one who found the store Florrie Brown-King's Attic."

Exhaling, my mom says, "Actually, it was Berkeley who picked out the final style."

My eyes gleam. "Really?"

"Yes," she says. "He stopped by one day while you were out, took a quick look at the short list, and, within two minutes, announced that this was the shoe you'd 'go loopy over.'"

"He knows me well."

"I'm gathering that."

Sipping his coffee, my father adds, "I hope they fit."

Smiling, Talula says, "If they don't, can I have them?"

Shaking her head, Brigitte says, "Any chance these shoes will end your silly quest?"

"We'll see," I say, flabbergasted that my birthday-shoe woes just got resolved because of shoes that Berkeley picked. *How cute!*

Arriving home around noon, I scour the house for an outfit worthy of accompanying the prettiest shoes on the planet. When I come up with nothing, I call Phoebe and drag her to the mall, where she helps me blow a double dose of grandparental birthday cash on a new outfit and new makeup.

By five o'clock, I have the results sprawled out on my bed: a sleeveless gray V-neck minidress, a long string of Phoebe's silver bobbles, a pair of my own thick silver hoop earrings, and sexy nude fishnet stockings.

As Phoebe and I stare at the stuff, I ask, "What do you think?"

She pats me on the shoulder. "I think it's a good thing you and Berkeley are spending your birthday in the company of Berkeley's parents tonight, where you'll be sufficiently chaperoned."

"Meaning what?"

She dips her head to the side. "Francie, that boy had it bad for you before you assembled this sexpot outfit. Wait until he sees you in it."

"Here's hoping."

She sits on my bed. "Am I sensing doubt?"

"A little."

"Why?"

I sigh. "I don't know. It's nothing specific, other than that for the last few months, Berkeley has seemed afraid of me."

"That's odd."

"Agreed."

"What do you think is causing it?"

"I don't know. Maybe it's because of the Italy thing, which we never talk about. Or maybe it's because of my scarred foot."

Phoebe sits on the bed. "Maybe it's the Shanna incident. Berkeley probably still feels guilty for what he did."

"Possibly."

She smiles. "If I were you, I wouldn't fret over it."

"Why?"

"Because it's blatantly obvious that you are the bee's knees for that guy, and it's only a matter of time before his sixteen-year-old urges remind him of that."

"So you think this outfit will help?"

Phoebe holds the dress up to my body, smiles, and replies, "Trust me—you prancing around in this will be a draw for ninety-nine percent of the entire hetero male population." Watching me shake my head, she adds, "With the remaining one percent suffering from delayed puberty."

I giggle. "You say the craziest stuff."

She sets down the dress. "I'll bet you one thing."

"What?"

"If you wear outfits like this one when you're in Italy, then you and Berkeley will have way bigger issues to deal with than his kid-gloving."

My face sours. "What's that supposed to mean?"

She stands up and heads toward the door. "In about two months, you'll figure it out."

Ignoring her, I say good-bye and start suiting up.

A few minutes before Berkeley is due to arrive, I'm sitting on my bed, ready and waiting, staring at my fabulous birthday footwear.

Loving the fact that they are delaying the reveal of my scar's current state but knowing they don't, at all, suit my currently accumulated me-shoe criteria, I wonder, *Are they so spectacular that I'd be satisfied to completely discard my research and crown a shoe style totally unexpected? Or are these shoes simply a temporary thrill brought on because they happened to suit my needs at this vulnerable point in time?* I expect it's the latter. Regardless, I think I'll give them a label that exudes extraordinariness: the Knockout.

From the top of the staircase, I see Berkeley standing at the front door, looking hot, as always—his hair is floppy and wild, his dress pants and button-up shirt fit like a glove, and his casual red loafers are the icing on the cake. He's listening to my parents babble about something pointless, but as soon as his eyes shift to me, he walks toward the staircase, zombielike, as if my parents don't exist, and says, "Wow! You look fantastic!"

"Thanks."

"And intimidating."

Giggling, I make my way down the steps and say, "Could it be the effect of my fabulous new shoes?"

Watching me descend to the bottom step, he answers, "I don't know, because my eyes haven't gotten past your face."

When my parents roll their eyes and wander off to another room, I look at my feet and say, "I can't believe you picked these out for me. They are so awesome. Thank you."

"What's awesome is how they got infinitely more gorgeous once they met your feet."

"Thank you!" I say, grasping his hands and heading out the door.

Seated in Berkeley's car, I say, "Good news for tonight."

"What's that?"

"My parents extended my curfew to one a.m."

Berkeley smiles. "That *is* good news."

Fluttering my eyelashes, I ask, "So what are you going to do with an extra hour of me?"

Blushing and gazing out the window, he responds, "I don't know. Probably play some board games."

I say, "Like Twister?"

He gives me a side glance, gushes with his eyes, and responds, "I do own it."

"Nice," I say, feeling hopeful.

Arriving at the Millses' house, I receive the sweetest birthday wishes from Berkeley's parents, Archer and Sarah, and swiftly wander outside to find a candlelit, flower-adorned poolside-table setup.

With eyes gleaming, I say, "This is so beautiful."

As Berkeley runs inside to turn on some music, Sarah quietly responds, "I'm not supposed to tell you this, but Berkeley put it all together."

"Really?"

"Yes," Archer responds, "he wanted your evening to be perfect for you, but don't tell him I told you that either."

I giggle. "My lips are sealed."

Wandering toward some lit torches, Sarah and I end up having drawn-out conversations on a variety of topics: the latest news, the latest fashion, the local goings-on, and some lighthearted pop-culture gossip. Though I've talked to her several times on numerous occasions, this is the first time she and I have had one-on-one time, which makes me realize she's an amazing woman and makes me understand why her husband is so smitten with her.

Glancing at my footwear, she says, "Those shoes are fabulous on you."

"Thank you. I love them."

"Berkeley often talks about your affinity for beautiful shoes."

Smiling, I reply, "Did he tell you I'm collecting research—and shoes—in an attempt to find a perfectly me pair?"

She chuckles. "No, he didn't mention that, but on that note, let me show you something."

"Sure."

Leading me inside the house and up the stairs, she takes me into her large walk-in closet to show me a collection she's spent years working on: evening bags.

As my eyes light up at the many beauties neatly organized on custom-made shelves, I exclaim, "This is amazing!"

She shrugs. "I may have overdone it a bit."

"Not at all," I respond, admiring what must be about a hundred bags, each in a different size, shape, and color; each unique in detailing; and each perfectly propped.

Taking hold of one, Sarah admits, "I've been amassing these since I was thirteen, and I will probably do so until the day I die."

"Do you have a favorite?"

"Yes, I do," she says, retrieving a round, glittery white one.

"It's so lovely."

"It's from my honeymoon."

"It looks vintage."

"It's from the 1960s, I believe. I found it in a quaint secondhand store on a tucked-away cobblestone street in London."

As she shows me several others, she says, "Feel free to borrow one any time you'd like. They could stand to get some use."

"Thank you," I respond. "I would love to one day."

Sighing, she looks at my shoes and says, "If only my feet weren't about an inch longer than yours, then the two of us could share shoes too."

Both giggling, we walk arm in arm back downstairs.

Following the yummiest meal ever—with an Italian theme that does not get lost on me—Berkeley excuses us and leads me by the hand into the family room.

Seated close by my side on an oversized cushion on the floor, he smiles and says, "I have something for you."

"I think you've spoiled me enough."

"Never—not ever."

As he sets in my lap a shoe-box-sized package wrapped in pink paper with an orange bow, I say, "More shoes?"

He shakes his head. "No, but I will tell you that there is a shoe factor involved."

"Sounds intriguing."

Opening the box, I pull out a handmade clay sculpture of something. Although I can't be certain, I think it's a female figure with a paintbrush in hand, standing before an art easel. As for the shoe factor, the figure is wearing large red shoes.

With his chin held high, Berkeley says, "It's a sculpture of you that I made in art class."

Furrowing my brow, I respond, "It's so, umm, interesting!"

Looking into my eyes, he adds, "I realize that art is not my calling, but I wanted my first birthday present for you to be memorable, and—"

Unable to contain myself, I burst out laughing.

Squinting, he asks, "Why are you laughing?"

"Because it's—what's the right word? Hilarious!"

Watching me laugh even harder, Berkeley yanks the piece out of my hands and says, "It's not hilarious. It looks a lot like you."

My eyes widen. "Are you sure? She has the body shape of a lizard and the nose of an eagle, and she's wearing clown shoes."

"Those shoes are your boxing-glove slippers, and they are not that big."

"Are you kidding me? Look again."

Berkeley does and says, "Okay, so the proportions could use a little work."

"Maybe just a little," I reply, taking the figure back. "Though it concerns me that this is how I appear in your eyes, I'm thrilled you made this for me. And I love it. Thank you."

With a puzzled expression, he replies, "You're welcome, I think?"

"I will cherish this always."

Grabbing his nearby guitar and positioning it in his lap, Berkeley says, "Let's move on to something less ego bruising for me."

Setting Clown Girl aside, I ask, "How's the strumming going these days?"

"With little progression, unfortunately."

"Why?"

"I've been busy—that's all."

"Will you play me a tune?"

"Sure, but keep your expectations low, because I seldom practice."

"Okay."

Opening with some pleasant-sounding chords that remind me of the song we first danced to, he says, "Remember this?"

"I do," I say. "You should make more time for that guitar. You're such a natural at playing it."

He grins. "I probably will in about two months."

As he transitions into a new melody, I say, "That sounds amazing, Berkeley. What is that?"

He looks up and responds, "New stuff I've been fiddling around with."

"Does it have lyrics?"

"Not yet."

"Well, you should work on some, because I think you've got something superfine there."

"Maybe."

Coyly smiling, I say, "I'm not sure if you remember, but on your birthday, you said you might write a song for me someday."

"You have a keen memory."

"Maybe you could come up with one now."

"You want me to just instantly create a song?"

I raise myself onto my knees and face him. "Yes, I do. Please. Put anything together."

After taking a deep breath, he replies, "Okay, give me a minute."

"However long you need."

Doing some practice strumming, he says, "All right. Here's what I've got. Take it or leave it."

"I'll take it!"

He grins. "This will be my second birthday present for you, to make up for the defective first one."

I giggle. "I can't wait."

After clearing his throat, he says, "Short and sweet."

"Just like me!"

Smiling, Berkeley continues with a few chords that make it evident the tune will involve a slow-paced country twang—nothing like the indie sound he normally plays. Several instrumental bars into it, he gives me a sheepish grin and lulls, "My darlin' Francie."

Grabbing his arm, I exclaim, "I love it already!"

Fake moaning, he says, "You broke the flow. Now I'll have to start over."

"Sorry."

After scolding me with a cute headshake, he carries on.

"My darlin', Francie, you are my fancy. 'Cause when I see your backside, it makes me antsy."

I plop my hands onto his. "Seriously?"

Attempting to keep strumming, he laughingly replies, "I can't help it. Your very fine behind was very deserving of its own song."

I give him a light shove. "I knew it; you are a typical teenage guy."

"Yes, I am."

I smile. "I'm surprised you didn't ask to make my very fine behind the subject of your photography assignment."

Blushing, he replies, "I won't lie. The thought crossed my mind."

My brow furrows. "Interesting comment coming from the guy who has stayed an arm's length away from me for all of the last three months."

Setting aside the guitar, he says, "I'm sorry about that."

I sigh. "Is it because my ugly foot is a turnoff?"

Standing up, he replies, "God, no! Why would you say that?"

I shrug. "Because the timing fits."

Giving me a strange look, he says, "No, not at all! Seriously, that's the craziest thing you've ever said."

"Well, what is it then?"

Exhaling, he responds, "I don't know. I think I've just become super manic about screwing up again."

Gingerly moving to the sofa, I quietly say, "Come over here."

After a pause, he hesitantly sits beside me, leans his head back, and says, "I would give my right hand to relive that day at school and not do something so stupid."

Staring at his profile, I say, "I thought we moved past that stuff."

Turning his head away from me, he replies, "I just can't get out of my head the disappointed look you had on your face that day."

Climbing onto his lap for the first time since Shanna-gate and positioning my face so the tips of our noses are touching, I say, "Everybody does stuff that's stupid."

"Not you."

As my mind fills with images of John the ski bum, I say, "Berkeley, I'm as likely as anyone to misstep."

He shakes his head. "I can't imagine you ever doing anything as hurtful as what I did."

I place my forehead on his. "Well, in the event that I do, please promise me that no matter how pissed you are at me, you'll forgive and forget."

He wraps his arms around my waist. "I could never stay mad at you."

Staring into his sweet eyes, I say, "On that note, I wonder what it would take to irk you."

"You could never irk me."

"Everyone has a threshold."

He shakes his head. "Not when it comes to you."

With a sheepish grin, I attempt to rattle him by crawling on the sofa back and maneuvering my knees onto his shoulders.

Chuckling, he asks, "What are you doing up there?"

"I'm being reckless with you."

Gripping my legs, he says, "Be careful. I don't want you to hurt your foot again—or anything else, for that matter."

"Around you? That would be impossible." Attempting to stand up, I start laughing and topple over, and in my downward tumble, I accidentally catch the heel of my shoe between the wall and a cabinet.

After hearing a sound like a tree branch snapping, Berkeley and I freeze and say in unison, "Oh crap!"

Twisting around, Berkeley exclaims, "What happened?"

Reaching toward my foot, I answer, "I think I broke my new shoe! Please tell me I didn't."

Checking out the damage, he says, "It looks like you popped off the end of the heel."

"Can it be fixed?"

"Yeah, I'm sure it can."

Stepping down from the sofa back and settling into Berkeley's lap, I mumble, "I can't believe how easily it snapped."

His brow furrows. "Probably because it wasn't meant for climbing."

Sporting a grin, I press my torso against his and say, "The extremes I have to go to in order to get manhandled by you."

Running his hands down the length of my spine, he smiles and replies, "Trust me, Francie—the thought of manhandling you is on my mind night and day."

Lifting my chin, I say, "Prove it."

After smoothly repositioning us horizontally onto the sofa, he gives me the most tingling-down-the-backbone-fantastic kiss ever, followed by some other stuff—of the Maverick-level variety—that sends the kid gloves flying.

When my fabulous shoes go flying too, I think, *Okay, Phoebe. Go ahead. Gloat.*

As some late-night thriller movie comes to an end, Berkeley clicks off the television and says, "I need to get you home."

Lying on the sofa with my back to him, I flip off our shared blanket and reply over my shoulder, "FYI, I'm willing to disregard my curfew tonight if you are."

Using his hand to follow the contours of my hip, Berkeley says, "I seriously wish I had the lack of decency to be all over that, but I have every intention of staying in your father's good graces."

Rotating to face him, I say, "What about the body-part photo you're supposed to take?"

His eyes spring open. "Oh, thanks for reminding me."

He climbs over me, grabs his camera, and starts taking random shots—some of them goofy, some of them too close to my scar for comfort, and some of them wandering.

Striking some corny poses, I say, "Thanks again for my unforgettable sculpture."

"You're welcome."

"And thanks again for my ass song."

"That was my pleasure."

Sitting up and slipping on my footwear, I say, "And thanks again for choosing these over-the-top shoes."

Still snapping pictures, he asks, "Will their recent breakage exclude them from being considered for your criteria?"

After thinking for a minute, I reply, "The fact that they're so fragile makes me want to enshrine them rather than wear them. So if I'm to take anything away, it's that my Francie shoe must be poised for anything."

He smiles. "I like that idea."

"Me too."

Setting down the camera, he pulls me toward him and replies, "And so the quest moves on."

I nod. "With hopes that the city of Florence puts its best footwear forward."

His smile dissipating, he replies, "August is coming up fast."

"Yeah, it is."

As thoughts of leaving Riverly Heights conjure up images of my life without Berkeley in it, I give my head a small shake and announce, "You know, you made this my best birthday ever."

"I'm glad to hear that."

"Thank you big-time."

"You're welcome."

I grin. "Same time next year?"

After planting a kiss on my lips, he replies, "And the next and the next and the next."

# foot note sixteen

MY LAST TWO MONTHS IN RIVERLY HEIGHTS BEFORE HEADING OFF to Italy are all about minimalism: skimpy outfits meant to beat the heat; only a touch of makeup, because I don't want to perspire it off; and a maximum of six hours of sleep per night so that I can stretch out my time spent with Berkeley.

I've been wearing easy-on, easy-off silver leather flip-flops—aptly labeled the Handy-Dandies—which have proven poised and ready to take on every activity I've exposed them to: hanging out poolside with Berkeley, where we've explored the concept of hot fun in the summertime; taking my driver's road test successfully; learning from Berkeley how to operate a car's standard transmission (it's a slow learning process, because I like the feel of his hand on top of mine); and spending time with Berkeley in the park, listening to him strum his guitar as I sketch him and shoes—moments that prompted Berkeley to regularly refer to me or my footwear as "cute as a button," which subsequently prompted me to add that feature to my me-shoe criteria.

I even wore my favorite flip-flops when applying for my first summer job as a sales clerk in a department store, where I was hired by—surprise, surprise—Mark Baker, the guy who sold me my first pair of Mary Janes when I was a kid, a crazy coincidence that I discovered over lunch on my first day, when the sight of his near-black eyes, glowing chocolate-brown skin, and expressive arm movements sent me many years back in time. After I mentioned the long-ago incident, he and I ended up having a conversation that revealed my ongoing shoe quest, following which Mark immediately moved me from women's fashion to women's shoes.

God, I love my job and passing on my fashion sense to customers and having them appreciate the help. It's too bad, though, that I've spent much of my newly earned money buying shoes for myself—a habit I acquired when I learned I get an attractive employee discount.

Berkeley is working this summer too, for his parents at the newspaper. He's learning the ropes and preparing for his predetermined future.

One day, when he and I went out for dinner after work, I got all giddy and exclaimed, "I love my work so much I would do it for free!"

Smiling, Berkeley responded, "That's great. Maybe someday I'll end up doing something that makes me feel that way too."

Grasping his hand, I said, "I do not doubt you will."

The downside of working nine to five is that I miss seeing Berkeley during the day every day, as we did when we were in school. On the flip side, the time apart is making for a good transition, because soon, he and I won't be seeing each other at all—something I have purposely avoided mentioning or thinking about.

Thinking about it now, I get a fluttering feeling in my stomach, and I try to ease the anxiety by telling myself, "It's only for nine months. How bad can it get?"

I start getting a sense of how bad it's going to become when, at the one-week-before-departure mark, I start saying my good-byes.

First up are my close friends, my teachers, and my grandparents. These good-byes are tough, but I get through them without any major outbursts.

Next up is Patrick Needle, whose eyes get weepy when I give him a final hug. Only then do I realize I've neglected my friendship with him since getting involved with Berkeley.

Following that, I say good-bye to Phoebe, which is the hardest so far, because we've been buddy-buddy since the first day of kindergarten.

Hugging me, she tearfully exclaims, "I hate Berkeley for coaxing you into moving away!"

Wiping away a tear, I reply, "Good. Please spread the word to every girl at school that he is horrible and should be avoided at all costs."

My comment makes her laugh.

Berkeley's parents are next on my list, and that good-bye proves to be as hard on them as it is on me, especially when Berkeley's mom says, "This is for you," and gifts me one of her evening bags: an almond-shaped blue-black bag with sequins that resemble stars.

As I hold it in my hands, I say, "Thank you. This is so wonderful."

"I hope you have occasion to use it often," she says.

Looking into her green eyes, I mumble, "Please make sure nothing bad happens to Berkeley while I'm gone." Then I burst into tears, realizing I'm going to miss Sarah Mills almost as much as I'm going to miss her son.

One day before my departure, a startled yelp from my own mouth awakens me. As my eyes spring open, I realize I've just had a dark dream about walking along a beach, about the tide coming in, about being swept out to sea.

As my brain reconnects with reality and verifies that I have not met my demise, I mumble, "Pull it together, Francie. The nightmare doesn't start until you leave town tomorrow."

Staring at the ceiling, I whisper, "Wow! This is really happening. In twenty-four hours, I'll be gone."

I look at my hands. They're shaking. My heart is pounding too.

145

Who knew that saying good-bye to those who hold the top spots on my list—Mom, Dad, Brigitte, Talula, and Berkeley—would feel so nightmarish?

*Egad. Where will I find the strength?* I hope I'll find it in what I'll be wearing on my feet when I meet up with Berkeley later today: a pair of tan espadrilles with aqua-colored ribbons, purchased solely because they conjure up an image of a stoic warrior princess—the persona I plan to fake today.

Around four o'clock in the afternoon, following several sweet good-byes with my workmates, I hop into Berkeley's car and say, "Hey, you."

"Hey," he replies, making eye contact with me only briefly.

"How was your day?"

"Pretty quiet. How was yours?"

"Good. Lovely. Mark arranged for a cake in the shape of a fancy boot."

"Pretty."

"It was until I cut off the heel and ate it."

"How did it taste?"

"Sweet."

Following a lull in the conversation, he says, "Are you ready for our surprise outing?"

"Are you ready to tell me where we're going?"

Glancing at me, he responds, "All I'm going to say is that it's private, serene, and special."

"So is there a reason I need to—as per your instruction—stop at my house and put on a swimsuit?"

"Yes, because the place has a small waterfall."

My eyes perk up. "Hmmm. Who knew there was a waterfall in the middle of the flat plains?"

"My dad knew, because he and my mom have been there before."

"Nice."

For many minutes, we wordlessly listen to the radio, observe familiar buildings, and wave at people we recognize walking on the street.

During a pit stop at my house, I make a quick change into a black strapless bikini, a white sundress cover-up, and my warrior espadrilles. I take a quick glance in the mirror and say, "This is the last image that's gonna get planted in Berkeley's brain."

As we drive off again, Berkeley checks me out and sweetly says, "Man, it is going to be tough not seeing you every day."

Feeling my insides firing off tinges of pain, I reply, "Yeah, tomorrow is going to suck."

Exhaling, he says, "How about we forget about tomorrow and concentrate on today?"

"Sure."

"Good."

Looking his way, I ask, "So what are our plans once we get to the waterfall?"

"Swim, bask, eat, linger, and, in my case, lust a little." Watching me giggle, he adds, "We'll do whatever makes you happy."

"Thank you."

After parking in a sunny spot under a weeping willow tree, Berkeley jumps out of the car, runs around, opens my door, and escorts me out. As I'm panning the tree-covered scenery, he grabs the supplies, lays out a blanket, positions a couple of cushions and some beach towels in the middle of it, and begins removing the contents of the basket.

Watching, I ask, "Did you put this together all by yourself?"

He smiles. "My mom may have helped."

"Your mother is fantastic."

"Yeah, she's a keeper."

Fiddling with his phone, Berkeley turns on one of my favorite songs—our first dance song—and pulls me into his arms for a quick sway.

Hugging him tightly, I say, "You think of everything, Berkeley."

Placing his mouth near my ear, he replies, "I'm doing what I can to send you off with a mind full of me."

Giggling, I say, "My mind is already on overload with you."

Releasing me, he says, "Let's go for a dip and create one more memory."

In water warmed by the summer sun, Berkeley and I splash around for at least an hour, never once losing touch of each other, especially as the waterfall envelops us and hides us from the world. With my head full of thoughts that this is the last time in a long time I'll be this close to this guy, I grip Berkeley around the neck as if I'm in the midst of a tornado.

"Are you cold?" he asks.

"Yeah."

"Then let's go warm up."

"Okay," I reply, climbing onto his back for my last-in-a-long-time piggyback ride.

After we wrap ourselves in towels, Berkeley and I sit down, pull our knees tightly to our bodies, and silently watch the sun as it taunts the tree line. Turning on another mushy tune, Berkeley eases me backward and lays his body tightly against mine.

Fixating on the song's heartfelt words—which are about missing someone, about distance causing the worst form of heartache—I look at Berkeley's face and say, "Don't you wish we could stop time?"

"Shush. Do not go there right now."

Deeply inhaling, I say, "I've got a question."

"What?"

I clear my throat. "Do you think you and I will be different when we see each other next?"

He nods. "Yes, I do."

My heart races. "How so?"

He pulls me closer. "For one thing, my legs will be hairier."

I giggle. "Mine might be too."

"I doubt it," he says, running a hand down my leg.

Calmed by the tenderness of his touch, I ask, "What happens if we feel different when we see each other next?"

Placing his forehead against mine, he asks, "Why would you ask something like that right now?"

"I need to. Because I'm worried."

"About what?"

I tearfully hiccup. "About being swapped out."

Locking eyes with me, Berkeley kisses me with more emotion than he ever has before and then whispers, "Never—not ever."

I place one of my hands on his face. "How do you know?"

After a pause, he snags a lose string from the blanket, ties it into a perfect bow around my left ring finger, and responds, "Because I tell myself all the time that one day, I am going to marry you."

"You do?"

"Yeah, I do."

Suppressing a river of tears, I fiddle with my new string and lightheartedly say, "When do you see that happening?"

Sweeping the hair away from my face, he answers, "How about when we're really old, like thirty?"

Nodding, I reply, "Okay, that should give me enough time to find the right shoes for such an important occasion."

He smiles. "For the record, Ms. Lanoo, you could wear shoe boxes on your feet and still cause me heart palpitations."

Feeling my insides warm, I sigh and say, "Thank you for that much-needed dose of sappiness."

As Berkeley smiles at me, a final burst of daylight hits our faces. Abruptly standing up, he exclaims, "Don't move!"

"Why? Is something crawling on me?"

He touches the top of my head. "No, you're fine." He grabs his camera and starts snapping photos, reminding me, "Stay still."

"What are you doing?"

"I'm creating a sanity file."

I flip onto my stomach. "I need a picture of you too, so let me shoot one."

"I've got a better idea," he says, positioning the camera on a nearby log, pressing the auto timer, plopping back down beside me, and waiting for the click.

After retrieving the camera, he sits beside me, scrolls through his work, and says, "This will do."

Reaching out, I ask, "May I see?"

Turning the screen toward me, he exposes an amazing close-up of us—our heads are side by side, the evening sun has turned our faces golden, and our smiles are faint and concealing like Mona Lisa's.

I position the camera close to my eyes. "This is my favorite photo ever."

"Mine too, because it highlights your adorable freckles."

I smile. "Will you send me a copy?"

"Sure."

"Thanks," I whisper as a huge lump in my throat causes my hands to quiver and my tear ducts to spring tiny leaks.

Setting the camera aside, Berkeley pulls me to a standing position and says softly, "Come here." He gives me a giant hug.

Inhaling short breaths, I say, "I never thought I could feel this sad."

After kissing me on the cheek, he murmurs, "Hey, this is all going to work out for you and me. You'll see."

I nod but say nothing, because he couldn't possibly know.

On the ride home, Berkeley and I sit in silence. There is no music, no chatter, and no sobbing—yet.

When the car stops in front of my house, I say, "So I guess this is good-bye."

"Only temporarily."

Sighing, I ask, "You aren't just saying that to make me feel better, are you?"

Pulling me toward him, he responds, "No, I'm saying it because in all seriousness, Francie, what matters most to me I'm looking at."

As I feel Berkeley's body tensing up, the enormity of what I'm about to do drops like an anvil, and I lose it, bursting into uncontrollable sobs for the first time in front of him. As I bury my face in his chest, I feel every part of me aching. My heart hurts the worst; it wants to burst out of my rib cage and drive away in the palm of Berkeley's hand.

Between outbursts, I look at him and say, "Please call me and text me and e-mail me all the time."

"I will."

"And please visit me soon."

"I will. I promise."

"And please don't forget to send me that photo."

"I won't," he says, lifting his T-shirt to dry my face.

Gazing into his eyes, I whisper, "I don't think I can do this."

Putting his hand on my cheek, he replies, "Yes, Francie, you can."

Placing my lips a hair's width from his, I mumble, "Please don't let me."

After swallowing and pressing his lips together, he says, "Francie, go and be amazing."

When he turns to face the driver's-side window, I solemnly accept what is expected of me and wordlessly slip away.

Bursting through the door of my house, I head for the front closet and toss my sandals inside, their appeal forever gone.

Sulking my way into the family room, I encounter my mother standing there, staring out the window.

Seeing my crumpled face, she joins me in a cry, mumbling, "Over the past sixteen years, I haven't been apart from you for more than a week."

My dad and sisters enter the room, and for many minutes, we embrace in a group hug and exchange sloppy sentiments.

"I wish I were five again," I say.

"I do too," my dad says.

As every inch of me turns cold and starts to shiver, especially my bare feet, I exclaim, "Please, time. Stop."

But it doesn't.

# foot note seventeen

It's four in the morning, and I'm leaving the airport at sunrise.

I have terrible insomnia—which sucks—brought on because my mind won't stop reeling from my farewell with Berkeley. Though I'm trying hard not to be, I'm a little hurt that when I mumbled, "Please don't let me go," he did. Making matters worse, I'm concerned that moment is a foreshadowing of what's to come; I'm worried that absence is going to make the heart swap.

I'm not alone in my sleeplessness. My sisters have visited my room several times throughout the night to talk, cry, and tell me they'll miss me. My parents have been awake too, mumbling nonstop in the room next door. More than once, I know I heard my mom weeping.

The worst part about my sleeplessness is that it's drawing attention to the fact that my feet are still freezing. Despite being buried in blankets and wearing thick white socks, I can't find relief. I wonder, *Are there any shoes out there with the ability to warm me?*

*What to wear? What to wear?*

I can't get over the fact that my feet are so cold. I don't think they've ever been like this.

I wish Berkeley were here right now to rub them warm.

I scowl. "Get Berkeley out of your head."

*I wish.*

Remembering that his feet are never cold, I consider what he often wears: sneakers.

I own a pair of sneakers decent enough to don in public—they are retro, classic black suede with white stripes, a near match to a pair that Berkeley owns. In fact, Berkeley gifted them to me with the whimsical explanation they were his idea of the ideal shoes.

*Yes, that will be my choice for today,* I decide. *Soothing and sentimental, with the potential to make one part of my body happy.*

If only I could wrap Berkeley's shoe around my heart.

I think I just figured out my next me-shoe characteristic: *heartwarming.*

I don't require an early morning alarm to wake me up. I've been wide-eyed all night.

After crawling out of bed, I take a long, hot shower and sob the entire time. Inside my closet, I mindlessly slip into some comfortable all-black yoga wear and my link-to-Berkeley shoes. As my feet warm within minutes, I sense the tears coming to an end—at least for now.

Following a heartbreaking fifteen-minute good-bye with my mom and my sisters and a twenty-minute taxi ride to the airport, where I feel dazed and unsure, I plunk into a noncushioned airport seat next to my father, fixate on the passersby, and, within minutes, notice a strong pattern regarding their choices of footwear: black and nondescript.

Stealing glances at the faces of those wearing such dullness and noticing that many look as unhappy as I feel, I consider that maybe it's human nature to be sad and unexpressive when departing.

As I'm wondering if the airport's arrivals level would be more to my liking, my dad turns to me, reads my face like a book, and says, "Life will get easier once you're settled into new surroundings among a new group of friends."

After exhaling, I reply, "But I'm scared that if I move forward, I might also move on—and that others might move on too."

My dad wraps an arm around me. "If you're referring to Berkeley, I don't think you need to worry, because that boy won't ever make a move that doesn't consider you first."

"I'm not so sure about that."

"Well, you should be sure, because he called me the other night and told me as much."

"He did?"

"Yes, he did."

Gathering our belongings to get in line to board the plane, I keep my father's latest words in the forefront of my mind and use them to help me walk the walk that an hour ago, I was certain I wouldn't.

Following a flight to New York, a two-hour layover in JFK Airport, and an overnight haul to Rome (which I sleep through), my dad and I arrive by train in Florence, step out of the downtown train station, and view the quaintest collection of old-world buildings with warm terra cotta roofs and happy yellow stucco walls. Each is attached to the next, as if they're holding each other up, with a crisp blue sky in the background.

Charmed at the sight, I breathe deeply, smile, and admire.

Noticing me, my dad says, "What do you think?"

Shrugging, I reply, "I won't perish here." Inside, I think, *Hurry up with the bags, Dad, so I can get busy and make my time here as fast moving as possible.*

Seated in the backseat of a taxi, I glance at my feet and wonder how day one of 273 (yes, I'm counting) is going for Berkeley. Does he still have my face as his brain's wallpaper? Does he miss me as much as I miss him? Is he, right now, wearing the same shoes I am?

My reminiscing comes to a halt when the taxi stops in front of a pair of ornate iron gates bearing an embossed bronze sign: Idea Incubatrice.

As my heart rate speeds up, my father rolls down his window and announces our names to the attending security guard. After handing us maps and giving us instructions, the guard waves us through.

A winding road takes us through a tree-covered, flower-adorned, impeccably maintained landscape. Opening the car window to let fresh air fill my lungs, I look at my dad and say, "The place isn't as horrible as I was expecting."

Smiling, he responds, "It's stunning. I can't believe you get to call this home for the entire next school year."

Our first destination is my dormitory building, which I know little about, because I couldn't bring myself to look at website photos over the last few months, out of fear I wouldn't like what I saw. Seeing the place for the first time, I unexpectedly release a smile. It's nothing like I pictured; in fact, it reminds me of my home—modern, flat roofed, and brick faced, with bright red doors. Looking beyond the building, I realize all of the architecture on the campus has been designed as such.

Shrugging, I say, "Okay, I probably won't suffer too much while I'm here."

Inside the dorm's main lobby, I discover common spaces filled with modern furnishings, sleek televisions, billiard tables, Ping-Pong tables, and even a cappuccino bar.

My second-floor dorm room is impressive too: it has floor-to-ceiling windows that overlook a lush landscape; more square footage than my room at home; warm white walls; creamy marble-tiled flooring; and sleek, modern furnishings in a wood finish that reminds me of liquid honey. With a smile, I take note of a stylish black lamp on the desk, a large frameless mirror on the wall, an art easel beside the window, and a dresser with eight spacious drawers. Of course, the closet is too small, but what closet isn't? However, I overlook that when I discover the private bathroom, a luxury I've never had in my life.

Taking a seat on the mattress, my dad says, "This place is so nice you may never want to leave."

Pursing my lips, I emphatically say, "That'll never happen."

Following a quick lunch in the cafeteria, where the food looks and tastes fantastic, my father helps get me settled in. Along the windows, we position two stacks of paisley cardboard boxes to hold all of my shoes. On the desk, we place a few mementos, including my Clown Girl sculpture. On one blank wall, we install a series of hooks in a grid pattern to hang a collection of brightly patterned scarves, all tied in bows. On the other blank wall, we plaster a series of magenta-tinted photographs, creating a collage of my life in pictures. The only one missing is the shot Berkeley took at the waterfall yesterday. But I've left a blank spot for it right over the bed's headboard and will tack it up as soon as I receive it and print it.

With the room fully assembled, I can't help but smile at the awesomeness that surrounds me, all of which is tolerable, happy, and me. The atmosphere makes it easy, after my dad departs for the hotel, to settle in for my inaugural sleep.

On day two out of 273, after slipping on my Berkeley sneakers, I set out to interact with the people who will accompany me on this Italian adventure.

First, in the cafeteria, I meet a woman named Allegra Giovanni, my dorm supervisor. She's in her midtwenties, has a face like a cherub, speaks four languages (Italian, French, Spanish, and English), and behaves so lightheartedly that I'm tempted to check her back for pixie wings.

She and I hit it off immediately as we wander around the building, discussing the ins and outs of laundry, curfews, television etiquette, and the like. From our meanderings, I learn that she too is an artsy girl (in fact, she once studied at Idea Incubatrice), loves words (especially old-fashioned ones, such as *kismet*, *bequeath*, and *zeitgeist*), and has a living space one floor below mine that's welcoming and wonderful, with garden gnomes positioned outside on the window ledge; tiny, round mirrors glued randomly on the ceiling; bedside lamps wrapped with beaded wires; blankets and floor rugs scattered everywhere; and many miniature paintings on the walls that she created in her spare time.

"The Antidepressant Zone," she calls it, and I could not agree more.

At the completion of the dorm walkabout, she smiles and asks, "Would you care to join a few of your future classmates as I traipse them through the rest of the campus and, afterward, the old part of Florence?"

I grin. "Are there any shoe shops along the way?"

"All the world's best!" she exclaims.

"Well then, count me in."

Giggling, she says, "I take it you're a fellow shoe girl."

My eyes gleam. "Are you?"

Throwing her hands into the air, she replies, "I am. In fact, I'm just two years away from a degree in fashion design, which I hope to complete after I make some money working at Idea Incubatrice. And after that, I intend to get a master's degree in shoe design."

I step back. "Wow. What a coincidence. That's what I'm hoping to do."

"Are you also hoping to one day open up a quirky little shoe shop on a quaint cobblestone street?"

I shrug. "I don't know. I haven't thought that far ahead."

Looking at my sneaker-clad feet, she asks, "So how many pairs of shoes do you own?"

Wishing I were wearing something other than my sneakers, I say, "Too many, but only because I'm on a quest to find my ideal shoe."

With eyes the size of melons, she responds, "What a fantastic idea. You must keep me abreast of your progress and let me know if I can assist in any way."

"Thanks. I will."

From there, Allegra takes me and four other new students—a Goth girl from Germany named Rita; a lanky, pretty blonde girl from Sweden named Inga; a petite, quiet, round-faced girl from Japan named Azami; and a polite, adorable redheaded Canadian named Aurora—on a tour of the campus's four different cafeterias, the library, the recreation building, the art studios, and the common green spaces. Along the way, I learn that each of the girls, like me, is living on her own for the first time; each speaks fluent English, which is essential since most classes are taught in English; and each is here for an education but also a good time.

Within a half hour, the conversation flows plentifully on the subjects of art, music, fashion, and people, making me realize I am in my element here. Grinning, I mumble to myself, "Maybe it won't be such a stretch to pretend this is home."

After becoming acquainted with a few of Florence's main highlights—Piazza del Duomo, Accademia Gallery, Uffizi Gallery, Palazzo Vecchio, Ponte Vecchio, and Pitti Palace—we end up deep in the city's heart at a tiny, charming shoe store called Montanini's, which Allegra claims is her favorite.

There, I make my first purchase of Italian footwear: a pair of quirky-heeled, square-nosed white patent-leather pumps. Though they are a shoe style my friends in Riverly Heights would probably mock or avoid like the plague, they are a best seller here in Italy—art for feet—and I can't wait to prance around in them on my first day of classes.

Back in my dorm room, with my feet exhausted despite the fact they've been in comfy sneakers all day, I lie on my bed and play the songs Berkeley gave me for Christmas. Though they're supposed to take my mind off of him, they don't. However, they do put a smile on my face, especially the one about a girl who uses her "kick-butt high-heeled shoes" to stomp all over some guy who has "done her wrong." Trust Berkeley to find all of the best words.

Curled up in bed, I realize I've hardly thought about home or Berkeley all day, which initially rattles me because I don't think a minute has lapsed since I met Berkeley that he hasn't completely permeated my gray matter. Feeling a pain forming in my stomach, I get the urge to hit number one on my speed dial. But after a minute of deliberation, I decide it's better if I don't, because I'm too worried what the sound of his voice might lead me to do.

On day three of 273, I bask in the sunshine while seated on a bench in one of the campus's green spaces and listen to some informative orientation lectures meant to quell the angst of living away from home, which they do.

In the evening, I enjoy an amazing Italian dinner with my dad at a quaint *ristorante* named Star Italiana, and after he escorts me back to my room, I say a tearful good-bye to the last link from my past.

Watching my dad hop into an awaiting taxi that departs and fades into the darkness, I wave and say, "Good-bye, old life."

# foot note eighteen

The school days are flashing by like lightning. It's October already. Where did the time go?

Here I am, eight weeks into the eleventh grade, feeling, at minimum, doubly smarter than I did in August. I've learned about art theory, graphic illustration, and artists I didn't know existed. My head is bursting with so much new knowledge that I often feel like it's going to exceed its capacity and explode. Though I would never have predicted it, I wake up every day excited about what I'll discover next.

In what little spare time I have, I keep my shoe pursuits alive by scouting out more shoe stores. Yesterday, from a quaint shop in a newer part of Florence, which Allegra took me and Canadian Aurora to, I made my second Italian purchase: a pair of skin-tight, midcalf eggplant-colored leather boots with laser-cut detailing up the leg to expose some skin. They're stunners, I've learned, because every time I've worn them out, I've received whistles from male gawkers. Never before has anyone whistled at me. *How unusual. How Italian?*

I've also spent my spare time hanging out with my new friends, who are bent on ensuring that we experience equal parts learning and fun, resulting in sleep deprivation and time deprivation—the reason

I haven't maintained contact with anyone back home, including Berkeley.

It's sad but true; I haven't spoken to him once since I got here. The silent streak started when I decided to wait to see how long Berkeley would go before missing me, which didn't happen until mid-September, at which time he regretfully informed me he would not be traveling to visit me this semester, because he's swamped with homework, his sports tournaments are many, his school newspaper work is sucking the life out of him, and Florence is too far to travel to for a weekend.

*Blah, blah, blah. Whatever. I get it.*

I sent him a message back: "No worries. I'm swamped too." Then, for reasons unknown, I completely shut him out. I don't know why; I guess I was just hurt. After all, he did promise to visit.

Truth be told, the occasional time I've felt the urge to get back in the loop with Berkeley, I've been unable to formulate words. I can't pinpoint why, and I obsess regularly about it, especially considering that Berkeley is more important to me than the air I breathe. I think I'm just worried that if I'm reminded of what once was, I'll want it again.

Yeah, I'm sure that's my problem.

Maybe that's why Berkeley hasn't stayed in touch with me. Or maybe there's another reason.

I sure miss him, though—oodles.

It's late October, halfway through my first semester already. My parents and sisters just called to say they've arrived safe and sound, and I'm ecstatic. I can't wait to spend time with people I love who love me. God, I've missed them. I anticipate tremendous waterworks when I soon head to their hotel—a place that my mom keeps raving about because the bed linens are made of actual linen—and from there, we'll go to dinner at a restaurant my dad picked, called Pitti Cantina.

Because my dad said the atmosphere will be elegant and upscale,

I've slipped into a chic black dress, sheer black stockings, and my stunning eggplant boots, which I'll never get tired of wearing. To finish off the look, I've styled my hair up and away from my face, and I've applied makeup in a way I would never have known how to six months ago (as taught by my friend Rita, who's been exposing me to all kinds of aesthetic tricks). Glancing in the mirror, I hardly recognize myself, which makes me smile and makes me wonder what my peeps back home, including Berkeley, would say if they saw me right now.

When I arrive by taxi and meet up with my family in the hotel lobby, Brigitte does a double take, throws her arms around me, and says, "Francie, you look fantastic. And way older than me!"

I smile. "Stick around, and Italy will have the same effect on you."

Hugging me, my dad says, "Italy is written all over you, and I mean that in a good way."

"Just wait until you see me at Christmas."

Joining in the hug, my mom adds, "Which can't come soon enough. Our home has a huge void in it with you gone."

Coming up from behind to join the hug, Talula says, "Except at the dinner table, because Berkeley sits in your chair about twice a week."

I dip my head to the side. "Really?"

"Yes."

Brigitte adds, "That guy misses you big-time."

My eyes moisten. "I miss him big-time too."

During dinner, my mom leans into me and says, "Berkeley requested I call him when I get back to Riverly Heights to update him on how you're doing."

Smiling, I reply, "Please tell him, specifically, I 'wear tenacity unexpectedly well.'"

Giving me a strange look, she lightheartedly notes, "I'm knitting him a sweater."

"What? You haven't knitted in years."

"I know, but I was starting to lose my skill, and I needed a project to work on. When I noticed how sad Berkeley's beautiful eyes were becoming, I wanted to do something to cheer him up."

"You are very sweet, Mom. Thanks for doing that."

Taking hold of my arm, she adds, "Berkeley told me that he fully intended to visit you in September, but neither of his parents were able to get away from work."

I half smile. "It's nice to know the thought was there."

Leaning in, she says, "I'm not supposed to tell you this, but Berkeley said he's holding off on contacting you until you contact him first."

"Why?"

"He's worried he'll disrupt you."

"Oh?"

With a furrowed brow, she says, "You should call him."

I take a deep breath. "Yes, I should."

After my family leaves, I do not call him, nor do I do so anytime over the next several weeks.

In a late-night heart-to-heart with Allegra, I bring up my hesitation, and she says, "How does your heart feel when you think of him?"

"It aches."

"Then your problem is a classic case of lovesickness. Because it hurts to miss him, your body has set up a defense to combat the pain."

I sigh. "Maybe that's the case, although the more I'm exposed to Italy, the more I realize what a great experience I'm having here. And I probably don't want Berkeley to know that."

Shrugging, she replies, "Or maybe it's like your shoe hunt, where you need to see what's out there before you make a decision on what's ideal."

I shake my head. "No, that can't be it. Berkeley is the surest thing in my life."

Standing up, she replies, "Maybe when you head home for the Christmas holidays, you should verify whether or not he feels the same way."

Walking toward the door, I say, "I will."

# foot note nineteen

WHEN I ARRIVE HOME FOR THE HOLIDAYS, I'LL BE EXPERIMENTING with symbolism through shoes, boasting without words how happy Riverly Heights makes me feel. To make that happen, I'm cladding my feet in simple yet stylish pointy-toed Christmas-green boots that I purchased from a shoe cobbler on one of Florence's tucked-away side streets. I'm calling this style the Holly-Jolly. I picked the pair up for a *vero affare* price that Allegra negotiated for me using Italian words that could have involved enrolling me in circus camp, for all I knew. *Note to self: start learning the language.* The deal was such a bargain that I had enough cash left over to purchase a new outfit—a black satin suit with "holiday dazzle" written all over it.

My dad arrived last night to escort me across the big pond again. He still thinks I'm too young to manage international airports on my own—a deduction he made when I wandered off in Rome's airport and he spent half an hour in a panic, trying to find me. Our flight leaves tomorrow, and man, am I anxious to catch it, especially after receiving a message from Phoebe informing me that at the recent Christmas dance, the mistletoe seemed permanently propped above Berkeley's head. At first, this news brought a tear to my eye, but after Phoebe's next message informed me that Berkeley posted my face on the outside of his locker, complete with daily countdown tabs and the header "Can't wait to kiss this girl under the mistletoe," my pouty face turned ecstatic.

My first priority when I set foot in Riverly Heights will be to make that kiss happen, which, fingers crossed, will tell me all I need to know about where our relationship stands.

God, I miss that guy.

I hope he feels the same way about me.

It's late and dark outside when the taxi nears my house. As the familiar boxy silhouette comes into view, its pretty pine trees beautifully decorated with warm white lights, I feel a pulsing sensation on both sides of my neck. Who will be waiting for me? Will the house feel familiar or strange? Has my mother made my favorite munchies? Will jet lag be less annoying because I've traveled west instead of east?

The taxi stops. I open the passenger door. While groggily jumping out, I look around, feeling hopeful.

Wandering toward the front steps, I say to my dad, "I forgot that winter is cold."

He smirks. "You've been away four months, and you're already forgetting this place?"

Giggling and shivering, about to the grab the doorknob, I hear the engine of a car. When it comes to a screeching halt in front of the house, I smile because I know that car. It's Berkeley's.

Instinctively, I toss my purse and carry-on bag into my dad's arms, turn around, and run toward the street.

Berkeley meets me halfway up the sidewalk, gives me the biggest hug ever, and says, "I'd planned to wait for you to call me, but my brain was veering toward an aneurism, so I decided to save my life by coming over."

"I'm so glad you chose life."

"Me too."

"How are you?"

"Great. How've you been?"

"*Molto bene!*"

"Good to hear ... whatever you just said."

As a wash of moonlight highlights Berkeley's eyes, I grin and say, "I've got so much to tell you."

"Me too, like at least a hundred different conversations that are stockpiled in my brain, all of which seem so secondary now that I'm standing here staring at your incredible face."

"Please don't stare at my face. I'm half-asleep."

"But I must stare at your face. I'm in awe."

As I blush, he glances at my feet and says, "Killer boots!"

Turning toward the house, I reply, "Yes, they killed my feet and deserve to be banished from my sight."

"I can help you with that," Berkeley says, swooping me into his arms, yanking the boots off of my feet, and throwing them into the snow-covered bushes.

"Thank you," I say.

Looking back at my dad, Berkeley says, "Hey, Mr. Lanoo."

"Good to see you, Berkeley."

As I'm grinning ear to ear and tightening my arms around Berkeley's neck, I hear vehicles arriving in front of our house. Out of them burst a barrage of our Riverly Heights friends: Phoebe, Beatrice, Silvia, Patrick, and Pierce. They noisily race toward us and smother me with hugs and well-wishes galore.

As the ruckus subsides, Berkeley returns my feet to the ground and ushers me inside, where my mom and sisters are waiting in the family room.

"Look who's home!" they say in unison, gathering around and suffocating me with more hugs.

When my friends fill the room, Berkeley and I plop down onto the sofa, sitting as closely as possible, and let the reacquainting begin.

Within seconds, I feel totally at home, as if I never left this place.

Smiling at the revelation that half a school year is done and only another half is left, I mumble, "I've definitely got this."

# foot note twenty

I'VE MOSTLY SPENT MY FIRST FEW DAYS OF BEING HOME FOR THE holidays on the family-room sofa, nursing my boot-damaged feet and being welcomed home by everyone else I know—grandparents, cousins, more friends, friends of my parents—all of whom act as if I just returned from being stranded on a desert island. While in their company, I politely smile and act nice, but secretly, I wish everyone would leave so that I could hang solely with person I've seen the least this week: Berkeley.

We've not been alone with each other once, and the most affectionate we've gotten is a quick peck on the cheek to say good night, which is agitating me, mainly because I can't get out of my head the images of Berkeley at the school dance, standing under the mistletoe with others.

I want my turn.

On Christmas Eve, still not having been alone with Berkeley, I'm ready to explode. Craving just one private moment, I convince Berkeley to skip a dinner with his aunt and uncle to join my family instead. When he texts me his acceptance and advises that he's already en route, I feel giddy from head to toe.

In preparation of making him notice me big-time, I throw on a slinky silver dress, silver stockings, and a pair of Brigitte's sexy black velvet pumps (seems the shoe bug has bitten her too). The label I've given them: the Merry Provocateur. Without a doubt, I'm wearing the most-attention-seeking getup my body has ever seen, but I'm pulling out all stops to ensure I get the attention I seek.

Berkeley is hanging out in the dining room when I come downstairs.

As I strut into view, he reaches out to put an arm around my waist, smiles, and says, "Whoa, you look stunning."

"Thank you," I reply with my best attempt at a sultry voice, which is, sadly, a work in progress.

"Hungry?" he asks.

"Very," I respond, smacking my well-glossed red lips together and making sure he notices me doing so.

After wiping his brow and taking a deep breath, Berkeley puts his mouth to my ear and says, "Please don't do that again with your lips; otherwise I'm gonna have to pour the punch bowl over my head to cool down some unmentionable body parts."

Of course, I laugh and want to lock lips with him even more.

During dinner, I'm barely able to focus on the conversation at hand, and instead, I plot how to get Berkeley somewhere—anywhere—in this house alone. After dinner, while watching a classic Christmas movie, I lie on the family-room floor under a blanket shared with Berkeley, and I hash a reasonable plan.

Looking toward my parents, who are curled up together on the sofa, I say, "Mom, given the fact that Berkeley is invited back here tomorrow morning for brunch, would it be all right if he sleeps over? In the guest room, of course."

As Berkeley gives me a surprised look, my mom locks eyes with my dad, exchanges an eyebrow raise and a shrug, and says, "Sure, that'd be fine."

"Thanks," I say, shooting Berkeley a cute look. I knew that would be my mom's reaction, not only because she loves Berkeley to death but also because the main-floor guest room is nowhere near mine.

When the movie ends and everyone stands up to head to bed, Berkeley and I saunter toward the base of the staircase but remain a foot apart because my parents are in the vicinity, locking the door, snuffing the fireplace, and picking up drink glasses.

With a smile, I say, "Be sure to keep your eyes tightly closed overnight, or Santa won't come visit you."

"Thanks for the tip," Berkeley says, moving in for a hug but pulling away when he hears my nearby father clearing his throat.

An hour later, as I lie in bed, twisting my nightshirt, I start imagining what Berkeley is doing one floor below me. I flip. I flop. I heat up. I cool down. Unsurprisingly, sleep eludes me. When I'm certain not a creature is stirring, I decide enough is enough—no more waiting. I am going after my moment alone with him.

To appease my freezing-cold feet and ensure my movement through the house is noise free, I forego my cozy rubber-soled slippers and put on a pair of thick hot-pink socks. Following verification that the coast is clear, I sneak out of my bedroom, close the door, and head downstairs, stopping by the front door to retrieve the mistletoe I intend to put to good use. After pussyfooting down a hallway, I enter the guest bedroom, lock the door behind me, and crouch on the floor beside the bed.

Berkeley is lying there on his back, fast asleep, so I take a stolen moment to admire his moonlit face and upper body, whispering, "Holy crap, the gods were having a stellar day when they assembled you."

As some passing clouds diminish the moon's illumination, I move my mouth to Berkeley's ear and sweetly murmur, "Ho, ho, ho."

Opening his eyes to my face hovering above his, he flips open the blankets and says, "Come here."

As I press my body tightly against his and feel our hearts beating in fast-paced rhythms, I whisper, "I brought something for you."

"What?"

"Mistletoe."

Quietly chuckling and sweeping the hair from my face, he asks, "What would you like me to do with it?"

Fluttering my eyelashes, I reply, "Whatever's on your mind."

When Berkeley's phone alarm quietly goes off at the break of dawn and I'm shocked awake by thoughts of what my parents would do if they found me here, I slither out of bed, take one last look at Berkeley's awesome sleeping form, do an unsuccessful search for my comfy pink socks, and tiptoe back to my room barefoot.

I don't mind, because my feet are now as warm as summer.

When my own phone alarm sounds at nine, I jump out of bed, throw on a robe, and head to the bathroom. As I look in the mirror and smooth my here-there-and-everywhere hair, I examine my beaming face and whisper, "Yeah, he's still into you."

Heading downstairs, I hear my parents and sisters banging around in the kitchen, so I stop by, give them each a big Christmas hug, and jest, "Did anyone check the fireplace to see if Santa got stuck in the chute?"

Smiling, my father replies, "I lit a fire and didn't hear any screaming, so I think we're good."

Giggling, I wolf down a freshly baked muffin, guzzle a glass of milk, and say, "I'm going to wake Berkeley."

"Good idea," my mom replies. "Because noon will be here in no time."

After darting out of the room as fast as I can, I face the guest-room door, straighten my robe, knock lightly, and say, "Berkeley, are you decent?"

After a pause, he eases the door open and groggily murmurs, "Around you, I struggle."

Seeing Berkeley's OMG body wearing nothing but green-plaid boxer briefs and the socks I sought, I smile and ask, "How are you feeling?"

Rubbing his eyes, he responds, "Very merry. Thanks for asking. How are you?"

"Cold footed."

"That's because you're not wearing any socks."

"Yeah, I seem to have lost mine."

He smiles. "Finders keepers; losers weepers."

Looking downward, I reply, "In my opinion, the hot pink totally clashes with the green."

Slipping into his dress pants and button-up, he responds, "I don't care, because sentimentality trumps fashion for me always."

Grinning, I grab Berkeley's black socks and say, "So I guess you won't mind if I borrow these?"

"Not at all. In fact, you can keep them if I can keep the pink ones."

"Deal," I say, putting them on and dragging Berkeley by the hand into the family room.

Plunking down onto the sofa, I say, "I have something for you."

"Please say it's a toothbrush."

"No, but I'll arrange one for you shortly if you'd like."

"I would like. Thanks."

I scoot toward the Christmas tree, grab a uniquely wrapped square package, and hand it to him.

"Thank you."

"It's entitled *She Sees Four Trees*."

"Great name."

"I dare you to say it ten times."

But he doesn't. He just pulls me toward him for a cute kiss on the forehead and peels off the gift wrap.

Uncovering a piece of artwork, he exclaims, "Oh, wow! You painted this. I can tell."

I nod. "It's the view outside my dorm-room window. I applied a coat of clear resin over the paint to give the illusion of looking through glass."

"It's spectacular!"

"Yeah, especially when the sun shines and illuminates the trees, the metal on the buildings, the flowers—"

He cuts me off. "I didn't mean the view. I meant the artistry."

"Oh."

"You've got some serious talent, Ms. Lanoo."

"The credit mostly goes to my new school."

"I think some should go to the guy who pushed you to go there."

I grin. "FYI, the school year is only half done, which means the eating of my shoes is still very much on the table."

He grabs my hand. "You and I both know that's never gonna happen."

"Beware of saying *never*."

Standing up and walking toward the fireplace, he replies, "It's not a problem when you're one hundred percent certain."

"One hundred percent?"

"Yup." After setting the painting on the mantel, he grabs a bow-tied box from under the tree and says, "I have a present for you too."

"Lucky me!"

Placing it in my lap, he instructs, "Open carefully."

"Why? Is it alive?"

"No, but it has a heart."

With twinkling eyes, I extract an intricate maple box with a quirky heart carved into the lid. "Oh, wow! This is beautiful."

"You're missing the best part. Open it up."

I do, and I hear a music-box version of the first song Berkeley and I danced to last September.

Swallowing a lump in my throat, I whisper, "Oh my!"

"Do you like it?"

Nodding, holding back a rush of mush, I reply, "I adore it."

My parents and sisters interrupt the moment by walking into the room with juice and munchies. They glance at our socked feet but say nothing. They just exchange hugs and greetings with Berkeley and fill the room with more merriment.

As requested, I find Berkeley a toothbrush and towels so that he can freshen up. Then I wander upstairs, step into the shower, and imagine Berkeley doing the same. Realizing I crave nothing more than getting closer to him, as I did last night, I consider the prospect of not returning to Italy. But when I step out of the shower and see Berkeley's socks lying on the floor, I accept the reality of my situation: Berkeley would find a way to push me back.

Standing in my closet, I consider for the first time today what shoes I should wear for the occasion. Back on the symbolism train, conflicted by the thought of footwear linking me to Italy, I forego deliberations and wear only Berkeley's socks, disregarding how absurd they look with my dressy pants and blouse.

Walking back into the family room, I discover everyone else primped, gleaming, and waiting for me. As the celebration commences with music, gift exchanges, food, and drink, Berkeley gravitates toward me, puts his arms around my waist, and whispers, "Who knew my all-time favorite clothing item would be a pair of your hosiery?"

As I giggle, my mom approaches Berkeley with the largest Christmas present in the room. "I hope you like warm and fuzzy."

His eyes expand. "I do."

Smiling, I add, "My mom made this for you."

Touching my mom's shoulder, Berkeley responds, "Mrs. Lanoo, you didn't have to go to any trouble on my account."

Side-hugging him, she replies, "I was happy to, because you're family around here."

After clearing her throat, Talula jests, "In fact, we prefer your company to Brigitte's."

Furrowing her brow, Brigitte retorts, "I heard that."

Giggling, Talula replies, "If you were as nice as Berkeley, you *wouldn't* hear that."

Berkeley quells the natter by aggressively removing the gift wrapping; uncovering the custom-knit sweater, which is taupe colored, with intricate cable and honeycomb stitches; pulling it over his shirt; and exclaiming, "Wow! Thank you so much for this. It's perfect!"

I touch the texture. "Mom, you've outdone yourself."

As she blushes, Berkeley says, "I'm starting to see where Francie gets her talent."

Checking the sleeves for length, she jests, "Maybe I'll make Francie one just like it, so you can be a matching pair."

Shaking her head, Talula says, "Please, Mom, tell me you'd never seriously do something like that."

Before my mom answers, Berkeley says, "If these sweaters were made readily available, half the city would be walking around matching."

As a wide grin forms on my mom's face, I become so happy that I want to crawl inside that sweater and live there. Trust Berkeley—and his words—to make my mom's day.

After the gift giving, glancing out the window at the snow-covered backyard, I wiggle my toes around in Berkeley's socks and realize that I have made no progress in my ongoing shoe research since recording the adjective *heartwarming* last August. Reviewing my other descriptors—*hurtless, harmonious, timeless, sparkly, uplifting, fuchsia, poised for anything,* and *cute as a button*—I wonder if it's my destiny to find all of my me-shoe characteristics here at home.

*Hmm. What a curious notion.*

Recognizing how much I've enjoyed being home for the holidays and how it would rip my heart out to ever miss being home for the holidays, I cross my fingers and hope I'm never in a position where I have to.

# foot note twenty-one

FOR NEW YEAR'S EVE—MY FIRST SPENT WITH BERKELEY—I'VE decide to go glitzy with a high-fashion outfit I bought in Italy: an avant-garde puffy black blouse, some skinny-legged silver jeans, and a pair of sweater-cuffed shorty boots embellished with metallic embroidery. I'm calling them the Minglers because they couldn't be more perfect for a social setting. I'm also trying out some new makeup: nearly white lipstick, silver eye shadow, and heavy black eyeliner that forms upward points at the outside corners of my eyes, which is drama-glam, to say the least, and I love it.

I sense Berkeley does too, because when he picks me up, he exclaims, "How is it possible that you keep getting hotter?"

His words make me grin.

We're spending the evening at the house of Berkeley's new close friend, Sam Nelson, a tall, blond, brown-eyed, dimpled cutie-pie who moved to town last September from Melbourne, Australia.

Greeting Berkeley and me at the front door, he puts an arm around me and, in his casual Australian accent, says, "As a result of about a thousand conversations I've had with Berkeley, would it be all right if I checked out your footwear?"

"Sure," I reply, laughing and showing him my Italian glitz.

Exhaling, he murmurs, "Those are sexy!"

Grinning and blushing, I reply, "Thank you."

"Do you like mine?" he asks, showing me a cool pair of lace-up canvas high-top sneakers in bold red with black stars.

Nodding, I reply, "Clearly you've got a shoe thing of your own going on."

Squinting, he says, "Yeah, which has got me wondering if shoe aficionados are something Berkeley's got a thing for."

Smiling at his observation, I understand why he and Berkeley became such fast friends.

Sam is one of eight new students in eleventh grade at Riverly Heights High School. As I make my way through the crowd and meet a few others—including some guy named Max, a stocky, brown-haired, weaselly eyed, loud-mouthed moron who keeps staring at me in a way that makes me feel as if I've got a snake crawling up my leg—I notice that pretty much everyone is dressed in jeans, bulky sweaters, and socks with no shoes. Though Berkeley has sort of bridged the gap by wearing black jeans and a striped button-up, I quickly start to feel like a Martian recently deposited on Earth.

To make matters more uncomfortable, I find myself conversationally out of the loop, missing out on many of the references made and wanting to interject for clarification but knowing it would squash the mood. Instead, I say little and go back to my ways of observing.

Later in the evening, annoying Max approaches Berkeley and me, puts an arm around me, and says, "Hey, Berkeley, I heard a rumor that Hannah has become so obsessed with you she's started running in front of your car when you're driving, in hopes that you'll hit her."

Removing Max's arm, Berkeley says, "Don't believe everything you hear, Max."

From that moment forward, Berkeley ensures I'm always drawn into the conversation and that I'm not left on my own for more than five minutes. As the clock nears midnight and the crowd begins a traditional countdown—"Ten, nine, eight, seven …"—he darts from the opposite side of the room, sweeps me into his arms, and, at the sound of "one," plants a kiss on my lips that reaches the count of at least fifty.

Seconds afterward, as part of a celebratory frenzy, the partiers begin spreading kisses in every direction. When Berkeley is yanked away for an array of friendly pecks, I become the target of the same— behavior I instantly disdain when Max sneaks up behind me, swings me around to face him, and slams his lips dead center onto mine. *Ewww!* The situation worsens when he hovers his face near mine and mumbles, "Please tell me you enjoyed that as much as I did."

I did not, but I say nothing. I just wipe the slobber from my mouth, slink away, and wish more than anything to leave.

Catching up with me, Berkeley looks at my pouty lips and says, "Hey, sorry, Francie. Everybody's just getting caught up in the moment. It doesn't mean anything."

Faking a smile, I reply, "It's okay. I understand how very kissable you are."

Flashing me a look, he proves me right by kissing me again so sweetly that I almost forget the lip-lock of two minutes earlier.

Staring into his eyes, I ask, "Hey, do you wanna go somewhere and do something with just me?"

Pressing his lips to my ear, he replies, "You just read my mind."

While we're putting on our coats, about to leave, I slip my hands into Berkeley's jean pockets and inquire, "Any chance you have a spare breath mint on you?"

His eyes perk up. "Around you, always." He pops one into each of our mouths, wraps his arms around me from behind, and ushers us out the door.

As we stroll hand in hand along the snow-covered sidewalk, Berkeley says, "If I'm going to stay the least bit sane between January and May, I need to absorb a four-month fix of you in what little time we have left together."

I grin. "I'm all yours."

He smiles. "For the record, last summer, when you left here, I had no idea how much I'd ache from missing you."

"Just ask me to stay, and the ache will go away."

But as expected, he doesn't.

As I hop into the car and mull over Berkeley's silence, it occurs to me that six months ago, I would have been in tears over his nonresponse. I would have felt hurt, broken, insecure, and afraid of being on my own. Now, upon reflection, I'm actually glad Berkeley didn't beg me to stay here. Otherwise, I would have missed out on the most-fantastic half year of my life, and I might never have learned how horrible I feel when I'm not with Berkeley. Most importantly, I would not be the person I now am.

Of course, I probably won't ever admit that to Berkeley—at least not right now while sitting in his parked car, making out with him.

Because I wouldn't interrupt that for all of the designer shoes in Italy.

# foot note twenty-two

I CAN'T BELIEVE IT'S JANUARY 4 ALREADY.

More so, I can't believe it's time for me to leave Berkeley again.

Since New Year's Eve, I've spent all of my free time with him, not wanting to share or be shared (especially not with the likes of that face sucker, Max), thrilled to feel us growing closer than we've ever been.

He is the love of my life. I will never doubt that.

Today, to reacquaint myself with my Italian life, I spend a few minutes flipping through some online pictures and posts of my friends from Idea Incubatrice, which, I have to say, are making me miss them. Rita has lost the Goth side and has become a plain-Jane brunette. Inga is sporting a jagged new hairstyle. Azami has spent the break creating the most-intricate origami on the planet. Aurora posted a beautiful picture of herself making a snow angel in the whitest snow I've ever seen.

The lot of them are soul mates of mine—something else I will never doubt.

With only a few hours left in Riverly Heights, I'm frantically packing up my suitcases and deciding which of my Christmas gifts will stay and which will come with me. I'm doing so while wearing my beloved sheepskin boots, which, I'm just now realizing, I never took to Italy and probably won't this time, because they're something I wouldn't wear there.

*Why?* I wonder.

Maybe it's because I'd feel out of place wearing such casual footwear amid an ongoing fashion show. Or maybe it's because I strongly associate them with home.

It's funny and curious how I do certain stuff in Italy and do other stuff in Riverly Heights. I miss my hometown friends when I'm there, and I miss my Idea Incubatrice friends when I'm here. I wonder, *What will happen in June, when I have to say farewells that could prove permanent?*

Speaking of farewells, Berkeley is on his way over to see me for one last visit. Though I loathe the thought of having to endure another parting with him, I expect that when I do so, my anxiety will pale in comparison to last summer's. I'm more relaxed. Berkeley seems to be too.

Maybe it's because we've been there and done that. Maybe it's because we're more capable of handling four months apart versus eight. Maybe it's because we have changed.

Following one last drive around town, Berkeley returns us to my house and walks me up the front sidewalk to the front door. As we stand face-to-face, staring deeply into each other's eyes, he asks, "How's the pen working out for you?"

I flash him a cute grin. "It's been fantastic. I use it all the time."

"I had a hunch you would."

"Do you need it back yet?"

"No, I do not."

I flutter my eyelashes. "Good, because I've grown attached to it."

"I hoped you would."

"Thanks again for letting me borrow it."

"You're welcome."

"I'll probably only need it for a few more months."

"It's yours as long as you'd like it to be."

"Okay," I say, taking a deep breath to suppress a pang that just stabbed me in my stomach.

Giving me an earth-moving kiss, followed by a body-warming hug, he says, "I'll call you tomorrow."

I smile. "And maybe once a week for the next few months?"

He smiles back. "I look forward to it."

As I watch him head down the front sidewalk, I feel a sudden ache in my chest, so I shout, "Hey, Berkeley!"

Spinning around and walking backward, he replies, "Yeah?"

"I noticed you haven't yet sent me that photo you took of us. What's up with that?"

He flashes me a mischievous smile. "Oh, right. I was supposed to do that awhile back."

Pursing my lips, I ask, "Are you becoming forgetful in your advancing age?"

"No, I'm just dazed and confused without you."

Giggling, I quip, "Do you think you'll find your way home okay?"

He shakes his head. "No, I don't. So I think you should get in the car and come with me."

With eyes gleaming, I reply, "When you eventually do make your way there, jot yourself a quick note as a reminder to send me that photo. Okay?"

He slyly grins. "I can't because I lent out my only pen."

I don't know why, but the sweetness in his voice makes me bolt off the steps, run down the sidewalk toward him, throw my arms around his neck, and say, "Please tell me how much you're going to miss me. Please send me messages on a daily basis. Please, please, please come visit me soon."

Kissing me again and again, he says, "Yes, I'll miss every inch of you. Yes, I'll keep in touch. Yes, I'm going to visit you. I'll even try for Valentine's Day."

My eyes widen. "Good, then you can give me another ridiculous card."

"See you soon, Francie."

"*Arrivederci*, Berkeley."

# foot note twenty-three

THE INSTANT MY SHOES TOUCHED ITALIAN SOIL A WEEK AGO, I went into frantic-preparation mode, readying my world for Berkeley's visit on February 14: researching quaint restaurants, compiling a list of interesting galleries, rearranging my dorm room, and preapproving romantic piazzas. I also committed to staying on top of my school assignments so that I won't be bogged down with homework during the five days Berkeley's here. Lastly, I began the hunt for a knockout pair of shoes to wear when I meet Berkeley and his parents at the train station.

My goal with all of this is to ensure Berkeley loves it here and leaves with travel plans in place to visit me a second time.

I'm nearly bursting, awaiting his arrival in five days, twiddling my thumbs at the thought of being face-to-face, eye-to-eye, and body-to-body with his fabulousness.

Unlike last semester, Berkeley and I are faithfully keeping in touch. Last week, I even snail-mailed him an old-style postcard that I found here, containing a weird photoshopped full-body image of Mona Lisa wearing a haute-couture outfit and a pair of amazing shoes. I hope it makes Berkeley laugh, as it did me.

God, I miss his laugh, his eyes, his minty-fresh breath, his arms wrapped around me, his swagger, his footsy playing, and his words.

*Stop it, Francie. Get your homework done so you're not doing it while he's here.*

Berkeley called me this morning to explain that he won't be visiting me on Valentine's Day.

The excuse this time: he has mono, as does half the school, apparently.

*Fine. Whatever.*

I'm now *not* missing Berkeley. I'm too angry to miss him.

It's now early March. As I'm lying in bed, thinking about Berkeley's latest plan to visit me—the makeup trip during which I intend to do some serious making up—I contemplate whether I should meet him at the train station wearing the same footwear I purchased for his February visit (a sweet pair of ruby-red slip-ons) or find something that looks less like Valentine's Day footwear.

I do have a new pair of platinum leather pumps that would knock his socks off. Yes, they're a better choice.

I hear my mobile phone ringing. I quickly clutch it. I see that it's Berkeley calling, so I answer before the second ring. "Hey, hi!"

"How are you?" he replies.

Noticing his tone is void of its usual zip, I say, "I'm well. Is everything all right?"

He exhales. "Well, no."

I sit up in bed. "What's up?"

"I'm not going to be able to make the trip this weekend."

"What? Why? We're supposed to celebrate your birthday together."

"My parents have a breaking news story to cover about some factory gas explosion, and they won't let me travel to Italy alone, so they've canceled the flights."

"Then fly alone."

"My parents won't allow it."

I lean forward. "Maybe my mom or dad could travel with you."

"I called them already, and neither is available."

After a deep sigh, I murmur, "But I had plans in place and people I wanted you to meet. I even bought some seriously head-turning shoes to wear when you arrive."

"I'm really sorry, Francie. It's just not going to happen."

My eyes perk up. "What about spring break? Can you visit me then?"

"No, I can't. Remember? It's my grandma's seventy-fifth birthday, and we're taking her to Hawaii—a trip my parents would kill me if I missed."

"Argh! What about another weekend?"

He inhales loudly. "Unfortunately, with basketball tournaments, exams, and the school ski trip, I'm fully booked right up until May."

Flipping my head back, I close my eyes and take a series of slow breaths.

Breaking the silence, Berkeley asks, "Francie, are you still there?"

"Yeah."

"I'm really sorry."

"I know you are."

"So tell me about your head-turning shoes."

My brow furrows. "No, there's no point. They've lost all of their appeal."

"I still want to see them."

I pout. "But how is that possible, when you're there and the shoes are here?"

"How about, on my birthday, you send me a picture of you wearing them?"

Looking at the shoes, which are still appealing, I say, "Sure, if you'd like."

"I'd like."

"Okay."

"God, I miss you."

"I miss you too."

Sighing, he asks, "So what's up for the day?"

I wipe away a lone tear. "I've got an art-history exam first thing this morning, which I need to do some last-minute studying for, so I should probably get off the phone and get to it."

"Okay. I understand."

"Well, have a good sleep, Berkeley."

"Have a good day, Francie. And good luck with your test."

"Thanks. Bye."

After hanging up the phone, I roll onto my stomach, mumble every expletive that exists in my vocabulary, and scream into my pillow, "Love sucks!"

It takes exactly four days for me to get out of the slump caused by Berkeley's no-show. Tired of scowling, I commence doing some yoga in my room (my latest passion), which is fantastic at easing my frustrated mind, and it puts me in a calm state for when I call Berkeley shortly to wish him well on his seventeenth birthday.

In that vein, I'm about to snap the photo Berkeley requested of me. In preparation, first, I slink into black stockings and a short black dress with a plunging neckline; second, I meticulously jazz up my face; third, I slip into the sexy pumps I bought with seduction in mind; and fourth, I summon a classmate—a guy named Arno—to snap some gutsy photos of me.

Arno resides a couple of dorm rooms down from me. He's a born-and-raised Italian and could not look or act more the part—he's dark haired, brown eyed, warm, expressive, mysteriously handsome, and stylish with everything he says, wears, and does. Also, he's easy to talk to (he speaks fluent English with the cutest Italian accent), he's an excellent student (he teaches me as much about the art world as any of the instructors), and he's become a very close friend, probably my best friend here. Though I've made him aware that I'm in a relationship with Berkeley, I do sometimes get the vibe he would like to date me—he makes it obvious with his lingering kisses to my cheeks every time he encounters me. Most days, I pay little attention to his affections and habitual flirting, but when he says stuff like "If I were Berkeley, I'd find a way to visit you every weekend," it's hard not to be flattered.

Arno arrives at my door, knocks, and wanders in, and after checking out my ensemble, he says, "Whoa. Now that's a birthday fantasy."

Rolling my eyes, I say, "Stop. I'm doing this to irk Berkeley more than anything."

Sighing, he says, "I can't believe he didn't move mountains to be here and see you looking like this."

I shrug. "He would if he could."

After Arno takes some photos, I text the campiest one to Berkeley with the message "Want to know what other clothing items I bought for your birthday that you can't see in this picture?"

Instantly messaging me back, he replies, "Are you trying to make me suicidal?"

Giggling for the first time in days, I flop onto my bed and shout, "Success!"

Eyeing my antics, Arno says, "Why don't you let me take you out for a delicious dessert?"

"I'd like that," I say with a smile.

Heading out the door, he mentions, "I wouldn't mind a copy of the photo you just sent Berkeley."

"No, that's not going to happen," I retort, smiling and playfully bumping one of my shoulders into his.

He's such an Italian.

# foot note twenty-four

A FEW HOURS BEFORE I'M ABOUT TO LEAVE FOR ROME TO SPEND spring break with my family, I receive a message from the Idea Incubatrice administration department, saying that I and three other students are being summoned to a meeting in the school president's office. The purpose is not stated.

As I trek in that direction, my brain fills with possible topics: A major assignment is being handed out, canceling my holidays? A witness has come forward after seeing a few of us sneak out of the dorm last Friday in the wee hours of the night? Some accolade is being given for a job well done?

As I'm sitting in the office's waiting area, wiggling my toes in a pair of casual tan sandals, which are perfect for travel, I watch Arno burst through the door.

"Hey, Arno!" I exclaim, smiling.

"Hey, gorgeous," he exasperatedly responds, parking himself beside me.

"Why are you out of breath?"

"Because I've been running around like a maniac, revising my holiday plans."

"I thought you finalized your ski trip weeks ago."

He smiles. "Are you still heading to Rome today?"

"Yes. Why?"

"Because my older brother, Enzo, is picking me up in two hours, and we're driving to Rome."

"Really? Why the change?"

He shrugs. "Enzo has free time, we haven't seen in other in months, and since he hates cold weather, we decided to drive south."

"Nice!"

Arno caresses my bare knee. "There's a seat in the car for you too."

Moving his hand back to his own knee, I reply, "Are you sure?"

"I am very sure."

I smile. "Well then, I'd be happy to take you up on the offer. Thank you."

"You're welcome."

Before Arno and I have a chance to discuss details, my friend Rita walks in, making her the third invitee, followed by Azami, who becomes the fourth.

As we all chat excitedly, the president of Idea Incubatrice—a soft-spoken, stylish, handsome, small-built fortysomething American named Thomas Garth—steps out of his office and ushers us into an adjacent boardroom.

After we take seats, he says, "We've summoned you here today because the four of you currently hold the top spots in eleventh grade academic performance. And because of your stellar achievement, Idea Incubatrice would like to offer you scholarships to return next year to complete your twelfth grade here."

"Wow!" Arno exclaims, nudging me.

Mr. Garth adds, "All expenses will be paid, including two trips home per year. And the advanced art-and-design curriculum will follow the same path it's currently on, at the end of the day, making you more than ready to enter any high-ranked postsecondary design program."

As we all open our eyes wide in amazement, Mr. Garth takes a deep breath and says, "There is paperwork in front of you, outlining all of the details. So please take it, discuss the offer with your families while you're away, and return to school with a response."

As the four of us wander back to our dorm, Arno says, "No question—I'll be returning."

Shrugging, I respond, "I'll be talking to my parents first before I plan anything."

"Me too," says Rita.

"Not me," says Azami. "I'm in."

As the girls say good-bye and head across the green space, Arno faces me and says, "For what it's worth, Francie, I'm pretty sure every instructor here thinks you're the most-talented student this place has ever seen, so it would be a shame if you did not come back and pursue what you were born to do."

I smile. "That's nice of you to say, but I don't want to rush a decision."

Dipping his chin, he adds, "For the record, it would make *me* happy if you came back."

I jest, "Why? Because you enjoy being beaten on every assignment?"

He grasps my hand. "Francie, when I'm around you, the last thing I care about is my grades."

Rolling my eyes again, I pull my hand away and start walking, ignoring the flocks of butterflies that just awoke in my stomach.

At the first sighting of Arno's brother Enzo—whom I would describe as a more-mature-looking, slightly taller, more-suave version of Arno—my jaw nearly drops to the ground. Murmuring under my breath, "Wait until Brigitte sees you," I extend my hand and say, "Hi, I'm Francie."

"Hello, Francie. It's a pleasure."

Smiling, I say, "I hope it's not a bother that I'm invading your brotherly road trip."

Grinning, he replies, "Someone as lovely as you couldn't possibly be a bother."

*Yep. They're brothers.*

During our drive to Rome, I've opted to sit in the backseat so that I can quietly enjoy the scenery while the brothers get reacquainted. I start contemplating what to do next fall. Should I return to Italy? I don't know. I'm tempted to. I want to. It's definitely in my best interest to. My hesitation in returning, of course, is Berkeley.

God, I miss that guy. I can't imagine another entire year away from him. I hate to think what might happen at the next Riverly Heights High School Christmas dance if I'm not there when the mistletoe gets passed around.

The counterpoint is that I've learned so much during my time here, and I could learn more if I stayed here. Also, I feel a kinship with Florence—as if I lived here in another lifetime (which would explain why I'm so easily picking up the Italian language).

"*Il panorama e bello,*" I spontaneously note, pointing to the hillside.

Looking over his shoulder, Arno responds, "Yes, but the sights in the backseat of this car are far more gorgeous."

Noticing Arno's delicious smile, I blush and look away. I should probably just sit back and be quiet rather than set myself up for more comments like that one.

In Rome, standing in a hotel lobby, my dad says to Arno and Enzo, "Please join us for dinner as a thank-you gesture for driving Francie."

"Sure," they say.

"Great!" say Brigitte and Talula, their eyes gleaming at the impending company.

Wandering down a street, we find a quaint family-run establishment with an outdoor table adjacent to the busy street. For three hours, we enjoy great conversation, amazing food, and lots of serenading. When the meal comes to an end, as expected, Brigitte opts to go evening sightseeing with Enzo.

Back at the hotel, Arno turns to me and says, "Maybe you and I could go for our own wander."

Worried about Arno's possible intentions, I smile and reply, "That's a lovely offer, Arno, but I haven't seen my family in months, and I really want to maximize what little time I have with them this week."

Exhaling and nodding, he says, "Okay, but Enzo and I insist that you ride back in the car with us next Saturday, because the idea of you traveling by yourself on a train is something that keeps me awake at night."

I smile. "That's very sweet. Thank you. A ride back would be very nice."

"I'm looking forward to it," he says.

"Have a nice break," I say, waving and walking away.

As much as I know that Arno and I could have a lot of fun together this week and that he would be the best tour guide and might even take me to some fantastic shoe shops, I don't want to lead him on when my heart is in the firm grip of someone thousands of miles away from here.

If not for Berkeley, though, who knows what might have happened between Arno and me?

An interesting observation crosses my mind: in all of the time I've spent with Arno, he has never mentioned my many shoes.

Maybe he's not into shoes.

Maybe that's a good thing, because the less he and I have in common, the more easily my world will spin.

# foot note twenty-five

WHAT STYLE OF SHOE DOES A PERSON WEAR WHEN STUCK BETWEEN a rock and a hard place? When battling between heart and head? When wanting to stay and wanting to leave at the same time? The only logical answer: she wears a different shoe on each foot.

It's an absurd concept, but I'm doing it anyway: wearing one flip-flop in white and the other in black as I frantically pace around the common spaces of my dorm building, attempting to make a choice.

I'm still undecided on whether to complete twelfth grade in Italy or to stay at home in Riverly Heights. I have only a day before I must commit yea or nay—a decision that I should have made a month ago, but I kept asking Mr. Garth for an extension, which, lucky for me, he accommodated.

The instructors of my classes have all encouraged me to return, telling me I would be shortchanging myself by not coming back. Arno is equally pro, pushing me over and over whenever we hang out together. Allegra, who's become like a third sister to me, has plans to return for one last year of dorm supervising and keeps telling me how much she'd love to spend another year together.

Even my parents and sisters see no downside, and they've said repeatedly that if I do return, they'll visit more regularly—because what's not to love about touring Italy?

Then there's Berkeley, who—I'm embarrassed to admit—is still in the dark about all of this. I was planning to call him about it today, but I am holding off until tomorrow, when he—I'm going out on a limb here—calls me to wish me a happy seventeenth birthday.

Who am I kidding, though? Berkeley won't see a downside to me returning either.

Only I do. Because I'm freaked about leaving Berkeley exposed for another nine long months.

Back to my birthday: I'm heading out to dinner in a few minutes with Arno, who asked if he could treat me to a birthday-eve celebration because my dad's arriving tomorrow to fly me home again, and there won't be another opportunity to see each other before I fly home.

I know I'm walking a fine line here by spending time alone with Arno, but I feel inclined to, because if I don't come back next year, I'll probably never see him again. If I could, I would buffer the evening by inviting some of my friends, but they all left for home today.

Arno and I are heading to a place called L'artista de Fuga, which, according to Arno, is *alla moda* (swanky), so I've dressed as swankily as possible, in the outfit I wore for Berkeley's birthday photo.

I know I'm walking an even finer line by dressing this way, but it is my birthday (almost), and I can dress up if I want to.

As a lone accessory, I'm using the pretty evening bag I got from Berkeley's mom last summer. It works ideally with my dress, and more important, it reminds me who my boyfriend is.

When Arno arrives at my dorm room—dressed in a sharp black suit, a chartreuse shirt, and snazzy shoes—he smiles and murmurs, "Francie Lanoo, you are elegance personified."

I jest, as I always do with him, "Didn't I read that exact description in one of our architecture textbooks?"

He walks up to me, takes my hand, kisses it, and says, "Let me start over. Francie Lanoo, you take my breath away."

"That's pretty good," I murmur, heating up in a way I never have before around him, so I break my gaze and walk out the door.

The jaunt to the restaurant drags out far longer than it should, not only because the heels on my shoes keep slipping into the cobblestone street's crevices but also because Arno regularly pauses to point out the historical detailing surrounding us.

The fact that he does so by standing tightly behind me (*Oh my!*) and placing his hands on my hips is causing some interesting chills down my spine, which makes me think I should have worn a sweater—a thick one like Berkeley's big, warm Christmas sweater, which looks amazing on him. *Yes, fill your head with thoughts of Berkeley.*

During our shared meal of amazing *rigatoni alla crema*, my phone starts to buzz.

In an act of silliness, Arno snatches it from the tabletop, answers it in animated Italian (saying something along the lines of "Francie is tied up"), and then hangs up.

Yanking the phone out of his hands, I yell, "What are you doing?"

"I'm having you all to myself for once."

I give Arno a twisted look. "Please don't answer my phone for me."

He flashes me puppy-dog eyes. "It was all in good fun."

"For you maybe."

When I discover the call was from Berkeley (per Murphy's Law, he had to ring me right now), I mumble, "Oh crap!"

"Is there a problem?"

"Maybe."

Though I shouldn't feel bad about what just happened—because nothing inappropriate is happening, is it?—I do. I also know that if I call Berkeley back right now, I'll feel obligated to explain what I'm up to and with whom, which could get awkward. So I don't.

A text on my phone catches my eye. I glance at it. It's from Berkeley, and it reads, "HB2U. Miss U sooooo much!"

Reminded that no one makes me feel like Berkeley Mills does, I say to Arno, "It's late. We should head back."

Exhaling, he quietly replies, "As you wish."

During the walk home, I slug it out in my too-high shoes, accepting the pain because I feel I deserve it. I should not be with Arno. I should not have agreed to this night out.

Looking up to the sky and seeing thousands of stars watching me, I fixate on Berkeley—the guy I promised a year ago to celebrate this occasion with—and after becoming overwhelmed by a sudden sense of longing, I accept that living far away from the person you most care about leaves an enormous hole, a painful one that no memory or sweet text message can ever fill.

This realization might be telling me I need to turn down the Idea Incubatrice offer.

When we reach my dorm room, Arno stands face-to-face with me and asks, "Have you made a decision about next fall?"

Breathing deeply, I reply, "No, but I'll decide tomorrow after I've talked to my dad."

He eases toward me. "Is there anything I could do to help you say yes?"

"No, Arno. There isn't."

"Not even this?" he asks, and before I take another breath, he slips his hand around my waist and kisses me.

Pulling away, I say, "You shouldn't have done that."

"I'm sorry, Francie, but I've wanted to do that for eight long months, and I feared this might be my only opportunity."

"But I'm—"

Before my sentence is complete, he leans in and kisses me again. This time, I let him—for many seconds—because with my eyes closed, I pretend he's Berkeley, the guy I'm dying to do this with right now.

However, when I feel a tingling sensation in several parts of my body, I pop open my eyes, pull away, and step back.

Grasping my hand, Arno exclaims, "I will absolutely lose my mind if you do not come back!"

I turn, hurriedly unlock my door, and reply, "I need to go, Arno. I have to get some sleep because my dad will be here very early in the morning."

"Sure, I understand."

As I sweep the door closed, I say, "Thanks for dinner."

"You're welcome."

"Good night, Arno."

"Good night, Francie." His words come to me so clearly that I know his face is pressed tightly against the door.

To the sound of his departing footsteps, I flop like a rag doll onto the bed, bury my face in a pillow, and say, "I need to call Berkeley."

I try, but he doesn't answer. He is probably taking a final exam.

Maybe it's better that I didn't reach him, because I'm not sure how'd I'd explain who just answered my phone—not that I feel the need to hide anything. Arno is just a friend, and friends are allowed to take you to dinner and give birthday kisses. Right? This notion leads me to a final thought for the evening as I remove my shoes: *If Arno is still just a friend, then why did I wear these shoes tonight—and this dress and lipstick in a shade called Kiss-Me Red?*

I know why. I like the guy.

Mad at myself for allowing these feelings to develop, I walk to the closet, pull out my suitcase, and commence packing.

It's time to go home, where I belong.

# foot note twenty-six

AS I RIDE ALONGSIDE MY DAD IN A TAXI AND RECOGNIZE WE'RE almost home, I slip off my traveling flats and put on my dad's birthday present to me: a pair of chic high-heeled white-patent penny loafers, which he bought at a shoe boutique while on a stroll yesterday. I've already established that they won't be contributors to my shoe list, because of their unforgiving tendency—the pure whiteness got badly scuffed on cobblestones when I wore them to dinner last night and, for the life of me, I could not get them completely cleaned.

In anticipation of seeing Berkeley—he just texted to say he's waiting at my house—I take a quick look in the small mirror on the back of the driver's seat, adjust my pinned-up hair, add a touch of hot-pink lip gloss, and take a deep breath. Never in my lifetime have I been so excited to see someone. Never have I needed to talk about life with someone, partly about the present but mostly about the future.

As the taxi pulls up to the front of my house and I see him there, I whisper, "He looks amazing," something I know I'll never feel differently about.

He's perched on the front step, tan and fit, and when he stands up, he's taller than I remember. When our eyes meet through the glass,

I feel my heart skip a beat, so I fling open the door before the car has even stopped, run toward him, and exclaim, "How are you?"

"I'm great now!"

"Me too."

After giving me a warm kiss with the best lips ever, he looks me up and down and says, "That suit is spectacular on you!"

"Grazie!"

"It makes you look thinner, if that's possible."

"No, it's just a monochromatic illusion—a trick I learned at school."

"It makes you look taller too."

"No, the credit for that goes to my snazzy heels," I say, lifting my pant legs to display them.

With eyes gleaming, he says, "Wow. Those are impressive!"

"Surprisingly comfortable too," I reply, loving the fact that he pays attention to the silly stuff that matters to me.

Pulling me into his arms and spinning me in a full circle, he says, "You have no idea how happy I am that you're finally home for good."

Though I know there's a clarification to be made here—the disclosure that I have committed to another year in Italy—I'm too tired to deal with stuff that won't matter for months, so instead, I reply, "Let's go find my mom and sisters."

"Sure. They're in the backyard, waiting for you."

"They'd better not be in my hammock."

"No, it's free and clear, waiting for you."

"For me and you."

As we're walking into the house, my father approaches from behind and says, "Hey, Berkeley, it's nice to see you, son."

"You too, Mr. Lanoo. Thanks for bringing Francie home safely again."

My dad sighs. "Well, next time she flies overseas, I'm pretty sure she'll be okay on her own."

Flashing my dad a look, I quickly note, "I'm starving. We should go out for dessert once we've had dinner."

"Sure," Berkeley replies with a cute smile, missing the facial attitude my father sends to me and the response I send back, implying, *I'll deal with it. Just give me time.*

Following a tearful reunion with my mom and sisters, I change into some short shorts, a T-shirt, and last summer's silver flip-flops to partake in a casual family feast out on the patio.

Afterward, Berkeley and I forego heading out for dessert, as jetlag has set in, and we do what I long for most: hang out in the hammock.

Comfortably knotting our body parts together, we commence babbling—not about Italy, the phone call Arno intercepted, or anything else about my other world. We speak only about us and how nothing else matters.

In honor of my seventeenth birthday—now belated—Berkeley surprises me with a stunning necklace: a fine silver chain with a pendant in the shape of an ornate key.

"I love it," I say with a sleepy hug.

Slyly grinning, he says, "Feel free to unlock me anytime."

As my eyes droop, I murmur, "Happy to."

Placing the chain around my neck and pulling me into his arms, he says the last words I consciously absorb before crashing: "I'm so sorry I didn't visit you."

I don't remember Berkeley carrying me upstairs to my bedroom last night, but I hear about it when he returns twelve hours later to have lunch with me.

Eyeing me with amusement as I enthusiastically inhale leftover lasagna, he says, "When I was leaving your room, you started talking in your sleep."

I drop the fork. "What did I say?"

"Something like 'Just gelato, Arno.'"

Half choking, half coughing, I reply, "I said that?"

"Yeah."

I shrug. "The fact that I obsess about food when I'm conscious and unconscious begs the question of how I only weigh a hundred pounds."

"Probably because you never sit still."

"Probably because I'm constantly chasing you."

"No, because I'd always let you catch me."

I giggle. "Yes, you would."

After a pause, Berkeley looks me square in the eyes and asks, "Is Arno a classmate?"

Without blinking, I say, "Yes, he's a classmate and nothing more than a classmate."

"Does he feel that way about you?"

I take a deep breath and reply, "I don't know, because I've never talked to him about it." After a pause, I add, "But he did kiss me on my birthday."

"Oh?"

I grab Berkeley's hand. "It didn't mean anything to me. Honestly. And was probably the result of him having had too much wine."

Berkeley exhales. "Yeah, maybe."

To end an awkward pause, I say, "I see you've been spending some time by the pool. The tan looks great on you."

"You're looking pretty sun kissed too."

"Yeah, but if you look closely, you'll notice my freckles are fading."

Berkeley smiles. "Uh-oh. Italy did change you."

Giggling, I ask, "Is your brain's wallpaper capable of installing an update?"

Smiling, he replies, "Yes, and it's currently overheating while doing so."

At that moment, I realize what I've missed most during my time away: the words that come out of this guy's mouth. I love every single one of them.

# foot note twenty-seven

FOR THE NEXT TEN WEEKS, BERKELEY AND I ARE SET FOR A NEAR repeat of last summer: he's working for his family's newspaper, and I'm working at the same department store, hired again by the even more-stylish Mark Baker, who is now the store's assistant manager. This time around, my job is in the merchandise division, where I'll be assisting two buyers, placing inventory orders for next year's shoe sales. My level of responsibility is low (checking other people's work for potential typos), but I don't mind, because I get to look at hot-off-the-press shoe styles all day long, and it's good for my pocketbook because I can't buy shoes that are currently unavailable to me.

Since I'll primarily be spending my work hours behind the scenes, I'm allowed to dress more casually than I did last summer, which means I get to wear last year's cute-as-a-button silver flip-flops anytime I choose. I had to glue the gemstones back on them because they fell off over the winter, but now that they're restored, they should last me the rest of the summer.

Outside of work, Berkeley and I fill our time with whatever activities this city has to offer to seventeen-year-olds—having and attending parties; hanging out in the park with guitar, camera, and sketchbook in hand; or sitting in a movie theater, watching the summer blockbusters. All of these experiences are happy ones, except for the occasional run-in I have with that guy Max (the creep who temporarily put a stain on the joy of kissing), which usually ends with Berkeley noticing the guy and dealing with it. Sadly, in a city of only 150,000 people, it's nearly impossible to avoid running into people you'd prefer not to—a worry that will come to an end once I'm back wandering street bazaars, perusing centuries-old libraries, and watching street performers in my Italian world.

It's the middle of July already. So when am I going to tell Berkeley about my plans? I've avoided bringing up the subject, because every time I look at Berkeley, I just want to stay in Riverly Heights. The problem is—I know that's not in my best interest.

Mid-August arrives far quicker than expected. As I lie here in the Millses' backyard, faceup on a poolside lounge alongside Berkeley, I realize that if I don't tell Berkeley today that I'm returning to Italy, I'm at risk of making my world ugly.

*No more pushing this under the rug,* I tell myself. My parents have signed the enrollment papers; we've booked my flight to Italy; and I've already met in secret with Mrs. Bouchard, my former principal, and notified her that I'll be away for another year.

*Say something to Berkeley right now!*

I look his way, drool a little, and quietly ask, "Hey, Berkeley? Are you awake?"

Turning his head and looking over the top of his signature aviator sunglasses, he sweetly replies, "Yeah, what's up?"

After taking a deep breath, I say, "I need to talk to you about something."

"Fire away."

I clear my throat. "Umm, the new school year is coming up pretty fast."

He smiles. "I'm glad you brought that up. You and I should sync up for a couple of classes so I don't spend the entire school day obsessing about you."

That's my cue. Standing up and slipping my feet into my beloved silver flip-flops, I say, trying to sound cute as a button, "Speaking of our classes—"

Before I utter another word, Berkeley pats his hand on an open spot next to him and says, "Come over here. I am missing you."

Wandering over and sitting on the edge of Berkeley's lounge, I say, "I'm in a pickle."

He runs his hand down my back. "A pickle?"

"Yes, a sour one."

"That doesn't sound good."

As I put my hands over my face, he says, "Francie, what's up?"

I drop my hands. "I've been invited back to Idea Incubatrice to complete twelfth grade."

"Oh!" he exclaims, abruptly sitting up.

Staring at my reflection in his signature aviator sunglasses, I say, "I know I should have told you sooner, but the timing never felt right."

Removing his sunglasses and squinting at me, he says, "So you've decided already? You're going back?"

"Maybe. Yes. No. I don't know."

"Well, did you commit to it?"

"Yes, mindlessly, last June. Which I know I should not have done without talking to you, but that's water under the bridge."

He shifts his body so that it's tight against mine. "So let me get this straight. You've already signed on the dotted line?"

"Well, I didn't, because I'm a minor, but my parents did on my behalf."

"So you're saying you are enrolled there?"

"Yes."

"Well then, what's your pickle?"

I look into his eyes. "You." As he turns his head away, I add, "I don't want to spend another year away from you."

He rubs his face with his hands, purses his lips, and says, "I don't understand why distance is such a big deal for you."

"Because I hate missing you."

"But you made it through last year without post-traumatic stress disorder."

"Yeah, well, something's different this time around."

"What?"

"I don't know, but it's making me want to stay put."

He leans back. "And here we go again."

"I knew you'd say that."

"Francie, you know you need to go back."

"No, I don't know."

Taking a deep breath, he stands up, walks away, and abruptly dives into the pool. For a long time, he doesn't come out; he stays underwater, swimming and swimming, occasionally coming up for air.

As I watch his body smoothly moving, my head fills with questions: *Why are my pretty flip-flops irritating my feet? Why is he being so nonchalant? Why am I feeling so reluctant? Why is Italy on the other side of the planet? What is happening to me?*

Closing my eyes, I take a deep breath and start answering myself: *My feet are irritated because my silver flip-flops are getting old and ragged; it's time to retire them. Berkeley is being nonchalant because it's in his nature to live carefree and easy. Damn that side of him. I'm probably feeling reluctant because during my last stint away, I fell in love with Italy even though I didn't want to, and I let another boy kiss me—and I liked it. With another four months away, who knows what might happen?*

As I open my eyes, Berkeley gets out of the water and saunters toward me, the water dripping off of his body, rendering him Adonis-like. Toweling off, he parks himself beside me and says, "To avoid going down the same road we did last year when you were in this position, I'm gonna ask that you factor me out of the equation."

"What do you mean?"

"Pretend I don't exist."

As my body starts to quiver, I murmur, "Berkeley, that's impossible. You matter more than anything to me."

"I was afraid you'd say something like that."

"What's wrong with putting you first?"

"Because it's proving yet again that I cloud your judgment."

"My judgment is not clouded."

He sighs. "You and I both know that if you weren't dating me, you'd go back to Italy in an instant."

"But I am dating you."

"So that's the obstacle."

A chill washes over me. "Berkeley, where are you going with this?"

Turning his back on me, he murmurs, "Here's how it's going to be. You are gonna go back to Italy. And when you do, you'll do fantastic stuff there. In fact, I predict you'll have your best year ever."

My face sours. "I don't understand what you're saying."

He sighs. "What I'm saying is that I'm about to do something extreme."

"What?"

"I'm breaking up with you."

"What! Why?"

"To force you to use your brain."

Fighting back the tears, I mumble, "So just like that? You don't care about me?"

He takes hold of my upper arms. "You know very well that I'm flat-out mad about you, but—"

"But what?"

"You and I are way too young to be controlled by us."

"But I like being controlled by us."

"And right now, that needs to come to an end."

Running my hand down his bare chest, I say, "Okay, fine. If you think it's best that I go to Italy, I'll go. Just please don't break up with me because of this."

Positioning his face so close to mine that I can taste his awesome breath, he replies, "You are going to be great on your own."

"No, I won't."

"Yes, you will. You just need to get away from me to realize it."

Wiping away tears, I say, "Your rationale sucks."

"It might, but it's for the best."

Looking away, I say, "I hate you right now."

Pulling me into a hold, he replies, "No, you don't. You love every bit of me."

I do, but I say nothing. I just cry quietly in his arms for as long as he'll allow me.

Once the waterworks run dry, I look up and meekly ask, "Are you breaking up with me so you can date other people?"

He squints. "That's not the point here."

"It worries me that you didn't answer."

"Yeah, well, it worries me that as soon as it's common knowledge you're single, every guy on the planet will try to date you."

I hiccup. "Except you."

"Francie, you know nothing could be further from the truth."

As my eyes spew more tears, he wipes them away and says, "One day you'll understand why I did this."

"Tell me now why you're doing this."

Pressing his forehead against mine, he says, "Because I care about you more than I care about anything."

Slinking out of his arms, I say, "You have a strange way of showing it."

Helping me gather my belongings, he says, "Let me drive you home."

I yank my bag from his hand. "No. I drove myself here. I can drive myself home."

Trailing me as I walk toward the gate, he says, "Don't leave town without calling me, okay?"

Moving swiftly, I mumble, "I won't be calling you."

"Francie, please don't be angry."

Shooting him a fiery stare, I reply, "How could I not be?"

He tries to stall me, but I refuse to let him.

Opening the gate, I say, "Have a nice year."

"Francie, wait."

Moving forward, I holler, "I'll have my mom drop off your pen next week!"

"No, I want you to keep it."

"Fine!" I yell, speeding up my pace.

With my head pounding, I hop inside my mom's car, lean against the steering wheel, and cry out whatever moisture is left in me. Then I drive home mindlessly, possibly running a stop sign, possibly driving in circles for a minimum of an hour, possibly covering twenty miles to travel one.

After parking in front of my house, I wander aimlessly through the front door, slip the silver flip-flops off of my feet, and throw them clear across the living room. "Be forever gone, cute-as-a-button shoes!"

Evidently hearing me, my family enters the room and gawks.

Softly, my mom asks, "Are you okay?"

With a furrowed brow, I yell, "Do I look okay?"

Talula exclaims, "You look horrible!"

Turning to my dad, I ask, "Can I change my plane ticket and leave earlier for Italy?"

"Yes, no problem."

"Tomorrow?"

"If you like."

"I'd like," I reply, running upstairs to start packing.

# foot note twenty-eight

I'M ON DAY ONE OF MY NON-BERKELEY LIFE, MARKING THE FIRST time in ages that I leave the house without showering, combing my hair, or caring about what I look like. I also, for the first time, leave the house wearing my unstylish sheepskin boots, and I have no explanation as to why. I just do.

To mark this turning-point day, I have chosen to renounce myself as a citizen of Riverly Heights. From now on, I am a citizen of wherever I live. Fill in the blank.

Presently, I'm midway on my solo trip overseas, on a flight direct from New York to Rome. In a few hours, when this plane touches down, I will meet up with my art-history teacher, Signorina Carlotta, whom my parents summoned last minute to accompany me on the train ride to Florence. For the record, I could easily have completed this journey on my own—it's old hat by now—but my parents are still being worry warts about me traveling alone, especially since I left the house crying, so to appease them, I agreed to be partially chaperoned.

Here I sit, feeling totally exposed in my midcabin aisle seat, noticing the distance between my past and future expanding. As my mind once again replays yesterday's breakup with Berkeley, I start to whimper.

Placing a hand on my lower arm, the passenger beside me, whose body language and shoes have "sweet grandmother" written all over them, quietly asks, "What's wrong, dear?"

Blowing my nose, I reply, "I just had my heart shredded."

As a typical grandmother would, she smiles and gestures for me to rest my head on her shoulder for a while. So I do.

Alerted by my constant sniffles, a few other passengers offer me candy, books, magazines, and whatever is on hand. An old lady sitting two rows ahead of me even gets up from her seat, hands me a twenty-dollar bill, and says, "Put this toward a little pick-me-up, so you'll feel better."

I try to refuse, but because she keeps stuffing the bill back into my hand, I say, "Thank you. You're very kind."

Later, an older gentleman sitting across the aisle hits the flight-attendant call button and says something to the flight attendant when she arrives.

The next thing I know, I'm being shifted into executive class.

I guess the guy in coach is either inherently compassionate or tired of my noises. Either way, I am grateful.

Nestled in my upgrade—spoiled by multiple desserts, expensive headphones, eye covers, movie options, pajamas, a pillow, and blankets—I start to feel like myself again.

I feel even better when an upbeat, tall, runway-model-gorgeous male flight attendant sits down beside me, learns of my sadness, and says, "By the looks of you, my dear girl, that boy has lost his marbles!"

I agree.

At the termination of my executive-class pampering, I meet up with Signorina Carlotta at the train station, consume a quick lunch, and board the train to what I'm now calling home.

The lush scenery along the way reminds me of the loveliness I am traveling to, enabling me to step off the train, tilt my head upward, and allow the Tuscan sun to seep into my body. Though I still hurt all over, I know I will survive. My friends at Idea Incubatrice will be the distraction I need.

On day two of my non-Berkeley life, I'm pleased to wake up dry-eyed for the first time since Berkeley dumped me.

I spent the night in Florence by myself at a prissy hotel in the heart of the city (a treat arranged by my parents), in a room that exceeds beautiful, with warm furnishings, a bathtub that could fit four of me, window shutters that open to the Duomo, sheets so soft that they facilitated a ten-hour sleep, and complimentary slippers that are the meaning of *hurtless*.

As I sit here on the hotel's outdoor terrace and eat a delicious breakfast, I plot my course for the day. I intend to heed that little old lady's advice and spend the twenty bucks on a pick-me-up (well, maybe more than twenty bucks). I'll do so by going shoe shopping, because (1) I want something showstopping to wear when I strut my way into my new dorm room, and (2) I want to further my me-shoe development, which hasn't seen progress in more than a year.

It somewhat surprises me that I did not add a single descriptor to my criteria during my last stint in Italy. Come to think of it, as of two days ago, I actually lost one with the deletion of *cute as a button*.

I've made a different kind of progress, I guess—revisionary.

My destination is a shoe shop I once visited with Allegra: E Punte, which means "Pointed Toes." As I head there in a taxi, I say to my driver, "Fermare qui, per favore," and I smile when he stops. After politely asking him to wait for me, I dash out of the car, scoot inside, and quickly browse for anything that catches my eye.

On the back wall, under a bright spotlight, I notice a pair of high-heeled, multistrapped sandals in cotton-candy pink. Though I don't necessarily love them, especially given that they feel tight on my toes, I do feel a sudden surge of energy in holding them, so I buy them spontaneously.

Jumping back into the taxi, I provide the driver with Idea

Incubatrice's address and change footwear for my impending single-girl strut.

Shaking my head, I wonder if shoe shopping is a problem for me. *Am I a shoe-aholic?*

There's no denying it: shoes are my go-to, my pacifier, my unconditional love, and my mood improver. But is that enough to cast me in the same light as an addict? I think not, because any damage caused by my vice is mendable.

I expect I'll be telling myself that again tomorrow, as I can feel new blisters forming already.

As I approach the door of this year's dorm building, which is directly across the main roadway from last year's, and sense its gravitational pull, I instantly smile. Only then do I accept that Berkeley was right. I'm meant to be here. However, because I'm still angry that he chose to break up with me to prove his point, I vow never to give him the credit he deserves.

Inside the building, I wander down the main-floor hallway in search of my new room; the taxi driver follows a few steps behind with my bags. In an adjacent lounge, I notice Arno sitting in a chair, holding an enormous bouquet of fresh flowers. As I make my way toward him—walking proudly in my perky-sounding, stunner high heels—he glances in my direction and bolts to his feet.

Smiling sweetly, he sprints toward me and exclaims, "Francie Lanoo! *Buongiorno!*"

"Hi, Arno."

"You look fabulous!"

"Thank you."

"I saw your posting a couple of days ago, mentioning that you were Idea Incubatrice bound, so I decided to move in early too."

"That's nice. We can keep each other company until our other friends show up." Rita and Azami will be back on scholarship, and Inga and Aurora will return on their parents' tab.

"How was your summer?"

I shrug. "Occupato."

His brow furrows. "Busy? That's it? Nothing more?"

After instructing the taxi driver on where to place my luggage and paying him his due, I add, "My summer was just okay. How was yours?"

"It lacked something."

"What?"

"You," he replies, pulling me into a tight one-armed hold.

Though his embrace feels warm and welcome, I slink away.

"Is something wrong?" he asks.

"No, I'm just exhausted."

"I understand. You've traveled far."

"I have."

"These are for you," he says, placing the flowers in my arms.

"Thank you. That's so sweet."

"You're welcome."

I smile. "I'll go put them in my room."

"Do you need any help?"

"No," I abruptly respond, "but thanks for offering."

As I turn to walk away, he adds, "If you need anything, Francie, day or night, just call me. I'm living four rooms to the east."

"Thank you," I say, moving quickly away from him before I weaken and take him up on his highly desirable offer.

Inside my barren new dorm room, I throw my suitcases onto the bed and—with my too-tight shoes still on—mechanically start pulling together what will be my home for the next nine months. Aside from the different outdoor scenery—I have a city view this time around—my new accommodations will mostly resemble last year's: the patterned boxes, the pretty bedding, and the multitude of scarves (all of which the maintenance staff relocated prior to my arrival). What will change, though, is the collage of photographs plastered on the wall behind my bed. This time around, I will replace the Riverly Heights nostalgia with an ever-changing array of Italy-based images (the people, places, and things here), which I'm hoping will remind me that I live in the present and not the past.

As a final touch, I am adding just two sentimentalities brought from home: Berkeley's pen, which I intend to use because it draws beautifully, and Berkeley's key necklace, which I intend to look at occasionally because it's the prettiest piece of jewelry I own.

Once I've assembled the room, I whisper, "It'll do." Then I sit on the edge of the bed and stare down at my pick-me-ups. Noticing that several open gashes have developed on my toes, I take the shoes off and mumble, "Never again will I be so impulsive."

Breathing deeply, I tell myself, *You'll hit your stride again. Just don't expect to in one day.*

On that note, I stuff the newbies into a box, put on my pajamas, and crawl into bed.

# foot note twenty-nine

THE FIRST NIGHT IN MY LATEST BED PROVES TO BE RESTLESS AND painful, which comes as no surprise considering the open wounds on my feet rubbing against my stiff cotton sheets for eight full hours.

In light of this new development, I forego my regular morning routine of primping and instead slip into comfy clothes and flip-flops and munch on a pastry left over from yesterday's stay at the hotel.

When done, I decide—with little hesitation—that it's in my best interest to put on hold any further me-shoe research until my feet no longer hurt. My rationale is that it makes no sense to move on to the next while still suffering from the last.

I stumble to my feet and force myself to get motivated, thinking, *Homework will resume soon, so enjoy the downtime.*

First, I head in the direction of Allegra's room, where I will be seeking advice on the treatment of the impulse-induced foot wounds. I would have called Allegra to announce my visit, but she doesn't use a phone or any form of technology, so I'm forced to make a cold call. *Sorry, Allegra, but you asked for it.*

After making a pit stop in the dorm's kitchen to grab a steaming-hot espresso for Allegra, I wander into my building of old, find her door, and lightly knock.

Hearing no response, I quietly murmur, "Allegra, are you awake? It's Francie."

She mumbles, "What time is it?"

"Seven."

"What are you doing up at this ungodly hour? And furthermore, what are you doing here two weeks before classes start?"

"It's a long story, but it starts with my feet seriously hurting right now." Faintly hearing her drawn-out sigh, I add, "I brought you an espresso," and much to my relief, she opens the door.

"May I come in?"

"Yes, you may," she replies, pulling me toward her for a hug.

"Thanks for getting up."

Taking the espresso, she gives me the once-over and notes, "You look awful."

"Thanks. It's great to see you too."

Her face softens. "How was your summer?"

"Eventful. How was yours?"

With eyes gleaming, she rambles on about her two months of travels through Western Europe; about every interesting detail of the cool hangouts, bistros, and boutiques she stumbled upon while there; and about some guy named Mauro, whom she met while wandering the streets of Barcelona.

Smiling, I inquire, "Are you going to see him again?"

With a twinkle in her eye, she replies, "He'll be traveling for much of the next year, but we're planning to meet up in his hometown of Milan next summer."

"Nice!"

After taking a deep breath, she says, "Now, tell me what is going on with those hurting feet."

I fill her in on my impromptu shoe purchase as well as the heartbreaking details of my Berkeley breakup, and she gives me a giant hug and then says, "To ease the foot pain—and to get you back into sexy shoes as soon as possible—I've got some skin-toned bandages that will heal those wounds within a week."

"Nice. Thank you."

"To ease the Berkeley pain—and to make you realize how much fun it is to be Francie Lanoo—I'm going to recommend you explore your new single-girl status by having a year of fun."

I furrow my brow. "I have no interest in fun that doesn't involve Berkeley."

"Honey, Berkeley is out of your life—at least for now."

"Not emotionally."

She sits up straight. "Listen to me, you silly Milly. You are young, you are beautiful, and you are living among the most-charming young men in existence. Go out with one—or two or three—and indulge."

"To what end?"

Her eyes widen. "To what end? Are you kidding me? At minimum, to jam-pack your love life with every experience imaginable."

"But I don't want that unless it's with Berkeley."

"Oh, stop being such a sad sap."

"Sorry, but I'm just being honest."

She looks me square in the eyes. "I think your hesitancy to date others is out of fear you'll be happier with someone other than Berkeley."

"Not true."

"How do you know?"

"Because Berkeley is it. I just know."

"But he's the only boy you've ever been with, which means you have no benchmark."

"I don't need one."

She raises an eyebrow. "He also hurt you. And isn't that telling you something?"

I drop my eyes to the floor. "It might be."

Placing her forehead against mine, she says, "Trust me—the best thing for you right now is to get back on the horse. In fact, I'm going to dare you to date another guy, even if it's for a short time, and come back to me with proof that the venerable Berkeley cannot be topped."

"I'm not going to date someone on a dare."

"Why not? There are a lot of hot guys out there worth spending time with—one gorgeous boy, in particular, who drools every time you walk into a room."

I shrug. "I don't think I'm cut out for playing the field."

"Why?"

"Because I don't want to get hurt again."

"Francie, not all shoes—and not all boys—cause pain."

"Yeah, but they all have the potential."

Nudging me, she says, "Come on. Do it. Get out there. Live your life fully."

Shaking my head, I slink off of the bed, wander toward the door, and say, "I don't know. I'm gonna be pretty busy this year with homework."

"Chicken."

"No, I'm not a chicken. I just know what's good for me."

Throwing a package of bandages at me, she says, "Do you?"

Opening the door, I reply, "Good-bye, Allegra. Thanks for your first aid and your time."

Shaking her head, she hollers, "You and I are not done discussing this."

I roll my eyes. "Yes, we are!"

Through the closed door, she yells, "FYI, I'm going to spread word that you're now single and loving it."

"Go ahead!" I reply, shaking my head.

Back in my room, I think about what Allegra just said and realize she might not be totally off base. There is a remote possibility Berkeley isn't the guy for me.

But then I ponder never being with him again, hearing his words again, or looking into those eyes again, which causes me to hopelessly crack open a whole new can of tears.

Slipping off my flip-flops, I add a bandage to the wound that is hurting most.

While wiping my soggy cheeks dry, I decide I'm going to put aside my love life and my quest for my Francie shoe and focus solely on excelling with my schoolwork. After all, that is the reason I'm here.

# foot note thirty

I CAN'T BELIEVE HOW FAST THE FIRST SEMESTER OF TWELFTH grade flew by. It feels as if I departed Riverly Heights, blinked twice, and am already heading back. I guess that's what happens when you put your nose to the grind and work, work, work.

Riding in the backseat of a taxi en route to the Florence train station, I have my first thought in four months that isn't related to my studies. I start to fret over what will be in store when I land in Riverly Heights twenty-four hours from now. My biggest worry, of course, is the source of my still-broken heart: Berkeley Mills. Do I miss him? Yes. Am I still hung up on him? Forevermore. Do I want to bump into him? Absolutely not.

So what happens if I do?

Dreading the thought, I start ripping at my cuticles. I need to think of something else—a diversion, a pacifier.

Like shoes. God, I've missed obsessing over them and searching for my me-shoe characteristics. Maybe it's time to browse the latest options and, if all goes well, discover something new, if for no other reason than I would love to wear a shoe style that connects me to Italy while I'm not here, something that reminds me of where I am happy.

*A quick shopping spree it is then.*

With my oversized backpack weighing me down, I traipse into a small shoe store just inside the train-station doors, where I zero in on a pair of hot-off-the-press deep-teal peep-toe pumps that make my heart go pitter-patter.

I try them on. I like the way they feel. I adore the way they tweak my posture. So despite the fact that my decision to buy them is as impulsive as my last shoe purchase was, I make them mine.

Taking my seat on the train, I remove my sheepskin boots, switch into my latest purchase, and don my first full smile in months.

As four different cute guys catch sight of them and also smile, I momentarily reconsider Allegra's recommendation about my love life and quietly say, "Nope. I'm still not feeling it."

After sleeping away most of the hours spent on an airplane, I'm wide-eyed in the backseat of a taxi, keenly observing the familiar sights of Riverly Heights. Twiddling my fingers and wiggling my toes, I watch with bated breath as my home's familiar facade comes into view, shiny with the evening sun beaming on it, glittery with its usual array of Christmas lighting. Spotting my parents, my sisters, and Phoebe exiting the front door, each one with flailing arms and a happy grin, I nearly jump through the glass window. After four long months of not seeing anyone from my past, my senses reawaken, and I accept that I do miss them.

To the beat of my racing heart, I force the passenger door open before the car has even stopped. Shouting, "Hello!" I rush like a lottery winner along the front sidewalk toward them.

As they collectively hug me—and my dad deals with the taxi driver and luggage—several conversations erupt: my mom analyzing the lack of color in my face, Phoebe filling me in on all of the goings-on at Riverly Heights High School, Talula asking what it's like to travel alone, and Brigitte informing me that my shoes make me strut like a runway model.

To the sound of voices overlapping, my eyes dart around to see if Berkeley is here, and my ears go on high alert too, in case his car is entering the vicinity. But there is no sign of him.

Of course there's no sign of him. Why would he be here?

As a tear forms in my eye, I look to my shoes and mentally tell them to take me forward, not backward. Then I further suggest that in the event I run into a green-eyed ghost from my past, may the runway-model strut serve me well.

The holiday season in Riverly Heights is brimming with its typical breathtaking winter-wonderland-ness: thick blankets of snow, an abundance of Christmas decorations, excessive food and drink, and lots of good cheer, all of which I am enjoying exclusively from the comfort of my parents' home, because that's where I feel cocooned, relaxed, and at ease.

Every day, without fail, Phoebe, Beatrice, and Silvia hound me to go out and do something fun. Usually, though, I tell them I'm still suffering jet lag (because I might be), after which I invite them over to my house instead. As often as possible, I wear my train-station shoes, and so far, they've helped me maintain a happy demeanor. Of course, that might also be related to the fact that no one has uttered a single Berkeley-related word since I arrived here.

When alone, I fill much of my holiday time reading the latest best-selling novels, baking cookies with my mom, or watching sappy, romantic movies, which I probably shouldn't do, because every one of them has made me weepy. Occasionally, I get caught up in reading messages from my Idea Incubatrice classmates—Rita, Inga, Azami, and Arno—many of which make me laugh and miss them.

Arno, in fact, messages me every day—this morning's note was a confession that he has had the urge numerous times to spontaneously hop on a plane to visit me.

"Please, no," I was tempted to reply, but I did not.

Deep down, I know Arno wants to date me—the blatant vibes first registered in my brain when he started slipping handwritten notes under my door, meant to make my day. Thankfully, he has not pushed the romance issue, probably because I've made it a habit to never be alone with him.

Truthfully, I do have the occasional urge to get involved with him, thereby testing Allegra's theory about benchmarks, but I've repeatedly talked myself out of it. I don't know why, especially since Arno is one of the nicest guys I've ever met. I almost caved on my last day in Italy, when he hung a piece of mistletoe above my dorm-room door and waited for me to exit.

When I eventually did, I stood face-to-face with him and let him give me a quick peck on the lips. However, when the connection reminded me of my last mistletoe encounter—the ultimate one—I pulled away and briskly marched to my first-period class.

*Berkeley. Mistletoe. Those lips. Those eyes. God, what's going to happen if I run into him while I'm home?*

"Don't let it happen," I say aloud.

At least I made it through Christmas Day without calling the guy. When the urge struck me the hardest—triggered by the sight of the guest-room bed—I slipped into my train-station shoes and pranced around as if I were attending New York Fashion Week.

My strut is getting better, I will admit.

I wonder what Berkeley would say if he saw how far it's come.

# foot note thirty-one

MY PLAN WAS TO SPEND NEW YEAR'S EVE AT HOME WITH MY parents at their twelve-guest dinner party, but at the last minute, Phoebe told me that the gathering would age me four decades and convinced me to go out with her instead. So I am—reluctantly.

I've kept myself cocooned inside the house for ten straight days. It's probably a good idea for me to get some fresh air, if for no other reason than because it'll clear a slew of stagnant thoughts out of my head.

As I start the process of getting ready for the evening, I mumble, "What vibe do I want to project today to express that I'm doing just fine in my post-Berkeley world?" *Indifference? Confidence? Or the truth—that I feel like a crumpled paper bag?*

With no regard for the brutally cold temperature, I say, "It's New Year's Eve, the ultimate party night. What better occasion to celebrate the girlie girl in me?" I decide on a short black skirt, a tight black pullover, and deep lavender stockings.

For footwear, since Talula is wearing my train-station shoes tonight (a decision made when I agreed to be the thirteenth member of the golden-oldie crowd), I'm borrowing a pair from Brigitte: high, sexy bronze platform shoes—footwear I went head over heels for after Brigitte debuted them at Christmas dinner.

Since dropping them off in my bedroom yesterday, Brigitte has been hanging out with me, taking an interest in my goings-on and sharing with me her own sordid personal tales. So maybe she misses me? I certainly miss her.

As she sits on the end of my bed again, witnessing the predeparture adjustments I'm making in front of the mirror, she notes, "I don't know why you're being so fussy. You looked great an hour ago."

"I'm just making sure I look reasonably mainstream to avoid a repeat of my last New Year Eve's space-oddity wear."

She laughs. "I do remember that getup."

"Yeah, it was a little over the top."

"Way over for a place like Riverly Heights."

As I'm checking my makeup and brushing off some powder foundation because it made my freckles disappear, Brigitte asks, "Is Berkeley going to be at this party?"

I freeze. "I don't know."

"If he is there, I bet I know what'll happen at the stroke of midnight."

"If he is there, I'll be out the door before the stroke of midnight."

"No, don't do that."

"Oh yes I will, because the last thing I need is to go back to Italy with him in my head."

"Based on your facial expression right now, I suspect he's already there."

"So?"

"So the best thing you could do is put you in *his* head."

"I don't think that's in the cards anymore."

"I wouldn't be so sure about that."

"Why?"

"Well, for one thing, he still stops by here regularly to chat with Mom and Dad."

"He does?"

"Yes."

I sit on the corner of the bed. "What does he talk about?"

Her face scrunches. "What do you think he talks about? You!"

I slump. "I should stay home tonight."

"Are you kidding? Definitely go out."

"To what end?"

"Well, if for no other reason than to strut around in those good-time-written-all-over-them shoes."

I look downward. "They are a party unto themselves."

Brigitte's eyes gleam. "I did really well picking them, didn't I?"

"Yes, you did."

Fluttering her eyelashes—something I've never seen her do—she says, "FYI, I won't hold it against you if you bring them back with a scuff or two."

I smirk. "Rest assured, I'll bring them back in perfect condition."

"We'll see."

As I walk toward the door, she adds, "Happy to cover for you if you get detained into the wee hours of the night."

Heading down the stairs, I holler, "Thanks, but that won't be necessary."

"Care to put money on it?"

"No, I do not."

When Phoebe arrives by taxi to pick me up, my eyes dazzle over how amazing she looks. Since I last saw her two days ago, she's cut her hair and dyed it auburn, she's applied makeup in an ultradramatic fashion (never have I seen lips so red), and she's dressed to entice the entire male population.

With wide eyes, I say, "You're too hot for Vegas."

She smiles. "It's part of my single-and-loving-it phase."

I giggle. "Have you ever had another phase?"

She taps her finger on my shoulder. "Don't knock it until you've tried it."

Furrowing my brow, I respond, "You and I both know I would not wear it well."

Looking at my footwear, she replies, "I don't know. You're rocking those hot-to-trot shoes pretty well."

Flashing her another eye roll, I follow her into the awaiting taxi and take many short breaths as we endure a brief ride to the house of our friend Pierce—memories of my last party there are invading my brain.

Joining the party in progress, I pan the living room for faces that are familiar, and when I spot Beatrice and Silvia, I head their way and position myself so that I'm practically hiding behind them. Only then do I start to relax.

Later, making my way into the family room, I run into the host of last year's New Year's Eve event, Sam. While engaging in a quick catch-up, I come close to asking him where Berkeley is tonight—he doesn't appear to be here—but I press my lips closed and refrain from going there.

Instead, I turn my attention to Sam's feet and notice he's wearing another cool pair of canvas high-tops (this version in bright cobalt blue with orange laces), so I exclaim, "Great shoes once again!"

"Thanks. I've adopted this particular brand as my trademark."

"It's a good one for you."

"I think so too," he responds, glancing at my feet and then adding, "I really like the provocateur thing you've got going on."

"Thank you, I think."

He looks me in the eyes. "'Tormenting' is what's written all over them."

"No, there'll be nothing of the sort tonight."

Smiling, he replies, "Sorry, Francie, but I don't think you're in a position to control that."

"Meaning what?"

"Meaning I need to stop talking, because I've had one too many drinks and need to use the boys' room."

"Too much information, Sam."

"Yes, so off to the loo I go."

Midsaunter, he turns around and asks, "Hey, Francie, have you been downstairs yet?"

"No. Why?"

He grins. "'Cause there's a pretty good vibe going on right now."

"Will I know anyone?"

He raises an eyebrow. "I can think of at least a dozen guys who would love to know you."

As I roll my eyes, he shouts, "Always a pleasure to see you, Footwear Francie!"

"Likewise, Shoe Man Sam."

*God, that guy makes me grin.*

Wandering into the kitchen, I see, across the room, that slobber-puss from last New Year's Eve, Max. As my mouth recalls his hideous tongue, I tell myself, *Not tonight.*

Noticing his eyes trailing me, I beeline to Pierce and say, "What's going on downstairs?"

"Come. I'll show you."

"Thanks."

With my hand gripped by his, I follow Pierce down a narrow flight of stairs and bombard him with questions: about his parents' whereabouts (they're at a party of their own), about his plans for college next fall (he has applied to study structural engineering at NYU), and about what I've missed at school so far this year. As soon as I hit the last step, though, my mouth freezes, and my hand drops, because my eyes see none other than Berkeley, standing across the room, leaning against a wall, surrounded by numerous classmates. *Some things never change.*

As my brain processes where I should go from here, he notices me too. Abruptly standing erect, he lifts a hand in my direction and sweetly smiles.

Though my heart is thumping so fast I feel it in both temples, I offer a warm smile back and try to act unfazed. I'm holding up pretty well, all things considered, until I notice a girl I've never seen before—blonde and pretty, wearing tight black pants and a low-cut red blouse, with curves that put my twiggy figure to shame—placing her hand on Berkeley's chest.

As I further observe her whispering into his ear, I go weak in the knees and wonder, *Is he with her?*

When she presses her body tightly against his, I have my answer. Yes, and I've been swapped out.

Caught up in what to do next—run, scream, or hide—I accept a beverage Pierce has brought me, move into a corner by myself, and try to stop the room from spinning.

As his eyes trail me, Berkeley must sense I'm freaking out, because he says something to his date and darts toward me.

Watching him approach me, I know I should turn and flee, but I'm incapable. I want to see him. I need to talk to him. I just wish he didn't look as if he'd recently dropped off of a fashion billboard.

Stopping within a foot of me, he says, "Your stockings would go well with my shirt. So maybe you'll let me borrow them sometime?"

Refusing to smile, I reply, "With your history of stealing my hosiery, I'm surprised you're asking permission."

"Well, it is the mannerly thing to do."

When I do not reply, he audibly inhales and says, "It's great to see you."

"You too."

"Italy must still agree with you. You look amazing right now."

I smirk. "Or the dim lights are just very forgiving."

Reaching over and giving my hand a quick squeeze, he asks, "How are you?"

Out of habit, I look directly into his eyes, but when I find him staring at me in a way I wish he wouldn't—not while he's in the company of a girl who's wearing a blouse I will never have the body to wear—I slink my hand away from his, stare into my beverage, and mumble, "I'm fine."

"Pierce didn't think you'd be here tonight."

"Blame Phoebe."

"I'm more inclined to thank her."

"Not me."

Inhaling, he says, "Hey, look, Francie. I know this is awkward, and I'm sorry. If I had known you were—"

"Berkeley, I'm a big girl. I can handle whatever you've got going on."

As his mouth opens to respond, the girl in the blouse hugs him from behind, prompting him to practically jump out of his skin and murmur, "Hey, Hannah. I'd like you to meet Francie."

"Hi, Francie."

"Hi, Hannah."

"Aren't you the girl who lives in Italy?"

Though I want to say, "Aren't you the psycho who jumps in front of moving cars?" I politely reply, "Yes, but I'll be back in four months."

Evidently, Hannah reads between the lines, because she gives me a snide glare and proceeds to rest her chin on Berkeley's shoulder, staking her claim.

Alarmed by the sight of someone else fondling the guy I'm still crazy about, I abruptly say, "Excuse me. I've gotta go."

"Sure, no problem," Berkeley quietly replies.

Without saying good-bye, I run up the stairs, grab my stuff, and bolt out the door with my adrenaline so fired up that I could sprint all the way to my house. I probably would if I weren't currently walking on stilts.

As my heart disintegrates into a thousand fragments, I pussyfoot about the snow-covered street while trying to retrieve my cell phone from my tiny evening bag.

As I'm calling for a taxi, I hear someone approaching me from behind. Praying that it's Berkeley—wishing for him to be away from her—I spin around and discover Max, whom I do not care to acknowledge or see.

Pursing my lips, I slip my phone into my pocket, give him the most-indifferent expression I can muster, and glance away.

Walking around to face me, he says, "How's it going, Francie?"

I fib. "Fine."

Edging toward me, he says, "I have to tell you that you've made my day by being here tonight."

Turning and walking away, I reply, "That's nice."

Jerking me around, he says, "Slow down, would you?"

With my face so close to his that I can smell his latest beverage, I yell, "Do you mind?"

"I just wanna have a conversation with you. Is that too much to ask?"

"Yes, because I'm trying to leave."

"Why would you split before midnight?"

"Because I choose to be elsewhere."

"Just give me five minutes of your time. That's all I'm asking."

"Sorry, that's not going to happen," I reply, bolting down the street as fast as these ridiculous shoes will allow.

When I glance back and discover him about three steps behind, I increase my pace to a trot, and doing so, I slide on some ice, twist an ankle, and fall out of one of my shoes.

"Stupid footwear," I say, reaching down to retrieve the delinquent.

Hovering over me like a dark cloud, Max grabs me by the upper arms, pulls me upright, presses his face against mine, and says, "You smell really good."

Trying to pull away, I reply, "Let me go, Max."

"But I'm not ready to," he mumbles, forcing my body against a car window.

With finger flexed beneath my silver gloves, I yell, "Get off me!"

But he doesn't; instead, he puts a hand over my mouth to stifle my cries and moves his hands to places I don't want them to be.

Slapping him, elbowing him, kneeing him, and not knowing what else to do, I close my eyes and wish for him to stop.

Then, as if summoned by my will, he does stop, his body swirling away from me as if it's been hit by a car.

As I bend over to catch my breath, a familiar voice shouts, "Max, you son of a bitch! Get the hell out of here!"

When I look up and see Berkeley standing a foot away from me, I fall to my knees and cover my mouth with my gloved hands.

With his arms outstretched, Max says, "Berkeley! Sorry. I didn't realize you two still had something going on."

With his fists raised and his brow furrowed, Berkeley yells, "And that gives you the right to do this?"

Smirking, Max retorts, "You're with Hannah now. What the hell do you care?"

As I stand up, I observe Berkeley breathing so intensely that he's emitting thick puffs of steam into the air.

Never having seen him so angry, and worried he's about to snap, I reach for his hands (as if I could stop him) and say, "Berkeley, please. Don't do anything crazy."

Stepping back, all the while keeping his eyes fixed on Max, he replies, "Fine, but only because you asked me not to."

When Max finally stomps away, I return my shoe to my foot and inhale several short breaths. As my body suddenly starts to shiver, Berkeley wraps himself around me like a cloak, places his chin on the top of my head, and quietly asks, "Are you okay?"

"Yeah. I guess so."

"Did he hurt you?"

"Only a little."

Linking his eyes with mine, he says, "Please don't ever do that again—run around outside at night by yourself."

My face scrunches. "I didn't know someone would come after me."

"Francie, you need to understand how vulnerable you are and that guys like Max can be really dangerous!"

"Okay. Fine. I get it!"

"Are you sure? Seriously, Francie, something really bad could have happened out here! What if I hadn't followed you?"

With lips quivering, I whisper, "I'm sorry," and I burst into a mess of tears.

As I cover my face with my hands, Berkeley opens up his coat and pulls me close to him, murmuring, "God, I'm such a jerk. I shouldn't be yelling at you for this. It's not your fault."

As I cry more intensely—less because of what just happened and more because being this close to Berkeley is making me realize how badly I miss him—Berkeley says, "So there is a downside to being Francie Lanoo."

Inhaling his sweet scent, I mumble, "What do you mean?"

"You make guys crazy—literally."

"Whatever."

Berkeley cups my face in his hands and asks, "Are you gonna be all right?"

"Yeah."

"Do you want to go back inside?"

I shake my head. "No, I've got a taxi coming, but you go ahead."

"No, I'm going to make sure you get home safely."

With pouty lips, I reply, "Thanks, but you don't need to watch out for me."

Holding me tighter than he ever has, he says, "Francie, whether you like it or not, I'll feel inclined to watch out for you until the day I die."

As I burst into another fit of sobs, Berkeley moves us to the curb, sits us down, and pulls me onto his lap. "What a night."

Sniffling, I say, "I'm sorry I messed it up for you."

"You didn't."

"Yes, I did."

"Actually, I'm happy to get away from the crowd."

"Me too. Except that it's really cold out here."

Taking his coat off and wrapping it around me, he replies, "I think your cold problem is the result of your ridiculous footwear choice."

"Not your favorite?"

He smiles. "They're the sexiest shoes I've ever seen you wear, but they are in desperate need of some rubber treads and fur linings."

I giggle. "They belong to Brigitte."

His eyebrows rise. "That makes sense, because I don't see a smidgeon of you written on them."

"Regardless, they drew me like a cat with a shiny toy."

Chuckling, he says, "So out of curiosity, how many pairs of shoes do you now own?"

"You don't want to know."

"Are you any closer to finding the ultimate?"

Sighing, I reply, "No."

He smiles. "Well, keep looking, because I know it's out there."

"I hope so."

After spending several more minutes absorbing his awesomeness, I say, "I miss this—us."

"I do too, which might explain why I wore your pink socks on Christmas morning."

I sit up straight. "You did?"

"Yep."

"Why would you do that?"

"Because I was dying to call you but suspected that might be a bad idea. So instead, I latched onto the closest thing I had to you."

"That's cute."

"You're cute."

"No, I'm not."

"Yes, you are."

When he kisses the top of my head, I say, "Can I talk to you about something?"

"Sure."

"Back when I was deciding whether or not to move to Italy, you promised that if I went, you'd be around when I came back. But that didn't end up being the case, and I'm wondering why."

After taking a deep breath, he says, "I said it because I meant it, but—"

"And you said you'd visit me in Italy but never did. And you said you'd send me a copy of that photo but never did. And what would have been the harm in you and me staying in touch, even just as friends?"

He leans back. "Okay, okay, I get it. You've got some gripes with me."

"I do."

"Well, cut me some slack, because I'm having a hard time with all of this too."

I slump. "I'm sorry. I don't mean to nag. I'm just frustrated because I have this gigantic hole in my heart because of you."

Grabbing my hand, he replies, "I'm not sure why I never visited you. Life got busy, and maybe I didn't want to get in the way of what you had going on over there." He exhales. "And I'm not sure why I didn't send that photograph. I guess it just slipped my mind. And—"

I interject, "Why did you swap me out?"

He looks away. "I didn't swap you out. I'm just passing time while you and I are on a break."

"So taking a break, for you, means getting physical with someone else."

"Is that a question?"

"No, it's just me being crazy."

"You're not crazy."

"I shouldn't have gone back to Italy for another year."

"Yes, you should have, because it was the best thing for you, and in a few months, you'll be home, so just hang in there."

I shake my head. "How is it that you're always so cool, calm, and together about everything?"

"I'm not really. I've just gotten good at keeping myself preoccupied."

"Yeah. With Hannah."

He sighs. "With stuff besides Hannah."

"Like?"

"Like macramé."

"As in the stringy stuff?"

He grins. "Yes, as in the stringy stuff."

"How offbeat of you."

He shrugs. "I chose it for therapeutic reasons."

My eyes perk up. "Will you make something for me?"

"Out of string?"

"Yes."

He looks me in the eyes. "Sure."

"Thanks," I say, fixating on his eyes as if I've been hypnotized.

Blushing, Berkeley asks, "How's school going?"

"Oh, it's pretty good. And I love it."

"How's the pen holding up?"

"Extremely well. I use it all the time."

"Good."

I show him my handbag. "I have it with me. Do you need it back?"

He tightens his hold of me. "No, I do not."

"Well, I'm happy to return it to you anytime you need it."

"I don't need it."

"Okay."

When the wind picks up and snow begins to fall, Berkeley stands us up and says, "We should go back inside before this storm gets worse."

"No, I'm gonna leave."

"Are you sure? Maybe just five more minutes?"

I smile. "No, I've detained you long enough."

"Impossible," he says just as the taxi pulls up and screeches to a halt.

As Berkeley and I stand there, staring at each other's face, we can hear the sounds of the house partiers counting down to midnight in the background. Then a blast of the taxi's horn startles us back to reality.

As Berkeley motions to the driver for one more minute, we hear the countdown sound of "One."

I smile. "Happy New Year, Berkeley."

Pulling me close to him, he replies, "Happy New Year, Francie."

Sweeping the hair away from my eyes, he leans in and gives me a kiss so heartfelt that it makes my cold body warm all over.

As we linger close together, I consider sending the driver away. However, when a second horn honk reminds me that Berkeley isn't mine anymore, I instead say, "Take care, you."

"You too."

Slipping out of Berkeley's coat, I smile and say, "Have some fun tonight."

Smiling, he responds, "I just did."

Getting inside the taxi, I stare forward and exhale slowly. Rehashing the last fifteen minutes of my life—the attack, the rescue, and the awesome kiss—I feel the waterworks approaching full force. Wiping away more tears, I'm struck by the notion that much about this trip home has made me sad, which makes me wonder if it's a sign that I'm meant to stay away from here.

Driven to thoughts of my happy life in Italy, I decide I'm going to make some changes when I return there. From now on, I'm going to start living where I live—just as Berkeley is.

As for my footwear pursuits, I have no desire to debate whether or not this pair of Brigitte's factors into my search. Berkeley was right. Not a smidgeon of Francie exists in them. Therefore, as soon I arrive home, I'm going to march them into Brigitte's closet and bury them deeply.

Shedding the last of my tears, I hear my phone ping. I pull it out of my pocket and see that it's Arno wishing me a happy New Year.

I smile. I cheer up. I text him back.

# foot note thirty-two

WHEN IT COMES TO WEARING FOOTWEAR IN ITALY, THE MORE chichi the style, the better. That's why I'm wearing a unique pair of metallic-gold sandals with ornate embossing and crisscrossing straps up the ankle.

An accurate descriptor for them would be *extroverted*, which is not a trait I would normally associate with me, but it's one I'm trying on for size as a means of expanding my horizons—something Arno has been encouraging me to do.

He and I are dating now and have been since the day I returned to Italy in early January. We didn't even discuss it or go on a first date. I just entered the Idea Incubatrice dorm building, walked directly to Arno's room, charged through the door, and kissed him passionately.

I've been having a blast with him ever since. The highlight happened on Valentine's Day, when he prearranged a romantic rooftop dinner, including wine (because seventeen-year-olds are legally permitted to drink wine in Italy), music, candles, flowers, and a view of the city that would make a rock weep.

So I guess Allegra was onto something last September, when she urged me to find out whether someone other than Berkeley could light up my life. Arno does all of the time. He exposes me to unique Italian food; encourages me to sketch and record much of what surrounds me; teaches me curse words in his native tongue; has taken me to the opera three lovely times; and introduces me to little-known museums, including one dedicated to nothing but shoes—a place that made me practically die and go to heaven. He has even driven me, in his little red sports car, to his family's winery, about a three-hour drive away from our school, which is the most beautiful, relaxing, and fascinating place on the planet—and the reason I now know which grapes are used for a shiraz, a pinot noir, or a cabernet.

We are on another road trip today, to do some studying for our final exams. We're heading to a quiet lake in the middle of the Tuscan hills, about an hour's drive from school.

As I gaze out the window en route, I become captivated by a lake of turquoise, crop-covered hills of yellow and green, and a large cluster of trees of such a brilliant shade of emerald green that I get lost in them and just stare.

Wondering why I'm fixating on this color so much, I realize it's because it matches Berkeley's eyes exactly. Rattled, I abruptly shift my eyes to the car's interior.

Glancing at my fabulous shoes, I remember my still-ongoing shoe search, which gets me thinking about Berkeley again (*Damn!*), wanting to know how he's managing in the world that doesn't include me.

According to Phoebe, Hannah is no longer in the picture. I should refrain from reading Phoebe's updates, because they tend to move me backward. Although, as the school year draws to a close, I am interested in hearing what everyone's plans are for the fall.

I suspect Berkeley will be heading to college somewhere. I will be—per a decision I finalized just yesterday—on a scholarship pursuing a four-year bachelor's degree in fashion design. Thus, effective mid-August, I'll be living in a city I've fantasized about since my sixteenth birthday: New York City, home to more shoe stores than any other city, or so I assume.

For the record, I contemplated messaging Berkeley prior to making a final college commitment, but because he hasn't contacted me (not once since our New Year's Eye encounter), I deduced that he's not factoring me into his future, so why should I factor him into mine? Maybe Berkeley hasn't gotten in touch with me because he's moved on to another pretty face—as he used to do before dating me. *No matter.* His feet are planted in one place. Mine are planted in another. That's just the way it is. *Chin up. Onward ho.*

Shifting my gaze out the window again, I feel uneasy about the fact that Riverly Heights feels like another lifetime to me. Why and how did that happen?

Maybe it's because by leaving Riverly Heights at such a young age, the nostalgic area of my brain became underdeveloped. *No, that's absurd.*

Maybe it's because I've drifted so far away from home that I've lost my way back. *Plausible.*

Maybe it's because I want to miss my old life, but it hurts too much when I do. However, if that's the case, then why, this morning, did I put on the key necklace Berkeley gave me for my last birthday?

*Good question.*

Playing with it in my fingers and remembering Berkeley's words, "Unlock me anytime," I don a silly smile. *God, that guy has a way with words.*

Grasping my hand, Arno says, "We're almost there."

Remembering where I am, I respond, "Your countryside is the most beautiful I've seen."

"All the more reason for you to stay here, because as you know, there are some amazing design colleges in Italy, and you'd be well received by any of them."

But my response is only a smile, because I know my time here is done—at least for now.

After parking the car at the water's edge, Arno directs me to the center of a small footbridge and says, "This is the best place to watch the sunset."

"I can understand why," I reply, leaning over the railing, enabling the key necklace to slip out from under my sweater.

Seeing it, Arno says, "Is that new?"

I clutch it. "No."

"May I look at it?"

"Sure," I say, removing it and handing it to him.

Rotating it, he says, "Did someone give this to you?"

"Yes—Berkeley."

"Really?"

"Yeah."

"Why are you wearing it?"

"I don't know. I don't usually. I just felt like adding some glitz today, and it's the only necklace I have here."

"No other reason?"

I glare at him. "Don't make this a bigger deal than it is."

Holding the necklace up in the air, he says, "I've always found it best to release the past and live wholeheartedly in the moment."

"You're not the first to tell me that."

Without hesitation, Arno lets the necklace slip out of his fingers and into the water, exclaiming, "There! Missione compiuta."

As my eyes nearly pop out of their sockets, I shout, "Why did you do that?"

"Because I'm going to replace it with something different."

"But I don't want something different!"

Wrapping his arms around me, he says, "It's Tiffany. I'll buy you another one, exactly the same."

I pull away. "I can't believe you did that!"

"I'm sorry, Francie. I was just—"

"I want to go back—now!"

As he tries to calm me in an exasperated mix of Italian and English,

I stomp to the car and plunk my body down into the passenger seat. Staring out the window at a world far less appealing than it was an hour ago, my mind starts spinning, wondering how I'll ever tell Berkeley that I lost something so precious. "Thank God I've never told Arno about Berkeley's pen."

Joining me in the car, Arno says nothing, or if he does, I don't hear him.

He remains silent the entire time we drive back to Florence.

As we near the city, I look at my sandals and curse myself for wearing something so clearly not me.

When we arrive at the dorm building, I get out of the car and start walking.

Arno catches up to me and tries to hug me and further explain, but I push him away and dart to my room.

Inside, I throw my sandals toward the closet, exchange my sundress for sweats, flop onto my bed, and bury my face in a pillow.

For an hour or more, I sob, scream, overheat, and quiver. Regardless of the fact that Berkeley and I are no longer together, I'd intended to keep that necklace for the rest of my life. Now I can't.

Knowing I could never forgive the person who took one of my favorite sentimentalities away from me, I decide my time with Arno is over, done, *finito.*

Through newfound tears, I say, "*Grazie molto,* Arno, for trying to take control of my destiny."

Something I will never let anyone else do again.

# foot note thirty-three

THE CLOSING CEREMONIES FOR IDEA INCUBATRICE ARE ALREADY a week behind me. To briefly recap, the event took place beneath a purple-hued sky at twilight, in a public square filled with crisp white tents, surrounded by family and friends. The celebration ended with an elaborate Italian feast and a dance that ran until dawn.

I wore a form-fitting, short soft-gold off-the-shoulder dress and a pair of elegant cream-colored high-heeled sandals—shoes that contributed nothing to my me-shoe search for one simple reason: while wearing them, I felt terrible sadness that I was about to end another chapter in my life.

My family came to share the day with me. I didn't have an escort, although I did spend part of the evening restoring civility between Arno and me. After I profusely apologized for my irrational behavior at the lake, I even danced with him once. However, I cut the dance short when he whispered into my ear, "I'd give up my right hand to be the guy you wish you were dancing with tonight."

The day after the ceremony, I said warm good-byes to fellow classmates Rita, Inga, Azami, and Aurora, which was doable because we've vowed to Skype on a regular basis. I also endured an agonizing farewell with Allegra, which left me sobbing buckets because her animosity toward technology undoubtedly means we'll lose touch before summer's end. When I expressed this concern to her, she attempted to allay my concern by saying that fate takes care of such matters, that kindred spirits naturally gravitate to one another throughout their current lives and the next ones, and that bonds rooted in love will simply always be.

I didn't tell her I feel skeptical about her theory and know from experience that absence drives humongous wedges between people, because I didn't want to put a bigger damper on an already-heartbreaking day.

The day after that, I returned to Riverly Heights, wearing footwear altogether uncharacteristic for me: unassuming, soft-soled, nondescript skin-toned flats. My attraction to them stemmed from a desire to walk quietly into town, unnoticed.

I didn't inform any of my friends as to when I was arriving. Actually, I've been here for five days already and haven't contacted a single soul, immediate family excluded. But I will once I've fully decompressed.

I'll have to join the land of the living eventually, because I'll be starting my summer job in just over a week, returning to the same department store and same department as last year, with the title of assistant buyer. My boss and pal, Mark Baker, hired me to pick shoes for next season, which made my day, because it's proof I'm moving ahead in this world of mine. *Yay, me!*

The only hometown friend I've spoken to since returning is Phoebe, but only because she ran into Talula yesterday and learned I was here. She kept the phone call brief, partly because she's prepping for next week's final exams and partly because she was pissed I hadn't called her. Before hanging up, she mentioned the Riverly Heights High School twelfth-grade graduation formal, which is happening on Saturday night. Phoebe has an extra ticket, and she claimed it has my name on it.

Caught off guard by the notion of socializing on that scale, I responded, "Give me a day to think about it."

Huffing, Phoebe said, "As if I'm going to take no for an answer."

An hour later, Mrs. Bouchard, who is still the school's principal, sent me a message regarding the same thing, stating, "I heard from Talula that you're in town, and since I still consider you part of this graduating class, I want to see your smiling face in the crowd."

Cursing Talula a second time, I replied, "Thank you for thinking of me. I will let you know by tomorrow."

To be honest, I'm reluctant to show up at a Riverly Heights High School event, because sadly, I don't feel like a part of that class anymore. Besides, if I were to go, what would I wear? Certainly not the clothes I wore to my Idea Incubatrice graduation. Oh, the horror of being photographed wearing the same ensemble twice.

I would have to go shopping, which means I would have to leave the house, which means I might run into someone.

Am I ready to?

Maybe?

# foot note thirty-four

IN THE WEE HOURS OF MONDAY MORNING, WHEN AN EXTREME case of jet lag strikes with a vengeance, which is odd because I should be over it by now, I crawl out of bed, untwist my baby-doll pj's, and grab the first pair of footwear I find in the dark—a pair of tan riding boots.

Wandering downstairs, I discover the house to be deathly quiet and lit only by moonlight. I haven't a clue what time it is. Maybe two? Or three? Or four? Not that it matters. I don't start work until next week.

Midyawn, I glance out the front window and notice some familiar lilac bushes dangling in the breeze. When the sound of their cat-scratching on the windowpane makes me smile, I wander outside and inhale the scent, something I haven't done in years. At the same time, I allow the summer air to warm my skin and love that it feels nice, reminiscent, and homey.

Closing my eyes to concentrate on breathing more deeply, I hear the sound of distant footsteps rhythmically running. As the steady beat nears me, I fixate on the streetlight's glare and wait for someone to intersect it. The instant someone does, I snap to attention and stare, because I know the silhouette and because I think a wish just came true.

As my heart balloons in size, Berkeley sees me too. As if slamming into a brick wall, he halts and then veers in my direction. Shaking out his T-shirt, he steps onto the sidewalk in front of my house, lifts his hand to wave at me, and squints to see better in the darkness.

Smiling, I bellow, "Would you call this a late-night or an early morning endeavor?"

Audibly exhaling and stopping about ten feet from me, he answers, "I'm an insomniac these days, so I could go either way."

"Clearly, we share the same sleep pattern."

"Lucky for me."

As my veins heat up, I ask, "How are you?"

"Extremely sweaty. How are you?"

"Exhausted but antsy."

"It helps to run. But maybe not in those boots."

I look downward. "You don't like them?"

"Quite the contrary."

Grinning ear to ear, I sit down on the steps, wrap my arms around my bare knees, and say, "It's hard to see you in the dark. Maybe you could move a little closer?"

"No, I'm in desperate need of a shower, so I'm gonna stay right where I am."

I giggle. "Okay."

"Out of curiosity, what city are you calling home these days?"

Sighing, I respond, "Since my time in Florence is *finito*, I guess I'm a Riverly Heighter again."

"I'm glad you are."

"It feels nice to be."

After the two of us briefly catch up on what's happened over the last semester, minus a few details, and discuss where we're attending school in the fall (he has received a prestigious journalism scholarship to a school in Orange County, California), Berkeley says, "Let's go for breakfast."

"Sure. Maybe around eight?"

"Maybe now? I can sprint home, shower, and be back in fifteen minutes."

I sit erect. "You do know that it's like three a.m."

"Actually, it's four thirty, but what does it matter if our destination is a twenty-four-hour greasy spoon?"

"Don't you have an exam in the morning?"

"No. I have one in the afternoon."

Filling my lungs with fresh air, I say, "Okay, Mr. Mills. Go home, clean up, and then come back and get me."

"All right I will, as soon as you go inside the house."

"Why?"

"Because I'm unnerved by the idea of you standing outside in the dark wearing that."

"You worry too much."

"Only about you."

"Still?"

Shaking his head, he says, "Jesus, Francie! Always."

Caught off guard by his candor, I say nothing further. I just robotically stand up, turn around, and open the door.

As I'm about to step inside, he murmurs, "Keep wearing the boots."

Spinning around to face him, I flash an ear-to-ear smile and ask, "Any other requests?"

Smiling, he replies, "Yes, a pair of my socks."

"Fine," I say, thrilled to know he's aware that I'm still in possession of some.

Upstairs, feeling champagne-bubbly all over, I attempt to apply mascara and soft pink lipstick, but I experience difficulty because an unmanageable grin is distorting my face. Slipping into skinny jeans, a form-fitting T-shirt, and Berkeley's warm and fuzzy socks, I wonder if Berkeley will notice that my body has added a few curves. Wearing this, how could he not?

At least I don't have to deliberate on footwear. Stepping back into my boots, I say, "Keeping doing what you're doing," and then I skip down the steps, scribe a quick note for my parents, and gallop out the door.

Berkeley is already out there waiting for me, leaning against his car. The minute I move in his direction, he stands up straight and moves swiftly toward me.

With the house lights now on full beam, I'm able to see how amazing his showered face looks, and the skiff of facial hair he's sporting is definitely working. Certain I'm out of earshot, I say, "I can't believe I used to kiss this guy regularly."

Evidently, in the still of the night, Berkeley hears me, prompting him to reply, "Nothing's stopping you now."

As my face flushes, he pulls me into a familiar embrace and lifts me off of the ground. As our lips instinctively link together like high-powered magnets (*Holy crap, that feels sensational*), I instantly release every sad second I experienced during the last nine months.

Gently setting me back on the ground, Berkeley says, "Honestly, Francie, you get more beautiful every time I see you."

As I inhale the sweet scent of his freshly washed everything, I reply, "Good thing for that, or you might stop looking my way."

Hugging me again, he says, "Never. Not if I were blind."

Meandering hand in hand with me toward the car, Berkeley says, "You know, I haven't slept a minute since I heard you were back in town."

I don a silly grin. "You're kidding, I hope."

He opens my car door and smiles. "Actually, I'm not. In fact, I've dashed past your house every day for the last week, hoping to catch a glimpse of you."

I take my seat. "You numbskull. Why didn't you just ring the doorbell?"

"Because then you'd have known I was stalking you."

"You're no stalker."

"No, I'm more of a gawker."

"And a serious sweet talker."

"And a habitual jaywalker."

Giggling, I say, "I can't think of another one."

After kissing me on the forehead, he says, "Man, you have a spine-tingling, mind-blowing, flabbergasting effect on me."

Right then and there, I fall head-over-heels crazy for him again.

As we sit in a dimly lit diner booth at the Novia Grill, consuming enough calories to last a week, Berkeley becomes the third person to bring up the Riverly Heights graduation formal. "Why don't you come with me?"

"Don't you have a date by now?"

"Uh, no. I do not."

"Why not? You're so irresistible and charming and so bloody hot."

Blushing, he responds, "I haven't asked anyone."

"I bet you've been asked over and over and over."

He looks into my eyes. "I didn't see myself celebrating with anyone but you."

I raise an eyebrow. "Even though you broke up with me?"

Moving forward in his seat, he says, "Even though you let me break up with you."

After a pause, I ask, "So if I were to say yes, how would you introduce me? As a friend? Acquaintance? Former classmate? Playmate?"

"I like the sound of *playmate*, but I'm good with anything as long as it nets me time with you."

"Well, it's kind of short notice. What if I can't find a dress?"

"Then come in your grandfather's pajamas. I don't care. Just come."

Getting lost in his mesmerizing eyes, I answer, "Okay, I'll be your plus-one, on the condition I'm allowed to eat your dessert as well as my own."

"Condition accepted."

"Excellent," I reply, extending my hand for a shake, which he turns into a warm double-handed squeeze.

As we wander back to the car, Berkeley says, "I hope you realize that because I'm now totally consumed with seeing you on Saturday, I'm likely to botch every exam I take this week."

"Picture me in my grandpa's pajamas, and you should be fine."

"Picturing you in pajamas of any kind will not make me fine."

"Well then, I guess you're just going to have to tough it out."

"Thanks."

Slipping into Berkeley's passenger seat, I playfully say, "You know, Sunday is my eighteenth birthday!"

Grinning ear to ear, he says, "Oh, I know. Believe me. I know."

Noticing his eyes are glued to my face, I reply, "I wonder what I should wish for."

When the sultry expression on Berkeley's face makes my toes curl in my footwear, I ponder no further, because I know.

# foot note thirty-five

IN PREPARATION FOR THE RIVERLY HEIGHTS HIGH SCHOOL graduation dance, I went shopping with the no-longer-mad-at-me Phoebe and purchased a strapless beaded white dress, a pair of stunning clear plastic high-heeled sandals imprinted with tiny emerald-green leaves, and a pretty rhinestone ankle chain ideal for concealing the scar that's still a part of me. I'm labeling the shoe style the Surrealist, in honor of how my evening with Berkeley is bound to feel.

Berkeley is waiting with my mom in the living room when I make my way downstairs in the ensemble. As I enter his view, he jumps to his feet and exclaims, "Oh, wow! Look at you!"

"And look at you!" I respond, my face breaking out in an ear-to-ear grin at the sight of his stylish black tux, black shirt, and distinctive Burberry tie.

As my mom fiddles with my hair, I face Berkeley, adjust his collar, and say, "You do the dress-up thing really well."

He smiles. "I've pulled out all stops to try to hold your attention for an entire evening."

"No worries there."

Grabbing my left hand, he says, "I brought you something."

"Did you?"

"Uh-huh."

Retrieving a box from the table and removing its contents—an amazing fuchsia-colored orchid corsage adorned with silver satin ribbons—he asks, "What do you think?"

"I think I love it."

"Me too."

"Did you pick it out?"

Tying two of the ribbons into a perfect bow around my wrist, he explains, "Sort of."

"Sort of?"

He smiles. "I walked into the florist shop and requested something related to shoes, and when the florist suggested a slipper orchid, I replied, 'I'll take it.'"

"Nice!"

"It looks perfect on you," he murmurs in a tone so sensual that I want to say, "To hell with graduation; let's go to my room."

The heated moment is interrupted when my mom loudly clears her throat and offers safety tips related to after-graduation partying.

"Thanks, Mom," I reply.

"Make good choices," she adds.

I roll my eyes. "We always do."

Touching my arm, she says, "Given the significance of this evening, I see no reason why we can't relax your curfew for one night."

Suppressing a laugh, I ask, "Do I still have one?"

"Fine," she mumbles. "Do whatever you want until whenever you want. Just come home alive, because I've got a beautiful birthday cake waiting for you, and I intend to watch you eat it."

After offering her a warm hug, I grab my satchel containing my after-graduation attire and follow Berkeley out the front door.

Reaching the passenger door, he slips an arm around my waist and says, "Thanks again for doing this with me."

As I take my seat and respond, "I'm still over the moon that you asked me," he retrieves his phone and starts snapping pictures of me.

"What are you doing?"

"Documenting this occasion so I can look back fifty years from now and fall in love with you all over again."

"How about this?" I ask, twisting my face and crossing my eyes.

Shaking his head, he responds, "For as beautiful as you are, you wear quirky very well."

"Maybe I should add *quirky* to my list of me-shoe criteria."

"Maybe you should make it number one."

So I do.

Hopping into the driver's seat, Berkeley says, "I realize I might be getting ahead of myself by asking this, but I was wondering if you'd be interested in committing to some other stuff with me—for next week and the week after that and the week after that."

I shrug. "I don't have any other commitments on my agenda, so sure."

"Great. I'll look forward to us being committed."

"Suits me fine."

After a pause, he says, "Now you've got me wondering about the best way possible to stockpile four years' worth of you by the summer's end."

With eyes gleaming, I respond, "When you figure it out, let me know so I can do the same."

Inside the paper-flowered, helium-balloon-decorated banquet room at the Grand Hotel Riverly Heights, many eyes gawk when they view Berkeley and me walking hand in hand through the doors.

Taking a deep breath, I smile at some faces nearby and then tentatively move deeper into the space. When Berkeley gets distracted by some friends, including Sam and Pierce, I zigzag my way through the sea of familiar faces and extend some warm hellos. When my greetings are met with long-lasting hugs, I feel all of the apprehension I had about attending this event flitting away.

Reaching the dinner table is the highlight of my arrival, because it's where I encounter Berkeley's parents.

As each of them plants a kiss on my cheek, Sarah quietly says, "It's lovely to see you here, Francie. You've absolutely made Berkeley's day by joining him."

Blushing, I respond, "Don't tell Berkeley I admitted this, but he's pretty easy to say yes to."

She leans toward me and says, "I have no doubt he'd say the same about you," which makes me feel warm all over.

We're sharing our table of eight with Sam, Sam's parents, and Sam's date for this night only (because apparently there's a rotation): a long-limbed, extroverted, stunningly gorgeous redhead named Jillian.

Over the entire dinner hour, the eight of us enjoy a plentitude of conversation and delicious food. When dessert is served, Berkeley passes his crème brûlée toward me and says, "Your condition is fulfilled."

Resting my head on his shoulder, I respond, "Could you get any cuter?"

Unexpectedly, during the formal presentation, Mrs. Bouchard reads my name as an official graduate and asks me to accompany the other graduates on stage. As much as I'm honored by the gesture, I am a little unnerved, because Hannah follows me, and I end up shoulder to shoulder with the person I'd hoped to stay clear of this evening.

Even more awkward, Berkeley is called up next and ends up standing on the other side of her. The situation takes a turn for the better, though, when, as I'm walking offstage, Berkeley comes up from behind and surprises me with a giant hug.

During the dance segment of the program, Berkeley rarely leaves my side; he dotes on me, dances numerous dances with me, and makes me feel as if I'm the only other person in the room. Discreetly, he also makes sure I'm clear of Max, who only once tries to approach me, his dance request thwarted when Berkeley gets in his face and emphatically says, "Not a chance, pal."

Before the evening ends, I shake a leg with a few other guys I've known for years, including my old buddy Patrick. After having my pretty shoes stomped on numerous times, I return to Berkeley, show him my scuffs, and say, "Well, that was painful."

Taking my hands, he murmurs, "I'm pretty sure I've told you this before, Ms. Lanoo, but you need to be pickier with your dance dates."

Pressing my torso against his, I say, "Well, what's a respectable dancer like you doing for the rest of the evening?"

Speaking only with his eyes, he drags me out to the middle of the floor and doesn't let go of me for the next half hour.

When the final song starts playing—a sappy ballad—Berkeley pulls me into his arms and whispers into my ear, "I have this urge right now to pull the fire alarm and make everyone else flee."

"With what intention?"

"Whatever you'll allow."

"Since when do you need to involve the fire department to figure that out?"

Exhaling, he says, "It's no wonder every bone in my body aches when you're not around."

Though I'm tempted to pull the fire alarm myself, I know there's no need, because I'm sure I'm going to get as much alone time as I want with this guy all summer long.

After changing into casual wear (Berkeley in jeans, a T-shirt, and flip-flops and me in a flouncy black minidress, a jean jacket, and my fab clear shoes), we head to the graduation's after-party located in City Center Park, where we hang out under a big white tent that houses poker tables, a dance floor, a boxing arena, and a buffet of food.

Around three o'clock in the morning, Berkeley and I are itching to be alone, so we wander off to an uninhabited children's play area, where we sit side by side on a couple of swings.

Swaying and savoring the moment, I look at my feet and consider whether this style will be a contributor to my ongoing list of criteria. But I quickly dismiss the idea, because no one in her right mind cares about shoes when in the company of Berkeley Mills.

During a session of mutual gawking, Berkeley outstretches his hand, grabs mine, and announces, "Hey, Francie, happy birthday to you."

"Oh, I completely forgot!"

"I lost track of time too."

Exhaling, I say, "I wonder what my first act as an official adult should be."

"It should be to get your adult ass over here, because I've got something in my pocket for you."

I mosey toward him. "You do?"

"I do." After shifting in his seat, he says, "Hop on. I'll give you a ride."

"Happily," I say, straddling Berkeley's lap and fidgeting with my dress so that I don't flash my adult ass to the world.

Setting the swing in motion, he smiles and offers me his closed fist.

Using my fingers to peel his fingers open, I discover a coiled string and ask, "What's this?"

"It's the wristband I made for you."

"Oh, one of your macramé projects!"

"It's the only one."

"Lucky me."

"I spent an entire month working on it and then quit doing macramé altogether."

Examining its braided intricacy and placing it on my wrist next to my orchid, I say, "Berkeley, this is beautiful, and it reminds me of my hammock."

Tying the loose ends into another perfect bow, he notes, "I think it's hippie-like and down to earth."

"I wonder if it'll keep me grounded."

"You're doing all right on your own."

"I wonder if it will shrink if it gets wet."

"Probably, so don't shower with it."

"I wonder if it will make me itch."

"If it does, then call me immediately, and I'll rush over to commence scratching."

As I giggle, he pulls me close and rests his chin on top of my head.

Burying my face in his chest, I say, "I'm sorry I didn't call you on your birthday. I wanted to, but I felt weird about it."

"It's okay. There'll be other birthdays."

"But I missed out on you becoming a bona fide fully grown-up, smokin'-hot adult."

He laughs. "Anytime you're interested in seeing how manly I now am, I'd be happy to show you."

As I look up and give him an eye roll, he says, "Hey, I take no responsibility for the thoughts that enter my head when you're this close to me."

"Should I go back to my own swing?"

"No, don't you dare! I've waited way too long for this."

"Me too," I note, and I plant a warm kiss on his lips.

When he kisses me back in a smooth-as-melted-chocolate way, I allow my shoes to drop into the sand and the rest of me to get caught up in whatever Berkeley's got going on in his head. Because why would I not?

Only when I hear rustling in some nearby bushes do I remember there's a crowd of people only fifty feet away. Sitting up straight, I say out of the blue, "I don't know why, but I much prefer a hammock to a swing."

Placing his hands on my hips, Berkeley replies, "I know why."

"Why?"

"Because it allows for a whole lot more than swinging."

Giggling, I put my mouth to his ear and say, "You've got the best answers for everything."

Smoothing my hair, he replies, "You inspire them."

Near dawn, Berkeley nudges me awake and says, "I should take you home."

Though my eyelids struggle to lift, I reply, "But I'm not tired."

Sweeping the hair away from my eyes, he responds, "Come on, party girl. You've got a big day ahead of you."

"Speaking of, I'd like to put in a request that you spend the next twenty-four hours in a row with me."

Helping me to my feet and retrieving my shoes, he says, "Yeah, you could twist my arm on that."

"Yay! My birthday wish has been granted."

Flashing me a heartwarming smile, he flips me onto his back for the journey to my house.

An hour later, as Berkeley eases me onto the front steps, I murmur, "Care to indulge in a celebratory birthday breakfast?"

Standing face-to-face with me, as he's one step lower, he replies, "I will if you let me make you a stack of pancakes."

Throwing my arms around his neck, I sleepily ask, "Will you put a candle on top?"

Batting his eyelashes, he responds, "I will if you'll let me light your fire."

Forcing my eyes open, I say, "God, I've missed you."

"May I take that as a yes?"

"You may."

Hip to hip, we share cooking duties, dance to some quiet music, and eat a conversation-filled breakfast at the kitchen island. After cleanup, we retire to my beloved backyard hammock, now hidden from the world by an overgrowth of greenery, and get cozy.

As a mix of swirling breezes and thick blankets enwrap us, I do learn exactly how manly Berkeley now is, and I direct all thoughts of the future far from my mind. I don't care that in August, one of us is heading west and one of us is heading east. I do not care that we will do so for four years. Because today—using Berkeley's line from two summers ago—what matters most to me I'm looking at.

# foot note thirty-six

IT'S THE LAST EVENING I'LL BE SPENDING WITH BERKELEY BEFORE we head our separate ways for college, and the thought of what I'm about to give up—the guitar serenading, the midnight pool parties for two, the wee-hours-of-the-morning pancake eating, the goofball photo taking, the other stuff—has me on the brink of tears. *Egad. How will I ever endure four years apart from this guy? Acupuncture for the pain? Hypnosis to suppress the memories? Macramé as a distraction?*

No, the void left in Berkeley's wake is impossible to fill, something I've verified from experience.

As he and I linger in the hammock one last time, I say, "In case you've forgotten, I'm still in possession of your pen."

"I haven't forgotten."

"Maybe I should give it back to you."

"Maybe I don't want it back."

"Okay, I will keep it. But be sure to let me know the minute you need it."

"I will."

Furrowing my brow, I say, "I still have to pack tonight."

"Me too."

"Are you taking your guitar and the music books I once gave you?"

"Yes, I am."

I smile. "Good."

"Out of curiosity, how many pairs of shoes are you hauling to New York?"

"Not enough."

"Are you still on the hunt for the Francie Lanoo?"

"I am, and I'm glad you brought that up, because I'm curious— have you ever thought about what my me shoe should look like?"

He tightens his hold of me. "Actually, I have."

"You have?"

"Yeah."

I grin. "Well then, smarty-pants, put it into words."

After a pause, he says, "First of all, to facilitate that irresistible strut of yours, I think it needs a heel that's about three inches high."

"Agreed, because my five-foot-four height needs all the help it can get."

"And because I know you'll wear it often, it needs to be comfortable and painless, like you're walking on marshmallows."

"Definitely a key to my overall well-being."

"Of course, it has to be in a color that looks fantastic on you, which I would peg as fuchsia—just like the corsage I gave you."

My senses perk up. "Carry on."

"Let's see. I imagine it will have a secure ankle strap so you're ready for anything, like running away from your many pursuers."

"And so I can hide my scar."

He furrows his brow. "That mark is barely noticeable."

"I can still see it."

Grabbing my flawed foot, he says, "I love that it's there."

"Why?"

"Because it's proof that you're actually human and not the otherworldly goddess that the male gender views you as."

I giggle. "That is so ridiculously untrue."

"It's so ridiculously true."

"Moving on."

He smiles. "Okay. Let's see. I like the idea of an open toe, to show your always-sexy, always-painted toenails."

"Very important."

"And I like the idea of a sparkle feature, something starry."

"To remind me of you."

"And to complement the fact that you shine inside and out."

"What a sweet thing to say!"

"Thanks."

"Is there more?"

"Yes, I think the shoe needs to be a little on the quirky side and, at the same time, sweet and easygoing."

I look him in the eyes. "Your attention to detail is pretty impressive. I think you've missed your calling."

He shakes his head. "No, I'm only gonna talk about shoes once and only because you asked me to."

"Then I'll consider myself fortunate."

Hugging me, he adds, "The shoe definitely needs to embrace being cute as a button, because it inherently is and always will be."

I giggle. "Even when it's old?"

"Even when, which leads to the last point: it needs to be timeless, so you'll love it forever."

"I like that idea."

"I knew you would."

Edging my head nearer to his, I say, "So does this shoe have a name? Because I am going to need one for reference."

His eyes light up. "Well, that's the easy part. It's called the Incomparable, after you."

As the touching words make my heart flutter, I look at Berkeley with moist eyes, prop myself up on my elbows, and kiss him big-time.

Keeping my lips near his, I say, "You are the most-amazing person I have ever known."

He sweeps the hair from my face. "Why, because I'm able to shoe speak?"

"Yes, among about a thousand other things, but right now because you just planted in my head the clearest image I've ever had of my ideal shoe."

"Well, I have had three years to put that shoe together."

My brow furrows. "So have I, but I've never made it feel real."

"Which proves something I've long suspected."

"What?"

"That I know what's best for you better than you do."

Knowing Berkeley isn't just talking about shoes, I stare deeply into his eyes and say, "I suppose that means I should consult with you before making any rash purchasing decisions."

Donning a poignant gaze, he replies, "No, I'm pretty sure the minute you decide what you want, you'll grab it and hang on for dear life."

"I guess I'd be crazy not to, right?"

After parting his lips to say something but exhaling instead, Berkeley gives me a hug and adds, "I can only imagine how many shoes you'll buy while living in New York."

"Well, now that I know exactly what I'm looking for, I expect my purchases will be fewer and more discerning. Thank you again for that."

He helps me out of the hammock. "My pleasure."

As we wander hand in hand through the side gate toward the street, Berkeley turns to face me, takes hold of my shoulders, and sweetly says, "Have fun in your new world."

Though I want to ask, "What will happen with us, and are we going to date other people, and should we keep in touch?" I'm unable, because my throat is clenching as if it's in a vice. Instead, I weakly whisper, "You too."

Half smiling, he says, "Don't miss me too much."

Suppressing tears, I reply, "I can if I want to."

Seemingly hesitant to walk away, Berkeley looks at me with softened eyes and says, "When I eventually see you on the flip side of all this, I hope you look at me the same way you are right now."

Unable to hold back the tears, I quiver and mumble, "I will if you will."

Giving me a giant bear hug, he whispers into my ear, "You know I will."

We seal our parting with the most passionate of kisses, followed by a wordless hand wave that turns me into a blithering sob machine. Then I watch the guy I can't live without walk away for what could be as short as four years or as long as forever.

With the heaviest heart, I wander inside the house, trudge up the stairs to my bedroom, and collapse onto the bed. As I rehash the last hour and conclude that I must be crazy to allow an entire continent to come between Berkeley and me, I locate Berkeley's pen and clutch it in my hand. Admiring it, I tie the picnic-blanket string he once gave me into a perfect bow around the middle of it and take solace in the fact that I'll have to see Berkeley at least one more time to return this to him. It is, after all, his.

# foot note thirty-seven

IT HAS ALREADY DIPPED BELOW FREEZING MORE THAN ONCE THIS week, which is odd for late September in New York, much to my chagrin. To make matters worse, the forecast is showing no signs of improvement anytime soon, which means I'll be saying hello to socks, stockings, and an assortment of closed-toe footwear. Though it saddens me to see my favorite season departing, I take solace in knowing that for the next many months, my feet will be coddled.

Today, to check out the streets of my current hood, Greenwich Village, I'm wearing jeans, a turtleneck, a suede blazer, and a pair of low-heeled black patent booties. Because my current shoes look nothing like the ones Berkeley described, I'll be traipsing around in them with zero visions of a footwear revelation.

Though I've only been in New York for five weeks, I already love my new surroundings: late-night diners, specialty tea vendors, art galleries, Broadway performances, tree-filled parks, and the most incredibly diverse collection of human beings imaginable. Every single day, I thank the stars that my life path has brought me here. Every single day, I come to the realization that I'm meant to be here at this point in my life.

My current living space is on the main floor of a college dorm;

the best description for it would be a sardine can. It has only basic furniture—a decades-old single bed (made bearable with my own white bedding), a small metal desk, a three-drawer dresser, and a ragged bookshelf. The lone window, positioned at the end of my bed, opens, but it's so small that even someone my size would have difficulty fleeing a fire through it. I've covered one wall with a collection of my own artwork; I've covered the other three with collages of patterned paper squares (my cheap version of wallpaper). On a large tackboard above the desk, I've added my traditional photo display, this year's version a collection of the people I expect to miss most. Berkeley is on it, in a photo taken at the Riverly Heights graduation dance, where he looked beyond awesome. However, the photo of Berkeley and me taken before I left for Italy is not there, but I remain ever hopeful Berkeley will eventually send it to me. Lord knows I've reminded him enough times.

The dorm rooms nearest to mine are home to my latest collection of gal pals: Pella, a fellow fashion-design major who is drop-dead gorgeous, has a pixie cut and sharp features, is innovative with wardrobe (putting together ensembles I would never think to), and is selfless enough to share her magical talent with the rest of us; Reese, an economics major who is off-the-charts intelligent and practical, is a little nerdy, wears heavy eyeglasses, has blunt brown hair, and hasn't used a descriptive word in all the time I've known her; Suzy, a political-science major who is a heavyset brunette, is a lover of business suits, is masterfully organized, and always offers practical tips of every possible variety; and Victoria, another fashion-design major, who's tall, blonde, pretty, bubbly, and always out there (which the rest of us tease her about) and who attracts all of the cute boys to our group when we go out.

We call each other flatmates (a term selected by Pella, who's Welsh), and we've labeled our dorm zone Shangri-la (a term chosen by Victoria, who regularly fantasizes about time-traveling back to the hippie sixties, often dressing for the excursion just in case).

Our five dorm rooms share a small kitchen, a tiny TV room, and a bathroom, which, over time, we hope to stop fighting over.

For the most part, the five of us get along famously; however, occasionally, a clash breaks out, proving that right-brainers are on a totally different wavelength from left-brainers. For example, is it imperative that we all eat dinner together every evening at precisely seven o'clock? Is it always necessary to hang coats on designated hooks? Does food in the cupboard need to be labeled with the purchaser's name?

The upside of being surrounded by four other people in a close-knit group is that I'm never lonely, and I'm rarely in a position to long for what I'm missing, which explains why I've not had any form of contact with Berkeley since the day I left town. I'm okay with that, because if I've learned anything during my last two years of being apart from him, it's that I'm less achy all over when I suspend the reality that he exists in this world.

Once in a while, though, I allow myself a momentary indulgence by taking a quick peek at his social-network links. However, each time I notice that his college life is as fun-filled as mine is, I shut down the electronics and move on to something else, especially when I see numerous tagged photographs of Berkeley alongside a petite, brown-haired, brown-eyed, smiling girl (*Hey, who does that sound like?*), whom Berkeley is definitely involved with—the sight of her hands all over him is a dead giveaway.

I hate that he and I parted ways on such an ambiguous note. I also hate that we're so comfortably good at it. Furthermore, I resent the fact that Berkeley prefers us this way—unlinked whenever we're untouchable. What's that about?

Sadly, I have no idea when I'll enjoy Berkeley's company next. I won't see him during the Christmas season, because I'm meeting my family in the Caribbean for two weeks of fun in the sun. I'm sad about spending my first holiday season away from Riverly Heights, especially since I feel such a strong association with it and the holidays, but on the flip side, I'm relieved to be avoiding snow (and a possible run-in with that monster Max).

Heading out the door with Pella and Victoria, I sigh at the thought of what it's going to feel like to get my college semester under my belt (never have I worked such long hours), get on a plane, head to a beach, and slip into a pretty swimsuit and a pair of lightweight sandals, as I do in the summer.

*Summer. Why does it feel a world away?*

# foot note thirty-eight

AT A RECENT VALENTINE'S DAY PARTY, ONE THAT I OPTED OUT OF because I was hung up on the idea of cruising as a single on the most-duo-oriented night of the year, my gal pal Pella met some guy named Garner Vale, whom she believes is a perfect match for me.

From what she's told me, he's a friend of a friend of a friend; he's edgy, quick witted, cool, and attractive in a dangerous kind of way; he's the lead singer of an alternative-rock band called Ill-Mannered Mimes; he's majoring in visual art at a nearby community college; and apparently, he's a portrait painter who prefers to work in the wee hours of the night with little or no clothes on.

In response to that information, I decide that Pella's belief in Garner's and my compatibility must be based on the premise that opposites attract, because I have never, nor will I ever, paint with little or no clothes on.

I've agreed to meet him this evening at a party and will be doing so with low expectations, because over the past few months, Pella has tried to sell me on various other guys, all with zero success.

Adding to my hesitation, I've not been in the company of a guy romantically, emotionally, or physically for more than seven months, and I'm feeling like a novice all over again. How do I behave? What do I say? What shoes will I feel most like myself in?

More important, why am I getting stressed out about this, when I have no free time to dedicate to a relationship?

The clock is ticking. Pella is dragging me out the door shortly. It's time to make some decisions. What would a musician find interesting? Probably not the scraggly jeans, plain white T-shirt, and comfortable flats I have on now, which have become my mainstay.

How about black skinny jeans, a black T-shirt, and a fitted black leather jacket? For a touch of color, I'll add a bold ruby-red shoulder bag, and for the icing on the cake, I'll put on a pair of high-heeled black boots I found in a vintage clothing store a few weeks ago. They intrigued me because the salesperson told me they once belonged to a well-known celebrity who wore them exclusively during her clubbing days back in the 1970s. Apparently, if they could talk, they'd have enough material to write a scandalous novel.

Lastly, I consider whether or not to wear Berkeley's macramé wristband, which I've faithfully tied onto my arm every day since receiving it. Staring at it, I decide that it kind of clashes with my current outfit, so I stash it in the dresser drawer and heed Pella's hollering.

Taking one last look at myself in the small mirror on the wall, I hope I look okay. Or not. I have no idea. *Whatever. Egad, I'm twiddling my fingers.* "Stop it, Francie. Just go to the party."

Meandering around the well-attended, sensory-overloaded soiree, I spot the guy I've been deployed to meet long before formal introductions are made. Pella's adjectives were correct: he's about six feet tall; he's good looking in a bad-boy kind of way; he has long, straight light brown hair that's draped across his face; he speaks expressively with his hands; and his aura oozes hotness.

Looking more closely, I notice he's wearing exactly what I would expect a guy like him to wear: black jeans, a black T-shirt, a black leather coat, and black motorcycle boots. As I'm thinking that if not for his many rings, chains, and earrings, he and I could be bookends, Pella grabs my hand and leads me toward him, each of us watching the other intently as the gap between us decreases.

Crookedly smiling, he says, "Clearly, we have the same stylist."

"Except she forgot your handbag," I say, flipping mine forward.

"Damn! That woman is fired!" he exclaims. Extending his hand toward me, he says, "Hi, I'm Garner Vale."

I take his grip. "It's nice to meet you. I'm Francie Lanoo."

Holding my hand for many seconds, he notes, "I've heard a lot about you, Francie Lanoo."

"Oh?"

"Yeah, our mutual friends have been filling me in on all kinds of fascinating stuff."

Darting a stern look at Pella, I reply, "Beware the risks of secondhand information."

Offering up a sexy grin, he says, "I like risks."

I spend the next half hour observing Garner as he interacts with the people around us. He's talkative, smooth, funny, and sometimes self-deprecating, which I find endearing.

Later in the evening, evidently noticing me watching him, he moves torso to torso with me, flashes me a suggestive glance, and asks out of the blue, "Wanna scram with me?"

Surprised to feel my body warming all over, I answer, "Yes."

"I was hoping you'd say that," he says, taking my hand.

As we're about to leave, several of the studs on my retro-party-girl boots pop off and roll around on the floor.

Stepping on a few and nearly taking a tumble, I scowl and curse them for misbehaving. But then I look at how fantastic and exciting they are and whisper, "Lighten up, Francie, and allow yourself the occasional thrill."

# foot note thirty-nine

I DID IT! I MADE IT THROUGH MY FIRST YEAR OF COLLEGE WITHOUT crashing and burning. Yahoo! And I did it rather well, scoring excellent grades, designing outfits I would definitely wear if they weren't only on paper, and squeezing in some all-night parties, further exploration of this amazing city, and dates with my always-entertaining boyfriend, Garner.

One evening spent with him, which I fully expected to be a one-night stand, has turned into a three-month-long relationship and, in all likelihood, will extend for another three now that I've decided to stay in New York for the entire summer break. How nice it's going to be for me to not have to pack up and move my belongings, something I haven't had the luxury of since the end of tenth grade when I first left Riverly Heights.

On a related note, I heard a few weeks ago (via Phoebe) that Berkeley isn't going home for the summer either, which came as a shock because I always assumed he had no choice but to return annually for summer employment at the *Tribunal*. I wonder, *Is Berkeley's absence the bigger reason I decided not to spend the summer there?*

No, I'm sure it's not. That would be silly.

I want to spend the summer in New York because it's the best time of the year to be here.

Aside from spending my free time lazing around on sun-drenched café patios, checking out new galleries, and becoming another subject in one of Garner's loud and colorful portraits, I'll be back in the lines of the employed, selling shoes at a department store—the flagship location of the same chain I worked for in Riverly Heights.

Mark Baker arranged the position shortly after I regretfully declined an offer to work another summer under his helm. To appease him when he said he'd miss our lunchtime shoe conversations, I promised to keep in touch by regularly sending him photos of all of the fantastic men's shoe styles exclusive to the NYC store that I could easily courier to him in Riverly Heights—an offer that thrilled him to no end.

The NYC shoe department is about ten times the size of the Riverly Heights one, and it nearly blew my mind when I first walked through it. Pumps, stilettos, flats, designer sneakers—basically, if it exists out there, it's on display in the store. One afternoon, I even came across a shoe that nearly satisfied my me-shoe criteria (a well-heeled, cute-as-a-button, open-toed, sparkly shoe with a touch of quirkiness), but unfortunately, it was lavender, not fuchsia. On the upside, the sight of it instilled a renewed belief that my ideal shoe is out there somewhere, which might explain why, when customers are few, I frantically scour the shelves in the name of my quest.

While doing so yesterday, I came across a pair of hot-off-the-press shoes that, for the first time in years, made me audibly gasp: pearl-encrusted, low-heeled matte-nickel leather sandals. Though the price tag made me gasp too (and is the reason I'm working extra hours whenever possible, to cover the cost), I rationalized it as an indulgent reward for a year's worth of hard work.

They're not my me shoe, but they're serving as good filler until the real deal presents itself.

The first occasion for my summer footwear is a ride-along with Garner's band, Ill-Mannered Mimes, when they play City Center Park in Riverly Heights, one of several stops on their summer-long tour. How cool is that? My boyfriend's band is doing a gig in my hometown.

We'll be traveling on a tour bus, which I've done a couple of times already this summer on short-haul gigs. Though the trek to Riverly Heights will require an overnight that'll have me sleeping vertically in a seat, at least when I arrive, I'll have an opportunity to visit with my family, hang out in some of my old haunts, and attend the show with some of my old friends. As a bonus, my family and friends will finally meet the new fabulous guy in my life.

Speaking of fabulous guys, I heard from Phoebe that Berkeley and his girlfriend of nearly a year (the one from the online photographs) might also be traveling to Riverly Heights this summer. I hope they're not in town at the same time as Garner and me, because that could prove to be awkward.

Pondering whether or not she and Berkeley are seriously involved, I imagine the stuff Berkeley might do with her while in town: introduce her to his family and our friends, show her some of the city's hot spots, and take her to a diner for pancakes. Maybe he'll even hoist her into an oak tree or take her for a dip under a waterfall and, afterward, piggyback her wherever she wants to go.

Feeling a lump forming in my throat, I give my head a shake and tell myself to be happy that Berkeley's making the most of his time in the California sunshine and not spending his days in a dark room, pining over me.

Who am I kidding? Of course I'd rather he be pining over me.

# foot note forty

I've come to grips with the fact that the band-on-tour lifestyle is a necessary means to gain notoriety, but I will never comprehend the associated groupie thing and why minimally clad female fans camp out at venues and hotels and flaunt their willingness to do anything. As I observe many of them here in City Center Park, wandering toward the stage for the Ill-Mannered Mimes' sold-out show, I give what I'm wearing—a black mesh teddy, supershort shorts, and my summer sandals—a quick once-over and think, *Jesus, Francie, you're one to talk.*

Alongside Brigitte, Talula, Phoebe, Beatrice, Silvia, and Patrick, I make my way toward the front-row seats that are reserved for us, and along the way, I notice a twentysomething girl at the end of the row, wearing the same footwear as me. Smirking and giggling, realizing the sandals are not as precious as I first thought, I arrive at my seat and take them off.

What a fabulous night it is for an outdoor concert. The air is warm, the winds are calm, the sky is clear, and the crowd is fired up. Though Garner's band is little more than a blip on the world-music-scene's radar, their show is a big deal for a place the size of Riverly Heights. No doubt, a good time is in store for all.

As the band takes the stage and opens with their first song, "Tattoo You," I grin and sing the words, which is easy for me to do, because I was in the room when Garner penned them. Scanning the crowd, I notice many girls in the audience already ogling Garner, throwing personal stuff at him, and flashing their body parts at him to see if he takes the bait. This is the tenth time I've sat in attendance at one of the band's shows, so I downplay the antics by reminding myself that on several occasions, Garner has whispered into my ear, "You're the only one who's ever seen the inside of the tour bus." He further reiterates this reassurance by catching sight of me in the crowd and directing his most-suggestive lyrics my way.

After the band completes its encore, my guests and I head in the direction of a large white tent a short distance from the stage, where an after-party is already in progress. While crossing the park's open green space, I have a flashback to a football scrimmage I once watched here, and I say to the gang, "I'll catch up in a couple of minutes, okay? I'm just going to check something out."

Nodding, Phoebe replies, "We'll wait for you by the picnic tables. Okay?"

"Sounds good."

Wandering to the children's play area and noticing the gorgeous stars twinkling above me, I become giddy, hop onto a swing, and, after several minutes of swaying back and forth, drift away for some serious daydreaming. As a warm wind graces my face, I feel a gentle hand gripping my shoulder. Assuming that it's Garner, I turn around and say, "Hi."

When I instead see Berkeley—*It's Berkeley?*—my pulse goes erratic, and I exclaim, "Wow! Hey! Hi!"

Smiling hotly (*Oh my, I wish he hadn't, because now I'm buzzing all over*), he replies, "Hey, you."

Standing up and moving toward him for a hug, I say, "Oh my God, it's so good to see you!"

"Same," he says, pulling back and sliding his hands onto my hips.

Admiring his tan, his slightly more-mature face, and the rest of his gorgeousness, I say, "Holy crap, you wear California well."

"Not as well as you wear New York."

I dip my head to the side. "I can't believe it's been almost a year since we've talked. Time is flying."

"I guess that means we're having fun?"

"Yeah."

Taking my hand and leading us toward a streetlamp, he eyes me up and down and says, "That is some outfit you're wearing."

"What? Too trendy? Too bold? Too shiny?"

"Too alluring—for me."

Giggling, I say, "God, I've missed you."

"And I you, which is why I'm so happy I was able to find you in the crowd."

"A lucky coincidence?"

"Or maybe it's because your mom is better than you at staying in touch."

"She's a conspirator, that one."

"I'm not complaining."

Facing me and sweeping the hair out of my eyes, he says, "The band sounded great tonight."

"Yeah, they're getting better and better all the time."

"I noticed the lead singer could not take his eyes off of you."

Realizing my mother has really been keeping in touch, I shake my head and say, "Onstage antics."

"Sure."

After taking a deep breath, I say, "So tell me everything about your world. How did school go this past year? Are you enjoying California? Where are you working this summer?"

Berkeley exhales. "Let's see. California is nice, almost always sunny and laid back. School is great, but the work is challenging. Lots of sleepless nights."

"I can relate."

"At the beginning of second semester, I realized I had less interest in running a newspaper and more interest in contributing to one, so I changed my major to photo journalism."

"That suits you so much better."

"I knew you'd say that."

"That's because I know you well too."

Smiling, he adds, "I'm spending the summer working at a newspaper in LA, which is hectic and mind-boggling but very educational."

"Great to hear. And how's your guitar playing coming along?"

"Actually, I haven't had any time for it."

"Why?"

He shrugs. "I've just been too preoccupied. And I've kind of lost my inspiration."

I touch his arm. "Don't worry. You'll find it again."

"I hope so."

"And your parents? How are they?"

"They're great, although my dad was disappointed when I told him I'd be spending the summer working for another newspaper."

"That's understandable."

"I think his angst has to do with the fact that he despises the conglomerates of the media industry, especially the one I'm working for, and is convinced they're the root of all evil, the end of journalistic integrity, and the instigator of biased news reporting."

"I sense you disagree."

"No, I just understand that the industry is evolving."

I dip my head to the side. "I bet your dad's disdain has more to do with the fact that he and your mom miss you so much it hurts."

"Yeah. Missing someone sucks."

As a lump forms in my throat, I quit babbling and simply nod.

Exhaling, Berkeley asks, "So what's new in your world?"

"Lots! Let me see. Fashion school is a truckload of work."

As I elaborate and start flinging my hands in the air, Berkeley trails my left wrist, grasps it, and says, "That's new."

I look. "Oh yeah, my tiny fuchsia orchid tattoo."

"When did that come about?"

"On my last birthday, after too many tequila shots."

"I hope the tequila numbed the pain."

"It did, but it also made the entire experience one big blur, except for the fact that the leather-clad tattooist's name was Hog."

"It looks great on you and suits you."

I run a finger over it. "Yeah, although I expect that when I'm eighty, it'll look as wilted as me."

"You've got nothing to worry about."

"Wait and see."

"I'm counting on it."

From seemingly out of nowhere, a girl approaches and says, "Berkeley, I've been looking all over for you."

Turning to face her, Berkeley says, "Hey, Shoshanna, I was just catching up with Francie. Let me introduce you."

"Sure."

As her face breaks out in a smile—and verifies she's the one from the photographs—I swallow hard and say, "Hey, Shoshanna. I'm Francie. It's a pleasure to meet you."

"It's nice to meet you too."

Watching her reach for Berkeley's hand, I experience the same burning in my chest as I did the last time I saw Berkeley with someone else. *Damn, why does that still happen?* As I force myself to look away, I feel a pair of strong arms wrap around me from behind.

Resting his chin on my shoulder, Garner says, "Hey, gorgeous!"

In jest, I reply, "Excuse me. Do I know you?"

After spinning me around and planting a giant kiss on my lips, he responds, "Allow me to introduce myself: I'm the guy who's madly in love with you."

As I'm shaking my head, Garner looks over and asks, "Who are your friends, France?"

"Shoshanna and Berkeley."

Exchanging handshakes with them, Garner says, "Hey, dude. I've heard a lot about you, that you and France once had a thing going on."

With pursed lips, Berkeley responds, "Yeah, we did."

Slapping Berkeley on the upper arm, Garner says, "Well, I'm glad you two moved on, because your loss is my gain."

Watching Berkeley's face sour—which might be because he's in the company of his girlfriend or because he has never seen me with someone else—I downplay Garner's cockiness by shaking my head and flashing Berkeley an ignore-this-guy look.

The gesture helps, because Berkeley gives me a look with his big green eyes that implies Garner is just marking his claim.

Turning to Garner, Shoshanna excitedly says, "Hey! Great performance tonight."

Smiling, he replies, "Glad you enjoyed it."

As the two of them start discussing some onstage details, Berkeley edges me away and asks, "How long are you in town?'

"I'm leaving tomorrow."

"Oh! Your mom said you'd be here all week."

"I planned to be, but then I got scheduled to work, so I had to cut my trip short."

After taking a chest-heaving breath, he says, "That seriously sucks because I was really hoping you and I would find some time to hang out."

"With or without our respective dates?"

Taking a step toward me, he replies, "Ms. Lanoo, I thought you'd know by now that whenever you're around, my sense of propriety automatically rejigs to you."

Tipping my head, I respond, "Mine too, with you. I wonder why."

Before Berkeley responds, Shoshanna is at his side, saying, "It's late, Berkeley. We should get going."

Sauntering to my side, Garner says, "Let's blast too, France. I could use a cold beer."

"Sure," I murmur, waving good-bye.

Waving back, Berkeley says, "By the way, *France*, your footwear choice is a departure from anything I've seen you wear before."

Grinning ear to ear and feeling a strong urge to grab hold of Berkeley's hand and run away like bandits, I reply, "Exactly the reason why, by tomorrow, they'll belong to Talula."

The next day, staring at my nondescript flip-flopped feet while seated next to Garner on the bus, I take a minute to rehash the encounter I had with Berkeley. Running my hands through my hair, I whisper, "I should have stayed home longer."

Lost in thought, I wonder whether or not there are any good fashion schools near Berkeley that would accept me as a transfer student. Although, moving west wouldn't guarantee that Berkeley and I would pick up where we'd left off. Glancing at Garner as he's penning a new song, I say, "No, stay in New York. It's good for you."

Turning to face me, Garner says, "Did you say something, babe?"

"No, I'm just admiring the Riverly Heights skyline."

He scoffs. "Does it have one?"

I sigh. "Yes. A really sweet one."

Feeling exhausted, I slip my hand away from his, pull my knees up to my chest, and close my eyes for a snooze. At that moment, I accept that despite the fact that I'm in a reasonably happy relationship with a guy I share a zip code with, I am, and only ever will be, in love with Berkeley Mills.

So what do I do about that?

Nothing, because my sole priority right now is to stay focused on my studies so I graduate. To ensure that I keep all distractions at bay, I intend to put all matters of the heart on hold—including shoes—until I'm gripping a college diploma in my hand.

# foot note forty-one

DURING THE LAST TWO AND HALF YEARS, I'VE BEEN SO INUNDATED with college studies that I've completely lost track of every aspect of my existence that doesn't involve being graded. A mere three activities fill my days: schoolwork, usually into the wee hours of the night; the occasional meal, which is purely about keeping my energy level up; and sleep, which I wouldn't worry about if my body didn't make such a fuss when deprived of it. Only a half semester left to go before I reach the finish line. It looks as if I'll make it.

So will my fellow fashionistas Victoria and Pella, whom I currently coexist with in a warehouse apartment with raw brick walls (plastered in my own insomnia-induced large painted canvases), expanses of hardwood floors (great for laying out fabric and clothes patterns), beds tucked away in the corners (concealed with personalized room-divider screens), and entertaining street noise (which travels freely through the many thin-paned windows).

Currently, we're each working on our final project: a collection of elegant evening-gown designs, one of which we are required to fabricate as our graduation dance dress. Once the assignment is complete, I intend to rejoice by searching for the most-outstanding pair of shoes in existence, which will serve as my graduation dance shoes. If the stars align, that selection will also be my me shoe—because how apropos would it be to strut into the banquet room while wearing something that perfectly reflects the all-grown-up Francie Lanoo?

By the way, I have no visions of doing that strutting on the arm of Garner Vale. Not long after his band's concert in Riverly Heights, I learned his numerous groupies *were* getting invited to see the inside of his tour bus, so I moved on. Or maybe that means he moved on—repeatedly?

I will admit, though, my relationship with him was fun while it lasted and brought out a free-spirited side of me, yet another facet of my personality I never knew existed.

I haven't dated anyone since my breakup with Garner, and I intend to stay unhitched until I'm a college graduate. *No stress. No mess. No cleanup.* The decision makes me wonder if Berkeley was onto something when he dumped me way back when. Specifically, the fewer complications one has during these growing-up years, the better.

Speaking of Berkeley, I haven't seen him in more than two years, not since Garner's concert in the park. He has been doing summer work in California, I've been doing summer work in New York, and I've spent my semester breaks in sunny destinations with my family. I do, however, have lengthy text exchanges with him every few months, wherein we update each other on the latest happenings. I prefer this method of communication to phone calls or Skype because it makes me yearn less and also eliminates the possibility of interrupting Berkeley in a compromising situation. He is still actively dating Shoshanna; I know from my online browsing.

Craving a piece of him, I open to a picture of Berkeley on my laptop, retrieve my phone, disregard that it's after midnight his time, and start texting. "Is there a Berkeley Mills out there somewhere?"

Instantly, he texts back: "Yes, and his ears are now perked to the max."

Smiling, I ask, "What's making you happy these days?"

He responds, "For starters, I recently thought of that Clown Girl sculpture and the expression on your face when I gave it to you, and I'm still smiling."

I reply, "I'm staring at her right now and must apologize for being so critical. You did a masterful job."

He says, "Don't try to flatter me now, Ms. Lanoo. The damage to my ego is done."

I say, "Do you want to borrow my clown shoes so you can kick my ass for being so cruel?"

He says, "Yes, but only because I like the idea of coming into contact with the world's most perfectly fine ass. And just to clarify, I mean contact in the nonpunishment kind of way."

I say, "No one has commented on my ass in years."

He says, "Clearly, you're hanging out with the wrong company."

I giggle. "Or maybe it's because I don't have time to keep *any* company."

He says, "Hey, here's something I'm sure you'll find interesting: I got dragged for my first pedicure yesterday."

Though I'm tempted to ask who took him for his first pedicure, I refrain and text, "Nice. How did you enjoy it?"

"I loved it, and now I understand why your feet are always so soft. Speaking of: how are your beautiful feet these days?"

"In desperate need of a pedicure because they've been taking a beating—literally—at my weekly self-defense class."

He immediately responds, "Did something happen? Did someone come near you?"

I say, "No, worrywart. Our landlady, Madge Hunter—a tough, stocky, streetwise middle-aged motorcycle enthusiast—recommended strongly that Victoria, Pella, and I take the class to prepare for the worst of our borderline-seedy neighborhood."

He says, "What's the class like?"

I say, "Picture a middle-aged, überjacked, loud-voiced former marine named Suki Majors teaching techniques for spraying mace, poking people in the eyeballs, and slipping our bodies out of a headlock."

He asks, "How are you and your roommates faring?"

I say, "We spend the majority of our time laughing at ourselves, at how unnatural our raging expressions look and feel, but we're getting a great workout."

He says, "Remind me to check out your muscle tone next time I see you."

Smiling, I add, "Here's something else I'm sure you'll find interesting: I turned your macramé bracelet into a window-ledge minihammock and saw a ladybug crawl into it. Seriously, it was the sweetest sight ever."

He says, "Did you take a picture?"

"No."

"Have I never mentioned how important it is to photo-record everything extraordinary so that the memory is retained forever?"

"You've never said it, but you've certainly demonstrated it enough times."

"Speaking of, could you do me a favor and send me a pic of you standing somewhere distinctively NYC, wearing your current favorite shoes?"

I reply, "As soon as you send me that pic from the day at the waterfall."

"Oh yeah, where did I file that?"

Noticing that dawn is starting to break, I say, "Why don't you go and get busy looking for it so I can complete some pattern pieces to cut that are due for an early morning class."

"Will do."

"Signing off. Take care, you."

"You too. Miss your freckles and such."

Leaning back in my chair, I feel even more inspired to find a spectacular pair of grad shoes so that I can make them the subject of a photo taken especially for Berkeley. That reminds me—Berkeley and I are both graduating soon. I wonder what will happen with him and me then.

*Nope, don't go there,* I tell myself. *Just get this evening gown designed and fabricated before it's due in two weeks, or you're going to miss out on the year-end bonus.*

The day after our final project is due, I'm scheduled to head on a field trip (*Who knew field trips existed beyond grade school?*), an end-of-the-program ritual for all fashion-design majors (which means Victoria and Pella are going too), intended to provide a close-up look at the fashion world's manufacturing process. Only those that hand in their final assignment are eligible to go.

For the previous five years, the destinations have been clothing facilities in exotic parts of the world, but as if I clicked my heels to make a wish come true, this year's choice is a shoe-making facility—*Yahoo!*—located just outside the city of Bucharest, Romania, which should be interesting.

Never having been to the eastern block of Europe before, I asked my professor what to expect, and she said that as the result of the country's fledgling economy, the accommodations will take us back in time, the local food (or lack of it) might result in some weight loss (i.e., we should bring along some energy bars), and our mobile devices probably won't have reception for much of the time there. Regardless, I still see this as a girlie-girl road trip with two of my favorite people, and I can't wait to go.

As an added bonus, we, the starving students, are being allowed to purchase up to three pair of new shoes each at the factory's wholesale cost. Since this facility produces footwear for some top-notch shoe brands, I'm feeling confident I'll be returning with not only a wealth of knowledge about the making of shoes but also a few samples that demonstrate it.

Maybe my Francie shoe is waiting for me on a shelf in Romania. How unexpected would that be?

# foot note forty-two

I GO FROM A TEXT-MESSAGING CATCH-UP ONE DAY TO OLD-fashioned longhand-letter-writing catch-up the next.

With next week's trip to Europe dominating my thoughts, I've been fixating on my former dorm supervisor, Allegra, wondering how she is, what she's doing over there, and where her shoe adventures have taken her. To try to find out, I'm about to reach out by way of a letter, which I intend to send to her parents' home in San Marino, Italy—the only known address I have for her.

Taking hold of Berkeley's pen, I start scribing.

> Dear Allegra,
>
> Hey, stranger. Remember me? Big news: I'll be visiting your continent soon, touring a shoe factory outside of Bucharest, Romania. So if you're not doing anything, why don't you come visit me? Just kidding.
>
> In case you're wondering, I'm almost done with my bachelor's degree in fashion design, after which I hope to complete postgrad studies in shoe design, if one of the schools I've applied to accepts me.

*What's the latest with your shoe pursuits? Are you still in school? Are you designing somewhere? Or are you doing something altogether different, like globetrotting with another cute Italian?*

After a pause, I grab my rendering markers and another sheet of paper and say,

*Regarding my me-shoe search, I'm now referring to the crowned jewel as the Incomparable, courtesy of Berkeley, who described it to a T and, in the process, totally blew my mind (as he always does). Anyway, as the result of his words, I now have the shoe's image firmly planted in my brain. See the attached sketch.*

With ease, I throw together the embodiment of painlessness, harmony, timelessness, sparkle, height, readiness for anything, cuteness, warmheartedness, quirkiness, and the color fuchsia—a detailed sketch that, if I do say so myself, is the best shoe I've ever created. I even take a picture of the drawing to use if I ever get back on the hunt.

Carrying on, I write,

*How's your love life? Did you ever see that guy Mauro again?*

*The latest on my relationship status is that I'm single and still hung up on Berkeley, but I'm pretty sure Berkeley is in a long-term relationship with a girl named Shoshanna and not hung up on me. In related news, according to my math, Berkeley has spent a lot more time in Shoshanna's company than he ever did in mine, the thought of which gives me chest pain so severe that I'm starting to worry I'm developing early onset heart*

> disease. So if there's a magical bandage in your first-aid
> kit meant for healing that, please send it my way.

Sighing, I close with the following:

> *Hope to hear back from you soon.*
> *Love and hugs,*
> *Francie*

Popping the letter into a mailbox I had to hunt to find (because who uses them anymore?), I cross my fingers that it finds its way to Allegra. I miss her and want to reconnect with her, and I would benefit greatly right now from one of her crazy pep talks on the inevitabilities of everlasting love. I hate that I'm losing hope.

# foot note forty-three

LOOKING OUT THE WINDOW OF AN UNDERSIZED HOTEL ROOM IN the old part of downtown Bucharest, I see nothing but water-drenched streets, dripping buildings, soggy pathways, and neutral-colored umbrellas. As I glance into the distance and see a landscape that appears painted over in gray, I curse myself for failing to pack a raincoat, rain hat, or rain boots and start digging through my suitcase for something other than the satin bronze trench coat and black suede boots I wore here last night.

Victoria, who grew up in the Arizona desert, is doing the same, her rising blood pressure turning her inherently golden skin a flustered pink.

However, Welsh-born seasoned-traveler Pella has brought all of the right stuff and says, "You two are such amateurs. Make do, or you'll miss the bus."

Heeding her words, I slip into jeans, a sweater, and a pair of retro sneakers I brought with me in case I had time for a nice evening stroll under the stars (or not). Afterward, I follow the gals into the hotel lobby and join Vivian in buying, from a small gift shop, a cheap rain slicker (clear plastic and unbearably unflattering). We belt our slickers, shake our heads, and giggle at the ridiculousness.

Our itinerary for this field trip involves two days of factory touring, followed by two days of sightseeing on our own. Since I did not see a single shoe store, clothing store, bookstore, or art gallery on the bus ride from the airport to the hotel, I'm guessing forty-eight hours of leisure time will be more than enough to experience all that Bucharest has to offer.

Out the door I go.

On tour day one, while wearing my soggier-by-the-minute sneakers, I endure a nail-biting bus ride along some narrow roads through steep hillsides, slog through endless mud, and make my way to an old brick building that our guide—a brunette, brown-eyed, petite twentysomething former gymnast named Cosmina—explains sat abandoned for decades before a group of Italians decided it would be ideal for the cost-effective manufacturing of high-end goods.

Inside, I enjoy a fantastic, informative, and eye-opening tour, on which I learn that at least one hundred operations go into the construction of the average shoe, thirty-five measurements from a footprint are required for a single shoe design, and these factory workers are trained to do most of the work by hand in order to make the finished products as close to old-world crafted as possible.

It's riveting stuff for a shoe fanatic like me. Seriously!

On tour day two, after learning how to do some of the handcrafting, our group visits a showroom containing hundreds of pairs of finished shoes—the eagerly anticipated shopping-spree opportunity—where I'm surprised to discover I'm not interested in trying on a single pair. Maybe my lack of interest is because my feet are currently stuck in waterlogged sneakers and don't feel worthy of slipping into pristine pumps hot off the press. Or maybe it's because I've seen what the hardworking factory employees are able to afford for their feet and I've been humbled. Or maybe it's because I keep thinking about the shoe sketch I sent to Allegra and do not see anything similar. Whatever the reason, I end up leaving the factory empty-handed.

On leisure day one, after spending another rainy day touring Herastrau Park, Cismigiu Gardens, the National Opera House, and the National Museum of Art, Victoria, Pella, and I return to our hotel room, feeling damp, cold, and exhausted.

Glancing at my sneakers, I say, "Sadly, my lovelies, you are about to be written off," after which I wrap them in plastic, throw them inside my carry-on bag, halt my brain from associating the shoe style with Berkeley (as has happened in the past), and start rooting around in my suitcase for something warm to wear to dinner. I settle on the all-back outfit I wore when I arrived in Romania.

Heading out the door, Pella looks at me and says, "The ready-for-a-funeral look is not your best." It's a comment that sends a shiver down my spine, for some reason.

Seated with Pella and Victoria in a cottage-style restaurant about a block from the hotel, I notice my brain yo-yoing to thoughts of home—my true home, Riverly Heights.

Even as the girls are talking to me, I'm preoccupied with what's going on there, what I've missed, and the possibility of heading there after I graduate. On the way back to the hotel, I become so distracted by thoughts of getting there that I veer off track and have to be physically shifted in the direction of the hotel.

With hands on my shoulders, Victoria says, "What's up with you this evening? Too much cheap Riesling?"

I shake my head. "No, I think my body is just so cold it's lost all sense of direction."

She smirks. "Hang in there. You'll be home in two days."

"Yay."

On leisure day two, a group of us do a minibus day trip through the picturesque—albeit rained-drenched—Carpathian Mountains to the

Transylvanian castle of Dracula, where I learn the place is actually called Bran Castle; its former owner, Vlad the Impaler, was spooky, with bulging eyes, an elongated nose, and a horrible mustache; and I'm probably going to have nightmares when I crawl into bed tonight.

In the middle of the night, sure enough, I wake up in a cold sweat with my heart racing. Alarmed that (a) I'm suffering a case of food poisoning, which is possible, (b) I've contracted a flu bug, or (c) Dracula is, in fact, real and is hiding in the closet, I climb out of bed and cautiously check every nook of the room.

Verifying that the coast is clear, I take a deep breath, return to my bed, and assume a seated position while I wait for daylight.

Curious to see what's happening in the land of the living, I retrieve my phone and attempt to connect—an effort that is thwarted by another no-service zone. I drop the useless device to the floor and mumble, "Damn this medieval world."

In the bed adjacent to mine, Pella sleepily mumbles, "Francie, are you awake or dreaming?"

"Both."

Rolling over, she asks, "What's wrong?"

Pulling a throw blanket over my head, I say, "Vlad is wrong. Sorry to disturb you. Go back to sleep."

To ensure my mind doesn't veer off on another wild ride, I mentally make a list of all of the things I have discovered on this short adventure.

One, the knowledge acquired from the factory tour has made me love and want to design shoes even more.

Two, I will never see a horror movie again.

Three, I could never live disconnected, as Allegra does. There's too much going on in the world that's bound to get missed.

Speaking of Allegra, I wonder if she got my letter.

# foot note forty-four

AS MY THIRTY-TWO FELLOW FIELD-TRIPPERS AND I ARRIVE AT Bucharest Baneasa International Airport, ready and anxious to head back to New York, everyone collectively screams at the realization that his or her cellular service is alive and well—everyone except me, because I accidently tossed my phone into my big suitcase, which is currently in the checked baggage system and not to be seen until the plane lands in NYC.

Reaching the departure gate, I hear over the airport PA system the final boarding call for our flight. Knowing I don't have time to borrow Victoria's or Pella's phone for a lengthy catch-up with my parents (the only people I truly need to be connected to), I board the plane, settle into my seat, and crash hard, desperately in need of sleep after my Dracula-induced insomnia.

After many hours high above the Atlantic Ocean—which passed by in an instant because I was unconscious for almost all of that time—I stand before the baggage carousel, retrieve my suitcase, quickly dig out my phone, and start listening to four days' worth of messages.

The first is from my mom: "Francie, I need to talk to you. Call me as soon as you can."

With furrowed brow, I say, "Her voice was awfully nasally. I wonder if she's got a cold."

The next is from my father: "Francie, your mother and I need to talk to you about something important. Call home as soon as you can. Please!"

The next three are from Phoebe, whom I haven't talked to in months. Skipping past them, I notice there's one from Berkeley. "That's weird. He hasn't called me in forever."

Moving on to text messages, I see my mom left five, all of which say, "Call me, please." And Phoebe left one: "I need to talk to you about Berkeley. It's important. Call me."

Feeling my forehead perspiring, with my mind filling up with wild imaginings—*Is he sick? Is he getting married?*—I hit the speed dial and say, "Hey, Mom. I'm back in New York. I got your many messages. What's going on?"

"Oh, Francie," she murmurs in a drawn-out moan.

With my hands starting to shake, I ask, "Mom, what is it?"

She sighs. "I hate to tell you this over the phone, but there's been an accident."

"Involving whom?"

"Involving Berkeley's parents. They were out for a run a few nights ago and were struck by a drunk driver."

My heart starts pounding. "Are they okay?"

"Archer is going to be, but Sarah ..."

"What about Sarah?"

"Honey, she didn't make it."

"What? No! That can't be right!"

Whimpering, she responds, "I'm so sorry you had to find out this way."

Collapsing to my knees and setting the phone on the floor, I exclaim, "This can't be happening!"

Crouching beside me, Pella and Victoria try to figure out what's going on, but I don't respond. I don't even see their faces, because the world around me is spinning like a top.

My mom repeatedly shouts, "Francie, are you still there?"

I take a deep breath and put the phone to my ear. "Yes. When's the funeral?"

"It was a few hours ago."

"So I missed it?"

"Yes, honey. I'm so sorry. We tried to get ahold of you several times."

With lips trembling, I mumble, "I need to wake up. Someone, please wake me up."

As Vivian and Pella start babbling words I'm incapable of absorbing, my mom says, "Honey, where are you?"

I look around. "In JFK Airport. I just landed."

"Are your roommates with you?"

"Yes."

"Good. Why don't you head with them to your apartment and call me from there?"

"Okay," I whisper, hanging up the phone, not sure if I should sit, stand, or crawl under a chair and assume the fetal position. With concocted images of the accident running over and over in my head, I cover my face with my hands, close my eyes, and try not to vomit.

When I finally tell Pella and Victoria what has happened, they do their best to console me, and they pick me up off the ground and hug me. When the truth finally strikes me, I become hysterical, and they lead me to a bench and dry my tears.

Taking my hand, Victoria says, "It'll be okay."

I shake my head. "But I should have been there for him."

"You didn't do anything wrong."

"Yes, I have done so many things wrong."

Once Victoria, Pella, and I clear US customs, I say, "I need to make a phone call."

Pella touches my arm. "Go. We'll take care of your suitcase for you."

"Thank you."

Arriving at a quiet niche, I, for reasons I cannot explain, retrieve my soggy sneakers and put them on my feet. Speed-dialing Berkeley's number, I start rehearsing various phrases to express my condolences, all of which I immediately dismiss because they sound insufficient.

After several rings, he finally answers and says, "Francie."

After taking a deep breath, I reply, "Berkeley, I'm so sorry I wasn't there for you."

In a voice beneath a hush, he replies, "God, I wish you were here now."

Bursting into tears, I respond, "I'll be on the next flight."

# foot note forty-five

AS I WALK DOWN A DIMLY LIT AIRPORT CORRIDOR AFTER deplaning in Riverly Heights, I hear my ruined-by-Romania sneakers making a strange quacking noise with each step I take.

Mad at myself for accidentally leaving behind not only my black boots but also my suitcase, because I ran to catch another plane before catching up with my roommates, I shake my head and say, "To hell with shoes." I could be in bare feet for all I care, and I don't just mean that in reference to today. I mean that from now on.

Working my way toward the building exit, I hear my phone ping. I look and read a message from Berkeley, telling me he's here, waiting to drive me home.

As my heart begins to race, I look down from the mezzanine level and spot him one floor below. He's standing with his back against a pillar, shoulders slouched, hands tucked into his peacoat pockets, and eyes fixed on a wall-mounted poster. As usual, he has no idea that many women—and several men—are taking second glances at his extreme handsomeness. Even when some of them pause nearby to try to get his attention, he remains oblivious.

When I step onto the escalator, as if by a sixth sense, he looks up and sees me. As our eyes lock, he lifts his hand in a wave and offers a half smile. When I reciprocate, he stands erect and starts walking in my direction.

The closer we get to one another, the faster his grief reveals itself. His eyes are sunken, his hair is disheveled much more than usual, and his forehead is lined with creases that weren't there before. He probably hasn't slept in days. How could he? How will he ever be able to again?

As I walk off the lowering steps, I ease toward him, wrap my arms around his waist, and quietly say, "Hey, you."

Giving me a hug so tight that I can barely breathe, he replies, "God, I'm glad you're here."

"Me too."

As he takes the carry-on bag from my shoulder, I clutch his free hand and say, "How are you holding up?"

"It helps that my head is sleep deprived and foggy."

"Do you need to be anywhere right now? Or could we go visit your mom?"

"I'm fine to do whatever you want to do."

"Thank you," I reply, and I turn my head away, because if I keep looking at his sad eyes, I'm going to crumble to pieces.

The half-hour drive to Riverly Memorial Park—in Berkeley's familiar first car—is eerily silent, neither of us up for even the simplest conversation.

When we turn into the cemetery, Berkeley breaks the silence. "Mom's plot is to the west of here, under some canopied trees."

I look to where he's pointing and say, "This is a pretty resting spot, Berkeley. Very peaceful, sheltered, and lush."

He nods but says nothing.

As we get out of the car and start walking, the clouds unleash a downpour. Though neither of us has an umbrella, we're not bothered. We just trudge through the soggy sod and do what we must.

Remaining tightly by my side, Berkeley points and says, "It's right over there, I think. But the headstone isn't in place yet, so I'll have to navigate from my memory. If I can."

"We'll find her," I reply as a sudden rush of my tears begins blending with the droplets falling from the sky.

After wandering for many minutes—past many rain-sprinkled flowers, many lost loved ones, and much sadness—we eventually locate a rectangle of freshly disheveled earth.

Standing before it, Berkeley announces, "She's here."

As I watch him stare downward, I notice his lips are quivering and say, "Berkeley, I'm so sorry this happened to you and your dad."

Facing me, he moves within inches of my body, rests his head on top of mine, and starts sobbing loudly and uncontrollably.

Wrapping my arms around him, I cry too, not only because I too feel as if I've lost a family member but also because I've never heard Berkeley cry before, and the sound is raw, tender, and heartbreaking. Wanting to make him feel better, I force my one-hundred-pound frame to stand strong and hold him upright for as long as he requires.

I have no idea how much time passes by. An hour, I'd guess? We stand there long enough that my feet become a swamp, and my spine turns into a riverbed. As the dampness turns me bitterly cold, I start to shake. When my teeth begin to chatter, I look up and whisper, "I don't think these showers are the least bit inviting of May flowers."

Wiping away his own tears, he opens his coat, pulls me inside, and holds me tighter.

Burying my face in his warm chest, I sigh and ask, "Are you going to be okay?"

Inhaling deeply, he replies, "I don't know."

I place my palms on his cheeks. "If I can do anything to make this easier, please ask."

"Thank you. That means a lot," he replies, motioning that it's okay to leave and leading us back to the car.

Nearing it, he says, "I can't believe how quickly you got here."

"It helps that I was already in an airport."

"Why was that?"

After hearing the story of the last few days of my life, he says, "It seriously saddens me that you were on the other side of the planet, and I had no idea."

I shrug. "We're both wrapped up in our own worlds right now. That's all."

"I hate that you and I have become so estranged."

"We're not estranged. We're just distracted."

"Yeah, but this relationship between you and me is the most important of my life, and I should never have let it get so messed up."

I grab his hand. "We are not messed up."

Looking to the sky, he mumbles, "I must have been out of my mind to ever break up with you."

"Berkeley, we were kids when that happened."

Dazedly, he adds, "And how stupid was I to go to school on the opposite side of the country from you? I should have moved to New York, where I could have spent the last fourteen hundred days waking up to the sight of your face."

I lean into him. "If it's any consolation, I still get bubbly-bodied at the sight of you."

He throws his arm around my shoulders and replies, "Thank God for that."

Smiling, I add, "On the upside, school's almost done."

He pulls me tightly to his side. "And it can't end soon enough."

"Fifteen days of classes and counting," I say as the phone in my pocket starts vibrating, reminding me that I recently interviewed for a job that would move me to London, and furthermore, a London fashion school recently accepted me to study shoe design—opportunities I'd be crazy to turn down, because I'd be furthering my skills and gaining work experience simultaneously. But in light of the fact that Berkeley's world just imploded, I don't dare share. I just reach into my pocket and turn the phone to silent mode.

Grabbing Berkeley's hand, I say, "My parents would love it if we joined them for dinner."

"That would be nice," he replies, opening the car door and ushering me inside.

On the way back into town, the two of us slip into another cone of silence, the occasional warm glance communicating all that matters.

When the car makes a turn onto my home street and its unfamiliarity unsettles me (*How long have I been away?*), I shift my gaze to the car floor and am instantly transfixed by the strangest realization: Berkeley's sopping-wet feet are clad in a pair of retro sneakers almost identical to mine.

With a smile, I say, "I like your shoes."

Looking down at our footwear, he shakes his head and replies, "I like yours too."

As my body starts dismissing the chill from fifteen minutes earlier and my mind starts reconciling the hand that fate has dealt, I think, *It's okay to still care about shoes.*

# foot note forty-six

IT MAKES ME CRINGE, LOOKING INTO THE BATHROOM MIRROR AND seeing myself decked out in my mom's soft-pink fleece leisure wear with a yellow polka-dot towel wrapped around my hair, alongside Berkeley dressed in my dad's bright orange tracksuit, which, in combination with his freshly showered slicked hair, has turned him into a character from a low-budget 1970s detective movie.

But I guess this is what happens when you slop through your parents' door, drenched from head to toe, and let them be parents again.

Funnier still is the sight of our clad feet: Berkeley is wearing brown plaid old-man slippers, and I'm stuck in a pair of my mom's soft-yellow puffballs, which could not be more un-Francie.

Slinking tightly beside me, Berkeley calmly says, "Aren't we a sight for sore eyes?"

Smirking, I respond, "We look like the poster people for how not to dress for our body types."

Throwing an arm around my shoulders, he adds, "For the record, if I were setting my eyes on you for the first time right now, I'd still wanna date you."

Giggling, I respond, "Likewise," and lean into the mirror to adorn my lips with a layer of my mom's pink lipstick—a shade that perfectly complements the powder-puff thing I've got going on.

Examining my mostly makeup-free face, Berkeley says, "You know, your freckles are still hanging in there."

Looking closely, I reply, "Huh! I think you're right."

"I'd forgotten how much I like staring at your face."

Scrunching my nose and bucking my teeth, I reply, "Because it's so pwitty and wovewy and thexy."

"It is."

Losing the lisp, I add, "And getting more wrinkled by the day."

Placing his hands on my hips, he says, "FYI, Ms. Lanoo, your kind of beautiful does not age."

Smiling, I reply, "And your ability to push the right buttons doesn't either."

After clearing his throat, he asks, "Are there any other buttons you'd like me to push right now?"

Caught off guard by his sudden lightheartedness, I burst out laughing and smear lipstick well beyond my lip line. "Look what you've done."

Flashing me a killer smile, he replies, "Let me fix that."

"How?"

After tossing my headwear towel to the floor, he lifts me onto the vanity, pulls me toward him, and gives me the mushiest kiss ever, smearing lipstick onto both of our faces.

Seeing a hint of playfulness in his eyes, I stop stressing about whether or not he's going to be okay. I know.

By the time my parents summon us to dinner, Berkeley's aura has regained some of its energy.

His positivity returns a little more when my dad enthusiastically says, "Berkeley, that tracksuit looks great on you. Why don't you keep it?"

Suppressing laughter and flashing me a cute smile, he replies, "Sure. Thank you. I'd love to."

As we consume several courses of delicious food, the conversation starts flowing without a lull—about the latest goings-on in Riverly Heights, about how Talula is doing on her high-school trip to Europe, and about how Brigitte is liking her new public-relations job, which has her living a three-hour drive away from home. All the while, the pouring rain continues to block out the view beyond the windows, eliminating any distraction that would take my eyes off of the people who matter most in my world.

When dinner wraps up, my mom takes Berkeley into the living room to talk privately. I have no idea what she says; however, knowing her as well as I do, I assume it's along the lines of "If you need anything, I am here for you."

Around nine, my parents announce they're heading out to a late movie—their not-so-subtle way of offering us some alone time. We take advantage of it by sauntering into the family room, lying on the sofa, and burying our bodies under several fuzzy blankets.

The rain soon intensifies, and an electrical storm erupts. Amid the house rattling, the sky illuminating, and the airwaves booming, a spectacular lightning strike cuts off the power inside the house.

Scrambling to our feet in the pitch-blackness, we scamper to light candles wherever we can locate them.

As the room starts to glow, I say, "You do know what this means, Mr. Mills."

"What?"

"That the clothes dryer has stopped, so we're likely stuck in these clown suits until morning."

He shrugs. "Fine with me. I'm totally comfortable in my new digs."

Giving him an odd glance, I ask, "Are you suggesting you'd actually wear that again?"

He sighs. "You may find this hard to believe, but living in California has turned everything about me more leisurely."

Meeting up with him on the sofa and straddling his lap, I ask, "Is there anything else different about you that I should know?"

His brow furrows. "Let me think." After a pause, he says, "Yes, my legs did get hairier."

"What a coincidence. Mine did too."

Running his hand up one of my pant legs, he responds, "They don't feel hairier."

"That's because I regularly wax them."

"Sorry, but I regularly do not."

"How un-Californian."

"That's because at heart, I'm still a Riverly Heighter."

Gazing into his flame-lit eyes, I ask, "Do you have any idea how fabulous it feels to be in the same room as you?"

"Yes, I do," he replies, slowly toppling both of us over and pulling our torsos tightly together.

Sighing, I say, "It feels like no time has passed since the last time we did this."

"And if I could make one wish, it would be to end each day like this for the rest of my life."

Examining his face, I reply, "You look exhausted. Maybe you should get some sleep."

Forcing his eyes open, he counters, "No, I don't want to miss a minute of being with you like this."

"It's okay, Berkeley. I'm not going anywhere."

With eyelids dropping, he murmurs, "Just five more minutes. That's all."

"Sure," I say, watching his eyelids immediately drop.

After carefully slinking away to snuff the candles, I return and stare at Berkeley's floppy hair, full lips, slight stubble, long eyelashes, masculine jawline, sharp collarbones, and bulked-up arms, which are all as perfect as they ever were.

When my gaze reaches his finely sculpted hands, I retrieve Berkeley's pen from my nearby handbag, grab his left hand, and scribe, "F ♡ B more."

Smirking, I put away the pen and snuggle in.

Before I allow myself to crash, I rest my head on Berkeley's familiar chest and savor the sound of his steady breathing. As the rhythm calms me, I smile at the realization of how ecstatic my shoeless feet feel while resting on Berkeley's slightly hairier legs.

# foot note forty-seven

THURSDAY MORNING ARRIVES WITH THE LOUDEST THUNDERCLAP I've ever heard. As my body bolts upright, Berkeley wraps his arms around my waist, eases me back down, and mumbles, "Are you okay?"

"Yeah, I'm fine. I just wish the rain would shut up and the wind would shut up and the trees would shut up."

"I wish you would shut up."

Smiling, I rest my head on his shoulder and grant him his wish.

As he drifts back to sleep, I reach into my handbag and grab my phone. Glancing at the time and surprised to see it's already nine—*We slept for eleven hours?*—I start reviewing the many messages I spent yesterday ignoring.

Discovering that I have an official response from a potential employer, I wiggle off of the couch and wander into the kitchen to contemplate what to do about it.

Munching on a scone, I read a short note my parents left prior to their departures for work, grin, and whisper, "Yay! Alone for the day."

Itching to get out of my current attire, I tiptoe toward the staircase and slink to the second floor. Entering the laundry room to restart the dryer, I consider my options for a temporary change. Lacking a wardrobe of my own, I saunter into Brigitte's bedroom to see if she has something worth borrowing.

Glancing inside her closet, I find that her clothes are completely gone and mumble, "Huh, so it's not just my life that's moving forward."

Wandering into Talula's bedroom, I'm surprised to see that the space has finally developed a personality of its own—ruby-red walls, ebony furniture, and stark white accessories have replaced my mother's old-fashioned pastels.

Smiling, I note, "Nice," and walk into Talula's closet, where I realize every item hanging has Talula's newfound style written all over it—I see a whole lot of teenage flash and skimpiness going on.

Commenting, "This too shall pass," I hold a few of the pieces against my torso and quickly conclude I won't be borrowing anything from this bedroom either.

Leaving Talula's room and skipping my mom's room altogether, for obvious incompatibility reasons, I wander into my own. As I turn on a table lamp and watch the space illuminate, my eyes grow wide with wonder. Every inch of the space is the way I left it when I went to college. In fact, I don't think my parents have moved a single thing.

Eager to reacquaint myself with the space, I wander around and pick up whatever item catches my eye, smiling as each associated memory surfaces.

Locating the music box that Berkeley once gave me, I turn it on and quietly hum along to its beloved tune. "God, I love that song."

Meandering into my closet, I discover that all of my old clothes have been put into plastic bins and stacked in a corner—all but my shoes, which remain lined up on the shelves precisely as I last placed them. Touching a few, I recall the specific times and places I wore them.

Coming across a pair that I once considered stylish but no longer do, I grin and mumble, "What was I thinking?"

Eyeing a special pair in the center of the top row, I reach for them, set them on the floor, and step into them. "The Debut-Taunters!" I say with a sheepish grin.

Despite the fact that the style is not anything I would wear now, I'm thrilled to prance around in the shoes for a few moments, happily recalling Francie and Berkeley sitting in a tree.

After completing a smooth pirouette, I pull a short, silky robe from one of the storage bins and proceed to do a quick change. About to glance in a mirror, I discover Berkeley propped against the bedroom doorframe, watching me.

"Good morning!" I say, my hands tying the robe's belt.

"Back at you," he responds, crossing his arms and sporting a cute grin.

Blushing, I reply, "How are you feeling today?"

"Pretty good after waking up to this," he responds, flashing me his scribed palm.

"Oh, that."

"Yeah, that."

Inhaling, I respond, "I hadn't used your pen in a while, and I wanted to make sure it still worked."

"Lucky for me, you felt the need."

"Lucky for me, I keep the pen handy."

Tipping his head, he quietly says, "What are you doing in there?"

"Putting on something more me."

"Nailed it."

Giggling, I reply, "I wish I could say the same about your getup."

Peering down, he says, "Yeah, in the light of day, it no longer resonates."

"So you're saying your good sense has finally returned."

He smiles. "All it takes is a few hours with you, and my perspective reverts right back to where it ought to be."

"Out of curiosity, did it happen to reinstate my face as your brain's wallpaper?"

He smiles. "Rest assured, Ms. Lanoo, not a day has passed since I first laid eyes on you that it hasn't been."

Feeling my heart flutter, I mumble, "God, I've missed your sappiness."

"It feels good to put it back into action."

As I smile, he looks at my feet and says, "I remember those shoes fondly."

"Yeah, they facilitated a pretty good night for me way back when."

"For me too."

"In my shoe-questing log, I called them the Debut-Taunters."

"That's about right."

"That was my quest's first entry, actually."

"What's happening with that these days?"

"Not a lot, except for a sketch I drew recently—based on your descriptors, you'll be pleased to know—that I thought held a lot of promise. However, in light of all that's happened recently, I'm starting to think my shoe obsession is a little silly."

Slowly edging his way toward me, he says, "Don't give up on it."

"Why?"

"Because you prancing around in great shoes is the best sight my eyes will ever see."

As my body warms all over, I reply, "I did not know that my footwear had such an effect on you."

After taking a deep breath, he says, "Let's just say that when you strut into a room, every cell in my body starts buzzing."

As I giggle and blush, he adds, "And on a more practical note, I'm anxious to be proven correct."

"So what you're saying is, to abate your gloating, I should carry on?"

Sauntering nearer me, he replies, "Yes."

Staring into his still-awesome eyes, I say, "Okay then. For you alone, I will take my quest to its end."

"Thank you."

"You're welcome."

Standing mere inches away from me, Berkeley slips his arms around my waist and quietly asks, "How long are you planning to hang out in that closet?"

Placing my hand on his chest, I say, "How long are you planning to hang out in these old-man duds?"

"Am I weirding you out in them?"

"Yes."

Smiling, he swoops me into his arms, carries me to the bed, and seriously lip-locks with me for the first time in almost four years.

To the sound of my phone ringing in the closet, he asks, "Do you need to answer that?"

Lost in Berkeley's everything, I reply, "Do you seriously think I would right now?"

Untying my robe's belt, he whispers, "God, I hope not."

As he starts setting every cell in *my* body buzzing, I say, "Looks like these shoes are about to facilitate another good time for me."

Pulling them off my feet and tossing them across the room, Berkeley says, "I think you should revise their name to the Taunters."

Giggling, I reply, "Done," after which I discover Berkeley has learned about a whole lot more than journalism while living in California. *Holy moly, hold on to my hat.* He knows how to push a girl's buttons.

It's supposed to rain heavily all day, which is ideal because it's reason enough to stay indoors, where I can have Berkeley all to myself. To ensure the two of us are fully disconnected from the rest of the world, I hide all laptops, place our cell phones in drawers, and close all of the window blinds. To further set the mood, I light the rooms with candles, rendering the setting cavernous and reclusive. *Perfect.*

Happily, the two of us are back to wearing our jeans and T-shirts, now clean and dry. Though Berkeley has put socks on his feet, I've opted to stay barefoot, rubbing my tootsies against Berkeley's legs whenever I have the chance.

We pass the time by exchanging stories about our school lives, watching a favorite old movie, jointly cooking brunch, and consuming several glasses of bubbly champagne, our newly realized shared favorite indulgence. Often, we steal glances at one another—but only until the gawker gets caught and breaks the stare with a shy smile.

My mother arrives home from work later in the afternoon. Running around the house, opening blinds and windows, she wanders into kitchen and says, "You two are missing the spring flowers that are erupting all over the yard."

Putting his arms around me from behind, Berkeley responds, "I'm only interested in the scenery here in the kitchen."

Fluttering my eyelashes, I say, "For that, Mr. Mills, you get to stay for dinner."

Rolling her eyes, my mom retorts, "On the condition that I don't have to listen to mush for three hours."

After kissing the top of my head, Berkeley says, "Francie, please get your mom some earplugs, because she's gonna need them."

As I start giggling, my mom replies, "You'd better grab a pair for your dad too."

My father arrives home around six, and by seven, the four of us are gathered around the dining-room table, eating, talking, and smiling. As the sun bursts through the clouds for the first time since my arrival in Riverly Heights, I notice that every inch of the backyard is glistening: the trees, the shrubs, the teak furniture, and some newly erupted pink tulips.

Sensing something is amiss, I lose the happy face and ask, "Mom, where's the hammock?"

Glancing outside, she replies, "Oh, I got rid of it."

"What? Why?"

"Well, it was starting to look ratty, and no one was using it, so I dropped it off at the Goodwill store downtown."

Sitting forward in my chair, I say, "I wish you'd told me first before you did that."

"Don't worry. I'm replacing it with a canopied swing that should be here next week."

Recalling the many happy moments spent in that hammock and fired up that there won't be any new ones, I softly say, "Why did you have to pitch it? Couldn't you have just stored it in the basement?"

My dad asks, "What's the problem, if we're replacing it with something that'll serve the same purpose?"

With furrowed brow, I answer, "That hammock was one of the things that brought me home."

Shrugging, my dad says, "Since you only venture here about once a year these days, I'm sure you can make do without it."

Setting down her cutlery, my mom adds, "And now that you're moving to London, I imagine you'll visit here even less often."

Dropping my fork and thinking, *Oh crap, why did she have to say that?* I respond, "For the record, I haven't finalized what I'm doing after I graduate."

As both of my parents look at me strangely (because they know otherwise), Berkeley looks at me, squinting, and asks, "Are you moving to London?"

"It's a possibility," I say, abruptly getting up from the table, walking toward the kitchen, and bringing the conversation to a screeching halt.

"I'll get dessert," my mom says, following me.

"Sounds good," my dad says.

Darting to my side, my mom asks, "Okay, what's going on?"

"What do you mean?"

"Well, a week ago, you told me you were moving to London, and now you're saying you may not be. Have you changed your mind?"

"Shush!"

"What is there to shush about?"

"I don't want to discuss this right now."

"Why?"

"Because I haven't mentioned it to Berkeley yet, okay?"

After loudly exhaling, she says, "Oh, Francie. Why not?"

"Because he's had enough to deal with this week."

Shaking her head, she replies, "Well, you'd better get it out in the open pretty quick, or you'll end up adding to his angst."

After taking a deep breath, I say, "I'm aware."

Returning to the dining room, I find Berkeley now pensive, his gaze directed anywhere but at me. Evidently, he's drawn the obvious conclusion that our on-again, off-again relationship won't be changing anytime soon, which is the last thing he needed to learn today.

To try to improve the room's vibe, I pass around some small plates and say, "I hope everyone likes coconut cake with cream-cheese icing."

As Berkeley takes his plate from me, he replies, "Sounds delicious."

Reaching for a plate of his own, my dad adds, "I bet you two kids haven't had a home-cooked meal in months."

In unison, we reply, "Nope," after which the entire room takes on another awkward silence.

While using my fork to peel away the layer of icing, I consider some conversational options: I could tell Berkeley that the internship and grad studies are only six-month terms and that I'll be back in North America soon.

No, being dishonest will only make the matter worse down the road.

I could invite Berkeley to move to London with me, but in light of recent circumstances, that's about as likely as me living at the North Pole.

Breaking the silence, my father asks, "So, Berkeley, are you planning to come back to Riverly Heights as soon as you've finished school?"

*Why did he have to ask that?*

Giving me a side glance, Berkeley replies, "Yeah, once I graduate, that is the plan."

Warmly smiling, my mom says, "Your dad is going to be so happy to have you back home."

"I hope so."

"Is he doing any better?" she asks.

"Physically, yes. Emotionally, no."

"I'm so sorry to hear that. Is he by himself right now?"

"No, he can't be left alone, which is why my aunt Jane has moved in for the next few weeks."

My dad adds, "He must be devastated after what has happened."

After taking a deep breath, Berkeley responds, "Yeah, that's an understatement. After having watched the only woman he ever loved die in his arms, he's become unreachable and spends most of his time staring blankly into space."

"Oh my," my mom murmurs.

Covering my mouth with my hands, I say, "I hadn't heard that that's what happened or that your dad was in such a state. I'm so sorry, Berkeley."

Pressing his lips together, Berkeley looks to the tabletop and replies, "We can't get him to sleep or go into the office. He's barely eating. And to make matters worse, over the next several months, he'll have my mom's estate to deal with, a lawsuit to launch against the driver, and a business to keep running, none of which will be easily accomplished if he remains in la-la land."

Grasping Berkeley's hand, my mom replies, "Thank goodness he has you."

As my eyes fixate on Berkeley's paling face, my mind goes into high gear, recognizing only now that Berkeley is not just tied to here but also chained to here—not only to transition the newspaper into someone else's hands, temporarily or otherwise, but also to make sure his dad comes through this tragedy in one piece. I want to help him, but I would only be in a position to if I'm willing to give up everything I've worked for. Under the circumstances, I should, and I could. But what happens to me if I do?

As the magnitude of the situation strikes like a guillotine, I begin to feel the blood pulsating in my veins. Hypnotized by the fact that some life-altering stuff is going on here, I cover my entire face with my hands and inhale a series of shallow breaths.

Gripping my shoulder, Berkeley says, "Francie, are you all right?"

"Yeah, I'm fine."

"Are you sure?"

Dropping my hands, I reply, "Yeah, I probably just ate too much, which I have a tendency to do, which is really stupid because a person my size only has so much capacity, and—"

My mom interjects, "You look pale, honey. Maybe you got a chill when you were outside yesterday."

"Maybe."

"Why don't you head to your room and lie down for a while?"

"Yeah, I should. I will. I'm going to," I reply, picking up my plate and wandering toward the kitchen.

Hot on my heels, Berkeley grabs the stuff out of my hands and wordlessly leads me where I need to go.

Upstairs, as I'm crawling into my bed, he sits beside me and places his palm on my forehead to check my temperature.

As he tucks the blankets under my chin, I look into his eyes and say, "I'm feeling very twisted right now."

"Something I did this morning?"

"No, silly. My mind is knotted."

"What's happening in there?"

"Heavy-duty stuff."

He sweeps the hair from my face. "What specifically?"

I take a deep breath and say, "You and I seem destined to be on different life paths."

Berkeley's brow furrows. "Where did that ridiculous notion come from?"

"From the conversation about your dad, your new reality, and life in general."

He shakes his head. "Don't worry about any of that stuff right now. Just concentrate on finishing school. Okay?"

Sighing, I respond, "I don't know if I can stop worrying, when it seems that with every passing year, you and I face a new obstacle."

Pressing his forehead against mine, he says, "As syrupy as this sounds, Ms. Lanoo, rest assured that there is not a barrier I wouldn't scale if I knew you were on the other side."

After taking a deep breath, I ask, "How can you so easily slight this stuff?"

Looking me in the eyes, he replies, "I just have to look at your face, and the whole world makes sense to me."

I squeeze his hand. "But specifically, how do you stay so unfazed?"

Sitting up, he answers, "I keep my eye on the ball—the ball being you—and worry only about the obstacle that's most immediate."

"I don't know how to do that."

"It's easy. Take right now, for example: the only thing between you and me is a mound of blankets, which I could easily bust through."

As he demonstrates by whipping the blankets away, I mumble, "How are you able to be so lighthearted amid the crisis you're now facing?"

"Because by keeping my stress level in check, I'll prevent myself from turning into a crumpled heap."

Watching him stand up and grab my ankles, I ask, "What are you doing?"

Grinning, he says, "Take hold of the bedposts."

Doing so, I ask, "Why?"

"So I can relax you."

As I grip the posts tightly, he gently pulls on my legs to make every muscle in my body elongate. For many minutes, he does only that, offering a smile when I whisper, "This feels so good."

Eventually, he lets go, gently rewraps me in blankets, and says, "There. You're all unknotted."

Watching him sit down beside me, I say, "If only I had you around whenever I need ankle yanking."

Smiling, he murmurs, "Whenever you're in need of anything, just call me, and I'll be there."

"Yeah, but if I'm living on the other side of the planet, your visit would only be temporary, and then you'd have to leave."

Webbing his fingers with mine, he replies, "Listen, Francie. All you need to know right now is that I will forever be out of my mind in love with you."

"Same here with you."

After leaning over and kissing me softly on the lips, he retorts, "Then quit overthinking this, okay? It'll all work out in the end."

I force a nod. "I hope so."

Standing up, he asks, "What time is your flight on Saturday?"

"Noon."

"Mine's at twelve thirty. Why don't we cab together to the airport?"

"Sure."

Tucking me in, he's says, "I really hate to leave you like this, but I need to give Aunt Jane a break."

Sort of smiling, I reply, "Give your dad a hug from me, okay?"

"I will. Sleep well. I'll talk to you tomorrow, and maybe we can get together."

As he heads to the door, I say, "Do you think it would be all right if I visited your dad tomorrow?"

Furrowing his brow, he replies, "Actually, Francie, I'm not sure that's a good idea. He's not handling company very well."

"Oh?"

"Save it for when you're home next. I'm sure he'll be better then."

I nod and smile but refrain from responding, because I'm too caught up in wondering when I'll be home next. It could be years.

With Berkeley gone, being barefoot loses all appeal, and my feet turn ice cold. From the floor beside me, I grab the Taunters and slide them onto my feet. While wiggling my toes around inside them, I notice they aren't the least bit soothing, warming, or comfortable, likely because they no longer fit me.

Wondering if maybe it's time to give them to someone else, I remove them, hold them tightly to my chest, and vow never to let them go, because I can't imagine something so dear to me on the feet of someone else.

# foot note forty-eight

FRIDAY MORNING IS THE POLAR OPPOSITE OF THURSDAY. INSTEAD of playing around with Berkeley in my bedroom and hanging out with him over brunch, I'm sitting in the living-room chair with my brain still knotted, my stomach feeling uneasy, and my fingers twisted into pretzels.

My phone rings. It's Berkeley.

"Hey," I say.

"Hey. Did you sleep okay?"

"Decent. Where are you, and what are you doing?"

He sighs. "I'm currently involved in some legal discussions regarding the accident, and then I have a meeting with the *Tribunal's* second-in-command to restore some order, and after that, I have to arrange home care for my dad and, at the same time, remove all of my mom's items from the house that he's being negatively affected by. So, regretfully, I won't be able to see you today."

"Can I help?"

"No, I'd rather you not have to deal with any of this mess."

"So then, I guess I'll see you tomorrow."

"Yes, the one thing I have to look forward to."

Hanging up, I realize that it's probably better I not see Berkeley today, because I don't want him to know that I'm about to defy his wishes by paying a visit to his dad. I must. I haven't seen Archer in what feels like forever. In fact, I can't remember the last time I was in the same room as him, and I need assurance he's going to be okay. But I'll make the visit short and sweet—just a quick expression of my condolences, followed by the warmest of hugs.

After a speedy shower, I dig through a clothing bin and recover the little black jumper dress I wore to Berkeley's after-graduation party, as well as a pair of still-stylish silver flip-flops—the ones I wore one summer repeatedly.

Checking my appearance in the mirror, I think to myself, *I hope I'm dressed appropriately.* I've never spent time with a widower before. Actually, I don't think I've ever even used the term before. *Widower*—what a sad-sounding word.

It's midmorning when I arrive at the Millses' house. Berkeley's aunt Jane, whom I've met several times over the years, greets me at the door with a smile and a hug. For the first few minutes, she and I exchange some polite conversation, and then, with a pensive expression, she ushers me into the den, where Berkeley's dad is sitting in an armchair beside a large window.

Nudging me toward him, Jane says, "I'll leave you alone with him for a few minutes."

"Thank you," I whisper, taking a tentative step.

Reaching the middle of the room, I see Archer's face in profile. At first, I fixate on a nasty scar that's far from healed on his forehead, but then I notice he appears frozen, almost mannequin-like. If I didn't know better, I'd think he was asleep with his eyes open.

Cautiously approaching him, I clear my throat and quietly say, "Hey Archer. It's Francie."

When he still doesn't acknowledge me, I pull up a chair, sit down beside him, and wait.

After several minutes of uneasy silence, I grasp one of Archer's hands, which is as cold as ice, so I clutch it with both of mine and try to rub some warmth into it. When this still fails to signal my presence, I discern that Archer's thoughts are a million miles away.

At a loss for what to do next, I take a deep breath and say, "Archer, I'm so sorry about what happened to you and Sarah," and then I start to whimper loudly and shake. *Oh no! No, not now, Francie! God, not now!*

Try as I might to maintain a stiff upper lip, I burst uncontrollably into tears—loud sobs that seem to echo in the room.

Pulling his hand away from mine, Archer tenses and shifts away from me.

Wiping away my tears, I murmur, "I hope I haven't upset you, Archer."

Turning his head away, he starts to whimper too, softly like a wounded animal.

Not knowing what else to do, I stand up and holler, "Jane?"

Within seconds, she is on the scene, propping Archer's slumping head upright, adding a blanket to his legs, and wiping the tears from his cheeks. "Just relax, Archer. Everything will be okay."

Watching him calming, I whisper, "I'm so, so sorry."

Turning to face me, Jane whispers, "Maybe you should come back another time."

I nod and pray for Archer to snap out of whatever spell he's under, but he doesn't. He can't. He's no longer the Archer he once was. As images of Sarah in his arms for the last time fill my brain, I dash from the room and run outside.

Struck by the fact that Berkeley is likely going to be caring for his dad for years to come, a responsibility I can now see I'm not equipped to help with, combined with the fact that I can't come to grips with the notion of ever suffering a loss as immense as Archer's and feel sick to my stomach when that thought conjures up images of Berkeley dying in my arms, I realize I'd rather spend my life detached and alone so that I never have to sink into such deep despair.

Alarmed that I have just entered a dark place, I run toward my mom's car with such speed that I tax my flip-flops to the max and tear the toe piece out of one. When the flip-flop flies off and lands in the gutter, I don't bother to retrieve it. Instead, I remove the other one and leave both of them behind, the sight of their pretty gemstones sparkling brightly in the sun making me cry even more.

Bursting through the door of my parents' empty house, I wipe the tears from my cheeks, pull my phone out of my purse, and formally accept the junior-shoe-designer internship in London. "It's done. I'm moving even farther away from here."

Heading into the sunlit backyard, staring at the place where my beloved hammock used to hang, I fall to my knees and say, "My life here is over."

# foot note forty-nine

RETURNING TO NEW YORK IS MY ONLY PRIORITY TODAY—A TRIP that can't happen fast enough.

Following my horrid encounter with Archer Mills yesterday, I've been in a state of numbness—mind, body, and soul—glued to the family sofa and doing little but counting the hours as they pass.

The only productive thing I've accomplished today is to bag up my severely soiled-in-Romania sneakers and haul them to the Dumpster. Throwing those shoes away has rendered me essentially shoeless, except for the several precious oldies in my closet that I don't dare look at, because too many of them remind me of Berkeley.

Needing a pair of shoes to wear on the plane and unwilling to buy a new pair, because it would necessitate leaving the house, I decide my only option is to borrow something from someone else near to me.

I can't borrow anything from Brigitte, because her closet is empty, and I'm not going to borrow from my mother. *God, no.*

That leaves trendy Talula. *Egad.* Walking inside her closet and turning on the light, I grab the first pair of shoes I spot—a pair of clunky, wood-soled 1940s Swedish platform clogs—and quickly slip them on my feet. Though they feel heavy and are not anything I would purchase, they do make me feel as if I'm someone else, which will be useful in getting me through the rest of this day.

Usually, Saturday is my favorite day of the week, but I have never dreaded anything as much as I do today.

I don't ride to the airport with Berkeley. I make up an excuse that I'm running late and will meet up with him there. Furthermore, I don't respond to his text asking why. I just stuff my phone into my purse and pretend it doesn't exist.

Arriving intentionally late to my gate, I see Berkeley sitting in a seat, staring at his phone.

As always when he's in my fifty-foot radius, my heart starts thumping, my cheeks start flushing, and my hands can't wait to be touching him. *Damn, I wish my body would turn off.*

Seeing me, he stands up, walks in my direction, and offers a sweet smile.

When face-to-face with him, I force a half grin, curse my body for having even more involuntary bodily reactions brought on by the nearness of him, look away, and say, "Hi."

Gently clutching my shoulders, he says, "Your last message worried me. Is everything okay?"

"Yeah, I'm sorry about that. I didn't sleep well last night."

"I didn't either. Yesterday was long and stressful."

After taking a deep breath, I say, "Berkeley, I need to talk to you."

"Sure, and then I need to talk to you too."

"Okay."

We walk toward a quiet alcove, and I lean my back against a wall, take a deep breath, and attempt to speak; however, a loud preboarding announcement regarding my flight blares from the PA system, interrupting my thought process.

Shifting to face me, Berkeley says, "We don't have much time. What did you want to talk about?"

Touching his hand, I mumble, "This is so hard, saying good-bye to you."

Lifting my chin so that he can look into my eyes, Berkeley says, "Hey, I'm not sure if I mentioned this, but it means everything to me that you showed up here when I needed you most."

"It was the least I could do."

"Seriously, Francie. If not for you, I'd be in a bad way."

Shaking my head, I reply, "Berkeley, your dad is in a bad way."

He sighs. "Yeah. I really wish you hadn't gone to see him."

"So much has changed in the past week."

Taking my hand, he responds, "Francie, I know the immediate future won't be easy for us, but I promise I'll come visit you soon, and—"

Staring into the distance, I interject, "No, you need to stay here until your dad is better."

"I know."

"Which leads me to what I want to talk to you about."

"Okay?"

I take a deep breath. "I don't think I'm equipped to handle everything that's going on right now."

"What do you mean?"

With lips quivering, I mumble, "I mean, I think you and I need to back-burner us." Whispering, I add, "Or maybe even remove us from the heat completely."

Stepping back, he responds, "What are you suggesting?"

"That you and I just shouldn't *be* right now."

Grasping my arm, he says, "Francie, you're throwing me off right now. What's going on?"

"A combination of so many things."

"You need to be specific."

"First and foremost, I am moving to London. Soon."

Exhaling, he responds, "I sensed you would be."

"Which means that in a few weeks, our worlds will be even further apart."

"That's one way of looking at it."

"It's the only way of looking at it."

Putting his hands on his hips, he says, "Francie, don't make a bigger deal out of this than necessary. I give you my word: as often as I can, I will travel back and forth overseas so we can be together."

I shake my head. "I don't want to make your life any harder than it already is."

Pulling me close to him, he replies, "Listen carefully to me, Francie. You, always and forever, are it for me. Everything you do, think, wear, or babble is like jet fuel for me, and nothing external—not death, distance, or the delirium you're clearly experiencing right now—is ever going to change that."

"Please stop saying such sweet things to me."

"Why would I stop?"

With fired-up eyes, I say, "Because I need to stop feeling about you the way I do."

"Why?"

"Because I don't want to be around to watch you die."

"What?"

"Which is why I can no longer be attached to you. I just can't. I'm not wired to cope with the emotions that come with it."

Left speechless, Berkeley wanders away and fixates on the Riverly Heights skyline, his perfect face now tarnished with a frown. For several minutes, he just stares into the distance, occasionally running his hands through his hair.

Following an urgent final-boarding announcement regarding my flight, he rushes toward me and abruptly says, "Don't get on the plane."

"What will that accomplish?"

"I don't know. Just don't leave yet before we figure out what's really bothering you."

"Berkeley, I can't. I'm drained. I can't give any more."

"So what are you saying? You're abandoning us based on some crazy notion about me dying?"

As the airline agent begins pressuring me to get on the plane, I move away from Berkeley, allow the agent to scan my boarding pass, and say, "I have to."

Exhaling loudly, Berkeley say, "Francie, don't."

But I do, darting through the security door and heading down a glass-walled hallway.

Watching me leave, he exclaims, "I cannot believe you're doing this!"

Looking back through the glass, I see Berkeley walking parallel with me, his face awash in disbelief and confusion.

As I watch his hands reach into the air, displaying the lasting remnants of the note I scribed on his palm two days ago, I shake my head, suppress my tears, and trudge on.

Trailing me, he pulls out his phone and sends a text.

When my phone pings, I expect to find a plea. But it's not a plea. It's just the words Berkeley wanted to say earlier: "My mother willed you her evening-bag collection, so my aunt is planning to drop it off at your parents' house next week. Call her if you don't want that to happen."

Reading the message again and hearing it in Berkeley's voice, I mumble, "Oh my God, how could I do this, when he just lost his mother?"

Looking up to find him, to somehow express how sorry I am for my heartless actions, I realize I'm unable because he has left the area.

Gazing into the crowd, I catch sight of Berkeley charging down the concourse, weaving in and out of strangers. Amid my throat constricting, I watch as he—without missing a stride—throws his phone into a trash bin that's at least ten feet away.

Whispering, "He even does that flawlessly," I observe him blending into the crowd and disappearing.

Realizing he's gone—*He's gone?*—I turn forward and resume walking. I don't allow myself to think. I just get the hell out of Riverly Heights.

At the airplane's door, a perky flight attendant greets me and says something my brain fails to register. Louder, she repeats, "You're free to move on."

Pausing to absorb the poignant words, I start walking and respond, "Yes, I guess I am."

Navigating my way into the middle of the cabin, I encounter another flight attendant, who greets me with a smile.

"Honey, you look like you just lost your best friend," she says.

For a second, I pause to consider what she means and then answer, "Yes, I did."

Settled in my seat, I close my eyes and mumble, "What is happening to me?"

As the cabin door closes and announcements are being made, I become so shocked by my actions that I begin to overheat. Only then do I accept that I've done the unthinkable, irreparable, and unforgivable.

Scrambling to find my phone, I exclaim, "I need to call him!" But when I realize Berkeley has no working phone for me to call, I become flustered and panicky.

I call my mom. "I did something terrible. I broke up with Berkeley. Forever."

"Oh, honey."

"Mom, I feel horrible."

"Well, I'm sure Berkeley does too."

I whimper. "He hates me, Mom. I saw it written all over his face."

Exhaling, she asks, "Why did you have to do this now?"

I sniffle. "Because evidently, I've gone crackers."

She huffs. "I'm sensing you have."

As the space around me starts to blur, I mumble, "Why would I do something so awful?"

Calmly, she says, "I'm sure it's because this week has been incredibly stressful for you. In fact, you might be in need of some grief counseling."

"Yeah."

She clears her throat. "Why don't you, when you arrive in New York, give Berkeley a call and make amends?"

"No, I can't."

"Why not?"

"Because the wind is out of my sails."

"What does that mean?"

"I'm finished with loving someone as much as I love him."

"Oh, honey!"

After taking a deep breath, I respond, "I'm just not emotionally equipped."

"Francie, you're being irrational."

"No, Mom, I'm doing what I need to do for me."

Sighing, she replies, "I hope you realize the enormity of what you're giving up."

Closing my eyes, I say, "Regardless of whether or not I do, the deed is done."

Before my mom can respond further, I add, "Gotta go," and heed the flight attendant's terse signal by hanging up.

As the airplane lifts off the ground and Riverly Heights gets lost in the clouds, I look at my shoes—Talula's shoes—and realize I've just discovered another dimension of me I didn't know existed: a harsh, cold, self-centered one. Perhaps it surfaced because of stress; I have a lot on my plate before the end of the semester. Perhaps it surfaced because I've never dealt with grief before. Perhaps it surfaced because after spending so many years on my own, I've grown to put my own needs first. Whatever the reason, I've morphed into a person deserving of a life spent alone—like a cat lady but with shoes.

Nearing New York, I press my face against the airplane window, curse myself for what I've done to Berkeley, and whisper, "Time to hit the restart button on everything."

To begin the process, I remove my non-Francie shoes and throw them under the seat in front of me. "Barefoot, I will start my new life."

Looking at my left foot and examining my still-there but slightly faded ski-trip scar, I say, "Should I try to get that fixed?"

After pondering the notion for a minute, I whisper, "No. From now on, you will shamefully display that wound as a sign of how horribly imperfect you are. It will be your penance."

# foot note fifty

FOR THE OCCASION OF THIS EVENING'S COLLEGE-GRADUATION dance, I'm wearing my finished-in-the-nick-of-time year-end school project: a steel-blue halter-style satin gown that fits me like a glove. But it could be a black garbage bag for all I care, because I just want to get through this day so that I can close out the first twenty-two years of my life and move on to the next.

I also don't care what footwear I add to the gown. I wanted to attend tonight's event in bare feet (I've been barefoot pretty much nonstop since returning from Riverly Heights), but Pella wouldn't let me.

"Too bohemian for the dress," she said.

So I'm wearing what she chose for me: a pair of her metallic navy-blue stilettos, which hurt like hell. I agreed to them because they're deservedly making me endure agonizing pain. I'm five minutes in, and the blisters are already forming.

I no longer care about what shoes I'm wearing or about finding the style that has "Francie" written all over it. In fact, I no longer care about anything that used to make me happy. Sure, I still admire beautiful shoes and still intend to design them as a career, but I will do so only for the purpose of shoeing someone other than me.

Yes, I'm in a serious funk these days. I feel gutted inside, as if my world no longer contains sunshine, music, or joy.

Try as I might, I cannot figure out what got into me a few weeks ago in the Riverly Heights airport. I guess I just lost it and snapped.

Haunted by the knowledge that Berkeley will never want to see my face again, I refuse to think beyond the specific moment I'm living. Worse, I haven't been able to talk to anyone about it, other than the brief phone conversation I had with my mom. I've just let the self-pitying backlog, thereby putting myself on the precipice of an emotional explosion at any given second.

My roommates know something is wrong, because I barely speak anymore. But whenever they try to probe me for details, I claim I have somewhere else I have to be and leave, because I'm too ashamed to confess my actions.

My friend Phoebe has clearly heard through the grapevine what happened between Berkeley and me—it's obvious by the more than twenty calls she has made to me in the last couple of weeks—but I can't speak to her about it either, not when I can't come to grips with the situation myself.

My family arrived in New York yesterday to attend my graduation, and my mom took me aside to try to talk and reiterate the idea of grief counseling, but I told her to leave me be until I wrap my head around my actions. Since then, my parents and my sisters are trying their best not to poke the sleeping dragon, ensuring all interaction with me is light and fluffy.

Eventually, I will face all of this crap and talk openly about it. Maybe I'll even try to make sense of my wretched wrongdoing. But I can't now. My body still hurts too much all over. In fact, the nightmares I am now regularly experiencing—either about Sarah dying in Archer's arms or about Berkeley dying in mine—are causing me headaches so severe that I'm doing meditation and popping herbal supplements to combat them.

I suppose it goes without saying that I'm attending tonight's event dateless. I could have invited someone—several college-guy friends would have jumped at the opportunity to eat a free fancy meal—but I'm aware that my current disposition would be torturous for even the most easygoing of acquaintances.

Even if Berkeley and I hadn't split a few weeks ago, he wouldn't be accompanying me, because his college graduation is taking place this weekend too, on the other side of the continent. I wonder if he's taking someone to his formal—something I would verify if I hadn't deleted all of my social-networking accounts upon returning to New York, which I did because I didn't want to know whether or not Berkeley blocked me from his. He should have. He should never want to speak to me again. He should, forevermore, hate me.

I, of course, do not hate him. Rather, the opposite is true, which will forever be my punishment.

I miss him. I ache for him. I think about him constantly.

I even snail-mailed him a note the other day that read as follows:

> *Berkeley:*
> *I hate myself for what I did to you and completely understand why you hate me too.*
> *I'm the worst, and you deserve the best.*
> *Sincerely, Cruella de Francie*

I wrote the note using Berkeley's pen, thinking the exercise would alleviate some of my misery. But it didn't. Rather, it escalated it, probably because for so many years, Berkeley was the face of my happily ever after—and with good reason, because he's the stuff dreams are made of—and he will continue to be as long as I hold him in my thoughts. I'm trying not to, but I can't help it, because I'm plagued with too many reminders: the sight of any pair of pretty shoes, my freckles, the orchid corsage my father ties around my wrist, the stars in the sky I can see through the window, and the breath mint my mom just offered me.

Even a recent photograph my father took of me is a haunter: I'm wearing an expression on my face that is an exact match to the one in the photo Berkeley took of him and me before I left for Italy—the image I, for years, desired to possess but am now glad I didn't receive, because it would just be one of a list of keepsakes in line for removal of some sort.

Getting rid of the old to make way for the new will be my priority and goal once this day ends. In fact, beginning tomorrow, I'll be sorting through all of my belongings and weeding out everything I don't absolutely need. I'll store the mementos I'm hesitant to part with in the antique chest I'm leaving behind while I decide if London feels like home, I'll donate the clothes I no longer wear to a homeless shelter, and the majority of my shoe collection will go either to my fellow size seven, Pella, or in with my clothing donation.

Just a few basic outfits and a single pair of plain black pumps are all I will be hauling with me across the sea.

Once there, I'll begin a life focused solely on my work and my continued education, nothing else.

*Please, city of London, help me make it through the next year without falling to pieces.*

# foot note fifty-one

IT'S BEEN JUST OVER A YEAR SINCE I MOVED TO LONDON. TODAY, AS I reminisce about the experience with refreshed eyes, I find it interesting how a change of scenery proved to be both rejuvenating and tempering. Gone are my days of looking in the mirror and cringing at what I thought to be a repulsive reflection. Here to stay is an updated version of me—a more-resilient one because of newfound traits, such as stamina, patience, determination, and a whole lot of tenacity. The reasons for my transformation are many.

First, I endured twelve long months, six hours a day, in a tiny studio space on London's Mayfair Street, cowering over an old oak desk while my boss—beautiful, grumpy, spastic, neurotic, control-freak shoe designer Candy Perkins—belittled every suggestion I had to offer, subsequently rendering me self-conscious about every move I made, including something as simple as serving tea. To make matters worse, I was forced to keep my hair in a ponytail, my wardrobe stuck in neutrals (as dictated by Candy, so as not to draw her eye from the drawing board), and my feet clad in plain black pumps—the one and only pair of shoes I brought to London with me—making me the most-unnoticeable person in the entire London fashion scene.

Second, I spent all of my other waking hours immersed in the study of shoe design. I learned new shoe-related terms, such as *cordwainery, jiggering, crimping,* and *bespoken*; I discovered men were the first to wear high heels, not women; and I dedicated more study hours in a single week than I ever did while I was in school in New York City, subsequently rendering me exhausted and void of all merriment. However, I did leave the school with a master's degree in shoe design, so I guess the short-term pain was worth it.

On the rare occasion when I had free time, I used it to wander the nooks and crannies of London's quaint neighborhoods, purchasing a diverse menagerie of knickknacks and oddities. During those wanderings, I felt a sense of equilibrium rerooting inside of me, enabling me, one day at a time, to stand up straight again, shift out of the dark shadows, and behave more like the Francie Lanoo I once knew.

When, about a month ago, I visited New York for a reunion with my former flatmates and heard Pella describing my aura as "no longer cloaked in gray," I chose to finally release myself from purgatory. The next day, in the company of Pella and Victoria, I attended a two-hour meditative yoga class; ate lunch in a prissy restaurant, wearing clothing that was not in a neutral tone; and spent the entirety of a Saturday afternoon meandering the streets of my favorite city—actions that reset me and netted me a sweet pair of soft, round-toed royal-blue suede pumps, which I used for some thoroughly enjoyable nightclub dancing later that evening.

The following morning, after tearfully murmuring to my gal pals, "I wanna come home," I began a search for a job in New York and landed one before I'd even flown back to London.

So as of two weeks ago, I'm a New Yorker again—*Congratulations, me!*—working as a design assistant at one of the world's preeminent fashion companies, the House of Elan, where I'm allowed to speak freely, prepare tea any way I choose, and, best of all, move up the ladder.

Laurie Nenson

Without question, this is my dream job; its atmosphere is vibrant, its coworkers are the coolest people on the planet, and its corporate culture puts humanitarian and environmental issues above profits. It's no wonder I'm now happy, calm, and—fingers crossed—on track to become a person I again like.

Also contributing to my fine state of mind, I'm again living in the same warehouse loft with my two best gal pals, Pella and Victoria. I'm loving the place's familiar and fabulous view, noise, vibe, and clutter. Today, on this sunny Saturday, I'm in my corner of the wide-open living space, about to kick-start the getting-settled process by picking through the storage trunk and cardboard boxes I left behind a year ago. I see this task as a form of cleansing as well as a way to make space for the vintage gloves, broaches, and earrings I brought with me from London—my little enhancements that I can't wait to put to daily use.

First on the block for purging are my shoes.

As I sit on the floor and sift through the first two boxes, I start to laugh when I count more than twenty pairs I left behind a year ago. What was I thinking? After realizing each pair is nothing I would ever wear today, I decide they must all go to charity, so I throw them into a discard pile.

As I make my way deeper into the trunk, I smile when I come across a few old handbags that, for some reason, I felt a need to retain. Holding each in my hands, I take a few seconds to reminisce— something I rarely permit myself to do.

After stuffing a few into cardboard boxes, I uncover the one that was my favorite: a soft-sided camel-colored hobo sack that I regularly used during my last semester of college classes. I was most fond of it because it had a stretchiness that enabled me to cart around whatever I needed—art supplies, rolls of drawings, a laptop, a wallet, lip gloss, my giant water bottle, and the occasional lunch. *Should I part with it?* I don't know. It's battered, and I don't see myself using it again.

As I flip through its interior pockets to clean out any left-behind

346

items—gum, tissues, lipstick—I find something unexpected. "Berkeley's pen."

With eyes expanding as wide as they're able, I take a deep breath and say, "I can't believe I went a year without thinking about this." Then it all comes crashing back: the pain I inflicted, the fact that I pushed such a critical issue to the back of my mind for as long as I did, and the verbal apology I never had the courage to make.

Tearing up, I mumble, "I'm such a monster."

Walking near my zone of the room, Pella interjects, "A pretty cute monster, I might add."

Looking up at her, I, for the first time, tearfully spill the details of what happened between Berkeley and me last year.

Crouching beside me, she asks, "Why did you keep this bottled up inside of you?"

"Because it was too ugly to face."

Stroking my hair, she replies, "I bet an apology to Berkeley would fix this."

"No, the damage was so enormous."

"How do you know that?"

"Because I read it on Berkeley's face. He despises me."

"I do not believe anyone could despise you."

Looking toward the window, I murmur, "I didn't deserve him in the first place."

She hugs me. "Just call him, you silly girl."

"I'm not sure I have it in me."

She points at my heart. "I bet you have it in there."

Watching her walk away, I quietly say, "I'd probably make matters worse," after which I hear those little voices reawakening inside my head, saying, *Maybe it was temporary insanity. Maybe it was sleep deprivation. Maybe it was your own way of dealing with grief.*

Shaking my head, I mumble, "Or maybe I'm just an insensitive evildoer."

Having suddenly lost interest in sifting through my old stuff, I abandon my housekeeping efforts and flop backward onto my bed. Sweeping my hands across the smooth covers, I discover I'm suddenly feeling lightheaded, disoriented, and anxious.

Staring at the ceiling, I say, "Apologize. That's what you need to do," which is something I've intended to do over the last year and, in fact, did try during my one and only trip to Riverly Heights last February, venturing to places I knew Berkeley frequented. But I didn't run into him once, which blows a monster-size hole in Allegra's wacky theories about destiny, because if Berkeley and I were meant to be together, we would have serendipitously crossed paths.

Rolling over on my bed, I pull Berkeley's pen close to my eyes. As the incoming daylight accentuates the gemstones, I sigh at how much it has meant to me over the years. Reminding myself that it doesn't belong to me and that I should give it back without delay, I say, "But what if I'm not done with it?"

As my mind starts filling with ideas, I pull out my sketchbook and do what comes naturally: I scribe, I scribble, I doodle, I construct. Having not considered in a long time a shoe style with me in mind, I ferociously throw new ideas across the page: curves, angles, shading, and texture.

Over and over, I make attempts. In fact, hours pass, resulting in a heap of discards in the middle of the floor. But finally, something of substance presents itself: a pointy-toed black shoe with an hourglass heel and minimal adornment, just a series of silky ribbons crisscrossing up the front.

Holding the image in the air, I say, "I believe you're the most-refined shoe I've ever drawn." Though I immediately know it bears little reflection of the Francie Lanoo I know myself to presently be, I imagine myself wearing it and wish it were real.

Feeling a renewed desire to pursue some version of a me

shoe—maybe an altogether new one, void of all previously accumulated descriptors—I clutch Berkeley's pen in my hand and ask, "Do I have it in me to finish this journey?"

*Is there even a reason to?*

# foot note fifty-two

FOR A REENERGIZED SHOE GIRL LIKE ME, THERE'S NO GREATER feeling than seeing someone strutting around town wearing footwear you've played a role in designing, which I occasionally get to do as a result of my employment at Elan.

Equally as exciting is physically wearing shoes I've played a role in bringing to life. And because Elan's products are founded in quality above quantity, I now strut around in the highest of heels all day long without ever suffering feet fatigue. Living in fear of shoe-icide? Never. Not ever.

Another high point of my fabulous, still-can't-believe-I-work-here job is that after only eighteen months of being here, I graduated from the position of design assistant to full-fledged footwear designer. *Yahoo!*

The other day, when told of my promotion, I was lucky enough to meet Elan's legendary founder, Jaiman, a tall, well-built, platinum-haired, bronze-skinned god-of-a-man so famous in his own right that the paparazzi stalk him like an A-list movie star. Even I went a little cuckoo over the sight of him, becoming so flustered that I introduced myself to him twice. How embarrassing.

But after he told me he'd like to have me working in the Rome headquarters within the next two years, I exclaimed, "Yippee!" and gave him a warm hug.

Pumped by all of this good-shoe karma, I've been sketching all kinds of unique shoes day in and day out and am now full-throttle chasing the elusive Francie Lanoo shoe, guided not by a single descriptor but, rather, by my trusted instincts. When I see the shoe, I'll just know.

After mentioning the concept to my coworker Reuben—a midtwenties English bloke who looks so much like my old pal Patrick Needle that I often call him by the wrong name—I now have an enthusiastic ally who regularly bombards me with concept suggestions, new shoe-boutique names, and magazine features containing the latest styles. Reuben is another reason I love my time spent in the office.

I'm especially excited to go there today, because we'll be starting the designs for Elan's new spring collection set to go to market two years from now. The process to make a single shoe is long and arduous but worth it in the end.

In need of an energy boost to get my day off to the right start, I stop to grab a smoothie at a shop called Jumpin' Jackson's, a cool hangout near work that I frequent more than my pocketbook would like. However, I can't stop, because with one sip of their beverages, I feel as if I could fly.

I wonder if caffeine is involved.

Today, as always, the place is jam-packed with early morning risers. Finally reaching the front of the line, I order my latest craze, Tropical Paradigm—a mixture of mango, pineapple, banana, and peach—and then lean against a wall for the ten-minute wait.

To pass the time, I review messages on my phone: Pella and Victoria wonder what I'm doing this weekend; my parents wonder why I don't call more often; and my sister Talula has informed me she and her latest boyfriend are taking a weekend off from veterinary school to visit me next month. *Yay!*

After a few minutes, I hear the attendant call out, "Tropical," so I saunter toward the counter, grab the nearest lidded cup, and head on my way.

I'm barely outside the door, when I notice my beverage reads "Blueberry Exposure." Knowing I've snagged someone else's drink, I spin around and rush back inside. As I approach the service counter, I spot a nicely outlined gentleman saying something about blueberry.

Scooting beside him, I say, "I'm so sorry. I believe I grabbed yours."

As he turns to face me, I look up and see a pair of coffee-bean-brown eyes staring down at me. Reminded of the long-lost concept of male–female attraction, I smile back and then go so far as to physically speak, saying, "This is completely my mistake. May I buy you another?"

Gazing without blinking, he uses his full lips to politely respond, "It's the least you can do after stealing mine."

The attendant pipes up. "We're happy to redo them both, if you'll just give us a minute."

"Sure," we say simultaneously, staring at each and blushing a little.

As he begins talking—about the weather, the latest news headlines, and how fantastic this place is—my memory begins recording his other attributes: stylish eyeglasses, custom Italian suit, button-up shirt, uniquely patterned silk tie, newly coiffed sandy-blond hair, and square jawline.

As he takes the dialogue to more-personal topics—where we live in proximity to this place, our favorite menu items, and the effects the drinks have on dispositions—I discover he's intelligent, witty, and bursting with charm.

Letting down my guard for the first time in what feels like forever, I share details about myself, giggle a little, and even flutter my eyelashes, something that feels good, normal, and right.

Grasping our proper drinks, the two of us head outside and converse for the length of an entire block.

After we reach the corner and go our separate ways, I realize I failed to get the guy's name—an oversight for sure. However, I won't forget running into him, because lo and behold, he was wearing shoes that I designed the stitching pattern for as part of my first assignment at Elan.

I wish I'd thought to mention that when I had the chance.

*Oh well. Out of practice. My bad.*

# foot note fifty-three

THE COOLEST PERK ABOUT WORKING AT ELAN IS THAT I'M ALLOWED
to test-drive any of the display shoes whenever I want, on the strict
condition I apply cloth tape to the soles and return them by nine o'clock the
next morning, looking new. It's something I have no problem achieving,
because I would never deface art and am always the first one in the office.

To head out to an event tonight—the first showing of an up-
and-coming abstract-expressionist painter from Brooklyn—I'm
borrowing a pair of Elan deep teal velvet stilettos with intricate star
cutouts on the ankle straps. I picked them because they're about to be
featured in a cool new advertising campaign—"One Giant Strut for
Womankind"—and because they perfectly match the teal cocktail
dress I bought for tonight.

The only downfall of these stunning shoes is that their closed-
toe feature conceals the spectacular mirrored-aluminum pedicure I
treated myself to yesterday.

*Oh well, I've compromised in worse ways before.*

Here I am, hanging out at this art show with about two hundred other
enthusiasts, and standing across the room from me is the guy I ran into
at the juice bar a couple of weeks ago. *Huh. What are the odds?*

From my position about fifteen feet away, I'm only able to view him in profile, but he looks as handsome as he did the first time I saw him. He's sporting a slim-fitting black suit, a pale blue shirt, a stunning silver tie, and another pair of Elan shoes (I can spot our product from a mile away). He's with a date—a stunning woman who looks like a runway model and whose non-Elan heels have her standing about six feet tall.

Panning the room, he catches sight of me. Raising a hand and offering me a warm smile, he whispers something into his companion's ear and wanders to where I'm standing.

"Hey, Tropical Girl!"

"Hey, Blueberry Boy!"

Shaking my hand, he says, "I was so rude the other day. I should have introduced myself. I'm Robert Matthews."

"It's nice to meet you. I'm Francie Lanoo."

"I like your name, Francie Lanoo."

"Thank you," I reply with a smile.

After I introduce him to my flamboyant workmates—my sidekick Reuben and Guido, a small-statured, dark-haired, expressive twentysomething Italian—we commence talking art, and Robert asks me, "Are you a fan of this artist?"

Shrugging, I reply, "I usually love abstract expressionism, but I'm not overly impressed by this body of work."

"May I ask why?"

I point to a few of the works. "Because each one is so similar to the next. In fact, I'm guessing the artist lined up twenty canvases and started a production line."

"Hmm. Now that you mention it, they do seem rushed."

I crinkle my nose. "I hope I haven't deterred you from making a purchase."

Dipping his chin, he replies, "You couldn't possibly, because I've already done so."

"Oh, I'm so sorry!" I exclaim, my face flushing.

Touching my arm (*Whoa, that felt nice*), he says, "No worries. I'll just give it to my girlfriend since she's the one who wanted it."

Tipping my head to the side, I respond, "Proving yet again that beauty is in the eye of the beholder."

"It certainly is," he replies, still touching my arm.

As he fixes his gaze on my face and awakens butterflies in my stomach that I was sure were deceased and buried, Robert and I exchange condensed versions of each other's life stories: he's a lawyer (*Like my dad!*) specializing in international business and corporate takeovers; he's originally from Seattle but has lived in New York for five years; he collects art passionately; and he's fascinated that I work for Elan, because it's his favorite shoe brand.

As the evening churns along, he remains by my side and makes subtle suggestions that he would like to get to know me better, but because he has a girlfriend—and because I still feel unworthy of dating anyone—I ignore his subtle flirting and pull my friends back into the conversation whenever possible.

Near midnight, as the event starts to wind down and patrons begin flocking out the door, Robert shakes Reuben's, Guido's, and my hands, looks me in the eye, and says, "It was a joy running into you again."

"Likewise," I reply, and then I watch him cross the room to rejoin his girlfriend.

I don't see him for the next ten minutes, but as I'm walking toward the exit, he catches up with me, leans his head toward my ear, and says, "Just so you know, if I were single, you wouldn't be."

Caught off guard by the smoothest line ever, I respond with a slight chuckle and a sheepish grin.

Embarking on my short walk home, arm in arm with my two best work buddies, I say, "That was a good party."

Leaning into me, Jonathan says, "That man you were talking to—he was dee-lish-us."

Looking at my spectacular shoes, I inhale a deep breath and happily reply, "Yeah, and I think he just turned my heart back on."

# foot note fifty-four

TODAY I'M WEARING A PAIR OF ELAN DEEP PURPLE SUEDE BOOTIES with twisted silver heels—the first shoe style I've followed since its conception, when its first sketches were passed around a boardroom, the first week I started here. Luckily, I was first in line to test-drive it, which is impeccable timing because it means I'll be strutting with maximum style for the inaugural walk into my brand-new private workstation, located along the highly desirable tenth-floor north windows.

I've been moved here to work alongside one of Elan's senior shoe designers: Donatella Kabb, the artist extraordinaire responsible for churning out many of Elan's masterpieces. It's an honor and a thrill that I get to collaborate with her, and if even a fraction of her magical powers rub off on me, I'll be forever indebted.

What a great way to start the week—my feet feel amazing, my new ergonomic chair feels amazing, and my view of the Meatpacking District's buildings is amazing.

As a smile breaks out on my face, my office phone rings.

Answering, I say, "Good morning. This is Francie Lanoo."

After clearing his throat, the caller replies, "Hey, good morning. This is Robert Matthews."

My eyes pop open. "Hi. It's nice to hear from you."

"Is this a suitable time to call you, or am I interrupting something?"

"It's not a problem at all, because we at Elan are never too busy to talk to our customers."

Chuckling, he says, "What's on the drawing board today that might interest me?"

Smiling, I reply, "You'll have to wait approximately twenty-four months to learn the highly coveted answer to that."

"Good thing I'm a patient man."

"Bad thing you didn't even try to bribe me."

Chuckling again, he asks, "How are you?"

"I'm well. How are you?"

"I'm doing well too, and in case you're wondering, there is a reason for my call today."

"What might that be?"

After audibly inhaling, he replies, "Since running into you last week, I've been thinking—pretty much steadily—about your comments on artwork, specifically about what makes a painting great, how to assemble a well-rounded collection, and how to best pair it with furniture."

I grin. "The artsy part of your brain has been busy."

"Yes, it has, and it concocted the most-brilliant idea."

"Please share."

"It told me to hire you to tweak my apartment."

Leaning back in my chair, I smile and respond, "You do realize that apartments are not what I do, right?"

"Yes, I understand that shoes are your thing, but I can tell by your style that you have excellent taste, and that's what I'm seeking."

Spinning my chair in a full circle, I ask, "How exactly do you imagine me helping you?"

"By allowing me to pick your brain—for one hour tops."

Doodling on a notepad, I answer, "I'd be okay with that."

"Great. When can we get together?"

Pulling up the calendar on my phone, I respond, "Evenings after seven or weekends work best for me. So pick a date, any date."

Exhaling, he says, "Well, due to a recent change in my personal status, I am free all weekend, so how about Friday evening at eight?"

Feeling my face warming, I reply, "Sure."

"If you'd like, I can have dinner ready when you arrive."

My eyes light up. "Well, since my brain is better for the picking when it's well nourished, yes, you may make me dinner."

"Excellent!" he exclaims, and he gives me instructions to his place.

"See you Friday," I say.

"Looking forward to it," he replies, and then he adds, "Oh, by the way, I hope you like coffee, because I just bought a deluxe espresso machine, and I'd love to break it in during dessert."

Shrugging, I respond, "I'd be happy to be your test run."

"Great. I can't wait."

"Ditto."

After a pause, he says, "Well, I should let you get back to your day."

"Yes, you should."

"Have a productive one, Francie."

Grinning, I reply, "I'll do my best."

Hanging up and looking at the shoe samples lying around my office, I start thinking about my footwear choice for Friday's outing. After little deliberation, I decide that what I'm currently wearing will do just fine.

As I lean back in my chair, Reuben peeks around the corner of my workspace and says, "Based on the sexiness I heard in your voice during that last phone call, I'd bet a thousand dollars you were not talking to a client."

Blushing, I respond, "It was Robert Matthews, the guy I introduced you to at the art show."

His eyes widen. "Oo-la-la! He's a hottie. Are you going on a date with him?"

I tentatively smile. "No, I'm going to test-drive his new coffee machine."

Dipping his chin, Reuben replies, "Now that's a euphemism I've never heard used before."

Shaking my head, I put a pencil to paper and say, "Ha-ha, go back to work, Reuben."

# foot note fifty-five

When out and about in the city, I'm encouraged to wear Elan shoes all the time for marketing purposes. However, when I'm casually hanging around home, I regularly wear my latest go-to footwear: unpretentious, soft, fur-lined suede moccasins.

At present, I own four pairs. Today's choice is in the palest shade of silver gray with delicate tone-on-tone embroidery. They're adorable and whimsical, to say the least, but what I like most about them is that wearing them is like giving my feet a hug—it's a soothing end-of-the-day luxury to counterbalance the fact that my life is churning faster than a mini–doughnut maker at a carnival.

My primary time sucker is, of course, my work, especially now that a series of shoes designed by Donatella Kabb and me recently moved into the production stage, which requires round-the-clock supervision to ensure every last detail is implemented to the highest level of quality. My secondary time sucker is my alive-again personal life, which has gone from zero to sixty so fast I'm already cohabitating with coffee drinker Robert Matthews.

He and I have been romantically linked ever since the evening he summoned me to his swanky SoHo apartment to pick my brain, a process that didn't end up happening, probably because the penthouse suite was already art filled, professionally designed, and in need of zero tweaking.

Later that evening, after Robert walked me home, I got the biggest uplift I'd had in years, when he kissed me good-bye and whispered into my ear, "I think I just won the dating lottery." That moment marked a turning point for me, propelling me into an emotional place finally free of self-loathing.

For many reasons, these days, I'm in a thoroughly content state of mind, probably because this relationship is based on 100 percent compatibility: we're both easy to get along with, we're both respectful of each other's space, we're both attuned to exactly the same passions (indulging in travel, exercise, and fashion; supporting arts, culture, and charities; gourmet cooking; and dining at New York City's finest restaurants), and we're both on the same page with regard to our careers (we're passionate about what we do, goal driven, and happiest when we achieve milestones). Best of all, we're both content to coexist independently, meaning neither of us is the least bit bothered when work-related activities result in us going days without interacting with one another.

My takeaway from this adult relationship is that I don't need to be the center of someone's attention to feel complete. I don't need to see fireworks in the sky when they're not really there. I don't need to get giddy and tongue-tied just because of someone's nearness. Most of all, I don't need to lose all sense of time when adoring eyes lock with mine across a crowded room.

With age has come wisdom; most notably, I have realized that true happiness is best when it's self-induced. *Wow! What a long way I've come since my idyllic days growing up in my hometown of Riverly Heights.*

Speaking of, a week ago, I received an e-mail from my old high school, inviting me to our graduating class's seven-year reunion. The heading read, "The Seven-Year-Itch Party." The subheading read, "It's seven years, not five, because two years ago, no one was missing anyone"—a message that first made me laugh and then made me think about all of the people I do miss seven years later.

*A high-school reunion! Already. God, I'm getting old.*

Taking a seat on Robert's expansive dark brown leather sectional, I start contemplating whether or not I should attend.

I pull out my phone and text my longtime friend Phoebe, whom, I'm happy to say, I've started doing biannual girlie-girl getaways with, and I ask, "What do you think? Yea or nay—me at the reunion?"

Immediately texting back, she responds, "Yea, or I'll never speak to you again."

"Fibber," I say.

Texting my other childhood buddy, Patrick Needle, whom I've kept in touch with but haven't seen in years, I ask, "What do you think? Yea or nay—me at the reunion?"

Within seconds, he texts, "I'm having a party on the Sunday following the reunion, and if you don't make an appearance, I'm going to project supersized pictures of the naked two-year-old you all over the walls."

"Scoundrel."

On my laptop, I review the RSVP list and learn that about half of the graduating class has already responded in the affirmative, including several people I'd love to spend time with. Additionally, Mrs. Bouchard and many of my former teachers are planning to be there, which is another draw.

After walking in the door and kissing me on the top of the head, Robert says, "What's making headlines in your world today?"

Smiling, I answer, "I'm trying to decide whether or not to attend a high-school reunion in Riverly Heights."

"When is it?"

"Six weeks from now—the last weekend in September, which is slow at work, so I could easily miss a few days."

"When were you last home?"

"Hmmm. It has been a long time."

Pressing his forehead against mine, he says, "I could go with you and finally meet your family."

Shrugging, I say, "Sure. Okay then. Decision done. I am going to the Seven-Year Itch."

As my head fills with pleasant images of the numerous encounters I'm bound to have, I feel my heart rate kicking into high gear.

Feeling a youthful smile uncontrollably forming on my face, I say, "I should get a new hairstyle, a unique mani and pedi, and, more important than anything, a new pair of shoes."

"You should."

Looking out the floor-to-ceiling windows into the distance far beyond the Manhattan skyline, I say, "Okay, Riverly Heights. I'm coming home."

# foot note fifty-six

My homecoming hairstyle is done, and my homecoming manicure and pedicure are done, but my homecoming shoes are not done, and I'm running out of time.

Sadly, I'm down to my last evening of shopping before the venerable fairy-tale-princess clock runs out (i.e., before Robert and I head to the airport tomorrow morning at six o'clock), and I'm about to hit the panic switch.

Uniqueness has been the key to what I've been seeking, but after four weeks of scouring shoe boutiques, department stores, and the obscure Florrie Brown-King's Attic, I've uncovered nothing that flips my pancakes, as I used to say. I didn't find anything even after I sorted through several of the new Elan samples sitting on displays throughout our office.

If only I'd had enough time to design and fabricate a shoe style myself. But I don't. So I'm down to my last shoe shop: a quirky boutique that just opened up in Brooklyn, recommended to me by my friend Pella, who discovered it recently while researching shoes for me. From what she's told me, and I am quoting Pella on this, "Every single style in the place is worth going into credit-card debt for."

*Perfect!*

The shop has a great name too: Kismet Married Happenstance, which has me intrigued before I even get there.

I'm en route now, keeping my expectations low to minimize disappointment.

Making a beeline in the direction of the stop, I ask, "Why is that name making me so giddy?"

It's probably because I still hold a soft spot for frilly, pretty, girlie words.

Maneuvering around a cluster of people, I see an oval-shaped sign hanging on a wrought-iron bracket, featuring the store's name hand-painted in ornate turquoise script. Approaching it, I notice that the backdrop is splattered with silver glitter; the sunlight catches the many surfaces, making each particle twinkle like a star. *Nice.*

Arriving in front of the shop's display window, I peer through the glass and pan what is, without a doubt, the most-unusual-looking collection of shoes I've ever seen.

Grinning ear to ear, I whisper, "Thank you, Pella, for leading me here."

As my eyes scan methodically through the displayed options, absorbing a myriad of details that are completely new to me—which is saying a lot, considering what I do for a living—I feel as if I'm visiting the establishment of an old-world cobbler, one who makes each precious pair by hand.

I love them all. I would wear them all. I want them all. But when my excessive enthusiasm makes my heartbeat go erratic, I murmur, "Concentrate, Francie. You're running out of time. Will any pair do for Saturday night?"

*Let's see.*

Within the top section, all choices are tantalizing, but none scream, "You can't live without me."

Within the middle section, I see some extraordinary options that

I'd wear to any event in New York City but that I know would be far too flamboyant to wear in Riverly Heights.

Within the lower section, as I scan meticulously from left to right, I stop, stare, and begin breathing so heavily that I'm at risk of hyperventilating. After all of my years of refining, sketching, searching, and hoping, I am—right here, right now—discovering that it exists.

Squinting, I mumble, "It can't be. I must be imagining this." But I'm not. I can see it. It's right there. Tearing up, I press my face to the glass and whisper, "Hello, you."

To the sound of imaginary horns, strings, and percussion sounding in my head, I lovingly admire each one of its attributes—matte fuchsia leather, randomly placed rhinestone sparkles, a square heel, sturdy, cute as a button, timeless, lovely, a little bit quirky, and altogether like nothing else.

Feeling a sudden twinge of panic that someone else will snap the shoe up before I do, I morph into a sprinter and fling open the shop's cherry-red door.

Inside, I see a man sitting behind an ornate antique desk. He is well dressed and short, appears to be in his midthirties, and has dark brown hair and a pleasant face. He's on the phone, speaking in a language I know to be Italian.

Rushing toward him, I wave my hands to get his attention, and after he says something into the phone and hangs up, I exclaim, "I'm sorry to interrupt, but may I please have your assistance?"

Quickly standing up, he smiles and says with an accent, "Of course. What can I help you with?"

In a frantic tone new to my ears, I say, "I need to see the shoe on the lower shelf in the window, right in the middle of the lineup—the fuchsia one with the platform sole, the square heel, and the open toe."

As the man's eyes light up, he politely says, "Please, show me the one you mean."

Walking to the window, I agitatedly add, "It has a strap that wraps around the ankle, it has an insole that's shiny silver, and it has adornments that glitter like stars."

"Oh yes, I know the one," he says. Reaching to retrieve it, he adds, "My apologies for being slow on the uptake, but this season's stock is quite diverse, and I'm still acquainting myself with what's what and what's where."

"There's no need to apologize," I reply, earnestly watching as he handles the most-incredible object I've ever seen.

"It's lovely," he says.

As it nears me, I ask, "Do you have it in a size seven?"

Looking at the shoe's sole, he replies, "This one is a size seven, so just give me a minute to find its match."

"Thank you!" I abruptly shout, exhaling in relief.

Motioning to a quirky, floral-upholstered chair, he says, "Please sit down, and make yourself comfortable."

"Thank you. I will."

Taking a glance at my fidgeting hands, he offers me the display shoe and says, "While you're waiting, feel free to take a closer look at how the shoe has been crafted."

"I'd love to," I respond, drawing the shoe close to my chest and hugging it as if it's a newborn baby, ignoring the odd glance the salesman gives me as he walks backward through a turquoise velvet curtain.

Waiting, I take off my skin-tone pumps, nestle my bare feet into the shag carpet, and try to be patient. As my anxiousness worsens, I exasperatedly mumble, "Where is he? What is he doing in there?"

As the words seem to echo, the salesman reappears carrying the most-beautiful shoebox imaginable: glossy chartreuse with embossed metallic-pink polka dots on the lid only.

"You found it!" I exclaim.

Reaching me, he wipes his brow and says, "Yes, but I have some news that you won't be happy to hear."

"What?"

Exhaling, he responds, "Well, first of all, this shoe is a sample only—a style that has not been reproduced—which means, unfortunately, that there's only one pair in existence."

"But it's my size, so that's okay."

"Actually, it was never meant to be on display—something I didn't realize. I put it out by accident."

"But I'm okay with the display model, so there shouldn't be a problem. Right?"

Tipping his head, he replies, "Yes, actually, there is, because this pair appears to be on hold for someone else."

"What? No!"

Shrugging, he explains, "There's a note inside the box, and I didn't see it until just this minute."

My heart drops to the floor. "That's terrible."

"I know. I'm so sorry."

Suppressing a bucket of tears and plotting out in my mind the many possible ways to make a deal with the person who's placed them on hold, I mumble, "Do you mind if I at least try them on?"

"Of course," he says, passing the box to me.

As it crosses my line of sight, I notice a label posted on the end. I read it, gasp, and abruptly say, "It's called the Incomparable?"

Nodding, he replies, "Yes, I believe it is."

With my hands shaking, I lift the lid, push back the chartreuse tissue, grasp the pink sticky note, and read out loud, "The perfect shoe for Francie Lanoo."

Sighing, the salesman says, "You see? This pair is spoken for."

Looking up at him, I pull my driver's license from my bag and numbly respond, "But I'm Francie Lanoo."

Slumping, he frantically says, "Oh! I'm so glad to hear that! Oh, thank heaven! Oh my God, my heart is now beating so fast I think it's going to explode." After pausing to take a deep breath, he adds, "There is nothing I fear more than a disappointed female customer. And when I saw the sad expression on your face a minute ago, oh my goodness, I wanted to crawl into a hole."

Barely registering his words, I say, "How is it that these shoes were put aside for me?"

"I can't answer that right now, but if you'd like, I'll do some inquiring over the next few days."

"Thank you. I'd appreciate that."

I wonder if Pella somehow set this up as a special gift to me, but I determine that she couldn't have, because I've never described any shoe to her. Could she have just instinctively known?

Smiling, the salesman says, "Let's make sure the shoes fit. Shall we?"

Wiping away a face full of tears, I reply, "Sure, but to be perfectly honest, I don't care if they hurt or cause blisters or tickle my toes, because I will love them forever, no matter what."

Smiling, he replies, "Then they deserve to be yours."

As I slip the shoes onto my feet, I feel my heart's affection spreading throughout my entire body. When I notice that the ankle strap doesn't cover up my now-faded scar but, rather, runs parallel to it as if to underline it, I feel myself beaming even more.

Standing up and walking in a circle, I ask, "How is it that these shoes are so marshmallow comfy?"

"It's because their soles are made of a unique blend of natural latex and pure heavea milk to maximize comfort."

"I'll remember that," I respond, making a mental note to introduce that exceptional feature into every new shoe I create from now on.

"Would you like to take a look at yourself in the mirror?" the salesman asks.

"I would!" I exclaim, and as I do, I feel my insides overheating.

After imagining—and doubting and dismissing—this moment so many times, I'm overwhelmed that it's actually happening.

As my emotions get the best of me and I start to whimper like a sad puppy, the salesman touches my shoulder, offers a tissue, and says, "Can I get you anything? Water? Tea? A shot of some lovely Scotch I've got stashed in the back?"

"No, I'll be fine. I've just never before experienced happiness on such a grand scale, and I'm going to need a minute to pull myself together."

"Take all the time you need. And by the way, the shoes are free of charge, so let me package them up for you."

"Free? Why?"

Shrugging, he responds, "Well, since my wife is the designer as well as the only other person who works here, she will have the answer."

"Would it be okay if I came back in a week to talk to her?"

"Sure, that would be very nice. I'd contact her right now, but she's adverse to all things technological, so I have no way of reaching her."

As my senses perk, I say, "I once knew someone like that."

He mumbles, "What drives me most crazy is that when Allegra enters one of her design modes, she ignores me for weeks."

My hands drop. "Sorry, but did you just say Allegra?"

He looks up. "Yes. That's my wife."

"Are you kidding me?"

Eyeing my wide-open mouth, he asks, "Is everything okay?"

Overjoyed again, I run around the desk, throw my arms around the salesman's neck, and exclaim, "Everything's fine! Thank you! Thank you! Thank you!"

"For what?"

"For more than I have time to share."

"Okay?"

With eyes wide open, I say, "Please tell Allegra that Francie Lanoo will be back very soon."

He nods. "I'll do just that."

Grasping the cloth shoe bag and walking toward the door, I stop and ask, "Out of curiosity, would your name happen to be Mauro?"

His dark brown eyes brighten. "Yes, actually, it is."

Heading out the door, I announce, "It's a pleasure to meet you, Mauro," and then I leave, wearing a smile so extreme that it couldn't be slapped off of my face.

For many minutes, I wander and meander, feeling giddy and skipping. En route to the nearest thoroughfare, I browse the feet of many passersby, and when everything I see pales in comparison to what I'm holding in my arms, I happily sigh.

Turning a corner, waving down a taxi, and hopping inside, I finally realize that my longtime search is done.

As an odd roiling erupts in my stomach, my mind fills with questions: How many hours did I spend looking at shoes? How many pairs of shoes have my feet worn? What triggered me to go after my me shoe in the first place?

Staring at the traffic, I slip into an otherworldly daze and replay some of my life-changing shoes: the Debut-Taunter; the Valentine's Day I Love You; the dazzling sweet-sixteen shoe; the leaf-print transparent shoe from the Riverly Heights High School graduation (a knockout style even today); and many more.

As the nostalgia elevates my spirits to a level unfelt in years, I conjure up an image of the guy who was alongside me for many of those milestones, the guy who knew me so well that he verbalized this shoe style for me, the guy whose simple question prompted all of this.

His name slips from my lips. "Berkeley Mills."

Looking in the rearview mirror, the middle-aged gentleman taxi driver interjects in an Eastern European accent, "Excuse me?"

Looking at his reflection, I respond, "Oh, nothing. I was just thinking out loud."

As my face takes on a warm glow, he catches sight of me in the rearview mirror and replies, "A very happy thought, I see."

Eager to share my big day with someone, I say, "Yes, of my high-school boyfriend."

"Your first love."

"And so much more, including a collaborator on my me shoe."

The taxi driver's face twists. "Did you say 'me shoe'?"

I giggle. "Yes, he once described a shoe to me, and then I sketched it and sent it to someone else, who fabricated it and left it waiting for me on the shelf of the sweetest boutique ever. It's a long, convoluted story."

"It sounds serendipitous."

"It is!" I answer, and after a pause, I murmur, "I wonder what Berkeley would say if he learned I found what I was looking for."

"Why don't you call him and find out?"

"Oh no! I can't."

"Why not?"

"Because he and I haven't spoken in a long time, and because I know he'd never answer the phone if he knew the call was from me."

"That's very sad."

"It is," I respond, and when my insides begin rumbling, I quietly add, "I was horrible to him the last time we were together."

Sighing, the driver responds, "I'm sure an apology would make everything better."

Recalling the last look I saw on Berkeley's face, I reply, "An apology now would be too little too late."

Smiling, he adds, "My wife often reminds me that as long as I'm still breathing, an apology is never too late."

I drop my eyes to the floor. "I'm too worried I'd say something to make matters worse."

"Maybe you could send a written note. Because sometimes the hand more easily conveys what the mouth struggles to say."

"That's true," I reply, and as images of inscriptions on palms fill my head, I add, "You know, at age fifteen, I would have sold my soul to spend the rest of my life with Berkeley Mills, and here I am, a decade later, wondering if I'd even recognize him on the street."

"Of course you would! It's all in the eyes—the link to the heart."

After a pause, I smile and reply, "Thank you for planting in my head the loveliest picture."

He smiles back. "I think the picture was in your head before I said a word."

Glancing out the window, I say, "You're very perceptive, sir."

"The wisdom of experience."

"Something I could use a little of."

Turning his head to look at me, he says, "You appear to be managing just fine."

As a lump has formed in my throat, I quietly respond, "I'm a work in progress."

Noticing we're nearing Robert's apartment building, I say, "I hope I wasn't too chatty today."

Parking out front, he rotates in his seat and replies, "Quite the contrary. You're the first customer all week that has said a word to me, and I couldn't be happier."

"Enjoy the rest of your day."

He nods. "You too, my dear."

After I hop out of the taxi, I meander into the apartment and make myself an afternoon coffee. But when the first sip tastes bitter, I pour it down the sink and pop open a bottle of my favorite champagne.

Guzzling it, I give Robert a call and say, "I have some exciting news."

"What?"

"I found my me shoe."

Chuckling, he replies, "Wonderful!"

"I know."

Sighing, he adds, "Maybe now you'll start searching for something different—like hats."

"There's an idea," I reply, hanging on his every word, because I have never worn hats, nor have I ever expressed enjoyment in wearing them.

After hanging up, I wander into my closet, change into a wispy white dress, pop a few gerbera daisies into my hair, and slip my happy feet into their best shoes ever. Feeling young and carefree, I sip more champagne, grab Berkeley's pen from my handbag, turn on some nostalgic music, crank up the volume, and flit around the space like a fairy with new wings.

Arriving in front of a full-length mirror, I look down and admire my feet, and after verifying once more that nothing could be more me, I shift my eyes to the mirror's well-illuminated reflection and stare. Unexpectedly seeing Berkeley's ghostlike image standing beside me, I calmly exhale and gleefully scribe on the mirror using Berkeley's pen: "If Not 4 U."

Smiling as widely as my facial muscles will allow, I think of my awesome friend Pella, call her, and explain in great detail all that has happened to me in the last few hours.

Excitedly, she responds, "Never have I heard a story so incredible. You should write a book about it."

Shaking my head, I reply, "No, I'm just going to properly thank the people who made it happen."

"How are you going to thank Allegra?"

"By purchasing her a cell phone, goddammit. Enough of this cosmic-connection stuff."

Giggling, she asks, "How are you going to thank Berkeley?"

After taking a deep breath, I answer, "Well, for starters, I'm going to formally apologize to him—somehow, some way—which I suspect won't make much of a difference in the way he feels about me but will help me sleep better at night."

"It's a long time coming."

"Yeah, well, it took me all of this time to wrap my head around the fact that I can live with the knowledge that he despises the sight of me, but I cannot live with him not knowing how sorry I am for what I did."

"Correct me if I'm wrong, but I get the feeling that you have more to say to Berkeley than an apology."

"Maybe."

After clearing her throat, she asks, "And how are you planning to thank me—you know, for leading you to where you needed to go?"

Smiling, I answer, "I'm going to let you borrow my new shoes whenever you want."

"As if you're ever going to take them off."

"That's true," I say, giggling and then adding, "I'd better go. I still have to pack for tomorrow."

"Have fun, and good luck with your apology."

"Thank you."

After a dozen songs' worth of dancing, which leaves me exhausted and out of breath, I stand and stare at my shoes, smugly smiling at the wonder of knowing how true, mad, deep love actually feels.

As visions of Berkeley start vividly dancing in my head, I flip his pen into the pocket on my dress, move to the kitchen counter, open my laptop, and search for the online registry of RSVPs to the Seven-Year Itch.

"Are you attending, Mr. Mills, or not?" I say aloud.

Scrolling to find his name, I slump in my stool and say, "You're not." As a lump forms in my throat, I add, *"Damn."*

The apartment door opens, and Robert walks in. "Hey, sweetheart. How are those fancy shoes working out for you?"

"Perfectly well," I respond, pointing their toes in Robert's direction.

Grinning at them, he asks, "Are you packed and ready for the flight tomorrow?"

"No, but I'll get started in a few minutes." After swallowing and wiping away an unexpected tear, I add, "You know, if you'd rather not hang out with a bunch of strangers, you are welcome to stay here this weekend."

Hugging me from behind, he replies, "No, I'm fully committed to this because I can't wait to visit the place that shaped the woman I'm madly in love with."

Exhaling, I reply, "Okay then." But what I really want to say is "I think you should stay, because I'm suddenly so confused with my emotions I haven't got a clue how I feel about you or anybody else."

Heading into the bedroom, I hold Berkeley's pen close to my eyes and whisper, "Gosh, I love you to bits." After a sigh, I add, "But my time with you is done, isn't it?"

Packing the pen in my carry-on luggage, I wipe away more tears and say, "The sooner you give it back, the easier it'll be for you to move forward."

# foot note fifty-seven

STEPPING FOOT IN MY CHILDHOOD HOME FOR THE FIRST TIME IN A couple of years, my first observation is that everything feels smaller than I remember. Maybe it's because it's been a full ten years since I officially lived here. Or maybe it's because Robert's apartment is so spacious—its kitchen pantry alone is equivalent in size to my parents' entire living room—that I have a skewed perspective on living space. Either way, it feels cozy and comfortable, and I can't wait to settle in.

As Robert and I stand next to the staircase, my parents emerge from the back of the house. Locking eyes with me, they turn as giddy as toddlers, pick up speed, and exclaim, "Hello!"

"Hello back," I excitedly reply.

Before I say another word, Brigitte, whom I haven't seen since last Christmas in Saint Lucia, jumps out from around a corner, and then the all-grown-up Talula does the same alongside her new fiancé, William, a dark-haired, brown-eyed, meek-mannered hulk of a man who towers over every one of us.

Together again under the same roof for the first time in a long time, we break out into rounds of hugs, kisses, and mushy tears.

Smiling, Robert extends his hand and introduces himself to each person individually, the last being my dad, after which the two quickly get into a law-related discussion that leads them into the kitchen.

Locking arms with me, Talula watches Robert walk away and whispers, "He is so handsome and well groomed."

"Yes, he's a looker."

Smirking, she says, "Let me guess. He irons his underwear."

Giggling, I reply, "No, he doesn't. At least not to my knowledge."

Leaning into me, Brigitte says, "His face is as smooth as a mannequin's. Does he get facials?"

"Yes," I reply. "We get them together."

Squinting, Brigitte adds, "Seriously, he is so picture-perfect he could run for public office and win on appearance alone."

"Maybe he will one day. Who knows?"

As my sisters and William head toward the kitchen too, it suddenly occurs to me that I could not feel more at ease right now. I have no woes, no hang-ups, and no angst about anything. I'm not even bothered by the fact that I'm living on only a few hours of sleep. Something has happened to me in the last day—something life altering, something settling—which might be linked to having found my shoes. Whatever it is, I feel as if I'm finally done with life's growing pains, as if all decisions I make from this juncture forward will be sound and sensible.

As I stand there smiling, my mom walks over and says, "You look so grown up right now."

Resting my head on her shoulder, I reply, "Maybe because after twenty-five years, my head is finally screwed on straight."

Patting my head, she replies, "That's nice to hear."

Throwing my arms around her neck, I say, "God, I've missed you."

"I've missed you too."

Tearing up, I add, "You know, I've meant to say this for a long time but kept putting it off: it's okay that you gave away the backyard hammock, and I'm sorry I reacted the way I did when you told me about it."

Squeezing me tightly, she responds, "I'm sorry too, because I definitely should have discussed it with you first."

"No, it was your decision to make."

Releasing me, she adds, "You should pick up a hammock of your own sometime. And start creating hammock-related memories set in your own world."

"Good idea."

As my mom heads into the kitchen, I grab my carry-on bag and head upstairs to my bedroom, and as before, I discover that my room has remained unchanged.

Staring at the bed and recalling the last guy who rolled around on it with me, I blush, call Phoebe, and say, "Hey, I made it to town, so you can continue speaking to me."

"I knew you couldn't live without me in your life."

Smiling, I say, "It looks like there's going to be a good turnout on Saturday evening."

Exhaling, she responds, "Yeah, all of us cool people—except, as you may have noticed, Berkeley."

"Yeah, he's probably missing the event to avoid running into me."

"No, I heard he's on vacation in Spain, maybe with his girlfriend, whose name is apparently Berlin or London or some other European city."

I swallow. "That's nice for him."

After clearing her throat, she adds, "I hate to be the one to tell you this, but I heard via the rumor mill that a marriage proposal may or may not be in the works for that trip."

I sit on the bed. "Oh, really?"

"Yeah." After a long pause, she asks, "Are you okay?"

Wiping away an unexpected stream of tears, I reply, "Yeah, but it seriously sucks that the feelings associated with first love never ever leave your system."

Releasing a sigh, she says, "If you want to meet up and talk about it, call me."

"Thanks. Will do."

Hanging up, I get lost in thought about Berkeley marrying someone else and about how happy he must be if he's ready to commit to someone for the rest of his life. I walk toward the music box he gave me, turn it on, and say, "You were wrong, Mr. Mills. This didn't end up working out for us."

Pulling Berkeley's pen from my bag, I stare at its loveliness and whisper, "One way or another, little one, this weekend, you are headed back to where you belong."

Sitting down at my desk, I scribe an accompanying note that sums up all I need to convey.

> *Berkeley,*
> *Thank you for encouraging me to find the Francie Lanoo.*
> *Sorry I took so long to get it accomplished, and sorry I caused severe pain along the way. In my defense, I had no idea it would be so much easier said than done.*
> *Love and hugs, Francie*

I'm going to have my mom do the handover for me so that there's no fuss, mess, or heartbreaking memory to forever haunt me. Of course, letting go will be incredibly difficult for me regardless, because that pen was—and still is—the most-special gift anyone has ever given me. It got me through an intense two years of high school on the other side of the world, it got me through four difficult years of college in a city that gobbles people up and spits them out, and it played a role in landing me a prestigious position with one of the world's preeminent shoe-design companies. Most important, it helped to make real a shoe that I will forever hold dear. For those reasons and more, I expect releasing such a prized possession is going to feel like losing a limb.

After looking in the mirror and fixing my makeup, I change out of my travel wear, slip into a retro black-and-white-checkered sundress, and wander into my closet, where I retrieve a youthful pair of flip-flops that I have not worn since one fun-filled night in a hot tub.

Heading downstairs and finding my dad, Robert, and William glued to a football game on TV, I grab my mom and sisters and say, "Let's go for lunch."

"Great idea," my mom replies.

We go to a quirky outdoor café that opened up near my parents' house, and afterward, we partake in a stroll through a new hoity-toity shoe boutique that sits next door. As the others try on footwear galore, I sit back and watch, realizing that I'll never grow tired of browsing for pretty shoes, but because I have successfully attained my me shoe, I no longer feel the thrill of the hunt. Consequently, I expect that any shoe I purchase from this point forward will exclusively be about fashion: as an accessory, as research for work, or as a gift for someone else.

When we arrive back at the house, I say to my mom, "May I borrow your wheels for a while? I'd like to take a drive around town."

"Of course, but be careful. There are a lot of bad drivers on the roads out there."

"I will," I say, touching her arm because I too will never forget the incident she's referencing.

The first part of my tour is along the old part of Main Street, where everything seems set back in time, a little worn, and also shrunken.

The second part of my tour includes a drive past the beauty salon where I received many a pedicure, followed by a cruise past the dance studio where, as a youngster, I learned a few fine moves. Turning a corner, I discover the department store that gave me my first job and say, "Note to self: stop in to visit Mark Baker before you leave town."

The third part of my tour includes a zip through City Center Park, the location of many of my fondest memories, including one on the open green space and two on the swings. From there, I visit my old high school, where I examine the many classroom windows I gazed out of, the art room where I learned many of my skills, and the cafeteria's outdoor patio, where I ate food that I'm sure I would cringe at now. I get out of the vehicle and wander over to the now-huge oak tree that garnered me the kiss that has never been equaled. A sweet smile graces my face when I recall the many life highlights that followed as a result of that unforgettable evening.

As I'm driving away from the school, I see my old hangout, still named Jule's. Realizing I haven't been there in years and that I'm seriously craving its delicious pizza, I vow to order some after tomorrow night's dance.

The fourth part of my tour takes me past the all-things-Italian restaurant where I sat at a table and debated a decision that would move me away from home at age sixteen and change my life and where I received, on loan, the gift I intend to soon return.

From there, I make a left turn and drive past the retro café, still named the Rosemont, where I once enjoyed a sixteenth birthday dinner with the loveliest family ever. Not surprisingly, this leads me to the cemetery, where I drop off a large bouquet of crisp yellow roses on the now-in-place headstone of my favorite other collector.

The last leg of my journey takes me outside of the city, where I visit a peaceful waterfall that served as a backdrop for what I know to be my all-time favorite day. As the memories of each poignant moment flood my brain—the swim, the string, and the photograph—I get out of the car and commence crying uncontrollably for a long time. I fall to my knees and watch tears drop to the earth below me.

As my heart begins to tighten, I surmise that I'm probably reacting this way because I'm experiencing the end of my youth—which I'm not yet ready to do. Wiping away tears, I murmur, "Please let me stay young just a little bit longer."

Knowing that no one is ever granted such a concession, I climb back into the vehicle, open the visor's mirror, and wipe the smeared mascara from my sopping-wet cheeks. Noticing in the reflection that the swept-off makeup has exposed the last of my childhood freckles, albeit in their faintest form, I remember several cute comments that my unforgettable first love made about them.

*Berkeley Mills.*

It saddens me that I won't have an opportunity to return the pen and apologize to him in person and that he and I will likely never restore civility between us. On a brighter note, tomorrow's festivities will enable me to resume relationships with many other people I've drifted away from, and that alone will make the trip home worth it.

# foot note fifty-eight

ALONG WITH THE MOST-STUNNING SHOES IMAGINABLE, I'M wearing a fitted white blouse, a dangling silver necklace, and a pair of floor-sweeping, wide-legged black pants that render my shoes invisible.

I'm well aware of the irony that I have chosen to conceal from the rest of the world the most-awesome part of my attire, but for some reason, today I have an urge to be humble about my good fortune. It will be my joy alone.

Robert and I arrive at Riverly Heights High School about an hour after the festivities begin. The delay is due to a wardrobe issue: I couldn't pull myself away from the amazing Sarah Mills's collection of handbags, which I sifted through for the first time this afternoon. At my mother's urging to hurry up, I settled on a metallic-teal leather folded clutch with a polished dark-wood wrist handle (very 1950s), the color of which is a dead-on match to today's toenail polish.

After stuffing a few incidentals into it, I looked at my ensemble in the mirror and couldn't tell which was making me happier: the fabulous shoes or the fabulous bag.

As Robert and I walk through the arched doorway and into the high-school auditorium, I catch sight of hundreds of silver streamers dangling from helium balloons high above the floor, all of them twinkling under the spotlights. With a smile on my face, I meander toward a multitude of well-dressed and well-coiffed former classmates, all idling in familiar clusters. Many of them look different—some are taller; some are heavier; some appear weathered; and some are even sporting wrinkles. *Am I?*

Gravitating to my own familiar cluster, I hug Phoebe, Beatrice, Silvia, Pierce, and Patrick and introduce them all to Robert.

As various conversations erupt, Patrick rests his hands on my shoulders and says, "You have the same face you had as a teenager."

Tipping my head, I reply, "God, I miss you."

Pulling me into his arms for a warm embrace, he responds, "Later, you and me on the dance floor for at least three tunes in a row."

"I'd like that," I respond, thinking back to how many dances he and I have experienced, how many strolls he and I have shared, and how many conversations he and I have had. What a great companion he was for me while I was growing up. *Mental note: stay in touch better.*

Likewise, with all the other wonderful friendships I've been blessed with over the years, I must put more effort into ensuring their longevity.

Scanning the crowd, I view more people I haven't seen in years, including Catharine Armour, who's on the arm of Daniel East— *Didn't see that union coming*—and Shanna, who coyly waves at me. I wave back, remembering that were it not for her kiss with Berkeley, I'd be living a different life.

As I ponder what that life might be like, Patrick pulls Robert toward the bar for an in-progress shooter contest, leaving me standing by myself. I spin around and wander in the opposite direction, unexpectedly crossing paths with the slimy guy who attacked me several New Year's Eves ago, Max. Though I try my hardest to stealthily pass by him, he gets in my face and has the gall to grab one of my upper arms to detain me.

Gripping me tighter when I try to wriggle away, he drunkenly slurs into my ear something along the lines of "You and me, later, on a swing set."

Scoffing, I abruptly turn and slam torso to torso into Sam Nelson, Berkeley's good friend. "Sam!" I exclaim, my eyes popping wide open.

"Hey, Francie!" he replies, discreetly shoving Max into a nearby wall.

Watching Max growl and slither away, I meekly say, "Thank you for that."

After leaning over and planting a gentle kiss on my cheek, he responds, "That guy never gives up with you, does he?"

"No, I don't know what his deal is."

"Well, if you saw yourself in a mirror right now, you'd figure it out pretty quickly."

Blushing, I respond, "I think he's just had too much to drink."

"Well, if his behavior becomes a problem tonight, just let me know, and I'll make sure he's removed from the picture."

"Thank you. That's very considerate."

Donning a wide grin, he asks, "So how are you?"

"I'm okay now. How are you?"

"I'm well."

"Good to hear."

Eyeing me up and down, he says, "Father Time has been kind to you. You look fabulous."

Blushing again, I respond, "Everyone looks fabulous tonight."

He shakes his head. "Not everyone glows."

I smile. "That's only because not everyone pays attention to where the spotlights are."

Grinning, he crosses his arms and retorts, "A comment totally consistent with everything I've learned about you over the last few years."

"Who's been teaching you?"

Wrapping one of his long arms around my neck, he answers, "No one. Forget I said anything."

"No, I want names."

Laughing, he replies, "I'm sworn to secrecy, but hey, on another note, you'll be interested to know I've ditched my signature joggers."

I glance down at his cushy black loafers. "You did! Why?"

"Out of necessity, actually. The long days at med school require something more supportive of my arches."

I smile. "How are you enjoying that scary place?"

"I love it. And I'm proud to say I was recently accepted into my chosen specialty of heart surgery."

My eyes open wide. "Good for you, and good for me! Soon I'll have someone to call whenever my heart is aching."

Placing a hand on my shoulder, he replies, "For all matters related to your heart, I'd be happy to take the call, day or night."

Giggling because his accent is still adorable, I say, "Thanks. I'll keep that in mind."

As we continue chatting—or whatever it is we're doing—I hear a voice in my head telling me to ask about Berkeley, but I refuse to let the words slip out, probably because I'm afraid of what I might learn.

Looking directly into my eyes, Sam asks, "So how's life going for you?"

Smiling, I reply, "I've been offered a promotion in Italy, and I intend to take it."

"Nice. How do you enjoy shoe designing?"

"I can't believe I get paid to do what I love most."

"How does it feel to be home?"

"So amazing. I should never have stayed away for so long." Waving Robert over, I say, "Sam, this is my date, Robert. Robert, this is Sam."

"Nice to meet you," Sam says.

"Likewise," Robert replies.

Touching my upper arm, Sam quietly says, "Would you excuse me for a minute? I need to take care of something urgent."

Nodding, I say, "Sure, of course."

Flashing me a mischievous grin, he adds, "Do not leave without first seeing me."

Poking a finger into his chest, I say, "I won't, because I'm still waiting for you to name names."

Sheepishly winking at me, he retorts, "Don't hold your breath, little lady."

Watching him walk away, I stand there perplexed, because I have no idea why that encounter has left me so bubbly.

Turning back to Robert, suddenly feeling the need to avoid one-on-one time with him, I say, "I hope you don't mind, but my childhood buddy Patrick asked for a dance this evening, so I'm going to seek him out and give my new shoes a go."

"By all means, do. And enjoy."

"Thanks. I'm sure I will," I say, locating Patrick across the room and making my way toward him. Adjusting my blouse, I accidently drop my handbag and dump out the contents. Crouching down to clean up the mess, I pick up Berkeley's pen in its box and murmur to myself, "Why did you bring this?"

Shaking my head, I officially commit to the idea that tonight, I'm going to leave here with Berkeley's home address, and tomorrow I will wake up early in the morning, slink over to his place, and stuff the pen into the mailbox, my note included. After that, fingers crossed, my past will no longer affect me.

Right now, though, as I commence shaking a leg with the first guy who ever invited me to, I will happily allow the past to affect my every whim. And I will mark this as the highlight of the evening, coming full circle in the same room.

At the stroke of midnight, as I marvel that my feet feel fantastic despite the fact that they've been subjected to several vigorous dances in a row, I decide I'm ready to leave.

Locating Robert chatting with Silvia, I walk over and say, "Let's be like bananas and split."

Giving me a furrowed-brow look, because he's never heard me say anything silly, he remarks, "Not before you and I have had a dance."

Never having danced with him before—not once in the many months we've been together—I return a smile and say, "Sure, let's. To cap off the night."

As we walk toward the center of the room, a new tune flows from the nearby speakers. However, when I recognize it as my beloved music-box tune, I feel an uneasy shadow beginning to hover. Even worse, when the words "Baby, I want you" ring out, I feel my mind traveling to another place and time.

Simultaneously, Robert pulls me into an embrace and moves us left to right, right to left. *Or is that left to left? Which way is he going? Which way am I going?*

Aware that Robert and I are not in sync at all and that his sense of beat differs greatly from mine, I try to follow his lead to mask the incompatibility, and by doing so, I make the situation even more awkward.

I don't know why, but our clashing rhythms turns me weirdly giddy, so I slump like a rag doll, cease moving altogether, and drop my arms to my sides.

Robert halts too and asks, "Is everything okay?"

Looking up and withholding a stupid grin, I explain, "Yeah, I've just got two left feet tonight."

Always the gentleman, he smiles and replies, "It's not you. It's the crowd. Let's move to where there's more space."

"Sure," I say, suddenly noticing that dancing seems to be making Robert nervous, which is odd, considering he's always in control.

Relocating to a quiet and private niche near a narrow flight of stairs leading to the stage, I say, "This is better." However, when I realize it's the spot where Berkeley and I shared our first dance—exactly ten years plus a day ago, but who's counting?—I feel my mind flooding with images that need not be there. Though I try my best to dismiss them and just dance, they appear with such vividness that I feel as if I am fifteen again.

Covering my eyes, I drop out of Robert's embrace and start stomping the floor to try to rattle myself back to the present day.

Touching my arm, Robert sweetly says, "Interesting dance style you've got there."

Dropping my hands, I reply, "I'm sorry. I was just thinking about the many other times I've danced in this room and have apparently unleashed the goofiness in me."

His brow wrinkles. "I find it hard to believe you were ever goofy."

My brow mimics his. "Wasn't everyone in high school?"

"No," he says, at which point I realize that this guy has probably never had a bad day in his life.

Smiling, he says, "You look tired."

I nod. "Yeah. Do you want to leave, maybe go somewhere else?"

"Sure. Wherever you'd like."

My eyes open wide. "I'd like pizza."

His eyes open wide. "I'd prefer sushi."

My shoulders slump. "Sushi it is then."

To the song's mushy chorus, Robert locks eyes with me and sweetly murmurs, "Hey, before we go, would you mind if I talked to you about something?"

Though I am not in the mood to talk about anything at the moment, I say, "I don't mind at all. Fire away."

After taking a deep breath, he says, "First of all, let me say this topic has been on my mind for many days now."

Losing the giddiness, I reply, "I'm listening."

After another prolonged pause, he presses his lips together and admits, "I'm at a loss for words on how to open this."

"This must be important, because I've never seen you at a loss for words—ever."

Releasing a warm smile, he says, "Francie, I'd like to talk about the possibility of ..."

"What?"

He inhales deeply. "Of you marrying me."

As my knees go weak, I mumble, "What? What did you say?"

"I'm broaching the subject of marriage, I think." Taking note of my blank stare, he adds, "Ineffectively, I now see."

As my brain works feverishly to engage, I ask, "What brought this on? Now? Here? Today?"

Gripping my hands, he replies, "The fact that I just realized you're the best thing that has ever happened to me."

"That's nice of you to say."

Squinting, he says, "You seem shocked by this."

Shaking my head, I reply, "I shouldn't be. I don't think I am. I just wasn't expecting you to ..."

Pulling me closer, he says, "Maybe I should expand on where this is coming from."

"Okay."

Exhaling, he says, "Ever since you told me about the job transfer to Rome, I've been giving our relationship a lot of thought."

"Uh-huh."

"The conclusion I drew is that I think the two of us should have some sort of commitment in place before you go."

"I see."

Sheepishly grinning, he adds, "Actually, my bigger plan is to coerce you into changing your mind altogether about going."

*What? Now I'm being persuaded not to go to Italy?*

As I stand there lost in a daze, he says, "Maybe I should have brought this up at another time."

I force a smile. "No, it's fine. We should talk about this stuff, because we never have." Looking off to the side, I whisper, "Especially now that my quest is complete."

Placing a hand on my cheek, he asks, "Francie, are you all right?"

I look up. "Yes, yeah, maybe. Sure. Uh-huh. Why wouldn't I be?"

"I don't know, but you seem a little out of it, and you're stuttering."

"I think it's just because I'm absorbing a lot of stuff at the moment."

"I've put a damper on the evening."

"No, you didn't."

"And I think I've diminished the importance of what I'm asking."

"No, it's all A-okay. Super fine. Really fine. Top-of-the-day fine."

"Are you sure?"

I tentatively nod. "Yes, I'm just taken aback because this seems sudden, or maybe my insomnia of late is clouding my thoughts, or maybe the oxygen in this room is depleting because it is very crowded in here."

"It is crowded."

Forcing a smile, I add, "Actually, I think I'm suffering from some dehydration. I'm going to get us drinks—tall ones."

Lightly taking hold of my shoulders and forcing me to lock eyes with him, he asks, "Francie, is something going on right now that I should be worried about?"

Recognizing my brain has switched to an image of me near a waterfall, where my heart is palpitating over the sight of a string on my finger and my lips are quivering because they want more than anything to scream, "Yes, yes, yes!" I hit some sort of sensory overload and yell, "Bloody hell, I need to get out of here!"

"Okay," Robert says, releasing me and stepping back.

Exhaling, I say, "I need to go to the ladies' room, so that's exactly what I'm going to do!"

Throwing his hands into the air, he says, "Okay. Fine. I'll just wait here for you by the steps."

"I won't be long."

"Sure. Take whatever time you need."

"Thank you," I say, quickly turning away before the dialogue in my head escapes through my mouth.

Like a mouse heading to a hole in the wall, I scamper through the crowd, swiping arms and knees with everyone in my path. Under my breath, I ramble, "Oh my God! This is crazy!" Loudly, I bark, "Excuse me, please. I'm in a hurry!"

Reaching a side wall, I come face-to-face with Phoebe, who is steadying an open bottle of red wine in one hand and two empty glasses in the other.

Placing my forehead against hers, I exclaim, "Thank God I ran into you!"

"Why? What's up?"

"I'm in a seriously messed-up state of mind at the moment."

"Over what?"

"Over Robert, over the future, over the past." After an exhale, I add, "Over the fact that I should be strictly prohibited from ever making a decision related to my own happiness."

Shaking her head, she says, "Uh-oh."

"I don't know what I want anymore."

Pressing her lips to my ear, she responds, "If you want my opinion, what you want is in Los Angeles."

"Meaning what?"

"Meaning Berkeley Mills. That's where he is right now."

I droop my shoulders. "Why did you have to mention him?"

"You know why."

Watching me shrug, she adds, "Rumor has it he dumped Vienna or Prague or whatever that girl's name is. And he did so because he's still hung up on his ex, which may mean California Girl, based on the fact that he's in California."

"From whom did you hear that?"

"From Edell, who heard it from someone else, who apparently

heard it from Sam, who must know what's going on, because he and Berkeley are joined at the hip."

Nervously twirling my hair with my fingers, I respond, "I've gotta get out of here."

Resting her chin on my shoulder, Phoebe says, "At what point are you going to finally face the fact that you totally screwed up with that guy?"

"Why bring that up now?"

"Because every time I'm with you, I can tell you're haunted by it."

Loudly exhaling, I say, "Okay. Yes, I admit it. I got Berkeley handed to me on a silver platter, and I messed up royally."

"Yup, you did."

Resting my head on her shoulder, I let a long-awaited volcano's worth of pressure release inside my chest, spewing lava with such force that it hurts. The burn spreads into my stomach, then into my arms, and, lastly, into my feet, which become so tight in their pretty shoes that I want to go barefoot. Overwhelmed, I start to cry.

Releasing a sympathetic sigh, Phoebe asks, "What can I do for you right now to make your life better?"

Wiping away tears, I stand up straight, take a deep breath to pull myself together, and say, "Do you see Robert in the corner of the room, near the steps to the stage?"

She looks over. "Yes, I see him."

"Could you keep him company for fifteen minutes or so while I wrap my head around some stuff?"

"Consider it done."

"Thanks. You're a good friend."

Smiling, she hands me the wine bottle and says, "Here—take this."

"Why?"

"It'll help with the stuff."

"I doubt one bottle will be enough."

Giggling, she responds, "I'll get more."

With the hint of a smile, I turn and march toward the nearest source of fresh air. Opening the exit door, I inhale deeply and perk up when the evening's coolness graces my skin. After placing a rock in the doorway to hold the door open, I move under a nearby light fixture, lean my back against the wall, and start guzzling.

Glancing at my feet, I say, "For your information, you didn't exactly make this a red-letter day."

Pacing back and forth along the school's perimeter, I say, "I need to break up with Robert. Now. Before I do something stupid and marry him."

Wandering into the darkness, I stumble over a landscaping edge and almost fall, but much to my surprise, I keep the wine bottle perfectly upright. Bending over to check on my shoes to make sure I haven't damaged them, I'm relieved to find that the toes have been scuffed only minimally—nothing I can't buff.

Reminded of how magnificent they are, I think about how I knew from the moment I laid eyes on them that they were mine. Sighing, I say, "Why can't all matters of the heart appear with such clarity?"

Shaking my head, I mumble, "Ah, but they do."

Resuming my tiptoed wandering, I hear someone from the party swing the exit door fully open, kick away the rock I placed, and charge in my direction.

Eyeing the silhouette, I whisper, "Is that who I think it is?"

*Yes. Crap. It's Max.* "Like I need this right now."

From about twenty feet away, I watch as he stumbles, almost falls, and murmurs, "Where did that vixen go?"

As my fists clench because I fear he might be hunting me, I move slowly toward a low wall of shrubbery, where I crouch, wait, and plot how I'm going to get back inside without him detecting me.

"Hey, Francie! Are you out here?" he yells.

"Dumb-ass," I whisper.

"Francie, I need to talk to you."

Shaking my head, I settle onto my knees to creep in the direction of the school's front doors, handbag and wine tucked under my arms. Unfortunately, as I near an area of low-lying ground cover, I cause a crunching noise that seems to echo in the stillness of the night.

Max evidently hears it, because he veers toward me and gets closer and closer. *Dammit.*

Standing erect, I hold my chin up, take a deep breath, and say, "What do you want, Max?"

Edging toward me, he murmurs, "I wanna have a conversation with you."

"Sorry, I don't have time."

"What's your excuse tonight?"

"I'm heading back inside."

Taking hold of one of my shoulders, he says, "But the door's locked, and you won't be able to open it."

As my muscles tense, I reply, "Then I'll text someone to open it for me."

Licking his lips, he asks, "What's the rush?"

"My boyfriend and I are about to leave."

"I just saw your boyfriend dancing with Phoebe, so I know he's not in a rush to go anywhere."

Exhaling, I say, "Listen, Max. I'm not in the mood for this right now. Okay?"

Smirking, he replies, "Well then, tell me what you are in the mood for right now, and I'll cater to it."

"I'm in the mood to walk away, okay?"

But as I try to, he grips both of my upper arms, pulls me toward him, presses his face against mine, and moans, "Let me tell you what I'm in the mood for."

Wincing, I whisper, "Please, no."

"Please, yes," he says, trying to kiss me.

As the veins in my neck start to pulsate, I know I only have seconds before this situation escalates out of control, so I close my eyes, envision a butch New York self-defense instructor named Suki, and summon every kick-ass ounce of adrenaline I possess.

First, I lean my upper body back and throw some wine right into Max's eyes.

"What the hell?" he yells.

Next, I drive my right knee into his nether regions, and when this causes him to release me, I step back and use my left foot to deliver another blow to the same area.

"Jesus Christ!"

Lastly, as his body doubles over in pain, I sprint as fast as I can in the direction of the school's main entrance.

To the sounds of Max's agonizing groans, I exclaim, "Run, shoes! Run!" And they do, with such speed they are surely setting records for three-inch-heeled platforms.

As Max's groans begin to fade, I think maybe the wine has messed with his vision. *Please, yes.* Or maybe my kick is more powerful than I imagined. *I can only hope.* Or on the flip side, maybe he's sneaking around to reach me from another direction. *God, no.*

Stepping on a concrete sidewalk, I hear fast-paced footsteps nearing me. Blitzing full speed ahead through the darkness, holding the handbag tightly to my rib cage and the weaponry wine bottle firmly in hand, I approach the corner of the building and maneuver the ninety-degree turn like a train gone out of control.

The next thing I know, I abruptly crash head-on into him. As I yell, "Oh shit!" my right foot delivers another nether-region assault that sends Mr. Obnoxious flat onto his back and into some prickly shrubs.

As much as I want to keep running, the law of momentum dictates otherwise, propelling me out of control, into the air, and facedown on top of him, after which wine splatters everywhere.

To the sounds of his highly descriptive curses, I feel my adrenaline spiking off the charts. Shifting myself to a straddling position on his chest, I ready the wine bottle for my next act of defense, and with gritted teeth, I go full-throttle berserk, bashing as ferociously as I'm able, screaming, "Why doesn't it register through your Neanderthal skull that I cannot stand the sight of you?"

Raising his arm in defense, he says, "Francie! Please! Stop!"

I instantly do, because the voice is not the one I most dread. Rather, it's the one I most love.

Placing my hand over my mouth, I whisper, "Berkeley?"

"Yeah."

Tossing the wine bottle away, I exclaim, "Oh my God! I'm so sorry I did this to you! Are you okay?"

"No, I am not okay!"

"What have I done?"

After taking a deep breath, he mumbles, "I'll tell you what you've done. You knocked the wind out me with your bony elbow. You injured my shoulder with some blunt instrument. You embedded twigs into my forehead. And what is this liquid? Did you pour wine on me?"

"Yes."

Releasing a drawn-out groan, he exclaims, "How the hell can someone your size cause me so much pain?"

Resting my hands on his more-fantastic-than-I-remember chest, I respond, "I honestly didn't mean to."

Running one of his hands through his hair and attempting to sit, he adds, "Jesus Christ, do you have any idea the damage you inflicted on my groin with your goddamn shoe?"

Feeling his torso nearing mine, I reply, "I've got a sense of it, because my toes hurt really badly too."

Shaking his head, he asks, "What the hell just happened?"

Shrugging, I respond, "I was running away from a mean and ugly troll."

"From what?"

"From that pain-in-the-ass Max. He was after me again."

Through gritted teeth, Berkeley yells, "Where the hell is he?"

I look around. "I don't know, but I think I inflicted some damage to his private parts, too, so I have a feeling he'll be lying low for a while."

"If he's out here, I will find him."

"No, don't. He's not worth your time."

Pursing his lips, he mumbles, "I should have properly dealt with that guy the last time he went near you."

"Or I should have, if only I'd carried around a wine bottle back then."

Maneuvering his body so that his face is inches from mine and placing his hands on my lower back, Berkeley quietly asks, "Are you hurt at all?"

"Not much."

"Okay. Good."

"Is your shoulder going to be all right?" I ask, gently touching his arm and squinting to see him better in the darkness.

Slowly rotating it, he responds, "I seriously have no idea. I'm too numbed by the fact that you're in my lap right now."

"Yeah, this is so weird."

"It's crazy."

Scrunching up my face, I add, "Berkeley, what are you doing out here?"

"I was crashing the party."

"Why?"

Slowly standing both of us on our feet, he answers, "I didn't expect to be here, because I was at a meeting in LA, but after I managed to catch an earlier flight and then got an urgent text from Sam, telling me to get my ass over here, I bolted off of the plane and arrived as quickly as I could. I tried entering through the front door, but it was locked, so I was coming around the back."

I huff. "Where stuff goes bump in the night."

"The very reason you shouldn't be wandering around out here by yourself."

I raise my chin. "I think I just proved I can take care of myself."

He sighs. "My throbbing groin might agree, but the rest of me cringes at the thought of what would have happened if Max had gotten his legs back. By the way, why aren't you inside?"

"Because I had to get away from inside, because things were not going well for me inside."

"What kind of a night are you having?"

"A complicated one."

"Feel free to elaborate."

My brain goes on overload. *Why is Berkeley here? He's not supposed to be here. I'm not prepared to see him.* My hair is a mess, my face is splattered with merlot, my blouse is stuck to my skin, my clothes are covered in dried flowers, and I hardly slept last night, so I'm probably zombie-eyed. I respond, "I brought a date to this reunion, and in the middle of dancing with him, it came to my attention that he's not a very good dancer, and—"

"Ms. Lanoo, how many times do I have to tell you? You need to be pickier with your dance dates."

"That's very cute, Berkeley, but if you let me finish, you'll see that dancing is not the point of what I'm trying to tell you."

"Okay, then blab on."

I loudly exhale. "Just as I clued into Robert's dancing deficiency, he …" I pause, look away, and murmur, "Oh my God, did he really ask me that?"

"Ask you what?"

"To marry him."

Snapping to attention, Berkeley exclaims, "Whoa! Wait. Are you getting married?"

"No," I say, and when my brain engages, I ask, "Are you?"

"What?"

"To Berlin or London or Oslo?"

"Do you mean Geneva?"

"Yeah. I heard the two of you went to Europe and that you got engaged, or you eloped, or you got back together with California Girl, or—I don't know."

"Ms. Lanoo, where are you getting your information from?"

"Phoebe."

"Well, that explains a lot," he says. Motioning us toward the auditorium door, he adds, "To set the record straight, yes, I did travel to Europe with Geneva, but that was several weeks ago."

"Okay."

Glancing at the ground, he adds, "While we were there, actually, she asked me to marry her."

My heart skips a beat. "She did?"

"Yes."

I slow my pace. "What was your response?"

He gently hip checks me. "That I had no intention of getting married until I was really old, like thirty."

Coyly smiling, I reply, "I'm sure that went over like a lead balloon."

"Yeah, attached to concrete weights."

"Yikes."

After taking a deep breath, he says, "I was in Europe again—in Barcelona, actually—for all of last week, on a vacation with my dad."

I turn to face him, and with wide eyes I ask, "How is your dad?"

"He's doing really well."

I sigh. "I'm so relieved to hear that."

"He's a trooper, that guy. Living proof that time heals even the deepest of wounds."

"I'm sure he has you to thank."

"And a whole lot of therapy."

As we step onto the sidewalk near the school's rear door and inadvertently position ourselves under a light fixture, I glance up and link eyes with Berkeley for what feels like the first time. I stop dead in my tracks and think, *Oh my God! This guy is perfect. Right down to his wine-soaked white shirt, his sleek black suit, his gorgeous dirt-and-blood-smeared face, and his tousled, leaf-infested hair.*

Realizing he and I are examining each other with equal intensity, I exclaim, "Holy moly, it's good to see you!"

Smiling sweetly, he replies, "You too."

"How are you?"

Attempting to lift his injured shoulder, he responds, "If I ignore some newly registering pain, I couldn't be happier."

Cowering, I say, "I can't believe I did that. Hurt you, I mean. Please know that I never would, at least not intentionally. Although, I know I once did—terribly, despicably, unforgivably—but that was when I was young and crazy and such an idiot."

Gently placing a hand over my mouth, he says, "Stop."

Through his fingers, I murmur, "Okay."

He smiles. "How bizarre is it that we're both here right now?"

"It's madness."

Removing his hand and using his sleeve to wipe some wine splashes off of my face, he asks, "So how's life treating you?"

I lean into his familiar touch. "Better than I deserve."

Raising an eyebrow, he says, "Besides the engagement thing, what's happening in your world these days?"

As I spastically ramble on—about how I'm not engaged, how I have the best job ever, how I'm moving to Rome, how great it feels to be in Riverly Heights again, how pretty the stars look, how sticky my blouse feels, and how I'm dying to eat some pizza—it occurs to me that none of these words matter, because all I want to do is kiss this guy right now—and every hour on the hour for the rest of my life.

Sweeping the hair away from my face, Berkeley flashes me a killer smile and says, "So you're moving to Italy again."

"I am."

Squinting his eyes, he replies, "Interesting."

"So what's new with you?"

After taking a deep breath, he answers, "Well, for starters, I'm unemployed."

"Why? What happened?"

"The *Tribunal* got sold, and I got my walking papers."

"When?"

"Today, officially. But the deal has been in the works for the last two years."

"Wow, I had no idea."

Looking to the sky, he murmurs, "God, it was such a relief this morning when those documents got signed."

Leaning my backside against the nearby brick wall, I say, "So now that you're no longer tied to the family business, what are your plans?"

Edging close to me, he softly replies, "Well, priority number one is to finally stop missing you."

Smiling, I say, "I can help you with that."

Placing his palms on the wall on either side of me, he puts his mouth on mine and—*Holy moly, holy Hannah, holy Toledo*—minty-breath kisses me for a long time.

As our lips part, I look into his eyes and say, "Please do that again," and he does—so amazingly that I feel every fiber of my being melting.

As my happy meter hits overload and explodes, Berkeley presses his lips to my ear and whispers, "Unless you've got an objection, Ms. Lanoo, from today onward, wherever you are, I'm gonna be."

Withholding tears of joy, I reply, "Despite the fact that I'm apt to give you gray hair before you're thirty?"

"Or sooner. I found my first one last week."

"Really? Do you think it was because of me?"

Easing our torsos tightly together, he replies, "Yeah, but only due to your absence."

As my eyes spill tears, he wipes them away and excitedly says, "Hey, I brought something for you."

"You did?"

"Yes, which is one of several reasons I traveled across multiple time zones in the past two days to make sure I crossed paths with you."

He reaches inside his suit jacket, pulls out an envelope, and hands it to me.

Gently grasping it, I say, "What's this?"

"Open it and see."

When I do, I find a copy of the photograph Berkeley snapped of us before I left for Italy. And it's as precious as it ever was. Holding it tightly to my chest, I say, "It's about time you gave me this."

"I was waiting for the right moment."

"Well, you picked a good one."

Leaning his shoulder into the wall, Berkeley says, "Another reason I'd hoped to run into you this weekend is that I'm in need of a pen."

My eyes dart to his. "You are?"

"Yeah, do you have one?"

"I do."

He sweetly grins. "I hoped you would."

I pull the pen box and the accompanying note from my clutch, hand them to him, and say, "Good as new."

Without reading the note, he retrieves the pen, inks it, removes the string that's tied around the pen and says, "Give me your hand, would you?"

When I do, he webs his fingers with mine, flips my left palm upward, and scribes, "B ♡ F most." Then, with care, he ties the string in a perfect bow on my ring finger, releases my hand, slips the pen and the note into his lapel pocket, and smoothly says, "There. Everything is where it belongs."

As my heart swells, I ask, "Without a scratch?"

Raising an eyebrow, he replies, "With a few scratches."

"Did they leave scars?"

Smiling, he responds, "I've always had a soft spot for scars."

Reaching for his hand, I remember that I've been absent from the party longer than anticipated. With a sigh, I say, "I need to go inside and take care of some stuff."

With sweet eyes, he replies, "Is there anything I can take care of for you?"

I shake my head. "No, but thanks for offering."

"Give me a minute to text Sam so he can let us in."

"Sure," I say, breathing deeply with my entire upper body, dreading the next hour of my life because it will be neither my easiest nor my finest.

Midmessage, Berkeley mentions, "After you've finished in there, I'm gonna need to be with you."

"Tomorrow for breakfast?"

He peers up from his phone. "No, as soon as possible, but carrying over to tomorrow for breakfast."

"Where would you like to meet?"

Slipping his arms around my waist, he replies, "On a rooftop terrace not far from here, a.k.a., my apartment, where a vintage hammock awaits its long-lost owner."

"Really?"

"Yes, where ice-cold champagne, mounds of blankets, and, if my injured shoulder holds up, some rusty guitar serenading awaits you."

"All of my favorites."

"I'm trying to ensnare you."

"You did a long time ago."

Entering his coordinates into my phone, Berkeley asks, "How much time do you need?"

"A couple of hours," I reply.

"Which is going to feel like an eternity," he says, and then he kisses me again just as the auditorium door swings open to reveal Sam.

Eyeing our disheveled, wine-soaked, foliage-covered bodies, he furrows his brow and says, "You two couldn't find a room?"

Hugging me, Berkeley replies, "What can I say? This girl's irresistible."

Shaking his head, Sam says, "So I've heard from you about a thousand times."

"A thousand?" I ask.

"At least," Sam replies with a smile, pushing the door fully open. Then he shakes Berkeley's hand while saying, "It's good to see you, buddy."

Giving him a firm pat on the back, Berkeley replies, "You too, Sam. Thanks for keeping in touch."

Brushing debris from Berkeley's lapel, he adds, "Come inside. Mingle. Celebrate this grand occasion."

"I intend to," Berkeley replies, placing his hand on my lower back to ease me across the door's threshold.

As I take a step, I lift up my pant legs and expose my footwear for the first time this evening.

Shifting his gaze downward like a moth to a lightbulb, Berkeley exclaims, "Oh, wow, Francie! Look at those shoes!"

Watching him crouch down to examine them, I reply, "I know. They're great, right?"

Looking up, he says, "They're beyond great. They've got 'Francie Lanoo' written all over them."

"Yes, they do."

Smiling, he replies, "They look reminiscent of something."

Smirking, I respond, "Yes, they are exactly as you once described."

After standing up and kissing me on the forehead, he says, "God, I love it when I'm right."

As I smile and shake my head, Berkeley gets swarmed by several classmates, all of them anxious to reconnect. Amid the kerfuffle, I get pushed to the periphery and commence strutting my way through the crowd, smiling and shaking my head at the fact that some things never change.

"Hey, Francie!" Berkeley shouts.

Spinning around and squinting to catch a glimpse of him through the masses, I respond, "Yes?"

As we gaze at each other—with what I'm pretty sure are the same love-struck expressions we had when we parted ways at age eighteen—he asks, "Did you already do your dandy dance by night in those shoes?"

I grin. "No, but I was thinking maybe tomorrow night?"

"All right then."

Admiring the sexiest expression I've ever seen on his face, I ask, "By chance, are you free to join me?"

With his breathtaking eyes gleaming, he answers, "As if you needed to ask."

# Epilogue

STEPPING ONTO BERKELEY'S CANDLELIT TERRACE AND NOTICING his shoulder is in a sling, I place my hands over my mouth and exclaim, "Oh no! How much damage did I do?"

"A small fracture."

Cowering, I respond, "I am such a brute."

"Yes, but a very cute brute," he replies, sauntering toward me and handing me one of two bubbling glasses of champagne that he has entwined in his free hand.

"Cheers," he says.

"Cheers," I reply, clinking glasses.

Locking eyes with me, Berkeley quietly says, "I did a lot of thinking while I was hanging out in the ER with Sam."

"About what?"

"About you and me."

My eyes grow wide. "Anything you'd care to share?"

"Yes."

"Okay, I'm all ears."

He smiles. "I think we should forgo waiting until we're thirty and catch the first beach-bound plane out of here so we can get hitched before the week is through."

Grinning ear to ear, I place a hand on his chest and reply, "I'm already wearing my fabulous string ring and my favorite shoes, so I believe I'm good to go whenever you are."

"Fantastic to hear."

"Right now though, I wouldn't mind hanging with you in my beloved old hammock," I say.

"Happy to oblige," he responds, following me across the terrace, allowing me to assist his wounded body into the familiar weave, and smiling when I settle in beside him.

As I lie there with my head on Berkeley's uninjured shoulder, staring up at a sky flush with stars, I think about the fact that my decade-long quest has officially attained its only goal. *Berkeley's question got answered.* Reflecting upon the experience, if I were asked for advice from someone embarking on a like-minded endeavor, I would say this: If the sight makes your eyes sparkle, your fingers tingle, and your heart flutter, then you have found what you are looking for. Immediately thereafter, clutch it, and hold on for dear life. Do not hesitate, look further, or wait for it to go on sale, because letting it get away, when you know you were meant to have it, will result in unimaginable heartache.

I've been there and almost done that, and I wouldn't wish it on anyone.

Printed in the United States
By Bookmasters